CHUMPY WALNUT CONQUERS THE WORLD

Will Viharo

THRILLVILLE PRESS

Seattle, WA

Cover art and design by Will Viharo
Formatting by Rik Hall –RikHall.com

ISBN-13: 979-8-218-59237-0

First Printing
Printed in the United States of America

Published by Thrillville Press

www.thrillville.net
www.willviharo.com

For David Lynch,
My Fellow Dreamer:
"In Heaven, everything is fine."

For Jean Rollin,
My Fellow Erotic Pulp Surrealist:
"I just happen to have an imagination that doesn't
correspond with those of certain
conservative people."

For Jim Jarmusch,
My Fellow Independent Spirit:
"It's a sad and beautiful world."

For Russ Meyer,
My Fellow Woman Worshipper:
"Nothing is obscene, providing it is done in bad taste."

For Quentin Tarantino,
My Fellow Pulp Writer, Foot Fetishist, and
Ex-Video Store Clerk:
"You're so cool."

Thank you all for the artistic inspiration and creative
camaraderie.

"Reality is contradictory. And it's paradoxical."

—Tom Robbins

Table of Contents

Chapter One
DREAM VERTIGO

Chumpy Walnut was feeling lost in place until one day when he finds himself somewhere he'd always been but didn't realize it. At the moment, and moments are notoriously fluid, he is in a sleazy Los Angeles motel with an exotically beautiful hooker with alopecia who looks like a cross between Pam Grier and Tura Satana as "Hollywood Bed" by The Blasters appropriately plays on the radio. The year is 1982. The dark, wood-paneled room reeks of stale desperation and dried-up dreams.

"So what brings you to L.A., if you're not from here?" asks the voluptuously nude prostitute with bald patches in her otherwise thick, curly, jet-black hair, lying beside the equally naked, relatively short, and innocent-looking young blond boy-man in the creaky old bed. She is captivated by her strange client, mesmerized by his luminescent blue eyes, silky blonde hair, and alabaster skin, which gives him a somewhat unsettling appearance, as if he were a ventriloquist's puppet. But it's his fanciful imagination (she's been paid to indulge worse) that makes her a little wary, despite this entrancingly otherworldly visage, so she is humoring him with idle pillow talk. She qualifies her query. "I mean, most people in L.A. are from someplace else, including me."

"I tossed my dreams up into the air and this is where they landed," Chumpy Walnut says to Alopecia, who wears a bright red wig when on the street. "Or rather, they tossed *me* up, and this is where I landed. I just went to sleep one night back in my world, like it was any other night, but while trying to wake up from a dream where I was being sucked into a vortex, feeling trapped in between consciousness and subconsciousness as my head was spinning violently like I had too many mai tais, I finally snapped out of it and woke up here, in this world, with you, a complete stranger, and we were having sex. I keep thinking I'm still dreaming, and unsure whether I want to wake up, because maybe then I'll be dead."

"Wow. That sounds like something from a movie."

"It does. Gasper Noe's *Enter the Void*."

"What? I never heard of that director or that movie."

"Neither did I till I just said it."

"I don't understand."

"That makes two of us."

"It makes *all* of us, sugar. None of us has any idea what the fuck is going on."

"Everything in my life is something from a movie, I suspect," Chumpy says. "My mission is to meet my creator. I have a few questions for him."

"Mission or *e*mission? Because *that* I've seen and felt for myself. I feel pumped fuller than a luxury jet engine."

"Mission."

"So you're really on a fuckin' *mission*? Like fuckin' Secret Squirrel? How so?"

"Well, my solitary, sacrificial quest is kind of like that movie *Trouble in Mind*."

"Never heard of that one either," she says, fondly fondling his impressive member. "You're quite the esoteric film buff. By the way, I'm from Hawaii, so I love mai tais. I drank them instead of milk growing up."

"Where is Hawaii'?"

"Seriously? It's that island in the middle of the Pacific Ocean, next state over from California. Bunch of islands, that is, semi-strung together like a broken pearl necklace. You know, surf, sand, palm trees, and all that jazz? I was raised in Oahu. I'm part African American, Hawaiian, Portuguese, or rather, Portuguesas since I'm female, in case you haven't noticed, and Dutch."

"I've never heard of any of those places, but that's very interesting. How can your heritage be so complex?"

"Because my background is complex, baby. I never met my father, though my mother told me he was a half-black dude from Portugal. My mother was Hawaiian and Dutch, and a hooker too, and her Johns were mostly sailors and tourists from all over. Anyway, tell me more about this movie. I love movies. That's why I came here, to be an actress, but that didn't work out because of my alopecia and a few other things, like I'll sleep with a dude for rent money, because that's practical, but not for a part in a fuckin' movie, because that's self-deprecating. I hope to go back to Hawaii after I save enough bread to take care of my mother."

"So, Hawaii is a tropical island?"

"Baby, you're good. I gotta get you on a game show and get rich that way. *Yes.* Palm trees, beaches, the ocean, *all* that jazz. You should know. You're wearing a Hawaiian shirt! Or you were before I tore it off you."

"Tikitian."

"Huh?"

"It's actually Tikitian, or at least it is where I come from. Hawaii sounds like a place called Tikiti, where I had my honeymoon, and where my wife was later held hostage to make porn movies and forced into a relationship with a hideous monster."

"Okay, wait, I can't keep up. Is this another movie or the same one?"

"No, it's just my life. I don't think the movie I was just referring to has even come out yet. In fact, it hasn't even been made, not for another five years or so, by my cognitive estimation."

"Then how have you seen it?"

"I haven't. I just know about it. The main male character leaves his true love to find himself. Or something like that. It's a vague premonition or maybe a recollection of someone else's dream. In any case, in the end, he drives off, imagining she's beside him as a very sad song plays, a song that plays in my head like a private jukebox. It's set in a city called Seattle, the movie I mean, where I'm headed, eventually, hopefully. I don't feel in control of my own journey. But neither does the man in this movie. Or any of us, I suppose."

"Thanks for the spoilers, asshole," Tanisha Alopecia says with a laugh. "I'll remember this."

"Premonitions always ruin the surprise. I'm sorry I shared it."

"But you can't be sure, right? Since it doesn't even exist yet?"

"I'm pretty sure."

"So you've at least read the script, then?"

"I don't think Alan Rudolph has even written it yet."

"Who is he?"

"The man who also directed it. Or will in the near future."

"How do you know so much about things you have no business knowing?"

"Because someone is putting thoughts in my head and words in my mouth, screwing up my life with all these weird, wild scenarios—including this one—and I intend to find him and ask why."

"How do you know it's a dude? Maybe your God, and mine, is a girl, though I doubt it would all be so fucked up if that were true."

"I agree. I know it's a him' because of the obsession with impossibly sexy women best described as bombshells.' My wife is one, though she didn't start that way. She was just pretty and petite. So are you."

"Petite?"

"Pretty. *And* a bombshell."

"Oh. Well, thank you. I guess. I do have an explosive temper, so tread lightly."

"Don't thank me, I had nothing to do with it."

"You're not a serial killer, are you? Hearing voices 'n' shit? I have mace in my purse since I meet one of you crazy ass clowns like once or twice a month."

"Killer clowns?"

"Sometimes, yeah, sure, why not?"

"I get the feeling killer clowns will become popular movie villains. They could even be described as Art.'"

"Most of these creepy dudes are too smart to be real clowns. That's what's so scary."

"You mean like Doctor Branesucker, The Brain Sucker? He was a serial killer, but now he's dead. Torn apart by horny zombies."

"Hm. Never heard of that one. What's it called?"

"*The Romance of Chumpy Walnut.*"

"But isn't that *your* name?"

"Yes. It's my life story."

"And it's a movie?"

"No, it's a book that doesn't yet exist in this world, but my world exists because it was published. Before that, I was in limbo for a long time after the first book, which was written in this year we're in now, was finally published many years from now, making my imaginary world a reality. At least to me."

"Sugar, you're confusing me. None of this makes any sense. You seem harmless, but this is some freaky psycho shit. How come no one knows this stuff but you?"

"Because no one here knows about the world I come from. The two books about me are stubbornly obscure, even when they're published. This book we're both in now will be too, I'm afraid. Your world just doesn't seem to care about me."

"Wait, okay, just stop and settle this so I don't *completely* freak out and call my pimp for an emergency rescue. When you say my world,' you really mean *this* world we're in now, right? *Our* world?"

"No, mine is a lot different in so many ways. It would be barely recognizable to you. Much more colorful for one thing. Like a live-action Rocky and Bullwinkle' cartoon, or rather, stylistically at least, it's more like a Tex Avery cartoon, but rated X. I say this as someone who has no idea who Tex Avery is, much less Rocky and Bullwinkle."

"Rated X, you mean like Felix the Cat'?"

"Is that Tex Avery?"

"No. Ralph something, I think. His movies are dirty cartoons, too."

"The reference feels familiar, so I'll say yes, probably. But I could be wrong since I have no idea what it's all about. My mission is to discover the truth behind all of this."

"I was on that mission once. Trust me, it's a waste of time."

"Maybe your time, but not mine. I have all the time in the world—yours *and* mine."

Tanisha Alopecia is charmed but apprehensive. "You *do* look like a cartoon character. I mean that in the nicest possible way. Not a goofy one like Rocky or Bullwinkle. A handsome one. Like Jonny Quest. Only…I don't know. More innocent. Like a doll. Yeah, that's it. You're like a living doll based on a cartoon character. You just don't seem…real. Especially your cock, which is like some kind of accessory for a much bigger monster doll that someone glued onto your plastic body."

"I'm not made of plastic, as you well know by now."

"I sure do, honey. That was clear when that long, thick, mean thang suddenly sprang up on me like a hungry boa constrictor."

"Sorry."

"Too late to apologize. It finally squeezed into my juicy pussy like a bear in a gopher hole, but it was worth the stretch. Just one more big reason you seem like an alien or an angel from beyond the stars. Or a time barrier, in your case. Even your eyes look like doll eyes, so blue and clear. It's fucking eerie. But beautiful."

"Why, thank you."

"Just callin' it like I see it, sugar."

"Why do you keep calling me sugar'?"

"It's what my pimp calls *me*. I'm just passing on the contagious confection."

"Well, maybe I'm not realistic by your standards, but I *feel* real. Well, I *remember* feeling real, which is like remembering a realistic dream. Here, in this time and place, I do feel strange and out of place and disoriented. Like, I don't actually exist, not in the corporeal way that you do. I just don't seem to fit in anywhere. I've felt that way my whole life, no matter where I was. It's very frustrating."

"You fit just fine with me, baby."

"You're bleeding."

"I'm on my period."

"Oh. Cupey never got those. She was barren, like my mother."

"How the fuck could you be here if your mother was barren?"

"She wasn't my real mother. My real mother died in a fire."

"Oh. I'm sorry."

"Not your fault."

"So if you ain't from here, which seems increasingly plausible, are you from some fucked-up dystopian future then? Maybe that's why. You haven't been born yet. You're like a hallucination, or whatcha call it, a…"

"Apparition?"

"Yeah, that's it! You sure are smart for a talking doll boy with a cock like an atomic vibrator."

"I read a lot in my old world, and some of it applies to this one."

"I was only kidding. I don't believe in time travel. But then I don't really believe in anything. And *some*thing has to be true, right?"

"I suppose. I don't know."

"Nobody really knows anything, sugar. That's the true lesson of Life, I've learned the hard way."

"That much I do know. But I'm not from your future. From what little I've seen, it's more like your past as viewed through the perverse funhouse mirror of my creator's damaged brain."

"Yeah, Hollywood has that effect on all you dumbass, gullible tourists. Anyway, that pretty much describes *all* of us, sugar. In *any* world."

"Trust me, we're very different. In my world, we couldn't even have sex."

"We can't in this world either unless you cough up the cash, Romeo."

"It's Chumpy."

"Yeah, I know, Casanova."

"I have the money, don't worry, but in my world, no prostitute or even a regular woman—"

"Gee, thanks."

"—would even consider me because we're incompatible."

"Why, you're broke there?"

"No, I'm broke *here*. In my world, I'm just broken. On the inside. I just meant any physical relationship with me would be too challenging unless you loved me and it was worth the effort. That's why I was so lucky to find Cupey, who accepted me as I was, even after she changed. I am already regretting ever leaving, since I'm not sure how or if I can find my way back to her after I've solved the mystery of my existence."

"Wait a minute, Sherlock Freud, I thought you said you had my money? I knew I should've asked up front. But you had such an innocent face. Like most psychopaths. I should've known better."

"When I was transported, I brought lots of money in my pocket for my trip. Here."

Chumpy reaches into the pocket of his cabana shorts on the floor and pulls out a wad of what looks like tiny Monopoly money.

"What the fuck is this?" Tanisha Alopecia says.

"Money."

"More like an accessory for a capitalist action figure. I hope you're kidding."

"Why would I be kidding? What, it's no good? In my world, that's what we use to buy stuff."

"Ignoring the fact that there is no other world but this one, but pretending there is for your pathetic sake, have you ever heard of the international currency exchange?"

"No, but this isn't international. It's cross-dimensional. So I'm not sure it's covered by your regulations."

"Yeah, okay, well, maybe I should call my pimp, who can come over and explain those rates to you."

"I told you several times I'm not from here, so I can only give you what I brought with me."

"But unfortunately for you, my pimp *is* from here. All six feet five of him."

"Wow. I'm really only a foot tall. I mean, I was in my world. Here I'm a foot *long*. I'd be too small to fit inside you before. Cupey used me like a human dildo. Now it's the opposite."

"Trust me, your big dick is the only thing saving your little ass right now."

"Maybe you just stimulate my reproductive organ inordinately, and my penis will shrink back to average size for my current height when I leave."

"Nice try, but flattery don't cover my debts. You're funny, I'll give you that. My pimp has a lousy sense of humor. I give you points for creativity, at least."

"I'm not making this up."

"Because you're a nutcase."

"Walnutcase, to be exact."

Tanisha Alopecia laughs. "So let me get this straight. Before you magically showed up here, you were the same size as your pecker? In your dreams."

"Twelve inches tall, to be exact. Actually, in my dreams,

I was normal-sized all over. I told you I was a freak of Nature. I still am. I guess there's no escaping my fate."

"You won't escape mine, either."

"Your fate?"

"Yes. Fate is my pimp."

"Oh."

"Anyway, back to what you were saying: so your dream came true."

"Which dream? I have millions, and only one has come true."

"To be normal-sized like the rest of us. Well, relatively. But equipped with an abnormal penis and apparently a brain to match."

"I did dream of being normal-sized, but not with an abnormal-sized penis. Like most selectively answered prayers, there's an unexpected caveat. My wife is really my only dream come true anyway, though. I wish I'd been this well-endowed when I was with her. We might still be together."

"So you're married to this woman you keep referencing?"

"Yes, in my world, at least."

"Stop saying that. In my world.' You're freaking me the fuck out with that shit already. Please stop. Even if it's true. Or you *think* it's true. I can barely handle the fact that my own fucked-up world exists."

"Imagine how I feel to wake up here, so far away from home. Though no matter where I go, I can't escape the underlying sadness of corporeal existence."

"Not sure exactly what that means, but I get the jizz. Gist, I mean. In any case, you do sound pretty sad. I was wondering why, but I never ask anyone why they're sad in this world. I only ask why they're happy."

"I'm lonely here, like I used to be before I met my wife. That's all."

"Do you miss your wife?"

"Of course. She's my best friend and true love. And a professional prostitute, like you. I think this is why I gravitated to another prostitute as soon as I arrived here. It's the comfort of familiarity."

"Oh! I'm…sorry?"

"Don't be. She lets me watch her work sometimes. I'm happy watching her give and receive pleasure, since I am physically incapable of satisfying her sensual desires."

"Oh, well, I'm still sorry, then. Though now you're finally speaking my language."

"No need to be sorry. It was a mutually rewarding arrangement, even though I did suffer from a poor self-image due to my inadequacies. She is aware of this, but there's not much she can do about it. She loves me like no one else, and that's all that counts. To me."

"That's some coo-coo cuckold shit, baby, but whatever floats your boat."

"Thank you."

"Anytime, sugar."

"Anyway, I plan to return to her someday, ideally retaining my current size. But commensurate, so I can pleasure her properly like a real husband should. But having a boner that pops out like a mutant Jack-in-the-box every time I get aroused is a drag. Literally. But it doesn't matter to her. My wife is bisexual anyway."

"Meaning she said bye to you?"

"Something like that. But actually, I said bye to her."

"What are you running away from? The funny farm?"

"I hope farms here aren't concentration camps like where I come from. They're not very funny for the animals."

"Huh?"

"I'm not running from anything, just toward something."

"What?"

"Whatever I find."

"And you think what you're looking for is in Seattle.

That's way the fuck up north, near Canada. So your time machine has a broken compass."

"That's my intuition, yes. But not yet. I misfired by several decades, so I'll have to wait, I guess. Unless I can find him here, even if he's too young to know he will ruin my life with the second book. There is a chance I can head him off before he writes it, and retcon my story."

"Who the fuck is this guy? Maybe I fucked him. He sounds like the type I get."

"I don't know his name, where he is, or who he is. Those details are all blocked. I know instinctively he once lived here in this city, though, because he thinks of this time and place often. It's also the year I was officially born, I mean, conceived as a literary character in a finalized manuscript, so it makes sense he'd be somewhere around here now."

"So now you're telling me you're a newborn? I wasn't born yesterday myself, sugar."

"In the sense that he finished the first book he wrote about me this year, and then he met his dream girl in a movie theater and gave her a copy in the hopes she'd fall in love with him even though he's a putz."

"Did they live happily ever after? I mean, you're straight outta some funky fairy tale."

"Considering what a mess he must've become, I doubt it. Though I think she was only his dream girl in the sense that he dreamed about her. Then she magically appeared in his life, a movie star lookalike who is also a movie star, sitting right in front of him at a movie theater showing two of the original movie star's movies, after he had dreamed about her while writing my life story, at least up to that point. I sense he finds his true love later on. Like I did. But not when he initially wrote me. In the first book, he channels his own childhood trauma into my own. Then he rewards me with something he desperately wanted but thought he could never attain, at least not for a long time."

"Sanity?"

"True love."

"Well, believing in *that* fuckin' myth is a sure sign of insanity."

"I don't really know any of this for sure. It's like he's sending me subconscious messages from an unknown place."

"Uh-oh."

"Nothing bad, just stuff with details I don't really understand. Yet. It's up to me to connect the dots to find my destination, like a map that is also a board game. Like right now, he's watching movies by a French filmmaker named Jean Rollin. I don't even know what French' means, but that's the information I'm receiving. The filmmaker's surname, which I assume is this thing called French,' is spelled as if his last name is pronounced Rollin', but it's actually pronounced Roll-*ah*."

"Yeah, that sounds like a French thang."

"Do you know his movies?"

"Never heard of him either, sorry. I guess those haven't been made yet, either."

"Maybe. All I know right now is that Jean Rollin is one of my creator's favorite filmmakers, and he's obsessed with an actress in some of his movies, named Brigitte Lahaie. I can say her name, but I can't spell it. She's in one movie that's called *Fascination*."

"Hm. That *is* fascinating. Funny you should say this to me now. For one thing, my birth last name is Lanai, my mother's maiden name, which sounds kind of like Lahaie. One of my Johns is French, and he was tellin' me about this movie that came out not long ago called *Night of the Hunted* that sounded really interesting, and this Bridget or Brigitte babe was in it. So that's probably one of this dude's movies, right?"

"*Night of the Hunted*. Yes! That sounds familiar now that you mention it. His movies are considered to be adult fairy tales,' just like *Trouble in Mind*. The connection is that this is how *my* story is characterized."

"By who?"

"My creator. This is why I think he's sending me subliminal clues about where to find him, or at least who he is. My quest, though, at least from my viewpoint, is to find out how he got that way. So far, his clues make no sense because I see no relation between obscure erotic horror cinema from the land of France and my life whatsoever, other than he seems like a sex maniac, considering all the strange sex going on in my world."

"You mean he's a pervert."

"Likely, at least by conventional standards. Like, at this very moment, somewhere in time and space, he's fantasizing about an actress named Joëlle Coeur."

"Nope, never heard of her."

"Maybe I'm mispronouncing her name. Again, I can say it, because I'm quoting the voice in my head, but I can't spell it. And to be fair, maybe he isn't actually masturbating. But the pictures I'm getting of her inside my head from a movie called *The Demoniacs* sure seem like he should be. I almost want to join him."

"A psychic circle jerk?"

"Possibly."

"Your so-called creator is a sick fuck, like mine."

"Perhaps. But there's more to him than perversion; otherwise, my story wouldn't be so complex. I mean, like, a Jean Rollin movie called *The Iron Rose* is stuck in my head, but what significance does an Iron Rose' hold to me, or anybody?"

" Iron Rose'? Beats the shit out of me, baby. I have no clue. Unless you give it to someone for Valentine's, but then beat their ass with it."

"Well, I have clues, I just don't know what they mean. Which makes them useless."

"That's how I feel all the time. It's all one big mind-fuck, sugar."

"If these clues have no meaning, then it's all meaningless."

"Trust me. It's meaningless."

"Still, I can't help wondering why these particular details are seeping through the barrier from his brain to mine, except my brain is linked to his brain."

"Well, if it's any help, this movie *Night of the Hunted* really exists, here and now, because one of my Johns—who is actually named John—saw it in France last year. I don't think it played over here, at least not here in Hollywood or in Westwood, where I go for most of my movies. At first, I thought he meant that movie with Robert Mitchum, but that's called *Night of the Hunter*. That's a good one, too. My mom used to watch it on late-night TV. It's easy to confuse those titles, but they're *totally* different flicks."

"I can't confuse them because I've never heard of either of them. So far, I've only heard of Jean Rollin, only because I can hear my creator's thoughts sometimes without seeing him, because his fantasies co-exist in the same place where I live."

"*The Twilight Zone*?"

"I don't get the reference, but that sounds about right."

"*Whoa*. That's deep. Deep into what, I don't know. But definitely deep."

"But something happened in between the first book about me and the second because the second book of my life is so warped and twisted and sick. I would like to know how he got that way because he ruined the innocence of my entire world with his corrupted imagination."

"How so, exactly?"

"By subverting my happiness with his perverted sense of humor. Why should he be happy when I am not? I think that's a line from a movie, too."

"Nothing you're saying makes any sense to me at all, so I guess anything's possible since normal rules no longer apply to this conversation."

"I'm still piecing it together myself. I only physically perceive certain details about his character, life, and world, meaning this one, and his place in it. These clues somehow selectively penetrate the veil that separates our dimensions. I don't know whether his demented mind sprang a leak or there's a spiritual snitch somewhere that is on my side. Or if he's planting them himself, just to mess with me."

"There are plenty of clues for anything to be true if you look hard enough. That don't necessarily *make* it true."

"You think that Truth is an illusion?"

"It is if you can't touch it."

"You don't believe in unseen truths?"

"Not since you told me you had my money."

"I do, just not the kind you want."

"Now *that's* some fuckin' truth right there. Nothin' ain't *never* what you want. Well, hardly ever."

"So you really think I'm crazy?"

"Don't matter what I think. What do *you* think, Chumpy Walnut?"

"I don't think I'm mentally ill, though I suppose that's a possibility. It's more like I feel like I've transcended to a place I only vaguely recognize, where I don't belong. But I don't feel like I belong anywhere. I've spent my entire life idling in No Parking zones."

"Maybe you're parked in a dream right now, ever think of that?"

"I think it's *all* a dream, but we don't know for sure until we wake up, and then it's too late."

"That's called Death,' my delusional new friend."

"But I'm not dead. I can never die, because I'm immortalized in print."

"Like I said, I never fuckin' heard of you or these fuckin' books you keep talking about."

"Well, it's sort of selective, subjective immortality."

"What's your life story in a walnut shell, baby? I got no time to read anything but a money order."

"I was found on a doorstep inside a bird's nest after a fire destroyed the village of my people, just outside a town called Lonesome Grove. The kindly couple who found me, Woody and Minnie Walnut, raised me as their own, even though I was much smaller than everyone else. I only grew to be a foot tall. The townspeople were very mean to me, as most people are to anyone different, so in that sense, from what I can sense, your world is the same as mine. Eventually, I ran away, mostly for my parents' sake. But two hoboes, Goosey Maloy and Jinx Hoolihan, found me and took me to a city called Excelsior, where I was exploited on the nightclub circuit, run by gangsters. Then—"

"Hold on, Homer. I said walnut shell,' not ghetto dumpster."

"Okay. I met Cupey on this nightclub circuit. She was half an inch shorter than I, the only other survivor of the forest fire. We were very happy back in Lonesome Grove, till she suddenly and mysteriously grew to be your size, and was kidnapped by a mad scientist and his monster assistant, who wanted to exploit her in a series of underground pornographic films, and—"

"Okay, *now* it's getting interesting."

"No, this is where everything went horribly wrong."

"If you say so, but I'd read *that* fuckin' book."

"Anyway, Paige Pinup made me forget everything with her Magic Theremin, or at least suppress my memories, so I'm left with only impressions, some vague, some vivid. But despite her effort to give me a fresh start, all of my memories, good and bad, have resurfaced in dreams. I can't even tell the difference between which are memories and which are dreams. Some of my dreams were of Landoli, the imaginary land of my ancestors, which apparently never existed."

"I think we're on the right track here because none of this shit ever actually existed. Go on."

"The Magic Theremin's powers have only succeeded in

confusing the meaning of my existence even further. So it backfired."

"What the fuck is a theremin' anyway? I know what magic is. I'm lookin' at it right now."

"Hard to explain. It's this weird thing that makes strange noises."

"Yeah. I've had a few of those, too. Who the fuck is Paige Pinup?"

"On your world, she's known as Bettie Page, only not nearly as...superhuman."

"Who the fuck is Bettie Page?"

"Don't ask me, it's your world, not mine."

"Who the fuck should I ask then?"

"Your own creator, I guess."

"*Shee-it*. That's like sayin' I should turn up the sound on a silent movie."

"Anyway, it's been nice talking to you, even nicer than the sex."

"Not for me, baby. Sex is my preferred language. I'm fluent as fuck."

"I need to return to my quest soon."

"Because you're Jonny Quest?"

"No, because I'm Chumpy Walnut."

"You sure are. So that's what this is all about? You want to find your so-called creator'? In L.A.? Good luck, chump."

"Chumpy."

"Yeah, I know. Now I see why that's a good name for you. Anyway, what do you expect him to tell you, anyway, if by some miracle you do hook up?"

"My question to my creator is simple. I believe you'd translate it as WTF?'"

"How do you know *anyone* created you? That's a big leap of faith I never took because I knew I'd fall into a bottomless pit."

"Part of it is instinctual, partly practical. If I quit

believing in something bigger than me, which is almost everything, I'd probably blow my brains out. The problem with that is they don't make guns that small. Well, not where I come from. Here I have a shot. As it were."

"I got a gun in my purse, too. It's backup for the mace."

"I don't want to die before my creator dies because that will leave too many unanswered questions. It's so sad that someday he will disappear. I want to meet him first."

"Won't you disappear when he does?"

"My life lives in the books, in a loop until the next one is written, meaning the one we're in now. Even if no one reads them, that's where I live. Forever."

"You need to cool it or the wrong person will think you're stone sicko and pop a cap in that cute little ass."

"Don't worry about me. I'll be fine."

"Oh, because already you're so fuckin' cool, Chumpy Walnut?"

"No. Because nobody cares enough about me to even notice my fears or tears. You're right. It really is like I don't even exist."

"You exist enough to be sitting here with me right now, don't you? Because I *definitely* exist, sugar."

"I don't really remember meeting you before waking up next to you. Do you?"

"Of *course,* what the hell? You were wandering down Hollywood Boulevard, all lost and lonely, so I asked if you wanted company, and you said yes, but like you were in a trance and I was your hypnotist. Since the Bowl Motel, where I normally operate, was just around the corner on Cahuenga, I brought you here, where I bring all my clients. This is my home base of operations. You don't remember *any* of that?"

"No, I don't. Though I do have impressions of your world that could only come from actual observation. I'm more of an observer of humanity than a participant. So it makes sense there was a period of adjustment that escapes me, at least for the moment, because of the sudden transition from one dimension to the next."

"Well, you did seem disoriented, but once we got naked on the bed, it all seemed to come back to you pretty fast."

"Hm. My last memory before this was being back in Thrillville, the name of the town where I live, or lived, and sleeping beside Cupey, who rolled over and crushed me by accident. Again. Then I started drifting back asleep when I got the vertigo. Now here I am."

"Uh-huh, well, okay, good luck with all that, Chumpy Walnut. Now there's a call I gotta take."

"From who?"

"Nature."

As Tanisha Alopecia goes to the bathroom to wash Chumpy's walnut juice off of her, his penis abruptly retracts like a turtle into its shell, shrinking like a popped balloon so it fits inside his underwear without conspicuously bulging. He puts on the aloha shirt and cabana shorts he normally wears back in Thrillville, which survived the journey not only intact, but properly sized for his new "normal" height of about five feet five inches, which isn't tall, but not short, either, at least by his previous standards.

When Tanisha Alopecia comes back out wearing her leather halter top, mini-skirt, and knee-high boots (inspired by her favorite Marvel comics character, "Nightshade, Queen of the Werewolves," created by Steve Englehart), Chumpy is still there, sitting on the edge of the bed.

"I need to find someone named Tom Waits and warn him he's in danger of being killed," he says. "It will happen close to here."

Tanisha Alopecia looks surprised, though she thought she was past that by now. "Tom Waits, the singer? *Small Change* and *Blue Valentines* and *Nighthawks at the Diner*? I have all his albums. He's actually a friend of mine. He lived in this motel called the Tropicana, where I have my other job. I haven't seen him in a while, though, since he doesn't live there anymore. And you think he's gonna be assassinated by a crazed fan or something, like the President?"

"Not on purpose. It will be an accident."

"By who?"

"My creator."

"Oh, I get it. You mean God. At least *your* god. Mine is an arrogant, mean prick who takes us *all* out eventually after makin' us suffer for no good god damn reason I can see. He's probably hiding inside one of those pissed-off lookin' Tiki God statues back in Waikiki, who gets off punishing people who don't deserve it. Well, I mean, except for politicians and preachers, who are also arrogant pricks, *they* deserve it, though they do tip me pretty well. And none of this shit ain't no accident. It's all part of His fucked-off plan. I think Tom Waits can Wait in line like the rest of us."

"Can you take me to meet him?"

"Who, your creator? I can't even meet *my* all-powerful bitch! I mean, not till I die. And I ain't in no hurry."

"No. I mean Tom Waits."

"Well, I misspoke out of vanity. I met him a few times at this coffee shop where I worked. But I don't *know* the cat, sugar. I just dig his music. He sings for and about people like me. I have a few extra copies of his albums in that closet there if you wanna take a listen. I keep some stashed here for when I get bored in between appointments, or just want to be alone with my thoughts."

"So you live here?"

"No, it's just my home office. I share it with another girl who has the night shift. She likes my albums, too. *Heart Attack and Vine* is our favorite."

Chumpy, curious to learn more about Tom Waits—and there's no better way to know an artist than through their art—nods enthusiastically. An hour later, he has listened to two and a half Tom Waits albums, lying still on the bed as Tanisha Alopecia smokes joints and lies beside him, both lost in a musically induced coma.

"What do you think?" Tanisha Alopecia asks Chumpy.

"I like all of them. A lot. But *Rain Dogs* is still my favorite. It just sounds more like *me*."

"He didn't do an album called that."

"Not yet. He will, though."

"I'm gonna hold you to that, Chumpy Walnut."

"Please do. Now I really have to save him so he can record his future albums, like *Rain Dogs* and *Swordfishtrombones*. Hey, can we go back outside and walk around for a bit? I'm hungry." "Look, sugar, you already got a free ride, which I decided is on the house since I would've paid *you* for that rare pleasure, but I can't be buyin' you no lunch 'n' shit."

"I'm afraid no one will take my foreign money and I'll starve."

"You got that right. Okay, how about this. I know this little joint up around the corner, Snow White's Cottage or someshit. It has all these murals of cartoon characters, all the creepy dwarves, and that privileged princess bitch, and feels like it should be at Disneyland. You may feel right at home there. I'll treat you to some eggs and waffles, how's that?"

"I don't eat eggs or any animal products."

"*What*? How are you even alive?"

"That's my question."

"Aw, fuck me. A vegetarian too. Toast will have to do, I guess. Snow White don't serve no alfalfa sprouts. You want that shit, you gotta go up to The Source on Sunset, where all my hippie clients eat. I ain't traveling that far because I'm workin'. I can do a quick lunch break, then you're on your own. Cool?"

Chumpy nods sadly. "Cool," he says softly.

Tanisha's hard-boiled heart melts despite herself. Chumpy reminds her of the son she never had but always dreamed of, except he'd be darker on the outside, not as dark on the inside.

The day is bright, breezy, and sunny, with blue skies, fleecy clouds, and less smog than usual. At the Snow White Cafe, where "No Other Girl" by the Blasters is blasting from the sound system, Chumpy continues relating his many life experiences as Tanisha Alopecia listens, fascinated by his imagination and seduced by his innocence. He is indeed entranced by the murals of Snow White and the Seven Dwarves lining the brick walls. The otherwise divey coffee shop has no official affiliation with Walt Disney. None of the depressed Hollywood Boulevard denizens seems concerned about copyright infringement.

Sitting in the hard red chairs of the sleazy but strangely soothing storybook sanctuary, Chumpy tells a mildly amused Tanisha Alopecia all about his many misadventures with mad men, monsters, mobsters, molls, and misfits in his distant dreamworld of permanently retro Space Age aesthetics and pulp-cartoon pulchritude.

"I think maybe *you* were the one who wrote this jazz in a book nobody read," Tanisha Alopecia tells him after he takes a breath. "Then you got conked on the head and woke up thinking you're your own creation. Maybe *you're* the creator of your wild-ass fantasies."

"I'm not a writer. I'm just a character."

"Like I keep sayin', ain't we all. How was your toast?"

"Dry."

"Why didn't you just have waffles?"

"They contain eggs."

"They don't kill the chicken for their eggs, sugar."

"No, they just torture and rob them. *Then* kill them."

Tanisha Alopecia sighs in surrender. "Well, you should've tried the BLT, damn good for a cheesy joint like this."

"I like pigs too much."

"I like em too. I ate a million of em at luaus 'n' shit."

"How sad."

"I was happy. Happier than I am now, that's for sure. How do you like this joint?"

"I like it. It reminds me somewhat of where I come from."

"Yeah, I figured you'd say that. Anyway, why don't you eat meat? Just another non-sensical enigma, mystery boy?"

"Animals are as sentient as we are. I can feel their suffering. "

"Yeah, well, I can taste it. Tastes fuckin' *good*."

"How depressing."

"So it's about empathy for innocent victims?"

"Yes."

"I can dig it. You are somethin' else, Chumpy Walnut."

"So are you, Tanisha Alopecia."

"Tell me, if you just showed up here all of a sudden, how do you even know you're on a so-called mission?"

"I was on this mission long before I came here. I think I thought about it so much my destination self-manifested, or at least, allowed me dimensional proximity to my goal."

"Have you always talked like this?"

"No. I used to be naive."

"What are you now?"

"Cynical."

"And that makes you use all those big words?"

"Cynicism is a complex state, especially when mixed with confusion. My research is simply a way to explain and understand it."

"Yeah? How's that goin'?"

"I don't know. It got me here with you. So I guess okay."

Tanisha Alopecia smiles and winks at him.

"I like your dimples," he tells her.

"I like your cock," she replies with a wink.

After lunch, Chumpy asks Tanisha Alopecia to take him into the Hollywood Wax Museum next door.

"I guess I ain't workin' today," Tanisha Alopecia says.

"You deserve a day off," Chumpy says. "I can tell you

work hard."

"Yeah, well, thanks, but I'm supposed to make it *look* easy, not just *be* easy."

"You do a good job. Take it from me. Enjoy an afternoon off."

"My pimp won't like it."

"I'll talk to him."

"Yeah, that I gotta see. Show him your cock and you'll make millions. He'll not only forgive me but give me a finder's fee."

Chumpy quietly considers this option.

Inside the tourist trap, grotesque statues of Frank Sinatra, Dean Martin, Sammy Davis Jr., Elvis Presley, and Marilyn Monroe trigger Chumpy's memories of their counterparts in his consciousness.

"I've met all these people," Chumpy says. "Most are zombies now. I mean, where I come from."

"Yeah, they're zombies here, too."

"They look like it. But these aren't real."

"Neither are you."

"Good point."

"They all got big cocks like you where you come from? I mean, except Marilyn."

"Frankie Sonata brags to everyone about his."

"Yeah, I've heard that, too."

"All of these are clues to my own creation since my creator obviously took inspiration from these doppelgängers of your dimension."

Tansisha Alopecia shakes her head. "I blew off my shift for a date with the fuckin' Nutty Professor. Come on, Chump E. Love."

Chumpy gets excited by the Chamber of Horror exhibit, featuring monsters he's seen in movies back in Thrillville, only they have different names here: Frankenstein, Dracula, the Wolf Man, the Mummy. "I love horror movies," Chumpy says as he gazes in awe.

"Then you're lovin' life, baby."

After leaving the museum, they continue down Hollywood Boulevard. The currently popular music of Blondie, Devo, the Go-Go's, the Stray Cats, the Blasters, the B-52s, and the Cramps provides the soundtrack, blaring from cars, record stores, and boom boxes, resulting in a singular sonic ambiance. Chumpy finds the sights and sounds of his creator's world quite revelatory, not to mention exhilarating and stimulating. He is on the verge of a sensory overload that might result in spontaneous combustion.

"I recognize all of these bands and songs," Chumpy says. "Same melodies. Different lyrics, though."

"Yeah, I bet they do, sugar."

Just past Hollywood and Vine, they encounter a disheveled older man who wears hard experience on his creased and pockmarked face like a badge of dishonor. He's deep in intense contemplation as he stumbles into the midday sunlight from the fabled Frolic Room.

"Hi Charles," Tanesha says flirtatiously to the old man, who really isn't that old, just brilliantly embittered.

Charles nods and just keeps walking.

"Who's that?" Chumpy asks.

"Charles Bukowski, the writer. My favorite writer, in fact."

"I thought you didn't read?"

"I don't, but he's my most entertaining john, or was till I met you. He reads me his poetry sometimes. I like that shit."

"So if I read you my story, you'd like it?"

"You can try. I'd have to charge you real money, though. No more freebies."

"I don't have a copy of the book. It's not even published yet, from your perspective. But it's my story, so I can tell you anyway. I have plenty more to share."

"I think I've heard enough for now, Chumpy Walnut, but

thanks."

"Wait a minute. Charles Bukowski? His name sounds familiar. He might know my creator."

"Hopefully *he* ain't your creator, or you are seriously fucked."

"No, he's not. But he has some connection. Can we catch up and ask him?"

"As long as we buy him a drink. I mean, as long as *I* do. You're running up quite a tab, Chumpy Walnut. Maybe my pimp can turn you out as a hustler so I can get reimbursed."

"Okay!" Chumpy says.

"I was only kidding, but you do owe me a few good, hard fucks with that overinflated firehose."

"Okay!"

Ten minutes later, Chumpy and Tanisha Alopecia are sitting across from Charles Bukowski in a booth at the legendary Hollywood restaurant Musso and Frank.

"This is where Tom Waits will have his last meal if I don't intervene," Chumpy says matter-of-factly.

'"That's enough for now," Tanisha Alopecia says. "Just concentrate on finding your creator to solve the mystery of your existence and all that jazz."

"And save Tom Waits."

"Hush."

" Hush'…that's a song on the soundtrack of *Once Upon a Time in Hollywood*, which has a scene set here."

"Nope, nope, nope again, never fuckin' ever heard of it."

"No one has. Yet. So don't feel bad."

"I feel great, thanks to that portable piston of yours."

As they sit down, Bukowski is already on his second beer with an open tab and halfway through a ham sandwich on rye, made especially for him. Since he has no ID to flash for a cocktail, Chumpy is eating French fries, and Tanisha Alopecia is snacking on a shrimp cocktail, even though she just ate, because she's temporarily cutting back on her drinking after the morning's inexplicable events.

Chumpy tells Bukowski all about himself. The grizzled poet maintains a nonplussed expression throughout, admiring the inventiveness, as well as the philosophical implications, but weary of the self-indulgence, which makes him quietly question his own literary method.

"I'm looking for my Higher Power," Chumpy says to Bukowski.

"He'd have to be pretty high to have created you," replies Bukowski.

"Don't you want to meet your creator?"

"Never."

"Why not?"

"Because that means I'll either be dead or too drunk to think straight."

"I might already be dead, but I'm not drunk. Yet."

"Listen, kid, have you ever considered whether your alleged creator is fictional, and you're the real one? Maybe he's a figment of *your* imagination and not the other way around."

"I'm not hallucinating," Chumpy says.

"Drink a dirty martini and fix that."

"I prefer mai tais."

"Mai tais are for sissies."

"I guess I'm a sissy."

"I guess you are. Nothing wrong with being a sissy. Few admit it, though. Anyway, I'm unable to help you. Never heard of you or your damn creator,' unless you mean *my* imaginary megalomaniac, but we're estranged. We don't talk anymore. He never did talk, not to me. I was talking to myself. I still do that, but I assume nobody is listening now. Let it go, kid. Stop looking for meaning. Life is Art for Art's sake, nothing more. Or less."

"Art the Clown?"

"*What?* What fuckin' clown?"

"Never mind," Chumpy says. "I don't know myself. So, why do you think your god ignores you?"

"Because I doubt he even exists. He takes it personally. Fuckin' insecure like most dictators. Or clowns."

"You sound like me," Chumpy says.

"I'm nothing like you, kid. I like hard drinks, not umbrellas dipped in pussy juice."

"That actually sounds tasty," Tanisha Alopecia says.

"You're a dirty whore," Bukowski says.

"So?"

"Don't call my friend bad names," Chumpy says.

"That was a compliment," Bukowski says. "I love dirty whores. If they're too clean, they're shitty in the sack and not worth my time."

"I still get the feeling we have a mutual friend," Chumpy tells Bukowski. "Or rather, you have a mutual friend with my creator."

"You mean *this* dirty whore?"

"Fuck you, prune dick!" Tanisha Alopecia snaps at Bukowski.

"You mean my face is a prune. My dick is a ripe butternut squash."

"I sense our mutual friend is an actor of some sort," Chumpy says. "A famous one."

"So another dirty whore," Bukowski.

"Just your type," Tanisha Alopecia says.

"I don't hang out with lowlifes, kid," Bukowski tells Chumpy. "Well, I do, but only for material and honest company. They're lowlifes due to circumstances, not their character. Regular people and people who play them in movies are as useless as a pool table with no pockets."

"So you mean a billiard table, dumbass," Tanisha Alopecia tells Bukowski.

"Exactly. Billiards are for uptight mid-to-upper-class morons."

"I just want to know why I was created," Chumpy says. "Is that too much to ask?"

"*Yes*," Tanisha Alopecia and Bukowski say in unison.

"Don't look at me for answers, kid," Bukowski says. "I sure as hell ain't your creator."

"That's painfully clear," Chumpy says. "I was just operating on a hunch since that's the only guideline I have."

"That's more than most of us got to go on," Bukowski says.

"Uh, oh, there's Fate," Tanisha Alopecia says nervously, looking over her shoulder.

"No such thing, " Bukowski says. "You make your own luck. Believing it's all predestined is one more way to chicken out and not take responsibility for your own actions."

"I believe in destiny," Chumpy says. "But I'm not a chicken. Although I like chickens."

"Fried or baked?" Bukowski asks.

"Alive and free."

"You really are a naive little fuck. I almost like you. But you're too weird even for me. You creep me out."

"You creep me out, too," Chumpy tells Bukowski. "But I still like you."

"Because you're better than me, kid. Better and weirder."

"Being weirder makes me better?"

"Being better makes you weird."

"You set a low bar."

"So I can reach my drinks from a prone position."

"You both better hope that dude lookin' for me ain't *both* your destinies," Tanisha Alopecia says, ducking down. "Fate rarely comes lookin' for me in fancy places like this. He must be pissed because he lost track of me after I left the Bowl, and he knows I had business there, so he wants his cut, even if it's a piece of nothing. We're *all* in trouble now."

"Speak for yourself," Bukowski says. "Like I said, I don't even believe in Fate the Pimp, so he has no power over me, either."

"You owe him money, too," Tanisha Alopecia reminds

him.

"Another narcissistic authoritarian on patrol." Bukowski gets up abruptly, downing the rest of his beer in an expedient gulp. "Gotta go."

"What happened to being responsible?" Chumpy asks Bukowski.

"I'm only responsible for my bar tab, kid. I don't pay for sex because those fluids are free. They come with the meat. Like gravy."

"Gravy is extra," Tanisha Alopecia says.

"Only if you swallow it," Bukowski says.

"That beer ain't no bodily fluid!" Tanisha Alopecia says.

"It is now."

"And my all-natural pussy juice ain't on tap!"

"My cock is your pipe dream, baby."

"What does that even mean?"

"Nothing, because everything means nothing and nothing means everything. It's spontaneous poetry."

"You owe me for my pussy *and* that beer!"

Bukowski jerks a thumb at Chumpy. "Except suddenly I'm supposed to be a guidance counselor for nut jobs like him. I don't work for chump or Chumpy change unless it's at the post office. At least they give me health benefits."

"Fat lotta good that does you!" Tanisha Alopecia snaps. "Greasy old wart hog!"

"I just drank my self-prescribed medicine on your dime. Consider it a health benefit for my consulting services."

"*Yo, Tanisha!*" Fate the Pimp yells after he spots her, aggressively pushing past two waiters and a maître d', which slows him down long enough for the prurient poet to impart one last bit of world-weary wisdom:

"Be tough and smart and you'll be fine," Bukowski tells Chumpy. "You weren't created, you popped out of a shell after dropping from a tree, fully formed and already fucked up from the fall. Just like the rest of us. We're *all* fuckin' nuts, kid. There. You're cured. Or cursed, what's the hell's the difference except for a single letter that stands for shit'? Call us even. Just don't call *me*. So long, saps." Bukowski walks quickly out the back, stiffing them on the check, but that was already factored into the budget.

Tanisha Alopecia looks over her shoulder to see her pimp looming over their booth. Fate the Pimp is a tall, slender black man wearing a black porkpie hat, a white pirate shirt, tight leather pants with sequins, black cowboy boots, a necklace of shrunken skulls, ornate rings on every finger but his thumbs, and a big grin that showcases several gold teeth he had installed as replacements for emergency currency purposes.

When he looks down at a shivering Chumpy Walnut, Fate stops smiling, and his safety deposit box is closed.

Chapter Two
MIDNIGHT IN THE MONSTER SEX MOTEL

"I miss my beloved husband so much," Cupey Honeysuckle says breathlessly just before Paige Pinup brings her to another reality-altering, orally-induced orgasm. It's actually her twenty-fourth orgasm of the day. Still, all the rest were results of transactional copulation with sexually voracious zombie-men, the leftovers from the semi-mini-Apocalypse that nearly destroyed the nation, or at least parts of it that most people don't know or care much about anyway, except for Las Velvis, where a whirlwind zombie outbreak came and went without much notice outside of the property destruction which was rebuilt quickly by Mob-owned contractors. These sad, social outcasts are regular clientele of the Monster Sex Motel, one of Thrillville's most popular attractions, who have been rejected by their wives and girlfriends due to their extreme unattractiveness. The fourteen rooms of the midcentury modernist-designed Monster Sex Motel are garishly decorated with grotesque zombie-tiki statues and lurid paintings of nude women and horny monsters, bathed in the neon-rainbow glow of various lava lamps, equipped with plush silk bedding and velvet drapes, sonically abetted by Exotica music playing non-stop over the sound system to perfect its pagan perfection. It is a profitable mercy mission and haven for hideously deformed heathens, including the Rot Pack, the regular musical act at Ivar's Tiki Lounge. In another dimension, they are dismissed as "incels," although in that case, their unattractiveness is primarily internal, not external, therefore of their own making. By stark contrast, the drooling zombie men of Thrillville are victims of a back-firing manmade disaster.

Even though she takes pleasure from giving pleasure to the ugly and unworthy, who shows the most appreciation for their salacious services, nobody can make Cupey climax like Paige Pinup, except of course for her fellow bombshells Monica Tiki Goddess, Hotsie Totsie, Lola Lovejoy, and Queen Exotica, co-madams of the Best Brothel in the West, as officially awarded by numerous news organizations, none of which are particularly credible or respectable, but the recognition is a nice gesture, anyway. The customers always leave happy, and that's all that matters. Except for the massive amounts of money that have made them all rich, of course.

Paige Pinup's attempt to wipe all memory of these events from Chumpy's mind via her Magic Theremin eventually failed, as it did with the rest of an apathetic population she attempted to hypnotize via television waves, because memories resurface in dreams and most people are self-delusional, anyway. Also, for it to truly work, Cupey would need to be completely complicit in perpetuating the mental mirage, and she is nobody's tool. Chumpy is Cupey's tool, and she misses him because, despite their extremely incompatible size differences, he will always be her true love, and no one else can fill that void, even if he keeps slipping out of it during intercourse. Apparently, he's fallen from one void into another.

"I miss Chumpy, too," Paige Pinup says, licking her lips and wiping her chin. "Not as much as you do, obviously."

"It's not the same without him watching."

"I understand. It's so strange he disappeared like that. Are you sure he wasn't kidnapped?"

"By whom? Shades Wheeler and all of our enemies are long gone. Plus, I had that vision of him floating in the air, then getting sucked into a vortex before totally vanishing. I thought it was a dream, but the fact that he's nowhere to be found in our dimension proves it was real."

Paige is puzzled. "What do you mean, our dimension'?"

"For the past year, he's been telling me about his dreams of other worlds, including one where the person he thinks is his creator lives. I told him I actually had a conversation with that megalomaniac once, and he's better off ignoring him."

"What? You talked to Chumpy's creator?"

"Yes. Mine too. And yours."

"I'm agnostic."

"Only because he made you that way."

"Bullshit."

"Nope."

"Excuse the hell out of me, Cupey doll, but I am in complete control of my own body, lifestyle, and destiny."

"Sure you are. Thanks to him."

"Hey, fuck off, Cupey, seriously. I thought you were a feminist like the rest of us."

"We're only feminists' by his sexist standards. Haven't you wondered why all of us are prodigiously promiscuous, pansexual prostitutes with big hair, hour-glass figures, and high heels even when we're naked, which is most of the time?"

"Because we're fashionable, sex positive, business-savvy bombshells?"

"No, honey, I mean, yes, we are, but that's because deep down we're just someone's warped perception of a liberated' woman. I mean, I'm fine with it because at least I'm rewarded with a lot of creature comforts, so to speak. As are you. But I know a pervert when I see one, even if I can't actually see him."

"I certainly have no complaints."

"Of course you don't. That would be out of character."

"So you're saying we have no free will at all? How depressing."

"Funny you should say that. His name is Will."

"Who?"

"Our creator."

"If you have a direct line to him, can't you just ask him where Chumpy is, and make him give your husband back to you?"

"No, he doesn't talk to me anymore. I think it freaks him out that I have his psychic number. It dilutes his sense of power over me."

"Even if he's the source of that power."

"Exactly why I choose not to think about it. It's a serious mindfuck. *And* soulfuck. Paige, I want you to fuck with my pussy, not my mind. I don't care whose sick idea it is. I need more relief and distraction and I need it *now*. Please."

"On it."

Orgasm #25 is now in progress.

Elsewhere in Thrillville, Mayor Will the Thrill is masturbating to a live feed on his martini-shaped "Thrillocitor" of his wife, Monica Tiki Goddess, pleasing a trio of zombie men in her private suite of the Monster Sex Motel, because, as he tells her, "I dig it dirty, like my martinis." She is happy to oblige his lounge lizard libido from afar, because it frees her to indulge her own tawdry tendencies.

While indulging his base animal urges in the privacy of The Thrillpad, Will the Thrill is wearing a leopard print fez, zebra-print robe, tiger-print sunglasses, a leaky boner, and a handkerchief on his lap to quickly spot clean any spillover on his fancy duds. However, his pending emission is interrupted by another transmission on the Thrillocitor, one he didn't initiate. After following the first-person roving camera for a few minutes, Will the Thrill deduces that this particular magical mystery tour is being projected from a place called "Hollywood." The images are strange but vaguely recognizable, hampered by poor reception, but Will the Thrill thinks he makes out the figure of someone familiar on the busy street. Zooming in on the object of his curiosity, Will the Thrill closely views the visage of

Chumpy Walnut amid the dense urban sea of poorly dressed strangers, who aren't much taller than Chumpy, some being even shorter.

Before he can react, the foreign frequency goes haywire, then refocuses on a highly entertaining piece of vintage cinematic schlock called *The Mummy and the Curse of the Jackal.* Like the previous broadcast via this alien wavelength, the world this movie inhabits is somewhat similar, specifically regarding the nearby resort town of Las Velvis, ground zero for the Black Widow Zombie Massacre. However, in this case too, much of the cultural landscape appears oddly distorted, as if replicated in a dream. A big fan of B movies, especially since he virtually lives in one of his own making, Will the Thrill is immediately absorbed into this alternate dimension of dementia, figuring the flick must be yet another bootleg broadcast of a pirated print. Then, towards the end of the film, the screen turns into static before suddenly switching back to Monica Tiki Goddess in the throes of orgasmic bliss, so Will the Thrill doesn't get to find out who won the battle to possess the resurrected Egyptian princess, the Mummy or the Werejackal, which is quite frustrating. It was as if he accidentally hacked into a forbidden mainframe, intercepting forbidden footage, and someone in charge abruptly changed the channel.

End Transmission. Start Emission.

Back at Musso and Frank, Fate the Pimp is about to change Chumpy's destiny.

"Well, shit, there he is, Screamin' Jay Superfly," Tanisha Alopecia sighs. "Stalkin' me again. Sammy Davis called, baby. He wants his jewelry back."

Ignoring Tanisha, Fate the Pimp grabs a frightened Chumpy by the throat and lifts him out of the booth as if he were still diminutive in size, as opposed to merely below average height in this universe. Tanisha's taunts turn into pleas for mercy, but they go unheeded. Like his namesake, Fate the Pimp has already made up his mind what is going to happen next and is not listening to rational pleas for fairness. She keeps trying anyway.

"Fate, don't hurt him. He's only a cartoon!"

Fate the Pimp is unmoved and unimpressed. "Where's my fuckin' money, Jonny Quest?"

"I know, right?" Tanisha Alopecia says.

"My name is Chumpy Walnut," Chumpy says defiantly with a gurgling sound as real oxygen struggles to keep pumping through his cartoon pipes.

"*Fate, leave him alone!*" Tanisha Alopecia cries, standing up and pounding her pimp on his muscular shoulder. Meantime, police sirens wail in the background, which is Fate the Pimp's cue to wrap this situation up and send it express airmail to the future.

"Bitch, you called me from the Bowl and told me this cartoon-faced sucker paid you with fuckin' *Monopoly* money! I went lookin' for you there, then everywhere, till someone told me they saw you come in here with that deadbeat Bukowski. But I can catch up with his wet cracker ass later. Right now, I'm gonna shake this little sucka till gold coins drop out his little Hanna-Barbera Disney ass. Fate needs more fillings."

Chumpy's arms are flailing as he insistently gasps, "I'm not Jonny Quest, I'm Chumpy Walnut! Leave me alone!"

"We talked about this back at the Bowl and decided he's more a Fritz the Cat type," Tanisha Alopecia says.

"*What*? He ain't no talkin' fuckin' *cat*!"

"Actually, I'm more like a Tex Avery character," Chumpy says. "At least that's what my intuition tells me."

"Tex Avery? Who the fuck is Tex Avery?"

"I have no idea," Chumpy admits. "I think he's the guy who did Bugs Bunny," Tanisha Alopecia says

"You mean Mel Blanc?"

"No, not the voice, the animator."

Suddenly, another voice volunteers for the chaotic chorus. "Though he's acknowledged as the one most responsible for honing Bugs' persona, Tex Avery did a lot more than Bugs Bunny," says a pasty, pudgy, middle-aged studio exec on a lunch break, pontificating professorially from a nearby booth. "This was after co-creating him with Chuck Jones, Friz Freleng, Bob Clampett, and Bob McKimson, so Tex shared some credit. But I agree. That guy definitely looks more like Jonny Quest, so I'm totally on your side there, sir."

"*Shut the fuck up, Mister Peabody*!" Fate the Pimp snaps at him, followed by immediate compliance. "Ain't nobody here that wants to hear your fuckin' bullshit!"

"I think his *world* is like a Tex Avery cartoon," Tanisha Alopecia explains desperately, but with little conviction. "Now that I think about it, I think Tex Avery did the one with that horny wolf whistling at the Red Riding Hood stripper. I kinda remember his name in the credits."

Fate the Pimp stops shaking Chumpy for a moment to consider this late-breaking tidbit of information. "Hm. That's my favorite. That *is* one sexy bitch. If I put her on the street, I'd be a millionaire. Didn't know it was some fuckin' cowboy who made it. But this freaky doll dude here is flesh and blood, not no cartoon dog."

"Wolf," Tanisha Alopecia says.

"*Whatever,* bitch! Fuck!"

"The point is he ain't from here, Fate! Give him a break!"

"I was thinking maybe Max Fleischer," another nearby nerdy studio exec nervously offers after raising a hand but not waiting to be called on. "You know, Betty Boop and Popeye. He also produced a series of excellent Superman cartoons, combining elements of pulp film noir and science fiction, which is why this guy can be so handsome, but in a vintage animation sort of way."

Fate the Pimp remains silent along with the entire restaurant for a long beat, his eyes closed, though his eyelids keep fluttering, as he attempts to contain his frustration.

Finally, he says in a threatening tone, "I said, *shut*, the *fuck*, *up, all* you cartoon-watchin', cereal-eatin' crackers! This piece of Play-Doh ain't no fuckin' little boop-doop-a-doop pixie *whore* and he ain't no wisecrackin' smart-ass drag queen rabbit neither! Now cough up my cash, cartoon boy!"

"All I have is the money I already gave her," Chumpy says. "Now I don't even have that."

"Then give me some gold! Ain't they got that in your Magical Mystery Kingdom?"

"I don't have any gold coins in my pockets," Chumpy says hoarsely.

"Then you better *shit* some from that Little Golden Book ass of yours, and right quick, chump!"

"Chumpy."

"Ain't that what I said?"

The sirens have pulled up out front. Fate the Pimp normally avoids classy joints like this because his colorful attire, including his skin, tends to attract the wrong kind of attention. Of course, his racial makeup pales in comparison to Chumpy's foot-long penis suddenly protruding from his pants, sending everyone in the restaurant, especially Fate the Pimp, into a speechless state of suspended animation.

Right after this shocking and, for some, stimulating revelation, which only compounds the confusion, Chumpy turns into an actual walnut and drops to the floor, rolling beneath the booth. Already accustomed to a series of suddenly surreal occurrences, Tanisha Alopecia bends down, picks up the walnut, stuffs it in her cleavage while ignoring the walnut's muffled cries, and splits without paying the check. She feels she earned it with this impromptu floor show.

Fate the Pimp stands in stunned silence for a moment of serious reflection, then heads out the back entrance at a cop-eluding gate. He once again considers renouncing his wicked ways and getting a job as a nightclub bouncer, like his mama always wanted. The Musso manager announces drinks are on the house for everyone, including himself.

Meanwhile, Tanisha Alopecia hops on a bus headed towards her home on Doheny Drive near Santa Monica Boulevard, just past the West Hollywood border, so she can brag she lives in Beverly Hills, even though it's just a simple, if spacious, studio apartment.

On the bus, Tanisha Alopecia holds Chumpy the walnut close to her ear, pretending she's leaning against her hand, which is pressed to the window. She is whispering intensely, ignoring the stares of fellow passengers. But in L.A., crazy people who talk to themselves on the bus mostly go unnoticed. "So are you a talking walnut or a cartoon porn actor?"

"Both apparently," whispers the walnut. "However, I'm not an actor. Or in pornography. Not that I have anything against it. My wife works in a brothel."

"Are you okay with that, or are you jealous?"

"I vacillate."

"You mean you masturbate with Vaseline?"

"No, I mean sometimes it bothers me, naturally, but she's a beautiful woman and she has to have sex with *some*one, and it's not me. Plus, she gets paid well. She's free to do as she pleases. That pleases me, too."

"Too bad you didn't have that big dick back in your world."

"No, it was commensurate with my stature. Like I told you earlier, I was basically a human dildo. But at least I was human. Now I'm just a talking walnut." Tanisha Alopecia laughs and tries to suppress it, but the more she does, the harder she laughs. Not just out of amusement, but from her accelerated loss of sanity. She's somewhat comforted by the fact that there were many witnesses to Chumpy's abrupt transformation in full view back at Musso and Frank, so it wasn't just her having a nervous breakdown. The incident definitely scared Fate the Pimp away, perhaps permanently, finally freeing her to start a new life.

Tanisha Alopecia gets off the bus at Doheny and Santa Monica and walks down to her apartment, with Chumpy ensconced within her bountiful bosoms. Chumpy the walnut is quite content with this unorthodox but conveniently cozy mode of transportation.

Inside her sparsely decorated pad, Tanisha Alopecia sets Chumpy on top of the kitchen counter while she undresses for her shower before changing into a waitress uniform for her shift at Dukes Coffee Shop at the legendary Tropicana Motel, back up Santa Monica Boulevard. Since she never brings her work home, Tanisha Alopecia sometimes trysts with clients in the motel rooms, both before and after her waitress shift, where she often encounters them. Several of her regulars are famous rock stars and actors visiting from out of town for gigs, while others are residents. She counts Joan Jett, Pat Benatar, and Deborah Harry as her personal friends, though she's never had sex with any of them. Yet.

"You'll have to wait here till I get back from work," Tanisha Alopecia tells Chumpy. "I can't bring you because I'll be too busy."

"Do you have a client who has a waitress fetish?"

"No, nut boy, I *am* a waitress twice a week. I'm saving up for an operation."

"You said earlier you *were* a waitress in a coffee shop, where you met Tom Waits. Past tense."

"This whole thing is making me *presently* tense, Chumpy. I lied because I was embarrassed. But yeah, I do whatever I can to make money for my operation. I'm just a way better hooker than I am a waitress."

"Operation? You look healthy and you're very pretty."

"I mean my alopecia. It's no longer responding to treatment. My wigs make my scalp itch. The procedure is called a scalp reduction,' which I need along with a hair transplant. Once that's done, I'm going back to beauty school. I can't make no one else feel fake-beautiful till I feel naturally beautiful myself, you dig, little walnut?"

"I'm hip to the lingo since it's common where I come from. So yes, I dig.' If I may ask, why are you a prostitute?"

"I never understand why people ask permission to ask something, then go ahead and ask it without permission."

"I'm not a person, I'm a walnut. At least at the moment. I'm just curious why you chose this particular profession, that's all."

"I could ask your wife the same."

"She feels she's providing a valuable service to zombies. And for the hot zombie sex."

"Hm. Never thought of it that way. Many of my Johns are like undead losers, though. And I do like the sex, sometimes anyway, and if I can help some poor zombie feel alive for a few minutes, I guess that's cool. It's like walking a dog. I get exercise, and the dog gets to relieve himself in a safe place. I know some guys who *wish* they could lick their own balls, too, but in that case, I'd be out of business. But helping lonely, ugly motherfuckers get off ain't why I do it. What keeps my legs open is the fact that it's the most bread I can make fast without robbing a bakery. Both are technically illegal, but prostitutes don't rub the fuzz the wrong way as much as stolen money. Especially since many of them are my clients, and they fuck for free, in exchange for my immunity."

"Makes sense."

"Says the talking walnut. So make yourself at home and try not to nut all over everything."

"Excuse me?"

"I'll leave the radio on for you. What kind of music do you like?"

"All kinds, but mostly jazz."

"Me too, but I don't know what station that is. I'll leave on KROQ, that okay? Lots of that music that reminds you of home is popular here, too, from what you've told me."

"Okay, thank you."

"You're welcome."

"I mean for everything. You're taking all of this really well. I imagine I'm quite a freak by your standards. Lately, I'm even freaking out myself, so I can't blame you."

"Honey, one thing that don't freak me out is freaks. I've met and fucked all kinds. Not *your* kind, cause I think you're a one-off reject from the freak factory, but now I can scratch you off the list, preemptively, since you weren't even *on* the damn list. I didn't see you comin'. Well, till this morning, when you came all over the place, and I couldn't miss it. Anyway, I'll see you either as a little walnut or as a big dick sometime after midnight, since my shift is dinner through late-night happy hour. Unless one of my regulars wants a midnight snack, if you can dig it. And I don't mean walnuts, so relax."

"I dig."

"Oh, do you sleep now that you're a walnut?"

"I don't know."

"I'm curious, so let me know later when I get back."

"Sure."

Tanisha Alopecia winks and leaves as "I Ran" by A Flock of Seagulls plays on the radio.

Chumpy stays perfectly still for hours, careful not to budge lest he roll off the counter and crack his shell. He isn't hungry since he is now part of a food group himself, though to some animals and zombies, humans are part of a food group, too.

Later that night at Dukes Coffee Shop, Tanisha Alopecia decides to tell her friends, Lux Interior and Poison Ivy of The Cramps, fresh from a gig up on Sunset Boulevard, about her experience with Chumpy Walnut, safe in the assumption that they'll think she is either crazy or high. Musicians are often crazy and high themselves, so they won't judge. They find her tale quite amusing, and Lux Interior says he wants to write a song about it, with her permission, or else without it. Tanisha Alopecia laughs and gives him all rights to the concept per a verbal contract.

"You really are a nut, Tanisha," Lux Interior tells her. "I guess this means you have relatives in town."

"I knew you liked nuts, Tanisha, but not the healthy kind," Poison Ivy adds.

"That fuckin' story doesn't sound too fuckin' healthy to me," Lux Interior says.

Poison Ivy laughs and says to Tanisha, "You should bring your pet walnut to the Whiskey-a-Go-Go for our gig tomorrow night."

"Maybe I will! I can sneak him in without paying!"

They all laugh again, as if she were kidding, not just insane.

At the next table, an elegantly, ethereally beautiful Australian actress with platinum blonde hair and perfect ivory skin, named Linda Kerridge, sits in solitude as "Down Under" by Men at Work plays on the sound system. Linda loves the sleek, simple style and permanent vacation vibe of the classic coffee shop, where she has breakfast almost every day, and other meals as well. It's her favorite rendezvous spot due to its convenience, as well as its comforts.

A couple of years earlier, Linda made a splash in a movie called *Fade to Black*, playing a Marilyn Monroe lookalike who becomes an object of obsession for a sociopathic movie fan. She lives in a comfortable one-bedroom apartment adjacent to the hotel. Lux Interior and Poison Ivy had offered her a seat at their table, but she said she wanted to read this manuscript a fan had given her. Linda can't help eavesdropping on her friend Tanisha's story, which she sees as a sign, since the book she's reading is about a guy only a foot tall, named "Chumpy Walnut." Linda believes the Universe is interconnected, and this is no accident. She tells Tanisha Alopecia that she overheard her story, and it reminds her of the book she's reading.

"Is it about a talking walnut?" Tanisha Alopecia asks.

"No, it's about a guy who's only a foot tall, named

Chumpy Walnut."

Tanisha Alopecia freezes, eyes bulging. "That's *my* talking walnut's friend, too."

Linda laughs. "Well. You'd better get that copyrighted! This book might actually get published!"

Tanisha Alopecia smiles tightly with a furrowed brow and says, "What an odd coincidence."

"Hey, you should meet me at the Pink Turtle tomorrow. I'm meeting the author there with his friend, Mickey Rourke. You know him?"

"The author?"

"No, Mickey Rourke."

"I loved him in that movie *Diner*, but as a waitress, maybe I'm biased. Anyway, he tried to pick me up once."

"*Get out!*"

"Well, not exactly. It was for someone else, actually. Happened just recently, too."

"I was in a movie with him!"

"You mean *Fade to Black*?"

"Yes, what else? It's not like I have a catalogue to choose from. But we had no scenes together, and this will be my first time meeting him, too!"

"Oh, right, right. He plays the bully, picking on Dennis Christopher, who dresses up as a cowboy and shoots his sexy-raggedy ass."

"Yeah, that's him! Oh, *please* show up there about ten tomorrow morning. You can meet Mickey and the author, too!"

Tanisha Alopecia's head is spinning with serendipity. "You ever get the idea that sometimes the Universe makes crazy sense when shit like this happens?"

"All the time," Linda says. "These are clues to our spiritual journey, to let us know that it all happens for a reason."

"Even if the reason seems unreasonable."

"Only to us."

"So it makes sense not to make any sense."

"That's my sense, yes." After her friend walks away, Linda sits quietly contemplating recent events as "Nowhere Girl" by B Movie plays on the sound system.

Tanisha Alopecia leaves work early to tell Chumpy she's already found his creator, but the walnut is nowhere to be found. It was all a hallucination, after all. She is somewhat relieved, somewhat worried, and very sad. Even if Chumpy Walnut was only the product of her imagination, she misses him already.

Chapter Three
BOOBY-TRAPPED

The next morning, after deciding she doesn't have to report to work on Hollywood Boulevard since she hasn't heard from Fate the Pimp, Tanisha Alopecia keeps her tentative rendezvous at the Pink Turtle inside the Beverly Wilshire Hotel. After settling into one of the pink booths, she sees Mickey Rourke engaged in a lively discussion with a tall, striking, strawberry blonde, whom she correctly assumes is his wife, and a teenage boy, who is also blonde, but not tall. Tanisha Alopecia figures it's the woman's brother, though she is incorrect in this assumption. However, it could be Chumpy's creator and proves that even though Linda is late, she isn't lying.

While surreptitiously staring at the teenager, who strongly reminds her of Chumpy due to his innate innocence, she experiences an enlightening if enigmatic epiphany, connecting all the loose dots of the Universe at once via lightning flashback, if only for a fleeting moment of clarity, before it goes all Big Bang again:

Recently, Tanisha Alopecia was walking the streets of Hollywood at night covering her friend's shift when a car with three occupants slowed down and inquired about her availability. She told them to pull over into the nearby parking lot to talk shop. Leaning inside the passenger window, Tanisha Alopecia recognizes the actor Mickey Rourke in the driver's seat and, in the front passenger seat, another actor named Lance Henriksen. Later, she'll remember this moment when she sees Lance in movies like *The Terminator, Aliens,* and *Near Dark.* At the time, he only looked vaguely familiar.

In the backseat was the same blonde teen now sitting in the booth next to hers at the Pink Turtle.

"It's for him," Mickey tells Tanisha Alopecia in her

flashback.

"What'll it be?" she asks.

"Just a blowjob," the blonde teen blurts out, obviously petrified by the possibility.

"*Ooo*, he's *nasty*, he wants a *blowjob*!" Lance says lasciviously as Mickey cracks up and the bashful boy in the back seat abruptly cancels the whole scenario, preferring to remain a virgin, at least for the time being.

"There's a reason for everything," Tanisha Alopecia whispers to herself while sitting in the Pink Turtle. "That *must* be Chumpy's creator," she privately concludes, given both this coincidence and the obvious physical similarities. She gets up to sheepishly say hello to them, but thinks better of it and sits back down, contemplating her options. Not wishing to further embarrass the shy teen or herself with an outrageous revelation of his well-hung cartoon doppelgänger, who turned into a talking walnut before he mysteriously vanished, Tanisha Alopecia quietly leaves the Pink Turtle without ordering, just missing her friend Linda.

Meanwhile, Chumpy is walking around Westwood Village trying not to get trampled upon and crunched into oblivion as he stops to soak in the sights. This is not an easy task, since not only is he back at his usual height of twelve inches, but he's apparently invisible. On the plus side, his penis now matches his size, making him sexually incompatible again, at least in terms of copulation with the natives. In any case, he won't trip over it, so that's good. For now, it beats being a telepathic walnut, which can only roll around so far. At least he feels like his true self again, and the invisibility feels like a bonus.

The previous night in Tanisha's modest Doheny apartment, Chumpy was dozing off in his walnut state as the vibrant New Wave music continued playing on KROQ. While asleep, he had a nightmare of living in a place called New Jersey, but he couldn't see much because he was hidden inside a closet, without any corporeal form that he could discern. He was simply a disembodied spirit awaiting actualization. However, he heard plenty, and it sounded like a psychological torture chamber out there, so he had no desire to explore outside his dormant domain, anyway. The nightmare lasted a long time, as if he inhabited yet another alternate dimension.

While in the closet, Chumpy often heard a boy crying, and sometimes the boy would stash stolen comic books next to Chumpy, along with monster magazines and model kits, as if hiding them. The only times Chumpy was aware of anything taking place outside the closet were when the boy sometimes scrawled comic strips and pictures of a talking walnut wearing a baseball cap, inspired by Joe Palooka bubble gum. Chumpy could see the boy drawing him, not from the closet, but from the POV of the comic strip itself. Chumpy actually felt himself being created from scratch and imagination. He then deduces he currently exists as this crude sketch, hidden in the closet with the shoplifted comic books, and this is his embryonic manifestation at this particular time in this particular place.

But it was the boy's incessant torment that dominated Chumpy's voyeuristic consciousness. Several times, as the boy was secretly reading his comic books as Chumpy stared at him from the sketch, the faceless woman angrily appeared and harshly grabbed the boy by the hair as he screamed, and dragged the boy away.

Chumpy was abruptly awakened from this seemingly endless nightmare vision by the sounds of the door lock to Tanisha Alopecia's apartment being jimmied, then terrified to see Fate the Pimp barging inside, inebriated and annoyed. Since Chumpy was only a walnut sitting alone in the dark on the kitchen counter, he had no immediate sense of fear, feeling safely hidden from plain sight, as he did in the nightmare closet. But after tossing the joint, Fate the Pimp spotted the subtly shivering walnut and stared at it for a full two minutes, studying it, waiting for it to budge or show any signs of sentience. Finally, Fate the Pimp had to directly address the walnut.

"Are you in there, doll boy?" Chumpy kept his non-existent mouth shut, but Fate the Pimp picked him and put him in the pocket of his fake leather coat anyway, heading back out into the crisp Beverly Hills night, which was almost as crisp as the West Hollywood night right across the street.

It was then that Chumpy felt himself transform back into a foot-high human, albeit invisible. He instantly outgrew Fate the Pimp's pocket and fell to the ground. Fate the Pimp heard the commotion and reached into his pocket for the walnut. But it was not there. The pimp thought he heard tiny footsteps racing down the sidewalk towards Santa Monica Boulevard, and almost followed them. Instead, he climbed back into his 1959 pink Cadillac and drove back to his lavishly funky pad in the Hollywood Hills, further reconsidering his life choices and how they may have adversely affected his mental state.

Reflecting on his own strange turn of events—strange even by his standards—Chumpy sits quietly unseen on an unclaimed seat of the blue bus gliding down Wilshire Boulevard, his invisibility to the denizens of this dimension proving to be a crucial stealth asset. Instinctively, he gets off at Glendon Avenue, in front of Ships Coffee Shop, a place that seems somehow familiar, like everything he's seen so far. As someone exits, Chumpy races inside before the door closes and enters the retro-futuristic restaurant, hopping up into an empty booth after a self-tour, which confirms the similarities in his subconscious. As he suspected, this establishment's midcentury modern interior design strongly resembles the diners back in his world, particularly in Thrillville, so he feels somewhat at home, despite the starkly incongruent differences in fashion. While he quietly sits in the booth, absorbing the ambiance, "Atomic" by Blondie is playing on the sound system, followed by "Rock

Lobster" by the B-52s, songs Chumpy recognizes, just slightly tweaked.

As an older waitress with a friendly face, large glasses, white hair pulled back, and the name tag "Dorothy" walks right past him, Chumpy asks as loudly as he can, "May I have a fried egg sandwich, but please hold the egg?"

Dorothy stops as if she hears him. But after looking around and seeing no one, she shakes her head and mumbles to herself, "I'm getting old," before circulating her station, refilling coffee. Chumpy is amused by his own secret powers, which came on suddenly and could disappear just as quickly, so he makes the most of them while he can.

Chumpy hops from the booth and climbs up a chair in front of the counter as a waitress named Patsy, per her tag, serves customers on either side of him. He enjoys watching her work. When no one is looking, he snags a piece of unbuttered toast from a plate next to him and scampers down the chair and hides beneath a table to eat it, bobbing his head to The Blasters performing "Marie, Marie" on the sound system. He wonders if this is Heaven, and he's already arrived at his answer to the question of his existence's purpose, which may be to exist for the sake of it. But there's much more to explore before he comes to that conclusion, and he's having so much fun with the journey that the ultimate destination seems somehow irrelevant. After finishing his toast, Chumpy waits for the opportunity to scamper back out into the bright Westwood day.

Continuing his magical walking tour, Chumpy is overwhelmed by the sights and sounds of the Village, particularly the mysteriously pungent odor of a certain hot tea emanating from the Good Earth Restaurant. Curiously aroused, Chumpy follows the seductive scent down the stairs into the basement, where the aroma of freshly baked bread and alfalfa sprouts is absorbed into the ambient scent.

Inside the restaurant, Chumpy takes a seat at a table beside a large, well-dressed man enjoying several desserts, savoring each bite from each one. His name is Marlon Brando. Chumpy recognizes him as an older version of an actor in his world named Brandon Marlo. The waitress is gushing over her celebrity guest.

"You're so wonderful," she tells Marlon Brando, to which he flirtatiously responds,

"No, no. *You're* wonderful." The waitress goes from gushing to blushing.

Another young waitress who resembles the actress Nastassja Kinski passes by, and Chumpy feels like he knows her, even though he has no idea who Nastassja Kinski is at this point. He hops down and follows her as she makes the rounds of her tables, careful not to get caught beneath her feet, or any feet. In the attempt, he accidentally falls between her fast-moving legs, and she winds up tripping over him, sending her tray of empty tea glasses flying. Chumpy is alarmed by the fact that these physical beings are accidentally interacting with him despite his incognito condition.

The waitress, whose name is Nancy, is likewise confused. Her fellow waiters rush to her side and help her up, and while a little shaken, she's fine, except for the fact that she can't explain why she suddenly tripped. "I'm just tired from studying and need a nap," she tells her fellow waiters, some of whom are fellow UCLA students, so they nod sympathetically.

Feeling like he is inadvertently being a nuisance, Chumpy runs back to the top the stairs, dodging incoming patrons, and back out on the sidewalk, gawking at the vibrantly vivid clothes, hairstyles, and wide variety of storefronts. The many movie theater marquees are especially entrancing since Chumpy loves movies and is curious to see how they look and feel in this world.

Turning off Westwood Boulevard and heading down Weyburn Avenue, Chumpy notices two large movie palaces situated across from each other, the Village and the Bruin.

The marquees, respectively reading *One From the Heart* on one side and *Chariots of Fire* on the other, don't immediately grab him, and after taking a tour of both majestic cinemas, he decides to wait until something is playing that he'd like to sit and watch.

After exiting the Village Theater, Chumpy sees a young blonde teenager and a young man walk right past him, crossing the street and heading down Broxton. Intrigued for reasons he can't immediately identify, Chumpy follows them down to the Regent Theater.

"Wanna go in and see *Diner*?" asks the man, who has puppy-dog eyes, a uniquely handsome face, and thick, unruly hair.

"Really? Yeah!"

"Let's see if they'll let us in."

Chumpy is standing right behind them at the box office, where the man identifies himself as one of the stars. The girl behind the glass recognizes him. "*Oh my god*! *Mickey Rourke*! Hang on, let me get the manager."

Moments later, Mickey Rourke and his teenage companion are escorted by the manager into the back of the dark auditorium, which is packed. Chumpy can't find a place to sit, so he plops down in the aisle to watch the flick. The movie is just starting, but Mickey is in the first scene, so Chumpy immediately makes the connection. There's something about one or both of these guys that resonates deep within Chumpy's psyche. He wonders if either could be his creator.

"This is the scene we ran lines for at the Pink Turtle," the teenager says to Mickey, whose character up on the screen is simultaneously sitting in a movie theater, watching *A Summer Place*, sitting beside an attractive girl. In the movie, Mickey's character, Boogie, is using a popcorn box to hide his pecker, which, on a bet, Boogie has purposely popped through the bottom, so the girl accidentally touches it and runs out of the theater, appalled, as Boogie follows her to give his irrational and untrue explanation. Chumpy can relate to this ambiguous response to an unwanted penis.

"This is why I didn't order popcorn," quips the teenager before another patron shushes him.

Due to Chumpy's invisibility, people going in and out of the lobby door for snacks or the bathroom keep tripping over him, unsure of what the obstacle could be, but it's too dark to discern. Finally, one big biker barges in and kicks Chumpy squarely in the head, knocking him unconscious. Chumpy is out cold for the duration of the movie, woken only when it's over by the hordes of patrons walking over and on him on their way out of the theater. Mickey and the teenager are already gone. Chumpy is crestfallen and very sore all over, especially his head, but also his heart.

Outside the Regent, Chumpy instantly and intuitively locks his gaze on the first passerby he sees, an olive-skinned, lean and muscular man with thick, slick black hair and dark sunglasses, dressed in black from head to toe in defiance of the late afternoon sunshine. Once again, Chumpy feels a strange sense of familiarity, though he has no idea how he could know this moody stranger from anywhere, even if it's only a dream. But once again, this comforting, if puzzling, familiarity acts as a mobile beacon.

Chumpy follows the Man in Black back up Broxton to a popular spot called Stan's Donuts, situated on the corner of Broxton and Weyburn Avenue. "Mongoloid" by Devo is blasting from the sound system. The Man in Black goes into the donut shop as Chumpy hides himself in the corner, out of the busy path of the customers coming and going. The place smells delicious, and the intoxicating scent is confirmed when a customer sitting at a window seat drops a piece of a donut, and Chumpy picks it up and eats it, not caring if it isn't fully vegan, since he is quite hungry by this point, though still wary of exposing his hidden presence with spectral participation.

Feeling his tummy rumble, Chumpy follows the Man in

Black down Broxton to Wilshire Boulevard, where the Man in Black turns right and then left on Veteran, crossing the street and entering a large, distinctively gothic-urban building that is at once foreboding and inviting, but only for the residents, like a vampire's castle.

Striding through the dimly lit hallways, the Man in Black nods at his casually hip co-inhabitants as he approaches his room, "Rockin' Bones" by The Cramps filling the air from an indeterminate source, incidentally suiting the organically seedy ambiance. Per the neighborly salutations, Chumpy discovers the Man in Black's name is Greg. Chumpy barely makes it inside the apartment before Greg closes the door behind him, and the first thing Chumpy sees inside the room is a snake in a glass box, which further augments the overall vibe of exotic punk decadence.

Leaving the bag of donuts on top of a table, Greg goes to his bathroom but leaves the door open since he thinks he's alone. Chumpy takes advantage of this opportunity to climb up the chair beside the table and quickly snag a chocolate donut with sprinkles, which for him is like lugging a tractor-trailer tire down a fire escape. Back on the floor, Chumpy rolls the donut to a spot behind the bed, lets it fall, and begins munching on it with the gusto of a starving rat devouring a discarded pizza, doing so quickly before his purloined meal is discovered, disrupted, and discarded.

Greg comes out of the bathroom and picks up his bag of donuts, immediately noticing one is missing. "God *damn* it!" he exclaims as Chumpy freezes, then hides under the bed.

Bringing the bag with him, Greg sits on the edge of the bed and notices the partially eaten donut on the floor. Picking it up, he lets out another expletive. "*Fuck*! When I find you, I'm feeding you to my snake!" Greg assures the unknown culprit, whom he assumes is a rodent.

Greg puts on an album called *Scary Monsters* by David Bowie, which mesmerizes Chumpy, who lies beneath the bed, listening. The song "Ashes to Ashes" speaks to him personally, perhaps because it seems to be about a lost astronaut, drifting aimlessly in the cosmos, like him, though it's actually about a junkie strung out on drugs following a traumatic space trip. Close enough. Greg is likewise lying on top of the bed, listening, as they both fall asleep by the time the needle lifts from Side B.

Chumpy is awoken by the sounds of copulation above. He sneaks out from under the bed to see Greg having wild sex with a woman who has very black hair and very white skin. The TV is on, tuned to a channel called MTV. Billy Idol is singing "Dancing with Myself" surrounded by zombies. Chumpy, familiar with this scenario, finds it much more interesting than second-hand hedonism, a voyeuristic vice he can always indulge in back home when he visits his wife at work.

After the couple lies in bed talking and smoking for a while, Greg gets up to take a shower. Chumpy can't help but marvel at the beauty of the nude woman, who seems satisfied, yet sad. "I'm really looking forward to the Cramps tonight," she tells Greg when he comes out with a towel around his waist. "I haven't been to the Whiskey in a while."

Greg seems lost in thought, as usual, and nods acknowledgment, then says to her, "I'd rather see them here at the Who's Who so we could just roll back into bed. I'm beat." Donning his trademark black shirt, pants, boots, and jacket, but not his shades since it's dusk, Greg and the woman, now wearing a tight black dress and black high-heeled shoes, exit the apartment, leaving the TV on, presumably for the snake. Chumpy is hypnotized by music videos for hours.

Later that evening, Chumpy grows restless. He goes back out into the neon-lit Westwood night and winds up at the Avco Theater across from Ships, attracted by the movie called *Cat People* on the marquee. He easily sneaks inside and scores a big, plush chair in the back of the spacious auditorium as he revels in the overwhelming sensual spectacle of fornicating felines on the massive screen, filling himself with some popcorn that had spilled on the floor. The ethereally beautiful female star of the film, Nastassja Kinski, reminds him of that waitress back at the Good Earth. He recognizes David Bowie's richly baritone voice singing the thunderous theme song playing over the end credits.

"It's all connected," he tells himself, with more desperation than conviction, since he still has no clue as to why he recognized this cool cat named Greg, whom he may never see again. Or so he believes until he walks back through the residential neighborhoods of Westwood on this unusually breezy night, the soft wind whipping up leaves that swirl around the sidewalks and the steps of high-rise apartment buildings as the full moon shines above, giving Chumpy a serene sensation.

Finally, after passing through the eerily quiet UCLA campus, Chumpy impetuously hops on a bus at a designated stop while the opportunity presents itself, taking a deserted seat as the bus continues down Sunset Boulevard. Chumpy stands up to look outside the window at the sumptuously surreal sights of Los Angeles at midnight. After passing through the emerald elegance of Beverly Hills, the neon lights of the Sunset Strip abruptly come into view and glow like celestial signposts from a decadent netherworld, reminding him of his hometown Thrillville, which seems so far away it's like an outpost in a dream. Chumpy recognizes the nightclub Greg mentioned, called the Whisky-a-Go-Go, with The Cramps on the marquee. So, he gets off the bus near the intersection of Sunset and Clark, hoping to catch up with Greg, the only connection he has to his purpose in this place, and a loose one at that.

Inside The Whiskey, The Cramps are already performing. The current song is "I Was a Teenage

Werewolf," which, for some reason, sounds to Chumpy like his creator's anthem, or one of them. Chumpy has trouble navigating the crowd, many of whom are dancing, while others stand around with drinks in their hands. The audience is mostly young, like Greg, and if not similarly decked out in black, they are sporting garishly colored clothes, and in some cases, they have hair to match. Many are simply attired in T-shirts and jeans. Several boast a Mohawk hairstyle in various hues, with visible tattoos and piercings to enhance the trendy aesthetic of punk exotica. Some are sequestered in dark corners, talking or making out. Miraculously, Chumpy finds Greg and his female companion, whom Greg refers to as Nina, standing in the back of the nightclub, directly across from the stage. Though most conversations are drowned out by the music, Chumpy can hear Greg clearly, like the volume has been turned up on earphones. It's as if Greg is inside his head, or vice versa. Chuckling to himself, Chumpy stealthily sneaks up on Greg and kicks him in the shin to get his attention, even though they are unable to communicate directly.

"*Ow*!" Greg says, looking down and around the source of the quick, sharp pain.

"What's wrong?" asks Nina.

"I don't know. I had a pain in my leg. It's gone now."

Chumpy giggles before someone accidentally kicks him, and he goes skidding across the floor, where more oblivious feet stomp on him. Feeling beaten, Chumpy manages to find one of those dark corners where couples are congregating for \amorous privacy.

That's when he sees Tanisha Alopecia, who is alone, bopping her head to the music, pensively dragging on a cigarette. As Chumpy approaches her, as quickly as he can in his physically downtrodden state, he suddenly feels himself rolling, not limping. He realizes belatedly that he has transformed back into a sentient walnut. Tanisha Alopecia feels the walnut hit the toe of her pumps, and is elated when she looks down and sees her little nutty buddy.

"*Chumpy*!" Tanisha Alopecia exclaims, picking up the walnut and smothering it with tiny kisses. She can hear Chumpy giggling as if he's being tickled. "Where did you go? And how did you get all the way here?"

"It's a long story!"

"Ain't they *all*, sugar! You can tell it to me later. Right now, I need you to meet someone!"

Ignoring Chumpy's barely audible pleas for anonymity, Tanisha Alopecia takes Chumpy backstage as The Cramps take a break before their final set.

"Look who it is!" Tanisha Alopecia excitedly says to Lux Interior and Poison Ivy, who are resting in chairs, sipping beer.

"Who?" Lux Interior says.

"Chumpy Walnut!" Tanisha Alopecia says, sticking the walnut in Lux Interior's bemused face. "Chumpy, say something!"

"Like what?" Chumpy whispers.

"*Anything!*"

"No point."

"*Motherfucker cocksucker, Chumpy, tell Lux I'm not insane!*"

"I'm sorry, I can't do that. They can't hear me anyway."

"God *damn* it!"

"Have you lost your mind?" Lux Interior says, grinning uneasily as he takes the walnut from her and studies it intently before passing it over to Poison Ivy.

"*No!*" Tanisha Alopecia insists, before tentatively adding under her breath, "At least I hope not."

"Maybe he's just afraid to come out of his shell," Lux Interior says with a wry smile, humoring Tanisha Alopecia out of a mix of amusement and uneasiness.

"Oh, I think he's adorable!" Poison Ivy says, going along with the gag. "Can I borrow it?"

"For what?" Tanisha Alopecia says, brow furrowed.

"I want to wear him for our next set!" Poison Ivy says, sticking Chumpy between her breasts, where it's snugly ensconced within her sequin bikini bra.

"No, you'll smother him!" Tanisha Alopecia says, grabbing at Poison Ivy's left breast.

"*Hey*!" Lux Interior says. "Relax! She'll give it right back after the gig!"

"Promise?" Tanisha Alopecia says.

"It's okay," Chumpy tells Tanisha Alopecia telepathically. "This will be fun!"

"Well…all right," Tanisha Alopecia replies reluctantly to Chumpy, though seemingly to Poison Ivy, with a jealous, possessive expression. "Just don't lose him."

"Don't worry," Poison Ivy says. "He's my good luck charm."

"Mine too," Tanisha Alopecia says.

"I love you the most," Chumpy tells Tanisha Alopecia.

"I love you, too," Tanisha Alopecia says like a worried mother.

"What?" says Poison Ivy.

"I'll only let you borrow him because I love you," Tanisha Alopecia says.

Poison Ivy winks as she then takes Chumpy out of her sequin bra and drops him down her sequin bikini pants before running back to the stage with the band, as Tanisha Alopecia gasps and Chumpy squeals with delight far beyond earthly earshot.

"Hey, this gives me an idea for a song," Lux Interior says to Poison Ivy as Tanisha Alopecia reluctantly returns to the floor, sticking close to the stage so she can monitor the situation. "All you need is a machine gun like in one of those videos."

"Write that down," Poison Ivy says to him.

"I can't right now, I'm a little busy at the moment."

"Then you'll forget it."

"It'll come back to me eventually."

"Or to me."

"Then you'll take the credit."

"Chumpy gets the credit."

Lux Interior and Poison Ivy are inexplicably laughing as they launch into "Goo Goo Muck" to a cheering crowd. Chumpy is happily suffocating, ensconced within the tight bikini pants and pressed against Poison Ivy's sweetly sweaty loins. Tanisha Alopecia is fretting.

After the gig, Tanisha Alopecia rushes backstage to retrieve her pet walnut.

"You know, it's just a walnut," Lux Interior says to her, somewhat concerned about her mental state.

"Oh no, I think I'm pregnant!" Poison Ivy says as she reaches down into her bikini pants and retrieves the walnut. "Too late!"

Tanisha Alopecia snatches the walnut from Poison Ivy and heads back out onto Sunset Strip, passing Greg and Nina.

"*Tanisha!*" Greg calls to her as he reaches his car, a 1977 black Camaro, parked down the Strip from the club.

"Oh, hi, Greg," Tanisha Alopecia says wearily. "Sorry, I'm in a hurry."

"Did you drive?"

"I don't own a car. I'm running to catch a bus."

"What's the rush?"

"Um...I gotta pee."

"I saw you in the club," Nina says. "But it was too noisy and crowded to say hello. You seemed lost in thought, and I didn't want to bother you."

"Why didn't you pee in there?" Greg asks.

"I just thought of it," Tanisha Alopecia says, holding her crotch as if it were about to spring a leak.

"We can give you a lift," Nina offers.

"Take it," Chumpy says to Tanisha Alopecia.

"Well...okay. Thanks. Just keep quiet."

"Huh?" says Greg.

"Not you."

"Me?" Nina says.

"Never mind," Tanisha Alopecia says. "I appreciate it."

"Are you high?" Greg asks her.

"*Yes!*" Tanisha Alopecia says, realizing this could be a blanket explanation for all impending conversations and conduct.

"Can Nina put me in her bra?" Chumpy asks.

"*Hell no!*" Tanisha Alopecia says.

"No, you're not high?" Nina says.

"Yes. I mean no. I mean, yes, I'm high, and no, I'm not...anything else."

"Like crazy?" Greg says.

"No. I mean, yes."

"You have the night off?" Greg asks Tanisha Alopecia as they climb into the car. "You seem like you could use one."

"From which job?"

"Dukes," Greg says. "That's the only place I ever see you."

"What's your other job?" Nina asks her.

"Doesn't matter," Tanisha Alopecia says. "I quit."

"I'm hungry," Greg says. "Let's stop at Canter's. You must be hungry, too, Tanisha."

"Why?"

"Munchies, what else?"

"Okay!" Chumpy says, feeling he's on a roll and anxious for new adventures.

"Okay," Tanisha Alopecia sighs in secret unison. "I could eat." Then she sniffs the walnut and grimaces.

At Canter's Deli on Fairfax Avenue, a popular late-night spot for L.A. hipsters and hedonists, they are all sitting in a booth. Greg and Nina are chatting over their meals while Tanisha Alopecia sits quietly, sipping coffee. The Go-Gos are performing "Our Lips Are Sealed" on the sound system.

"Are you okay?" Chumpy asks her.

"Yes," Tanisha Alopecia lies. "Can I show you something?"

"Sure," says Greg.

Tanisha Alopecia reaches into her bra and pulls out the walnut. "Tell me what you see," she says to them.

"A Rorschach walnut?" Nina says, tentatively taking it from Tanisha.

"Yes, okay, but now tell me, what do you *hear*?" Tanisha Alopecia asks them.

Chumpy is not talking, just in case anyone hears him.

Nina puts it to her ear like it's a seashell. " The Nutcracker Suite'?" she says, cracking up Greg, who takes it from her.

"I don't hear anything, but I sure smell something," Greg says, sniffing the walnut. "Where has this walnut been?"

"Does it stink?" Tanisha Alopecia asks.

"No, quite the opposite," Greg says. "I just can't place the scent."

Nina takes it and sniffs it. "Smells like…sex. Probably just from your car."

"Right," Greg says.

"What's so special about this walnut?" Nina asks, genuinely fascinated.

"You're not fucking it, are you?" Greg asks.

"Let's not judge," Nina says.

"Hard to explain," Tanisha Alopecia says. "Let's just say I have a sentimental attachment to it. Just not *that* sentimental."

Then she sees Mickey Rourke walk in with his wife Deborah, and Tom Waits, with his wife Kathleen.

"Hey, there's Mickey Rourke!" she says. "I just saw him this morning," she adds, mostly for Chumpy's benefit.

"Yeah, and Tom Waits too, wow," Greg says. "We just saw him in that new Francis Coppola movie. He does the music too. It's great."

"Oh, I know Tom Waits," Tanisha Alopecia says.

"Maybe I'll go say hello after they've settled in."

"*Tom Waits!*" Chumpy yells. "*We have to save him!*"

"Hush now," Tanisha Alopecia says.

"What?" Greg says.

"Sorry, I'm stoned."

"Anyway, the soundtrack is the best thing about it," Greg says. "You can tell him I said so."

"What's the movie called?" Tanisha Alopecia asks. "I'll mention it."

"*One From the Heart.*"

"*Damn!*" Chumpy says.

"It co-stars Nastassja Kinski," Nina adds.

"*Double damn!*" Chumpy says.

"*Enough!*" Tanisha Alopecia says.

"Enough what?" Greg asks.

"Coffee. I've had enough coffee."

"The waitress didn't even ask you," Nina says.

"Well, in case she does and I'm in the bathroom."

"I'll try to remember that," Greg says.

"So where did you see Mickey Rourke this morning?" Nina asks Tanisha Alopecia.

"At the Pink Turtle. With his wife and a cute teenager. I saw that same blonde teenager a little while ago when Mickey and Lance Henriksen tried to pick me up to give him a date."

"Mickey wanted to go out with you?" Greg says.

"No, it was for the teenager. Mickey wanted to set us up, I guess. You know, on a date, just a regular date, nothing, you know, *bad* or anything."

"Funny, I have a blonde friend who is nineteen who knows Mickey well," Greg says. "That must've been him."

"What's his name?" Tanisha Alopecia asks.

"Will," Greg replies.

"Will what?"

"Viharo. Why? Did you take his cherry? I think he would've told me since that's all he ever talks about.

Besides Elvis."

"What girl?" Tanisha Alopecia asks, growing more agitated as the conversation progresses.

"Her name is Linda Kerridge," Greg says. "She's an actress."

"I know her! She lives by the Tropicana."

"Small world," Nina says.

"Not for me," Chumpy adds.

"Will has a big crush on her," Greg says. "Maybe he wanted you to give him some training before he makes his move, which he won't anyway."

"I think it's gross he expected you to sleep with a stranger, like you're a hooker or something," Nina says.

"That's all right, I was flattered," Tanisha Alopecia says. "He chickened out anyway. I mean the kid."

"Figures," Greg says.

"How do you know Will?"

"He's a busboy where I work as a waiter."

"Where's that?"

"Santo Pietro's in Beverly Hills. I thought I told you at Dukes sometime."

"Oh, maybe you did. Tell me, is Will a writer?"

"Yeah, how did you know?"

"What does he write?"

"Just one unpublished book so far. He just finished it when he was in Houston, staying with his mother's family."

"What's the book called?"

"Not like you could've heard of it," Greg says.

"Tell me anyway!"

" Chumpy Walnut.'"

Chumpy screams semi-silently.

"Wait here," Tanisha Alopecia tells Greg and Nina as Chumpy continues to hyperventilate.

"Where are you going?" Greg asks. But she's already run over to Mickey's table.

"Hello, sir! Remember me?" Tanisha Alopecia asks Tom

Waits.

"Tanisha!" Tom Waits says after squinting at her for a second. "I haven't seen you in a while. You still at Dukes?"

"Yes! How are you?"

"I'm okay. You know Kathleen here."

"Hi, Kathleen!"

"Hi, Tanisha!"

"*Tell him he's in danger*!" Chumpy shouts from within Tanisha's bra, but she tunes him out.

"And this," Tom Waits says, "is Mickey."

"Yes, we've met," Tanisha Alopecia says.

"How?" Debra asks with suspicion.

"Oh, around Hollywood," Tanisha Alopecia says.

"I don't recognize you, not from Dukes anyway," says Mickey. "I usually come here to eat, at least late at night."

"And the Pink Turtle. I saw you and your lovely wife there this morning. You were with a blonde teenager."

"Yeah, Willie," Mickey says with a slight smile.

"Yes, that's right."

"You know him?"

"We've met."

Mickey is losing interest. "Okay, well, I'll tell him you say hi. It's been nice to meet you or see you again or whatever. We're busy talking here, though."

"Yeah, Tanisha, I'll be sure to come by Dukes sometime," Tom Waits says. "Good seeing you."

Tanisha Alopecia stands pat in stubborn defiance of the gentle brush-off and says urgently to Mickey, "Well…um, can I meet your friend Will again?"

"I thought you were friends?" Mickey says.

"Well, I have a present for him and we've sorta lost touch."

"I can give it to him," Mickey says, hoping this will get rid of her.

Tanisha Alopecia pulls out the walnut and hands it to Mickey.

"*You're in danger!*" Chumpy keeps yelling at Tom Waits, even though only Tanisha Alopecia can hear him.

"Fuck is this?" Mickey says.

"It's his creation. His name is Chumpy."

They all laugh. "Oh, I get it," Mickey says.

"You know what I'm talkin' about?" Tanisha Alopecia says, wide-eyed.

"Yeah, sure. I love Chumpy. You know Willie, all right."

"So you'll give it to him then?"

"Sure, I'll give it to him."

"Promise?"

"Yeah, yeah, of course. He'll love it. We're having a conversation here. Take care."

Tanisha Alopecia finally takes the hint and leaves them alone to rejoin Greg and Nina.

"Mission accomplished," she says to a baffled Greg and Nina. "Now, where's that menu? I'm hungry!"

"What mission?" Greg says.

"Never mind, but I really need to thank you."

"For what?"

"Taking me here. If you hadn't, I wouldn't have run into Mickey and given him the walnut after you confirmed the blonde teenager Mickey tried to hook me up that I saw at the Pink Turtle when I went there to meet my friend Linda was indeed the same one you work with, which is too coincidental to be a coincidence, and before that, if Chumpy hadn't manifested as this flesh-and-blood cartoon character with a giant cock then told me, someone who's met all types in my line of work and has natural empathy for weirdos and social outcasts—as a waitress, that is, not a hooker or anything—someone who wouldn't dismiss him as just another lost cause, he told *me* his story and all about his mission to meet his creator, and if I hadn't taken him to lunch at Musso with Bukowski and if Fate the Pimp hadn't found us there to kick his ass and Chumpy hadn't turned into a walnut as some sort of magic defense mechanism, which enabled me to carry him around incognito since a telepathic walnut is easier to hide if not explain than a cartoon boy with a big dick, and then if Lux hadn't invited me to come to the show tonight at the Whiskey and told me to bring my pet walnut with me and I went even though I was depressed because I thought I'd lost Chumpy or my mind or both since he just disappeared, well then I'd have never reunited with Chumpy who by some other impossible chain of related events was already there at the Whiskey, like he was waiting for me, and then if I hadn't gone outside just when you did so you could see me and offer me a ride, and if you weren't hungry and insisted we stop at Canter's even though I wasn't hungry because I was too excited about our reunion, and if Mickey and Tom Waits hadn't happened to come here while we're here, well…*whew*!…if none of that had happened just as it did when it did, then none of *this* would've happened? It's all connected! It's *all* magical! Just like my friend and Will's dream girl, Linda, told me! She was totally right! I can't wait to tell her!"

"I wouldn't do that," Greg says.

"Oh, c'mon!" Tanisha Alopecia says. "Can't you see? Life is magic, and we're all gonna be okay! That's my takeaway, anyway."

Greg and Nina stare at her with a shared mixture of wonder and concern. "You need to be taken away, all right," Greg says.

"What the hell are you babbling about?" Nina asks as nicely as possible.

"Don't you get it? Your friend Will is about to meet his own creation!"

"*Who*?" Greg says.

"Chumpy Walnut!"

"Okay, I'm taking you home now," Greg says. "Or I can just drop you off at the nearest mental hospital for a checkup."

"But I'm hungry!" Tanisha Alopecia says.

"They'll feed you," Greg says.

"Is that why you're talking like this?" Nina says. "Low blood sugar?"

"And wasted, don't forget!" Tanisha Alopecia adds.

"That explains everything," Greg says. "What the hell are you high on, anyway?"

"Life, baby! *Life*!" Then she orders French Fries with gravy, like Mickey did in *Diner*, to keep the serendipity rolling like a walnut across an ice rink.

Just then, Fate the Pimp shows up out of nowhere and grabs Tanisha Alopecia's arm. Chumpy, who can hear everything happening due to his psychic connection with Tanisha, throws another fraught fit inside Mickey's breast pocket.

"Fate, leave me alone! I don't work for you no more!" Tanisha Alopecia says, pulling free, at least temporarily. "You been *following* me?"

"Fuck yeah! Your ass is *mine*! Get back to work!"

"I thought it was your night off?" Greg says.

"Not any more!" Tanisha Alopecia yells at Fate the Pimp."I told you, I *quit*!"

"You can't quit till I say you can, bitch!" Fate the Pimp smacks her sharply upside the head, alarming Greg and Nina, who remain still for the moment, mostly due to shock.

"Are you her manager at Dukes?" Nina asks Fate. "If so, I'm going to complain to the owner."

"He's my fuckin' *pimp*!" Tanisha says. "I *am* a hooker! And so the fuck what?"

"Nothing, I think it's awesome you have two jobs!" Nina says. "I can barely hold onto one."

"Makes sense," says Greg. "I mean, that he's a pimp, not that you're a hooker. It would be rather extreme for a coffee shop manager to resort to harsh language and brute force, at least in a totally different coffee shop, unless you're an exceptionally skilled waitress. In my experience, you're just okay."

"Fuck you, I'm an exceptional waitress *and* an exceptional hooker!" Tanisha says, spitting in her pimp's face again.

"I'll have today's special either way," Greg says as Nina punches his arm.

"So Mickey Rourke wanted to actually hire you to get Will laid, not just as a random favor," Nina says. "Small world."

"*Not small enough*!" Chumpy yells from Mickey's breast pocket. Mickey is also paying attention to the increasingly tense scene and preparing to proactively respond.

"Shut the fuck, *all* y'all!" Fate the Pimp yells. "I'll show you brute force,' motherfuckers!" Fate the Pimp pulls Tanisha out of the booth, kicking and screaming. Greg tries to intervene.

"Back off, T. J. Hooker's sidekick!" Fate the Pimp warns Greg, pulling out his switchblade.

"Who?" Nina says.

"Everyone thinks I look like Adrian Zmed," Greg says with a frown.

"Oh my god, I never realized it, but you *do* look like that hot dude in *Grease Two*!" Tanisha Alopecia says before she kicks Fate the Pimp in the nuts and runs outside. Brandishing his blade at Greg and Nina, Fate the Pimp attempts to chase after her. Mickey steps up and punches Fate in the face, sending him sprawling backward, the blade clattering across the restaurant floor.

"Mickey!" Fate the Pimp says, holding his bloody nose. "How you gonna do me like that, man? I thought we were street cool, brother!"

"Sorry, man, but you were out of line," Mickey says in his softly intimidating voice.

"Now, how do you know *him*?" Debra asks Mickey.

"Friend from the old days."

"I'm so glad we went out tonight!" Tom Waits says. "I

could get a whole album out of this!"

"*You'll be dead by then*!" Chumpy warns Tom Waits before demanding of Mickey, "*Take me to my creator*!"

Mickey helps Fate the Pimp up, pats him on the back, and walks him out.

Once outside, when he's sure Tanisha Alopecia is out of harm's way, and Fate the Pimp isn't hiding somewhere to grab her, Mickey takes the walnut from his pocket and chucks it across Fairfax Avenue as Chumpy shrieks and hits the sidewalk hard, cracking his shell as he lapses into a coma before rolling unconscious beneath a bush.

"Mickey, you shouldn't have done that!" Debra chastises him as Tom Waits chuckles and Kathleen concurs with her.

"That chick is nice but she's crazy," Mickey says. "Anyway, I got a much better present for Willie than a fuckin' walnut." Debra smiles knowingly. Tom Waits gets a chill and buttons his jacket, but that doesn't help.

Meanwhile, Chumpy's soul spirals down a long, dark tunnel into an even darker void, which is 1970s New Jersey. There, for what feels like years, he witnesses many more bizarre incidents of physical and psychological abuse from the safety of his creator's closet, wishing he could help the beleaguered boy escape this suburban torture chamber. But Chumpy is trapped inside his own hell-shell now, too.

Chapter Four
SHELL-SHOCKED

Halloween night, 1982. Mickey Rourke, Debra Feuer, Linda Kerridge, Sean Penn and his girlfriend Pamela Springsteen Springsteen—whom Sean Penn met while filming *Fast Times at Ridgemont High* and who would later star in two horror movies from the *Sleepaway Camp* series—pile into the white 1964 T-Bird with dice painted on the doors, a present from Mickey to Will, for a night on the town, Will, decked out as Marlon Brando in *The Wild* One, is at the wheel, which causes some uneasiness, since he had earned his driver's license only a few months prior while in Houston, while finishing up the final draft of his first novel, and he barely passed the test. Miraculously, they will all survive the evening. Chumpy, still a sentient walnut, wakes up inside Linda's pocketbook, unsure of where he is or how he got there. He listens closely to what people are saying for clues, though he has no idea what they're referencing.

"*Hey, bud, let's party!*" Chumpy hears someone, apparently the car's driver, repeatedly saying to Sean Penn, until Mickey jokingly tells Sean Penn, "Just hit him."

They get out in a parking lot off Hollywood Boulevard and walk around to check out the freaks and festivities. That's when Tanisha Alopecia sees them and says hello to Linda, Mickey, and Will without addressing the latter two by name. She is then introduced to Sean Penn and Pamela Springsteen. Chumpy recognizes Tanisha Alopecia's voice. He yells her name, but she doesn't respond, possibly because his telepathic signals are muffled inside the pocketbook. But unknown to him, it's also because his skull/shell is cracked and his powers of telepathy are effectively muted. Tanisha Alopecia has no way of knowing that her missing walnut friend is right in front of her, concealed from view, just like Chumpy has no idea his creator is right in front of him.

"Did Mickey give you that present?" Tanisha Alopecia urgently asks Will.

"You mean the car?" Will says, in his usual state of confusion.

"What present?" Mickey says.

"Who are you?"

"Nobody," Tanisha Alopecia says as Debra stares her down.

"I thought you two were friends," Mickey says. "You and Willie, I mean."

"I guess Will doesn't remember me. But you do."

"Yeah. Canter's."

"So did you give Will that present I gave you to give to him at Canter's?"

"No, I lost it," Mickey half-lies.

"*Another* present?" Will says.

Mickey leans over and whispers a reminder in Will's ear regarding the night he took him out with Lance to pick up a hooker, since Mickey indeed recalls where he first met Tanisha.

"Oh yeah," Will says, nodding at her. "Man, I sure wish I had *that* present! I was an idiot!"

"What is this all about?' Debra asks.

"I can't believe you lost it!" Tanisha Alopecia says to Mickey.

"Well, I did lose it finally, just not with you," Will responds anyway.

"Lose what?" Tanisha Alopecia asks Will.

"My cherry," Will replies. "My father set me up with a friend of his after Mickey tried and failed. She's a nurse. Of course, it turned out he fucked her, too."

"Wait, Mickey fucked *who*?" Debra says.

"No one but *you*, baby!" Mickey assures Debra.

"No, no, my *father* pre-fucked the nurse," Will explains quickly, "so I got Pop's sloppy seconds. That's how I finally lost my cherry."

Tanisha Alopecia is impatient with the information overload. "Not *your cherry*. I meant your *walnut*."

"Walnut?" Will asks.

"I gave Mickey a walnut to give to you."

"Why?"

"It's a very *special* walnut."

"That's funny, I found a walnut a few months ago when I was at the Farmer's Market," Linda says. "I've been carrying it around with me as a good luck charm. I'm not sure why. I guess it reminds me of Will's book. It has a cracked shell, and I felt sorry for it."

Mickey shakes his head as Debra laughs. "*What*?" Tanisha Alopecia says to Linda. "Do you have it now?"

"Yes, it's in my purse."

"Can I see it?"

"Um, okay!" Linda takes the walnut out of her pocketbook and hands it to Tanisha Alopecia.

"This isn't the one," Tanisha Alopecia says, shaking her head. "Mine wasn't cracked."

"Why the fuck are women saving walnuts all of a sudden?" Mickey asks rhetorically. "Is there a shortage?"

"I think I started a thing with my unpublished book," Will says. "A weird thing, but a thing."

"Yeah, it's also weird that I heard about all this already," Sean Penn says. "I thought it was a joke."

"From who?" Linda and Tanisha Alopecia ask him in unison.

"Never mind, just kidding," Sean Penn says, though, as an excellent actor, he could also be an excellent liar on short notice.

"There's a name for this," Pamela Springsteen says.

"I'll say," Sean Penn says. "I have a few words for it

myself."

"It's called anthropomorphism," Pamela Springsteen says. "It's when people have empathy for inanimate objects."

"So you're calling me an *anthropomorphite*?" Linda says, laughing. "I resent that!"

"*I'm totally animated*!" Chumpy is yelling at the top of his lungs, or would be if he had any lungs. But his telepathic voice is feeble and faint, like the titular hybrid human insect in *The Fly*, and with all the street noise and rowdy revelers, not even Tanisha Alopecia can hear Chumpy pleading with her as she hands the cracked walnut back to Linda, who then puts it back in her pocketbook.

"Wait, can I see it too?" Will asks, his curiosity aroused.

"*Yes, for the love of God, please*!" Chumpy yells, within earshot of no one.

"Sure," Linda says. She hands the walnut to Will, who studies it, even shaking it next to his ear. Chumpy is elated to have finally tracked down, albeit accidentally, the reason for his mission, belatedly realizing they'd already crossed paths back in Westwood. Unfortunately, in both cases, Chumpy is unable to communicate directly with his creator due to his incapacitated state. "You can keep it if you want," Linda tells Will, as Chumpy figuratively jumps for joy inside her pocketbook.

"*Yes!*" Chumpy yells. "*Finally!*"

"Can you hear anything?" Tanisha Alopecia asks Will, who is also picking up some strange signals.

"Like what?" Will says.

"Anything out of the ordinary!" Tanisha Alopecia says.

"You mean like a seashell?"

"No, Will, like a *walnut!*"

Everyone stands quietly still for a second, listening for anything out of the ordinary, which means everything on Hollywood Boulevard.

"No, I don't hear anything," Will finally says as Chumpy

starts sobbing. "I don't know why I put it to my ear. It just seemed like the thing to do." Chumpy is still screaming at his creator's ear to no avail. The creator is different from what Chumpy imagined, but then he had no idea what to expect. Certainly not a blonde teenager dressed, to quote Mickey, "like a male hustler on Christopher Street in New York."

"There's something about this walnut," Linda concurs. "I don't know what it is. In fact, I was going to give it to Will when I found it. But I decided to keep it. I've become quite attached to it."

"What the fuck is with you people?" Mickey says.

"I want you to have it," Will says, handing it back to Linda. Will's motivation for such generous philanthropy is that he wants to give Linda a present as an expression of his infatuation, even if it's just returning a walnut that she found first. He likes that it reminds her of his creation, and that she carries it around with her, like a de facto memento of their secret romance inside Will's head.

"Willie just doesn't seem to want any of your walnuts today, ladies," Debra says wryly. "Sorry."

"Where did you find it again?" Tanisha Alopecia asks Linda.

"Fairfax Farmers Market, on the ground. I guess it broke when it fell."

"That's nowhere near Canter's," Tanisha Alopecia says. "Though it is on Fairfax, so maybe it rolled all the way down fuckin' Fairfax? It does seem suspicious that you found a walnut and decided to keep it. Did it say anything to you?"

Everyone laughs again, except Linda. "I might've *imagined* something," she says, recalling some odd moments she chalked up to loneliness. "But walnuts don't talk." Or so she once thought.

"Wait a minute, give that back," Tanisha Alopecia demands.

"*No!*" Linda says. "It's *mine!* Go find your own walnut!"

"It found *me,* Linda! Then I gave it to Mickey to give to Will because it's not just any walnut, it's *Chumpy!*" More laughter, all nervous.

"It's *my* Chumpy now!" Linda says, grabbing the walnut back from Tanisha, resulting in a struggle that stops short when the walnut falls and rolls into a street gutter. Chumpy screams as he plops down in the sewer river, the rats laughing at him.

Tanisha Alopecia starts crying, and Linda almost joins her. "Poor Chumpy!" Linda says sadly. Will is upset about it, too, though he isn't sure exactly why.

"Well, that's that," Sean Penn says stoically. "The tragic end of a magic walnut."

"Hey, is Fate the Pimp treating you okay?" Mickey asks Tanisha Alopecia, changing the subject, and patting her on the shoulder.

"I haven't seen him since that night at Canter's," Tanisha Alopecia says with a sniffle. "So yes, in his absence, I'm doing okay."

"Well, I kicked his ass, that's why."

"You did? I think I must've left by then."

"Yeah, baby. I don't like dudes who beat up on women."

"Thank you for your chivalry."

"So you really *do* know each other from the old days," Debra says to Tanisha Alopecia.

"Tanisha is the hooker I almost got for Willie that night," Mickey finally reveals to Debra.

"What?" Debra says incredulously. "Willie, you passed this up for some woman your father fucked first? What is *wrong* with you?"

"Odds are *any* woman Willie fucks in this town would've been pre-fucked by his father," Mickey says.

"I guess I was holding out for true love," Will says, quickly glancing at Linda before looking away, blushing.

"Yeah, I'm sorry too," Tanisha Alopecia says. "You're

pretty cute. Even if you are dressed like a male hustler."
They all laugh again, except for Will, who remains
confused. "Anyway, thanks again, Mickey, for cleaning
Fate the Pimp's dirty clock. That must be why I never saw
him again. I guess that's just one more dot connected."

"I can disconnect his dots again if he steps out of line,"
Mickey says gallantly. "Let me know." Then he tells the
group, "C'mon. Let's go to that stupid fuckin' party up in
the hills, though nothing could be as much fun as this."

"I was thinking anything else would be *more* fun," Sean
Penn says.

Tanisha Alopecia sashays away, and Will watches her
walk, wondering what might've been, already forgetting the
walnut. The group heads down Hollywood Boulevard back
toward the parking lot where the T-Bird is parked.

Meanwhile, Tanisha Alopecia arrives at her new job in a
beauty salon further down the Boulevard, which is offering
last-minute Halloween hairdos. She belatedly remembers
Mickey played a hair stylist named Boogie in *Diner*. She
appreciates the irony, even if it doesn't signify anything
significant, and wishes she remembered to tell Mickey that
she worked in a salon now, too. But she was and is too
preoccupied with the walnut to think straight. This means
she is not prepared for the next surprise.

At the salon, unimaginatively and unironically called
Beauty Aids, Fate the Pimp is waiting for her, sitting
patiently in a chair, like a python waiting for its prey to get
too close.

"What are you doing here?" Tanisha Alopecia asks,
upset and alarmed by the surprise visit from someone she
never wanted to see again.

"I have an appointment," Fate the Pimp smiles, flashing
his golden molars. "With *you*."

"You don't need no damn fright wig. You're scary
enough naturally."

"No, I don't no further embellishment, that's true. I'm

perfect as is. Unlike you, right?"

"That's plain *mean*, Fate! I can't help it! It's a condition! Once I make enough money, I'll get my operation and never see your slimy ass again!"

"There's only one way for you to make that kinda bread in a hurry, and only one person who can help make it for you."

"I don't do that anymore. I've already moved on. I guess you haven't figured that out."

"That particular service is not what I mean. I'm talking about something much more valuable than a balding hooker."

"Get the fuck outta here, Fate, I'm busy."

Fate the Pimp looks around at the empty salon, which is brightly painted in New Wave pastels, as "Bela Lugosi's Dead" by Bauhaus plays on the sound system.

"There ain't no other customers, and no other hair stylists, neither," Fate the Pimp points out.

"There should be two other people here!"

"I gave them the night off."

"You don't have the authority!"

"Don't I?"

"It's not like you own it!"

Fate the Pimp smiles wider than the Cheshire Cat, saying everything by saying nothing.

Tanisha Alopecia feels utterly destroyed by the implied revelation. "Oh, fuck me. Please tell me that you are *not* the owner of this salon!"

"I'm only a co-owner, partners with two other cats. Both your co-workers used to work for me, too. Still do. And so will you unless you do what I say."

"Why don't you just be a nightclub bouncer like your mama wanted and stop bothering people, or at least stop bothering me!"

"Well, actually, my mama wanted me to be a nightclub *owner*, but she didn't think I'd be competent enough because I was such a fuck-up as a kid, in and out of juvie, so she downgraded her dream to a fuckin' door man. I even considered it recently when I thought I was on the verge of a nervous breakdown from all the pressure. You know. Seeing and hearing things that ain't there?"

"No, I don't know."

"Yes, you *do*. We both saw it that day, and I think you know where it is."

"Fate, I can't take this anymore. Why can't you just leave me be already?"

"I've been missing you, sugar. Not just as an employee, neither. I was so distraught, I was even thinking of killing myself."

"Oh, *please*, you're *always* thinking of killing yourself, you bipolar bastard. At least when you're not thinking of killing someone else."

"I'd never hurt you, sugar."

"Then just leave me alone, Fate. *Please*."

"I can't. I'm your Fate, sugar. Your forever Sugar Daddy. We're meant to be."

"Your daddy was a jailbird junkie and your mama was a strung-out slut, and you're an insecure, self-destructive manic-depressive with sexist power issues!"

"Yeah, that's all true. Thanks for the rewind rundown. *Anyway*, as you know, cancer robbed my poor mama—who loved me despite her drawbacks—of witnessing my success in a popular field with heavy demand, if not a traditionally respectable one. I was born with a good business sense. Just not the nightclub business."

"And now you know how to run a fuckin' beauty salon? Please. You dress like every god damn day is fuckin' Halloween."

Fate the Pimp laughs and nods. "Every day *is* Halloween in our profession, sugar. You're both the trick *and* the treat."

"And you're nothin' but a dime store pimp. That's all. You got no business running *any* business, and you know it.

I don't even believe you're an owner, anyway."

"Believe it or don't, sugar. Truth never needs nobody's corroboration to feel secure in its own conviction. Anyway, like many business owners, I don't actually *do* anything. Not around here, anyway. This is just a front for drugs and prostitution, and other technically illegal but highly profitable enterprises. I'm only a titular partner, if you get my meaning."

"God *damn* it! I *knew* there was a reason I got this job without credentials or references! And Beauty Aids is such a *stupid* name for a beauty salon! Not to mention insensitive!"

"I'm sure you'll live up to it, sugar, then die of it, given time."

"*Fuck you!*"

"Another time. Right now, I need you to tell me where your well-endowed walnut friend is."

Tanisha Alopecia shuts back down. "I don't know what you're talking about, Fate."

"Hell you don't. I went by your pad the night after he and I met. I found the walnut, but it vanished into thin air. Then, when I was leaving Canter's after Mickey Rourke did a number on me with this bullshit chivalry, I saw him toss something and wondered what it was. Across the street from Canter's, I found a cracked walnut on the sidewalk, partially hidden under a bush. I took it home and waited for it to turn back into a born porn star. But no dice. I kept it in my pocket. Then, when I was at the Farmers Market on Fairfax, I lost it again. I had a fuckin' hole in my god damn pocket, can you believe that shit? From all the keys to all the private businesses and personal residences that I have an interest in. I noticed last time I stopped by that you changed your locks again, but that didn't stop me. But I *know* I had that damn walnut when I got to the market, because I always feel for it like it's my third nut. But when I was having coffee in the market Cafe, I felt for it and it was missing, though I still got the two that I needed even more. I looked all over the market, even going through a bin of walnuts in silly desperation, hoping one would say something. But it was gone. I figured it had to find its way back to you."

"Well, it *didn't*!"

"Oh. Well, too bad for us, especially you." Fate the Pimp pulls out his switchblade, flips it open, and flosses his gold teeth.

"Fate, it was all in our imagination! I can't help you find a fuckin' mass illusion!"

"You don't have to look hard for no mass illusion, sugar. That's what makes it a mass illusion."

"Even if it's everywhere, it's *still* an illusion!" "You sayin' everyone at Musso was under mass hypnosis now? I saw what everyone else saw, and it was some fucked-up, surrealistic shit. I never heard about it on the news, the papers, or nothin'. It was a case of mass embarrassment if anything. They're literally covering it up because the truth is too damn crazy to believe, as the most valuable truths often are."

"And what truth is that, Fate?"

"That walnut is our ticket to a palace in the Palisades, sugar. Neither one of us will ever have to work again."

"How the hell do you figure that?"

"You seriously askin' me how a pretty boy with the biggest cock in the world, even bigger than Ron fuckin' Jeremy's, who can turn into a walnut at will, couldn't turn into a walkin' talkin' fuckin' ATM, too?"

"What, you're gonna pimp him out?"

"Hell yeah, I'm gonna pimp his cartoon ass out! I'll charge bitches access to that atomic salami by the motherfuckin' *inch*! Male *or* female!"

"But he's a walnut now—*oops*."

Fate the Pimp stares at Tanisha Alopieca and grins triumphantly. "That's what I thought. Thank you. I didn't even have to resort to subterfuge, which just makes you more credible, or physical force, which is frowned upon in most circles, if not ours."

"Get to the fuckin' point, Fate."

"See, sugar, if we're both hallucinating, then so was *everyone* at Musso, because trust me, I saw their faces, and they *all* witnessed that giant cartoon cucumber cock before it turned into a legit legume and dropped to the floor."

"Walnuts ain't legumes, dumbass. Only peanuts are."

"Oh, well then, excuse the shit out of me, Professor Peanut. But you dig what I'm sayin' anyway."

"Fate, I seriously don't know where Chumpy is, and why are you here anyway, after what Mickey did to you?"

"Mickey is a busy man these days, bein' a big star now and all. He don't have no time for old nobody friends like us no more. Now, you either cough up that Magic Motherfuckin' Walnut or you're back on the street. Or I'll just set you up to operate from here, like you do at Dukes. I *know* you're sellin' that snatch on the side, sugar. You think I don't know?"

"Fate, please. I thought we were all done with this. I'm done, anyway. I don't know how to find a fuckin' walnut in Los Angeles. I'm sorry."

"Maybe if he turned back into a dick with legs, he might find us."

"What do you mean?"

"I'm putting the word out on the street that fits his description."

"A cracked walnut?"

"*Or* a cute little cracker with watermelon balls. Either, or. Meantime, you need to help me with the bait."

"How am I gonna do that?"

"Your friend Linda, for starters."

"What? How do you know Linda?" Tanisha Alopecia wonders how long he's been following her.

"I don't, not personally. But you do. And I saw her at the market that day."

"So?"

"She must have my walnut."

"How do you figure that?"

"Mutual acquaintance."

"Of whose? Mine or hers?"

"Yours."

"*Who*?"

"Tom Waits."

"Tom *Waits?* What does he have to do with this?"

"That's what I'm tryin' to figure out, sugar. See, Tom Waits recently went to Dukes lookin' for you, you weren't on duty, and he sat next to Linda, who showed him her walnut, which he recognized. It was cracked. I know this because I got it from a reliable source."

"Who?"

"Another mutual acquaintance."

"Who?"

"Sean Penn."

"*You're* cracked, asshole! You don't know Sean Penn!"

"I don't have to, not directly. He's doin' research for a role in a movie called *Bad Boys*, opposite Esai Morales. A friend of a friend knows Esai. Tom Waits told Sean Penn, who told Esai, who told a friend who told my friend."

"Oh, for fuck's sake, Fate, you're all a bunch of nelly gossip queens! That's complete fuckin' nonsense!"

"Is it?"

Tanisha Alopecia has exhausted her reserve of implausible denials. "All right, fuck it. I'll call Linda if you promise to leave me alone." She has an ulterior motive, since she knows Linda is no longer in possession of the walnut, and she has no idea what happened to it after it bounced into the gutter following their tussle. Tanisha Alopecia inwardly smiles at the irony of Fate the Pimp waiting for her in the salon and just missing his chance to grab the walnut himself. "I don't want no part of his exploitation, though," she tells her gloating pimp. "That's between you two." She hopes that if Chumpy is widely exposed, as it were, then his creator will know how and where to find him. So perhaps that is meant to be, too.

A couple of days later, Linda is at the Orange Grove house of her friend Tessa Richarde, a breathy, busty, bodacious blonde whom Chumpy recognizes from her role in *Cat People*. Linda is telling Tessa "the walnut story."

"*Oh my god!*" Tessa exclaims, wide-eyed. "You won't believe this, but I found a walnut in my toilet this morning!"

"Your *toilet*?" Linda says, equally flabbergasted. "How did it get there?"

"I have no idea! I didn't buy any walnuts recently, and even if I did, I wouldn't drop them in the toilet! It's not an appropriate bathroom snack!"

"Do you still have it?"

"Yes! It's a mystery I have to solve! One of several!"

"You mean besides the meaning of existence?"

"That too! But I gave up on that one!"

"I did too until recently," Linda laughs. "One walnut can change your life! That's all you need! Good thing you looked before you flushed!"

Tessa grimaces with a giggle. "Oh my god, that's so gross! But totally true! Let me go get it, and don't worry, I thoroughly washed it!"

Tessa goes to the kitchen and removes the walnut from a drawer, then hands it to Linda.

"Hey, it's got a crack!" Linda says, wide-eyed. "It's the same one I lost!"

"How can that be?" Tessa says.

"The perennial question!"

"Oh my god, that is so weird! You know what else is weird?"

"I'm not sure I can stand any more!"

"I could've sworn the walnut talked to me, but its voice was garbled and barely perceptible, so that I couldn't make anything out!"

"Same here!" Linda said. "I was too afraid someone would think I was crazy!"

"But everyone *already* thinks you're crazy!" Tessa laughs.

"Oh well, no harm done then!" Linda laughs along with Tessa.

"Of course, this means I'm crazy too!" Tessa says. "That's also old news!"

They laugh some more until the walnut yells quite audibly and irritably, "*Shut up!*", and they both freeze.

"Did you hear that?" Linda whispers to Tessa.

"Only if you did!"

"I did!"

"Then so did I!"

"What do we do?"

"I don't know!" Tessa says. "Report it?"

"To who?"

"The authorities!"

"*What* authorities!"

"*Any* authorities!"

"Then they'll lock us both up!"

"At least we'll be together!"

"With our adopted walnut!"

"Unless they take him from us!" Tessa says, half-jokingly. "What's his name, do you think?"

"*Chumpy!*" Linda and the walnut both say in unison, equally audible to all.

Linda and Tessa stare at each other in silence, waiting for the walnut to say something else, but Chumpy has passed out from stress mixed with the toxicity of struggling actor sewage seeping into his cracked shell.

"I need to call my friend Tanisha," Linda says. "Can I borrow this?"

"Of course, it's yours, right? Tanisha, the waitress from Dukes?"

"Yes."

"Why?"

"She found a talking walnut, too."

"*Wow*! So there's more than one?"

"*Just one*," the walnut meekly clarifies with a cough before lapsing back into mental limbo. Chumpy is no longer having someone else's nightmares. He's drifting into a blank, empty expanse, barely remembering who or what he is. The only thing keeping him from slipping away into eternal nothingness is the fear of death before he finds his creator, or his creator dies, since his creator isn't eternal like everyone else's, apparently. Their recent close call sustains his survival instinct on a subconscious level. But it's not his survival instincts keeping his soul alive inside that cracked, waterlogged shell.

Linda uses Tessa's phone to call Tanisha Alopecia at her Doheny apartment. There is no answer, but Linda knows Tanisha Alopecia is working at Dukes that night. After she leaves Tessa's house and arrives home at her Tropicana adjacent apartment, she reads a bit more of "Chumpy Walnut," looking for answers to her present predicament, wondering whether to tell her friend Will about it and risk his respect for her relative sanity. She appreciates his admiration even as she gently keeps him at arm's length, amorously speaking. He's so much younger than she is; she can't imagine why he's even attracted to her, chalking it up to an innocent byproduct of naive youth.

Both Will and Linda wonder why they even met in the magical way they did, when she sat in front of him at a double bill of *How to Marry a Millionaire* and *Gentlemen Prefer Blondes* at the Nuart Theater in West L.A., shortly after he returned from Houston, where he finished the final draft of "Chumpy Walnut" while obsessing over her role in *Fade to Black,* itself is a movie about a film nut stalking her character. Will is harmless, or at least she hopes so.

It must all mean something, or nothing means anything. They have different ideas of what that could be. At the moment, Linda thinks it has something to do with Chumpy Walnut, though her trips to an ashram with her new friend Debra have made her consider that this spiritual connection is the true purpose of the improbable encounter. How a talking walnut fits into this puzzle is a piece she can't seem to place, but the fact that it followed her and found its way to her via the sewer system must mean something, too. She is hoping Tanisha Alopecia can give her more clues, although her part in this remains a mystery as well, unless Tanisha Alopecia is merely a conduit to deliver the walnut to Linda, whose role perhaps is to then pass it on to Will? She just tried that, and he rejected it. Of course, Will doesn't know the walnut communicates with her telepathically, however cryptically and sporadically, and it obviously didn't speak to him, unless it did, and he's lying, too.

At Dukes, Linda is starting to wish she had never met Will or found that walnut, which has only complicated her already unstable life as she sits and waits for Tanisha Alopecia to get to her table. "Our Lips Are Sealed" by the Go-Go's is playing on the sound system.

"Linda!" Tanisha Alopecia says, snapping out of her stupor. "I was going to call you!"

"Oh yeah, why?"

"About our mutual friend, the walnut."

"Funny, that's why I'm here. I found it!"

"What? That's amazing! Where?"

"You don't want to know, trust me."

Tanisha Alopecia nods. "Gotcha. Anyway, can I have it? I need to give it to someone."

"Who?"

"My pimp."

"*Why*?"

"So he'll stop harassing me."

"Why is he harassing you?"

"He thinks that walnut is his lottery ticket."

"*Why*?"

"Well, I didn't tell you this because I thought you'd think I was psycho, but since this psychosis is apparently contagious, I will now. When I met Chumpy, he wasn't a walnut. He was a real dude with a giant penis!"

Linda laughs until she realizes Tanisha Alopecia is not joking. "What are you talking about?"

"I know how it sounds, but at least his being a normal-sized kid with an oversized dick is less outrageous than a talking walnut, so it's all relative. Fate wants to see if he can make Chumpy switch back to male hustler mode so he can pimp him out, which ain't happenin' on my watch, or yours. I just need to stall him and buy some time."

"What's your plan?"

"We need to get that walnut to his creator." "You mean Will?"

"Yes. Mickey will protect them both."

"I agree. Let them deal with it! It's too much for us, obviously!"

"Exactly. So you got the walnut?"

"Yes, it's right here." Linda takes the walnut out of her pocketbook but drops it because her hand is trembling with relentless anxiety. She watches the walnut roll toward the door.

"Not again!" Tanisha Alopecia says.

Just then, Tom Waits walks in, inadvertently kicking the walnut, which ricochets off a chair leg, then rolls back out the open door, like a wayward pinball. "Tanisha!" Tom says with a smile. "Finally!"

But both Linda and Tanisha Alopecia push past Tom Waits in pursuit of the walnut, which is nowhere in sight. But someone else is.

Chumpy sits up and realizes he is no longer a cracked walnut but a normal-sized human again, with a headache and an inhuman penis. The reverse-metamorphosis was triggered by the impact of being inadvertently kicked around, Chumpy surmises, for lack of a better theory.

"There you are!" Tanisha Alopecia says as Linda's eyes bug out at the sight of the bulge in Chumpy's pants. Fortunately, when he transitions between his three different manifestations, his clothes come with him, except when he's a walnut, of course.

Tanisha Alopecia and Linda help him up. "He looks like Will!" Linda says excitedly. "Well, except for...you know."

"How would *you* know?" Tanisha Alopecia asks with a raised eyebrow.

"You can't hide a thing like that unless you're wearing a barrel!"

"What's happening?" Chumpy says, feeling groggy, like he just woke up with a hangover.

"Who is this?" Tom Waits asks. He had followed them out the door.

"I know you!" Chumpy says to Tom Waits. "You need to stay away from my creator! He's going to kill you!"

Tom Waits is naturally taken aback by this admonition. But before he can respond, Fate the Pimp rolls up in his Caddy alongside the curb out front of the coffee shop, flashing both his gold-toothed smile and his pearl-handled pistol, which is pointed right at them.

"Get in or I'll shoot your fuckin' friends," Fate the Pimp says to Chumpy and Tanisha Alopecia. "I mean it now. Both of you. *Move it*."

Tanisha Alopecia stands protectively planted in front of Chumpy, who is leaning against Linda, as she implores her ambitious pimp for mercy. "*No! Enough*! Fate, *please*!"

"Ain't gonna ask you again," Fate the Pimp says coldly, cocking the piece.

"You've *still* been following me!"

"Damn straight, sugar. Ain't no escaping your Fate." Then the pimp sees the famous musician standing in Dukes' doorway. "Yo, look who it is! Tom fuckin' Waits! Hey, Tom Waits! Check it out, man! That there cartoon cocksmith is really that talkin' walnut Linda told you about."

"What walnut?" Tom Waits asks, increasingly perplexed.

"He means the one I told you about when you came looking for Tanisha that time," Linda explains.

"That ain't no walnut!" Tom Waits says, pointing at Chumpy. "That's a dirty limerick waiting to be written!"

"Why don't you get to it and set it to music," Fate the Pimp says. "You'll have your next hit song."

"I don't write hit songs," Tom Waits says.

"Fate, you put that fuckin' gun down *now!*" Tanisha Alopecia demands, still shielding Chumpy.

"Tanisha, I've got no problem shooting straight through you. Now *move.*"

"Fate, you wouldn't *dare!*"

Fate the Pimp fires a bullet right through her, hitting Chumpy square in the penis. Chumpy screams in agony as a broken ketchup bottle erupts from his wounded wang, gushing all over Linda, who is also screaming as she kneels beside her unconscious friend. Miraculously, the bullet didn't hit any of Tanisha Alopecia's vital organs, but she passed out from the trauma and is bleeding profusely. Linda doesn't know this yet, though, and is trying desperately to revive her friend. "Tanisha! *Tanisha*! You okay? *Tanisha*!"

"We'd better call an ambulance," Tom Waits says urgently. "I'll get someone inside to do it."

Dazed and confused, Tom Waits goes back into Dukes, where the patrons are all shell-shocked by the eruption of violence. The police have already been called, and the sirens are already wailing, a familiar scenario for Fate the Pimp. He gets out of the idling Caddy, pulls a wobbly Chumpy up by his arm, and tosses him into the passenger seat, even though he'll bleed all over the upholstery.

Linda is too preoccupied with Tanisha to notice or care. "This is worse than my stupid movie!" she sobs as the ambulance arrives under police escort and takes her friend away. Meanwhile, Chumpy in any form is long gone, now in the nefarious hands of a cheap gangster who sees him as a passport to prosperity, at Chumpy's expense. Just like old times.

As he lies bleeding on the zebra-patterned seat cover, Chumpy belatedly realizes he was better off back home in Thrillville with Cupey. His creator's dimension is even more dangerous and demented than the one created for him. In this world, he feels not only marginalized but mortal.

Back home from Dukes, having told the police exactly what he witnessed in excruciatingly incredulous detail, Tom Waits tells his wife Kathleen all about the sordid action scene.

"It's weird because—well, for all the obvious reasons—but also because of the warning that kid gave me just before it happened, about me being in danger from his creator."

"He probably meant God?"

"Your guess is as good as mine. God kills all of us eventually, though. Nothing I can do to avoid it."

"Maybe that bullet was meant for *you*," Kathleen says. "And that kid stopped it!"

"With his penis."

"If you say so."

"Wow," Tom Waits says with a whistle. "Now, *that's* a fan."

Back in Fate the Pimp's Hollywood pad, garishly decorated with African artifacts, voodoo dolls, tribal masks, velvet paintings, nude male and female statues, and Witco furniture, Chumpy's big penis is bleeding all over a tiger-print blanket spread over Fate the Pimp's waterbed. Fate the Pimp is trying to bandage it up, but it keeps leaking essential fluids like a busted catheter.

"I need a doctor," Chumpy says weakly.

"I *am* a doctor," Fate the Pimp says, unwrapping the blood-soaked gauze so he can replace it yet again. "Just call me Doctor Fate! You know, like the comic book dude."

"No, you're not a doctor, or a comic book character! *I*

am!"

"I'm not a fuckin' cartoon, but I *am* a fuckin' surgeon when it comes to shit like this. I've dressed a hundred bullet holes, including my own. At least the bullet fell out, flushed out by all the blood from this super-sized syringe you call a cock, so you'll be okay and ready to work soon. But in the meantime, they can trace that bullet back to me if they find it, so what I need you to do is, when the cops show up here, turn back into a walnut. I'll pretend you can talk, which you can, but they don't know that, so if they take me in anyway because of all the witnesses, I can plead insanity."

"I have no control over my physical appearance," Chumpy says. "Not since I got there." But in his mind, Chumpy has taken note of the abrupt, radical changes that expeditiously respond to a particular situation, not to mention the circuitous yet circular nature of his journey, which always leads him back to his chosen path regardless of his state of mind or being. Chumpy doesn't have a map, but he must have an unseen guide. "I won't say anything to protect you," Chumpy says, crying. "You killed my friend!"

"What, you mean Tanisha? Please. I've shot that bitch twice already. She always pulls through. Well, I shot *at* her twice. This is the first time I actually *hit* her. The others were warning shots. This time, I didn't have time to play no games."

"It's not a game."

"Yeah, well, that's where you're wrong. It's *all* a motherfuckin' game with winners and losers. No in-betweeners."

"I'm not playing this game. I'm from a different board."

"We're on the same board *now*, motherfucker."

"You didn't have to shoot Tanisha."

"Yeah I did. That was the right move to advance my pawn. Which is *you,* motherfucker."

"Why?"

"Because you're not a player, you're just a game piece."

"I can't believe you shot Tanisha. She should've left you a long time ago."

"She tried. Those were the warning shots. Actually, now that I think of it, I've shot at her *three* times before, but only actually shot her *once,* just now. So I'm ain't *that* bad a husband. Just a poor shot."

"Husband? I thought you were her pimp!"

"The difference being?"

Chumpy is angry and confused. "I don't understand why anyone would take such abuse, no matter how much money they made."

"Mutual security."

"You mean toxic co-dependency."

"Whatever with your pop art psychology, Cartoon Boy. Forget it. Now that I've got you, I don't need her or any of my bitches no more. You're gonna inject that super-sized syringe into so much pussy and ass it'll pay off better than a plastic surgery clinic, which was my backup plan."

"I'm not a prostitute like my wife."

"*What the fuck*? Wait, stop the motherfuckin' presses. You got a wife, now that's a newsflash, but the fact she's a *hooker* is the bombshell headline."

"She's not a hooker. She's a high-class zombie love companion."

"So she's a hooker."

"That's not how she self-identifies."

"Well, however she chooses to promote her pussy, where the fuck is she?"

"Thrillville."

"Ha-ha, I mean for real, Kookie Byrnes."

"It's a real place, just not in this dimension."

"So you're from another dimension. Solid alibi. Otherwise, none of this would make any god damn sense. And it *still* don't, even with this information. Why'd you leave this Thrillville for here, anyway? It must be pretty bad there."

"Better than this."

"That's a low bar, but never mind. Anyway, if you can Star Trek your wife's ass my way, I can set you both up as a duo, like Louis and Keely, only for sex, not showmanship. Though eventually it'll be a creative combination of both, I imagine. You could do live sex acts on stage as a preview of coming attractions, and by coming attractions I mean the audience who'll be creaming all over their motherfuckin' seats."

Chumpy finds Fate the Pimp quite tiresome. "Look, Mister Fate—"

"*Doctor* Fate."

"—I'm not doing anything for you. I just want to find my creator, so he can send me back home. I'm sorry I ever went looking for him."

"I coulda told you tryin' to find God in Hollywood is even harder than tryin' to find a fuckin' talking *walnut* in Hollywood, but now you know. Anyway, once you're patched up and recuperated, I'm gonna promote you as the Cartoon Cocksmith of the Century through my professional underground grapevine because I don't want you attracting the wrong kind of attention from the fuzz or the competition. Then, after you've earned a few hundred thousand or so, word will naturally spread, like a virus, and this shit will advertise itself. You dig?"

"No, I don't dig," Chumpy says. "Both of my heads are broken now. I can't perform with either of them."

"You'll find a workaround once you hear your cut," Fate the Pimp says.

"I don't want money. I just want to complete my mission."

"Well, I'm changing your mission statement, motherfucker. Your mission now is to make a ton of motherfuckin' money with your God-given assets."

"I do want to ask my creator why he invented this particular iteration. It seems pretty extreme, emphasis on the x'."

There's an urgent knock on the door, and Fate the Pimp freezes, recognizing its rapacious rap.

"*LAPD, open up!*" Fate the Pimp recognizes that bossy tone of voice, too.

"Aw *fuck*! Chumpy, do your thing, man!"

"What thing?"

"Turn into a fuckin' walnut, man, what else! Or a banana or a prune or *any* kinda fuckin' fruit or vegetable that won't incriminate me! Unless you wanna wait and do it in front of em. It'll blow their minds so hard they'll forget all about me. Yeah, maybe that's better."

"*Open up now or we'll force our way in,*" a cop's voice says.

"I told you it's not within my power," Chumpy says.

"Bullshit! You turn into a walnut whenever you're in trouble. I fuckin' *saw* it, so don't try to con me, man! We ain't got time for this shit now!"

"I've noticed that circumstantial convenience, too, but it was still random, and it wasn't something I *made* happen. It just happens. Plus, I'm not the one in trouble. *You* are."

"*We know you're in there, asshole!*" declares the other indistinguishable cop voice. "We can hear you talking, asshole!"

Fate the Pimp is in a full-blown, sweaty panic. "*Fuck!* Chumpy, just put your arms together and blink like fuckin' Jeanie! You gotta at least *try*, man! We're in this together now!"

"You're on your own," Chumpy says. "You'll get no help from me. Despite your self-justifications, you're a very bad man. I know your type. They have them in my world, too."

"Yeah, I know your type *blood*, motherfucker! You think I wanna clean this stain out? I'm gonna have to throw this fuckin' blanket away now!"

"Whose fault is that?"

The cops continue pounding on the door and issuing legally authoritarian threats.

"Chumpy, c'mon, man! All I wanna do is make you rich! Then you can go home to your wife in Fuckville or whatever the hell it is, loaded with so much cash she'll wanna come back with you to make even more! Or you can both retire, I mean, once I got my own island!"

"Let me see Tanisha Alopecia first," Chumpy says. "If she's all right, I'll think about it."

"We ain't got time for that shit neither! Just take my word for it, the bitch is fine, or at least not critical! C'mon, Chumpy! This is all for you, man!"

"Your kind always say that. And they're always lying."

The police are furiously knocking and kicking at the door. Finally, one shoots off the doorknob.

"*Chumpy!*" Fate the Pimp yells as Chumpy sits stone-faced on the bloody blanket, casually watching two of the four cops drag the struggling pimp away in cuffs.

"You'd better come with us now, sir," says an impressed and curiously aroused cop, his eyes glued to Chumpy's big, bloody boner.

"I can't. I have to find my creator. That's the only reason I'm here. I know what he looks like now, at least. Sort of like me. But not as pretty, per common consensus."

The cops look at each, and then nod in agreement. They know his kooky kind, generally speaking, but not quite *this* kind of kook. "You'll meet your maker if you don't get that thing looked at," says one of the cops, trying not to stare at Chumpy's mutated, mummified member.

"One more reason not to see a doctor," Chumpy says adamantly. "Nothing can stop me from completing my mission."

The cops ignore him, except for his penis. "We also need you to formally identify the suspect and testify against him, assuming you press charges."

"I'm not helping you either," Chumpy says. "I have

better things to do. Apparently, according to the locals, I'm a cartoon character in the flesh, even if it's mutated flesh. It's still *cartoon* flesh. We get shot and run over and blown up all the time. It's no big deal. I'll be fine as soon as I get back to my real home."

Despite their professionally apathetic efforts, the cops are skeptical and stunned in equal measure. "Well, you can tell that to the prosecutor. In any case, besides two attempted homicides, that asshole faces charges of Disturbing the Peace and Reckless Endangerment, to name only a couple. He's going down with or without your cooperation. In any case, you require immediate medical attention. Let's go."

"Attempted? Tanisha, Alopecia is still alive?"

"The whore? Yeah, she'll pull through. It's a miracle, really."

Chumpy almost cries with relief. "That's all that matters to me. She's not a whore, by the way. She's my friend and she saved my life."

"You mean she saved her livelihood," a copy smirks with a nod at Chumpy's mutilated meat muppet.

"You can help her by helping us," the other cop says, snickering like a schoolboy.

"But she's not going to die. So you don't need me."

"You have to come with us anyway. We have to file a full report about this, and you're a big part of it. No pun intended. Well, actually, that pun was totally intended. Anyway, you can't just limp away. For one thing, you'll trip." Both cops continue to guffaw like giddy goofballs.

Chumpy sighs as each cop takes one of his arms, lifting him as gently as possible, but the topsy-turvy surface of the waterbed makes it difficult to retain sure footing, much less maintain a grip. Refusing to make it easy for them, Chumpy has gone completely limp, except for his penis, which is damaged but fully erect as the cops do their best not to touch it, or more importantly, not to let it touch them. Chumpy is concentrating hard, harder than his penis.

They almost have him up on his feet when they suddenly realize they've got a tight hold on nothing but the air between them. Then, just as suddenly, the waterbed springs a leak, and several liquids simultaneously pour all over the cops, who slip and trip into each other before falling flat on their flabbergasted faces.

Invisible Little Chumpy sets down Fate the Pimp's switchblade, which for him has become more like a harpoon, and then he scampers out the door, down the stairs, and back onto Hollywood Boulevard, right where he started. "Let's try this again," he tells himself, determined to never get detoured from his destination, which lately feels like a mirage.

Chapter Five
SHRUNKEN HEAD TRIP

Chumpy Walnut needs a mai tai. Since he wants to be able to blend in well enough to order a drink, while in the back of the bus, he concentrates and manages to morph from an invisible twelve-inch person to one of short but not uncommon height, but with a huge penis that he has learned to retract and suppress like a box spring barely hidden within a flimsy mattress. Gradually, he is learning to master his own visage, adjusting it from the known options to suit his circumstances, which are constantly in flux. He is still wearing an aloha shirt, but it's a fresh one in a different pattern. His loafers are likewise newly polished, and his cabana shorts are clean. Inter-dimensional travel and body morphing are not an excuse for poor grooming, at least per the style-conscious conduit.

The bus driver and passengers don't remember seeing Chumpy get on, because at the time, he was an invisible little man who didn't have bus fare, so his appearance was immaterial anyway. Now they can't help but notice Chumpy, though no one recalls him boarding the bus, including the driver. Their stares at the bulge in his cabana shorts don't stop him from politely inquiring where he can score a good mai tai. He gets plenty of answers from the women and a few of the men.

Naturally, Chumpy feels sad about what happened to Tanisha, even if she will survive the shooting. She is suffering because she is his only friend in this dimension. But not even his concern for her can distract him from his mission. He realizes this is selfish, and doesn't care, because that's part of being selfish. His distant empathy will have to suffice.

Taking some informed advice from a fawning gay man, Chumpy gets off the bus at the intersection of Wilshire and Santa Monica Boulevards in Beverly Hills, then enters an establishment within the Beverly Hilton Hotel called Trader Vic's. His aloha shirt makes him feel right at home, and the Polynesian Pop decor reminds him of Ivar's Tiki Lounge back in Thrillville. This place isn't quite as gaudy, since it sports a casually upscale elegance in its faux-tropical aesthetics. Instead of exotica music, though, the sound system is currently playing "Don't You Want Me" by the Human League. Chumpy takes a seat at the bar, expecting service.

"I.D.?" the burly, alpha-masculine bartender asks Chumpy. The bartender's name is Vincent Vincerelli, but people who know him well call him Vain Vinnie, or they don't call him at all. He's really an actor who needs a break, as he eventually tells all of his customers, particularly those in the industry. So he's not unique in this town. He only thinks he is.

"Excuse me?" says Chumpy. In Thrillville, nobody needs an "I.D." to drink, not even children, which could be construed as illegal or at least unethical, which is why no pesky procreation is permitted in Thrillville.

The bartender sighs. "I need to see your ID, sir. If I can even call you sir'."

"You may."

"I may what? See your ID?"

"What's ID'?"

"Identification, but if you don't even know that, that tells *me* all I need to know."

"Please, I just want a mai tai. I've had plenty in my time, so I can handle it. I want to see if they're as good as the ones at Ivar's."

"Ivar's? Never heard of it. Unless you mean the restaurant in Seattle."

"No, the one I mean is not around here. Please, sir. I've had a very weird and hard day. You can't even imagine how weird and hard it is. You'd have to be my creator to even imagine it. Literally."

Vain Vinnie gives Chumpy a blank stare, then says, "I'm not going to imagine anything, including verification of your age, so cough it up, baby face."

"Hm. I guess those are the rules here."

"That's right. Same as anywhere, Son of Stranger in a Strange Land."

"Well, if I can find my creator, he can show you his manuscript, which tells my life story, at least until the time I meet Cupey. This will verify the length of my existence. The second one won't be written for several decades. I have issues with the direction he took my life and world. It's why I'm here. Your world, not this bar, though I guess my desperation makes me thirsty. I'll come back here with the manuscript later, once I've found him. I don't think you have time to read all of it, but you'll get the gist. So just put it on my tab, as they say back in Ivar's."

The bartender stares again at Chumpy for a somewhat longer beat, shakes his head, then sighs and walks away. He comes back with a glass of water, which Chumpy drinks with disappointment.

Still feeling thirsty for something tangy and intoxicating, Chumpy scans the room for someone who can order him a cocktail in this prejudicial, ageist establishment. His eyes stop and lock on an incredibly attractive, blonde woman with deep, beckoning cleavage sitting alone in a booth. She is wearing sunglasses even though it's dark inside. There is a Scorpion Bowl on the table that is still full. Chumpy has found his mark. He leaves the bar and walks over to her table.

"May I join you?" Chumpy asks the gorgeous lady.

The woman smiles curtly as she says, "No autographs, please. I'm waiting for someone."

"I wasn't going to give you my autograph because it's worthless around here."

The effortlessly glamorous woman takes off her sunglasses and looks at Chumpy for a few seconds, then bursts out laughing. Feeling inexplicably entranced, she says, "I'll do much better than that, handsome. I'll give you something more memorable, even if it won't last long."

"A drink?"

She laughs again. "A memory."

"Time is fluid," Chumpy says. "Fast and fleeting, like it sprang a leak. Then it suddenly runs out and you're left holding an empty bag as your dreams circle the drain."

"Well, that's pithy. Who said that?"

"I did. Just now."

She smiles again, but broader, mysteriously enchanted by this beautiful alien being. "Take a seat. At least until my friend Yvonne arrives."

Chumpy is unsure why the woman laughs at him, but he's learned to take inappropriate laughter in stride, especially in this realm. "What's your name?" he asks her.

The woman seems taken aback. "You can call me Stella. I guess you've never seen *The Poseidon Adventure*."

"Never even heard of it."

"Really? I mean, talk about springing a fatal leak. What planet are you from?"

"It's a planet like this one, but not in outer space. It's just in a different dimension. I live in Thrillville, which is in an imaginary dimension. Imaginary to you, anyway. I'm just visiting. I'm looking for my creator."

Stella Stevens keeps smiling, but a bit nervously. Before she can reply, her beauteously brunette, buxom friend Yvonne Craig shows up with their mutual friend, petite, perky, and pretty actress Deborah Walley.

"Hey Stella!" says Yvonne with a smile.

"Hi, Stanley," Stella says with a Tennessee Williams savvy grin.

"I hope you don't mind I invited myself," says Deborah.

"Oh no, never!" Stella says. "I ordered a Scorpion Bowl, so there's plenty for everybody."

"Sorry I'm late," Yvonne says. "I had to drop Meridel off at an appointment. She says she's sorry she couldn't make it, but Deborah volunteered to take her place. And who's this? Your long-lost son?"

They both laugh. "A complete stranger."

"So he *is* your son!" Yvonne says, and they laugh some more. "What's his name?"

"I don't even know," Stella says. "We just met like five seconds ago. Isn't he cute?"

"Adorable," Deborah says. "In an 'E.T.' sort of way."

"He's not from outer space," Stella says. "I already asked, since that was my first guess, too. But apparently he is from a different dimension, so that checks."

"What is your name, sweetheart?" Yvonne asks.

"Chumpy! Chumpy Walnut."

"Like Bond, James Bond," Stella says. "Or James Blonde, in his case."

"So are you, like, a secret agent from another dimension?" Yvonne asks.

"Sort of. I am on a mission."

"I see," Yvonne says. The ladies have all been charmed out of their skepticism.

Vain Vinnie skulks over to their table and again asks Chumpy for his ID. "Sorry, ladies, but this guy won't show me his ID."

"He's with us," Stella says. "I promise he won't drink."

"Much," Deborah adds with a giggle.

Chumpy looks forlorn, and Stella winks at him.

"I'm sorry, but he looks underage to me," Vain Vinnie says with a scowl.

"Chumpy, how old are you?" Stella asks him.

"I'm ageless," Chumpy says. "So I'll always look younger than I am."

"I need some of whatever he drinks then," Deborah adds.

"That's good enough for me," Stella says. "Like I said, we'll make sure he doesn't drink."

"Much," Chumpy adds.

Just then, a fourth, ravishingly red-haired glamour goddess approaches the table and says hello. "Who's this cutie?" she asks everyone in reference to Chumpy.

"This is Chumpy Walnut," Stella says. "He's an imaginary being visiting from Thrillville."

"Well, you don't meet one of those every day!" Ann-Margret says.

"I'm sorry, Miss Margret, but I'm afraid he'll have to go since he has no ID," Vain Vinnie says with a conflicted mixture of urgency and awe.

"If he's with them, he's with me," Ann-Margret tells Vain Vinnie with a wink at Chumpy.

Perpetually starstruck, the bartender is now suffering from advanced Goddess Worship Syndrome. "Whatever you say, Miss Margret. I'm holding you responsible. By the way, I'm a big fan. Of *all* of you!"

"Then make like a fan and blow," Stella says.

"Can I show you all my headshot and resume?" Vain Vinnie asks them. "I have them handy, just in case."

"In case of what, a fire?" Yvonne says.

"Not now," Ann-Margret says with a polite but impatient smile. Then she asks Stella, "Can I sit with you? Roger must've flaked on me. Or I flaked on him."

They all move over to accommodate her. Then they proceed to share personal anecdotes about their respective co-starring roles with Elvis Presley: Ann-Margret in *Viva Las Vegas*, Yvonne in *It Happened at the World's Fair* and *Kissin' Cousins,* Deborah in *Spinout*, and Stella in *Girls! Girls! Girls!*

"I wish my friend Julie Parrish were here," Deborah says. "She was in *Paradise, Hawaiian Style*."

"I love Julie," Yvonne says. "We should get together

with her soon. Oh, and Annie, too!"

"Anne Helm?" Stella says.

"Yes, she was in *Follow That Dream*," Yvonne says.

"I know," Stella says.

"I think Anne Helm has a connection to my creator," Chumpy says. "It's just a feeling. I go mostly on feelings. They're all I got."

"Hm, well Annie *is* very spiritual," Yvonne says.

"Is she still married to Robert Viharo?" Deborah asks Yvonne.

"No, they split up and he married a famous French singer or something like that, last I heard from Annie."

"That's a shame," Deborah says.

"For who?" Yvonne says, and Deborah giggles.

"Wait, who was married to this Robert Viharo?" Chumpy asks. "That name sounds familiar, too."

"Our friend Anne Helm," Deborah tells him.

"Does this Robert have a son named Will? And is this Annie his mother?"

"I only know Annie has a son named Peter and a daughter named Serena," Yvonne tells Chumpy. "Peter is from a different father. Serena is Robert's daughter. But Robert has kids from other marriages. I haven't met them, though."

"Now that he mentions it, I feel like I know this Will," Deborah says, "or will someday."

"Funny, so do I," Yvonne says.

"Me, too," says Stella. "How about you, Ann?"

"Where's Annie?" Chumpy says. "She's here?"

"No, sweetie, I meant *her*," Stella says, nodding at Ann-Margret.

"Sorry, I took my needless introduction for granted," Ann-Margret says to Chumpy. "I'm Ann-Margret, but you can call me Ann since you seem to be one of the gang now.

"Do you know Will?" Chumpy asks her.

"I don't know Will, but it already feels like I do."

"Definitely next time we should invite Annie and Julie," Deborah says. "You know, all the casting directors used to confuse Yvonne and Annie."

"I know!" Yvonne says. "All the time. We could've swapped roles. Sometimes I wish we had."

"You're real life 'Kissing Cousins!'" Deborah says.

After they collectively suck up a couple more Scorpion Bowls amid many more amusing anecdotes, Chumpy is rather drunk, forgetting for the moment he even has a creator, or not caring whether or not he finds him. That's when he begins tipsily telling them his own life story, including the subjectively controversial future sequel. The ladies find this story incredibly riveting, misinterpreting it as the treatment for a screenplay, and instantly deciding Chumpy is a creative genius with a brilliant future. They are especially impressed by all the glamorous pinup bombshells in Chumpy's inner orbit.

"Okay, that absolutely needs to be a movie," Yvonne says. "Sounds like there are plenty of parts for us."

"You certainly have the parts for it," Deborah quips.

"He may not have an ID, but he certainly has an idea," Stella says.

"I'd sign up for it," Ann-Margret says, and they all concur. "Have you written any of this down?" she then asks Chumpy. "In either treatment or screenplay form?"

"No, but my creator has," Chumpy says.

"By creator, you mean your co-writer?"

"You could say that, since I'm living his words in his world, at least in the world he created for me."

"So he's your agent," Deborah says.

"If so, he's a lousy one," says Chumpy.

"You have a rather unique perspective," Stella tells him. "It's refreshing to hear something so original. Can we meet your creator, as you call him?"

"If I ever find him, sure," Chumpy says. "Though you may not need me for that since you'll meet him eventually, anyway. Well, some of you."

"I can wait," Stella says.

"I sometimes have trouble finding my agent, too," Ann-Margret says, and they all laugh while Chumpy sits with a nonplussed expression.

Eavesdropping on the entire conversation, including the "film treatment," Vain Vinnie is seething with jealousy. He wants to punch the stuffing out of this living doll's face till its glass eyes pop out and Vain Vinnie can pop them like bubble wrap.

Stella and Ann-Margret have pivoted to a private discussion of their roles opposite Dean Martin in two of his Matt Helm spy films, *The Silencers* and *The Ambusher*s, respectively. At the same time, the other ladies converse about family and other matters, in between eavesdropping on each other. Chumpy is more attuned to the conversation between Ann-Margret and Stella.

"We have a Dino Martini where I came from," Chumpy says, interrupting them during a brief pause. "But now he's only a zombie after being injected with venom from a giant black widow spider. He's part of the Rot Pack, which used to be the Pack Rats."

There is a lengthy pause by all, before Deborah says, "Oh my god, we have to put that in our movie!"

"Dean isn't quite a zombie yet," Ann-Margret says.

"Give it time," Stella says dryly. "He's still working on it."

There is a bit more tipsy conversation about handsome leading men they have in common before Deborah says, "I need to go to Neiman-Marcus to pick up a dress. It's one reason I tagged along with Yvonne, and I'm sure glad I did. Would any of you care to join me on a little shopping spree?"

"Sure!" Chumpy says.

"Of course you do," Stella says, hugging him. "You're lucky you're so cute!"

"I know," Chumpy says.

"Actually, that's so funny, because I'm meeting Raquel at the Club Room," Ann-Margret tells them. "Want to have lunch with us there? I need to eat something substantial to soak up this booze, and the food here is a bit heavy and greasy."

"Me too, I'm starving!" Chumpy says, and they laugh again.

Leaving their respective cars behind with the valet, who is tipped extra even though he'd have paid them to stay as long as they wanted, the ladies then pile into the limousine Ann employs for shopping trips. It drops them all off in front of the Neiman-Marcus department store, which is located up a few blocks on Wilshire Boulevard. Ann-Margret's bombshell friend Raquel Welch is waiting for them inside. The famous five and their trippy-looking tag-along attract a lot of attention, but people know not to disturb the stars in this particular constellation.

They take the escalator to the fourth floor and enter the restaurant, heading into the adjacent Club Room, where they squeeze into a large booth. "Obsession" by Animotion is playing on the sound system. By this time, Raquel Welch has already been brought up to speed about this semi-fictional character named Chumpy, and she is equally enchanted. The waiter on duty is the same nice man who recommended Trader Vic's to Chumpy on the bus. He is muscular and clean-cut with a thin mustache. His name is Jimmy. Seeing his idol Ann-Margret with her famous friends, as well as the angelic alien, makes him even happier than he already is.

"I see you did better than a mai tai," Jimmy tells Chumpy.

"I had a Scorpion Bowl!" Chumpy says. "It was bigger than the ones back home!"

"I'm your biggest fan," Jimmy says.

"Thanks!" Says Chumpy.

"Oh, I'm sorry, I meant them," Jimmy says, pointing to Ann-Margret and Raquel Welch. "*All* of you! I've seen *Viva Las Vegas* and *Kitten with a Whip*, oh, I don't know how many times. And of course, I also love *Batman*, *Gidget Goes Hawaiian*, *The Nutty Professor*, and *One Million Years B.C.*, all of which I've seen countless times. This is like a diplomatic luncheon in Hollywood Heaven. My family back home in Houston will never believe me. It's a dream come true. Thank you."

"Thank Chumpy," Stella says. "It's like he brought us all closer just by being here." The ladies find Jimmy very endearing. Ann-Margret is especially touched by Jimmy. Later, when Jimmy is in the hospital dying from AIDS, his friend Ann-Margret will call him and tell him to get better and eat his veggies.

"Where is this Houston'?" Chumpy asks Jimmy. "I believe that is where my story was completed."

"It's the one in Texas," Jimmy says with a bemused expression.

"That's probably the one I'm thinking of," Chumpy says. "Do you know my creator?"

"No, I don't, not yet," Jimmy says. "But as Warren Beatty would say, 'Heaven can wait.'"

After Jimmy has taken their orders—the Beverly Hills Diet Lunch but with the house specialty, popovers—two more radiantly attractive women enter the Club Room and recognize the familiar constellation of fellow stars.

"Julie!" Deborah squeals, getting up to hug her good friend Julie Parrish, who warmly hugs her back. Julie beams with organic luminescence. "We were just talking about you!"

"I was thinking of you, too!" Julie says. "You popped into my head suddenly, out of the blue!"

"We must be in sync," Deborah says.

"I've noticed that happening a lot lately," Chumpy says.

"Who's this fairy tale creature?" Julie asks Deborah.

"His name is Chumpy," Deborah says.

"I feel like we've met already?" Julie says to Chumpy.

"You probably met my creator, or will someday," Chumpy says, shaking her hand.

"We all will eventually," Julie says.

"And of course you know the rest of us," Deborah tells Julie.

"I haven't met them all in person, but I certainly recognize them," Julie says, exchanging pleasantries with each one.

"This is Myrna," Julie then says, introducing her cosmically comely companion to the group. "Myrna Hansen." Myrna looks like a living old-fashioned pinup, and there's a good reason for that.

"Oh, the Gil Elvgren model!" Deborah says.

"Yes!" Julie says. "And an actress."

"If you can call *Cult of the Cobra* acting," Myrna says dryly. "Nice to finally meet you all." Then she says to Chumpy, "Especially you, little man. I agree with Julie. You do seem familiar, but also like no one else I've ever met."

"Not yet," Chumpy says.

"You've been on so many of my ex-husband's calendars!" Deborah tells Myrna.

"That's nice," says Myrna, who hears that way too often.

"So, what brings you here?" Deborah asks Julie. "Just following your tingling ears?"

"Oh, Myrna and I were shopping and decided to have lunch. It was like a sudden attack of hunger only a popover could cure."

"Well, thanks for popping over!" Deborah says.

"Join us!" Stella says. Jimmy is already putting two tables together in the center of the room to accommodate the assemblage of ageless actresses, who migrate over with their drinks.

Deborah asks Julie to share some of her Elvis stories from *Paradise, Hawaiian Style*, and she obliges. Chumpy is enthralled.

"I was in an Elvis movie, but nobody even noticed it," Raquel Welch says. "That was before the dinosaur movie, though."

"You mean Bikini Beach B.C.?" Yvonne asks, and they all laugh. Yvonne and Deborah co-starred in *Ski Party*, which is part of the "Beach Party" series, except it's set in the snow.

"Which Elvis movie were you in?" Ann-Margret asks Raquel Welch.

"I had a cameo in *Roustabout*."

"I think I saw that," Yvonne says.

"Not me if you blinked," Raquel Welch quips.

"Are you an Elvis fan?" Ann-Margret asks Chumpy.

"No, not exactly, but I am a fan of Rocky Rolemodel. They sound a lot alike. Except Rocky Rolemodel is a zombie now, too."

"Hm. I never heard of him," Ann-Margret says. "But Elvis is definitely undead"

Chumpy raises his hand politely and asks the group, "Do you mind if I excuse myself to use the restroom?"

"Talking about Elvis usually makes me want to avoid the bathroom," Stella says.

"I promise to be careful," Chumpy says, and they laugh.

"It's just out the door and around the corner, sweetheart," Stella tells him.

At the urinal stall, Chumpy's penis is swollen with naturally filtered rum juice, and he has to stand back from the stall so he doesn't spray the second-hand spirits all over the restroom. Of course, it still spills outside the designated goal, accidentally splashing the astonished man at the stall next to his, a bespectacled playwright named Neil Simon, who quickly shakes his own comparatively modest member before wiping himself down with a paper towel and exiting the restroom in a hurry, back to the table in the Club Room where his wife, actress Marsha Mason, is waiting for him, having already paid the check. She is thoroughly appalled by the large, wet spots not only on his crotch but all over his sweater and pant legs, and is only more disgusted when he frantically explains that it isn't even his urine. They divorce the following year, though no direct connection has been established.

Back in the restroom, after Chumpy's humongous piss-hose has been fully depleted, it goes limp, and he stuffs it back into his pants like he's hastily burying a used body bag.

Sitting at the bar of the Club Room is a strikingly handsome, effortlessly suave young actor named Jon Lindstrom, who once worked here as a waiter. In a few years, he will become a popular soap opera star, then eventually an acclaimed and successful novelist. Jon is visiting his old friend Jackie, who is tending bar. She is a tall, leggy, blue-eyed, platinum-banged beauty from England who was once a showgirl in Las Vegas, where she had a fling with Elvis Presley. As Chumpy walks by on his way back to his table, Jon looks at him and exclaims, "Will!"

"I was going to say, he does remind me of Will," says Jimmy, who is collecting drink orders from Jackie. "I'm not my creator, though apparently I resemble him," Chumpy says.

"I thought he was Will when he first walked in, too," Jackie says. "But he's even prettier."

"Yeah, sorry," Jon says to Chumpy. "I mistook you for a good friend of ours."

"What can you tell me about Will?" Chumpy says.

"Will was a busboy here for a few years, when I was a waiter here," Jon explains.

"He still comes in from time to time to say hello," Jackie says.

"Has he come in lately?" Chumpy asks.

"Not for a little while, I'm afraid," Jackie says.

"He has family in Houston, like me," Jimmy says. "He just got back into town after staying with them for a few months."

Chumpy nods. "Yes, I figured, since he wrote the final draft of my story there."

"His mother was actually Miss Houston in nineteen-sixty," Jimmy says, "but then she was diagnosed with schizophrenia while he was still in her womb. It ruined her career as an actress, so Will never really knew her. It's a very sad story."

"And then he was raised in a cult in New Jersey," Jackie adds. "It's amazing he's not up in a tower shooting people."

"Well, we haven't seen him in a while," Jon says, and they laugh. "But I guess we would've heard about that."

"I figured mental illness runs in his family," Chumpy says.

"Like a marathon," Jackie says.

"That explains a lot. About my story, that is."

"What's your story about?" Jon asks Chumpy.

"My life."

"Wow, it must be pretty interesting if someone wrote a book about it," Jon says. "Did you write it? Is it a memoir?"

"No, my creator wrote it."

"So you mean it like a metaphor," Jackie says to Chumpy.

"I guess it's like a metaphor of my creator's own life," Chumpy says to Jackie, who nods politely.

"I'd like to write a book someday," Jon says. "Where can I find this book?"

"It's not published, and won't be for almost thirty years. And then it will be self-published."

"That's what I call planning ahead!" Jon says with a laugh.

"Have a little more faith than that!" Jackie says to Chumpy.

"No point," Chumpy says. "It's already happened in the

future. Your future, anyway."

"So you're a time traveler," Jackie says to Chumpy.

"We're all traveling through time," Chumpy says. "And it's traveling through us, too."

"Hey, Will wrote a book, too!" Jon says, deciding it's best to move on.

"I know," Chumpy says. "He's my creator."

They're all too stunned to say anything right away, but then Jon says, "So you must be the inspiration for Chumpy Walnut."

"I *am* Chumpy Walnut."

Jon goes along with the gag. "Forgive me, but I thought you'd be much shorter."

"Who put you up to this?" Jackie says. "Will?"

"No, I put myself up to it. I've never met Will. Do any of you know where I can find him?"

"Last I heard, Will is a busboy working up the street at Santo Pietro's," Jon says.

"I thought he was at Larry Parker's Diner?" Jackie says.

"Really?" Jon says. "Maybe. He moves around a lot."

"You mean he gets fired a lot," Jackie says.

Jon nods and grins. "His talents definitely lie elsewhere."

"He's meant for other things," Jackie says. "Like you."

"We'll see," Jon says.

"I'll go look for him at those two places then," Chumpy says. "Thank you. How can I find them?"

"Both are nearby," Jon tells Chumpy. "The diner is on Beverly just off Wilshire, and Santo Pietro is back up Wilshire a few blocks, then around the corner on Camden. Easy to find."

Expressing acknowledgement and gratitude, Chumpy heads straight back to his table, where he is introduced to a couple now occupying their vacated booth, which has been cleared and cleaned by Jimmy. They've all been chatting in Chumpy's absence.

"Chumpy, this is Olivia Hussey and her husband, Akira," Stella says to Chumpy. Chumpy shakes both their hands. He finds Olivia Hussey ethereally lovely and is already envious of her suave Japanese spouse.

"My, I just got an electric shock!" Olivia Hussey says to Chumpy as she quickly withdraws her hand from his grasp. "You must be magic!"

"We think so," Stella says to Olivia Hussey. "He just showed up out of nowhere and charmed our pants off. Not literally, but he might as well have."

"We've been telling Olivia, Julie, and Myrna about your movie," Deborah says to Chumpy, "and they'd like to be in it, too!"

"Some of the women in it sound like they look like me!" Myrna says. "Or how I once looked."

"You're *still* gorgeous!" Julie tells Myrna.

"Well, thank you, so are you," Myrna tells Julie.

"Are you an actor?" Olivia Hussey asks Chumpy.

"Oh, I've played various parts lately," Chumpy says cryptically. "I have a wide range."

"Really?" Olivia Hussey says, wide-eyed. "Have I seen any of them?"

"You're looking at one right now."

Olivia Hussey furrows her brow. "Well, whatever your role in this world may be, you have an absolutely other-worldly quality."

"How did you guess?" Stella says.

"Anyway, I'm sorry, but I have to go find my creator now," Chumpy tells them all, waving as he backs away.

"Parting is such sweet sorrow," Olivia Hussey says, blowing him a kiss.

"What about our movie?" Deborah asks. "We really want to help make that happen!"

"It's not possible to make it a movie yet," Chumpy says. "Please forget everything I told you."

"Well, *that's* impossible," Stella says, writing down her

phone number on a napkin. "Here's my home number. Call me and we'll set up some meetings. You can bring your so-called creator. We'll cut him in on the deal. Okay?"

Chumpy takes the napkin and puts it in his pocket. "If I meet my creator, I'll pass it on."

"Don't wait *that* long," Stella says.

"Nice meeting you, Chumpy!" Deborah says, and then all the other ladies echo the sentiment as "Call Me" by Blondie joins the chorus via the sound system.

Once Chumpy has left after one last goodbye to Jackie, Jon, and Jimmy, Ann-Margret says to the group, "Anyway, what were we talking about?"

"I can't remember," Raquel Welch says. "My mind is suddenly blank."

"Mine too, as if I were kidnapped by aliens and brainwashed," Yvonne says, and they all concur.

With a group shrug, the lovely ladies return to their luncheon, with no further mention or memory of Chumpy Walnut, as if he never existed.

Ten minutes and a few blocks later, Chumpy walks into Larry Parker's Beverly Hills Diner and sees that actor from *Diner* again with two other guys, both actors, Lance Henriksen and Leonard Termo, neither of which are Chumpy's creator, though they sometimes hang out with him. "Rock this Town" by the Stray Cats is playing on the sound system. Chumpy walks straight to Mickey's table, where Mickey is currently engaged in conversation with the owner, Larry Parker, who appears to be constipated as he stands upright and uptight.

"Mickey, Bruce Springsteen is not right for the atmosphere here," Larry is telling Mickey in his whiny, nasal voice. "This isn't a cafe in Greenwich Village. This is a hangout for teeny boppers and tourists."

"Then maybe this isn't the right place for me," Mickey says coolly.

Larry Parker doesn't want to lose the cache of Mickey's

patronage. "Don't you like the Stray Cats?"

"Yeah, of course, but I'm not in the mood for them right now. I need some Bruce."

"Yeah, Bruce is the Boss around here," Lenny Termo tells Larry in his usual gruff manner. "Not you."

Larry sighs and puts Springsteen's latest album, *Nebraska,* on the sound system, bringing the brightly lit retro-styled diner's carefully calculated mood down to Mickey's street level.

Once the matter has been settled, Chumpy sees an opening to approach Mickey. "Hi, you don't know me, though I've seen you, and I know your friend Will. Can you tell me how to find him?"

"Wow, you look like Willie as an action figure!" says Lance, who would later co-star with Mickey in *Johnny Handsome.* He has a distinctly deep, sardonic voice.

"Only handsomer," adds Lenny, who would soon co-star with Mickey in both *Year of the Dragon* and *Barfly.*

"No, Willie's handsomer," Mickey says.

"Willie's okay for jailhouse chicken," Lance says, and they laugh. "But this guy is better. Gourmet chicken. Willie is just a greasy bag of KFC."

"Like Charlie Chicken Wing," Mickey says, referring to a friend of Mickey's from New York, who also happens to know Chumpy's creator.

"Did Willie ever finally get laid?" Lenny asks Mickey.

"Yeah, his father set him up with a friend of his. I think he was fucking her too, according to Wiliel."

"At the same time?" Lance says.

"That's sad," Lenny says. "Will's young and could have any pussy he wants. Well, almost."

"Willie told me his father's wife Jeane tried to set him up with that sexy cowgirl from *Apocalypse Now*, and Willie chickened out at the last minute."

"He's chicken in more ways that one," Lenny observes.

"I know who you mean," Lance says. "Cindi Wood. She

was a Playmate."

"You gotta be fuckin' kiddin' me," Lenny says. "The babe in the cowboy hat dancing at the UFO show?"

"Yeah," Mickey says. "Jeane arranged a meeting at her house, and apparently, the cowgirl was down for it, but Willie was too scared. This was a little while ago, after he first got here from Jersey, and we just met."

"How did you meet again?" Lenny asks Mickey.

"Sandra Seacat and her daughter Greta picked up from work at Neiman-Marcus one day, and he sat next to me in the back seat. I told him he kinda looked like Elvis, so we hit it off right away."

"So let me get this straight," Lance says. "We took Willie out to pick up a Hollywood hooker, which we would pay for, but *after* he already turned down a freebie with a Playmate in a famous movie? And then he bails on the hooker, too?"

"He's an idiot," Lenny says.

Mickey nods. "I know. He's still hung up on Linda Kerridge."

"That's a fantasy," Lenny says.

"I've tried telling him."

"She's too big for him," Lance says, and they laugh again. "Willie needs someone like Betty Boop."

"He's too shy to even talk to girls," Mickey says.

"Even cartoon girls?" Lance says.

"Them, too. I think it might have something to do with his upbringing in New Jersey. He was taught sex was evil or something. So now, he thinks he needs to be a successful writer before anyone will take him seriously, especially girls, *any* girl, because he thinks he's too short and he's self-conscious, so he needs to compensate. I always tell him, You don't need to be tall, just tough. Plus, he has a nice face, and that's all that matters in this town, more than talent sometimes. He won't listen, though."

"You're saying, in his mind, he needs to be a bestselling

novelist before he grows the balls to fuck?" Lenny says. "He'll die a virgin."

Lance nods with a sigh. "Yeah, we talked about his insecurity when he drove me around in the T-Bird one day, running errands. I paid him for it. We all have insecurities, I told him. I wanted to take him to meet Al that day, since he was shooting a scene for that gangster movie over at Universal and invited me to swing by, but we ran out of time."

"You De Palma's *Scarface* remake?" Lenny asks.

"Yeah, it's mostly set in Miami, though," Lance says, before asking Mickey, "What's going on with Willie's book, anyway?"

"I don't fuckin' know. I told you I took him down to Zoetrope to meet Francis and Fred Roos, and had him audition for *Rumble Fish*, but he got cotton mouth and fucked it up."

"He's not an actor," Lance says.

"Yeah, I know. Too bad. He's got the right look."

"Can't you help him with the book?" Lenny says.

"What the fuck else can I do? I did have him send the manuscript to Fred Roos for a potential movie, but Fred passed."

"That would've changed everything," Chumpy finally interjects, absorbed in the information overload, feeling newly enlightened about his creator's motivations. "Especially the second book, which is why I'm looking for him."

"He only wrote one so far," Mickey says.

"He'll write a sequel soon, but it won't be published until he rewrites it many years from now, only retaining the title and a few fundamental concepts."

"Oh, so now you're from the fuckin' future?" Lenny says.

"*Your* future. Or maybe mine, I've lost track. But it doesn't matter in my case. I'm timeless."

"What the fuck are you talking about, Flesh Gordon?" Lance says. "Or is it Fuck Rogers?"

"Let's just say I have insider information," Chumpy says.

"How the fuck do you know so much about Willie if you don't even know where to find him?" Mickey says.

"I don't know him yet, but he knows me. He just doesn't know I'm looking for him."

"He owes you money?" Lance says.

"Get in fuckin' line," Mickey says. "Who the fuck are you anyway, kid? Stop fuckin' around and shoot straight."

"My name is Chumpy Walnut, and Will is my creator. I have a few questions for him."

They all sit in silence, then laugh. Mickey says, "Nice try. Willie ain't here, Chumpy.' Beat it."

"Isn't Chumpy supposed to be like a foot tall?" Lance says.

"Something like that," Mickey says.

"I'm only a foot tall in my dimension," Chumpy says.

"So is Willie in *this* dimension," Lance says.

"No, I think Will is at least *two* feet tall," says Lenny.

"I bet Willie has a big dick, though," Mickey says.

"Not as big as mine," says Chumpy. "It can grow up to twelve inches, same as my former height."

"*Whoa!*" Mickey says.

"*Hey Baba Rebop!*" Lance says. "You really *are* Fuck Rogers!"

"Now I *know* you're a fruitcake," Lenny says.

"You a hustler, kid?" Mickey asks.

"Not on purpose," Chumpy says.

"Last time a guy named Chumpy Walnut popped up around here, he was actually a fuckin' walnut," Mickey says with a grin.

"Yes, that was me, too," Chumpy says. "You cracked my shell when you tossed me across the street, and I crashed on the concrete. I was in a coma for a while. I'm appearing to you in this more socially acceptable form so you can't do it again."

Mickey is speechless because he has no idea how this stranger could be privy to such a private event. He assumes it's all a prank, but Will doesn't have the guile for that. In any case, Mickey's grown uncomfortable. Lance and Lenny are also weary of the weirdness. Mickey has hit his limit.

"Look, psycho, I don't know you, or how you know this shit, or what you think you know, but that's all you're gettin'. I'll tell Willie some freak was lookin' for him."

"I need to talk to him directly."

"He was fired," says Larry Parker, now standing behind Chumpy with Mickey's French fries and gravy. "Will doesn't work here anymore. Worst waiter on the planet."

"There you go, Chumpy," Mickey says. "Adios."

"Can I have some money first?" Chumpy says. "It will help me on my quest."

"He really is just like Willie," Lance says. "Fuckin' freeloader."

"What do I get for it?" Mickey says.

"The satisfaction of helping someone find your friend Will."

Mickey thinks for a bit, then, as if compelled by cosmic forces, reaches into his jeans and pulls out a hundred-dollar bill. "Sorry, this is all I got."

"That will do." Chumpy thanks him and quickly leaves before Mickey changes his mind.

"So you're fucking crazy, too!" Lenny says to Mickey.

"You should've at least made him blow you in the bathroom," Lance says.

"There was just something in his eyes," Mickey says pensively. "Anyway, I can't wait to tell Willie about this."

"About what?" Lance says.

"Yeah, tell him what?" Lenny echoes.

Mickey ponders this for a second and then says, "Fuck, I can't remember. Probably wasn't anything important."

Crestfallen but equipped with cash, Chumpy is looking around Santo Pietro's Pizza for someone who looks like him, only somewhat less attractive. A waiter asks him if he needs any help. Chumpy recognizes him as Greg, from that crazy night on the town. "Avalon" by Roxy Music is playing on the sound system.

"Hey, I remember you," Chumpy says to Greg.

Greg looks at him suspiciously. "From where, here?"

"Um, okay, sure. Is Will working?"

"You know, when you walked in, I thought you *were* Will, but he doesn't work here anymore. Are you related?"

"Yes. Sort of. Do you know where I can find him? It's an important family matter."

"I really feel like we've met somewhere besides here. Recently."

"I kicked you in the shin at that nightclub. It was an accident."

"*What*? At the Whiskey? I didn't even see you!"

"It was dark. I just need to find Will now."

"Well, he's working over at the UCLA Faculty Center, where I used to work."

"Where's that?"

"At UCLA, of course. In Westwood."

"Thanks!"

"Wait a minute! Why the hell did you stealth-kick me in the shin?"

Chumpy runs off to the nearest bus stop on Wilshire. He's getting to know the area pretty quickly, especially since his path keeps bringing him back to the same places, like vultures circling a carcass or water circling a drain. Since he assumes the bus driver won't break a hundred-dollar bill, Chumpy reverts to his invisible small self in full view of a few gobsmacked onlookers and hops on a bus that goes straight down Wilshire Boulevard into Westwood Village. Feeling hungry after all that drinking, Chumpy concentrates hard as if forcing out feces, then morphs back into his normal-sized self and gets off at Ships. Inside, "Tainted Love" by Soft Cell plays on the sound system. Dorothy is working the floor while Patsy is behind the counter, as usual. Chumpy nods at Patsy, who nods back with a bemused expression.

"Can I help you, cutie?" she asks.

"No thanks, I'm going to sit in a booth."

"Okay, help yourself. Here's a menu."

"I already know what I want, but thanks. I'll take it anyway, because I like the design. Reminds me of home."

"You're welcome, doll."

While perusing the aesthetically fascinating menu, Chumpy hears a voice from above. "Say, you look like Will!" Dorothy says.

"So I've heard. You know my creator?"

"Creator? He's just a guy who sits in my station. Very cute. But not as cute as you."

"So people keep telling me."

"Can I get you anything, dear?"

"I'll have a fried egg sandwich with French fries and coffee, please."

"That's what Will always orders! Are you related?"

"Not technically. Spiritually."

"So you *do* know him!"

"No, but I know who you mean. Does he come here often?"

"Yes, he does. At least once a week. He was just here a couple of days ago."

"Oh. So he won't be in for a while," Chumpy says, disappointed.

"Well, you never know. I'll get you that fried egg sandwich."

"Oh, wait. Hold the egg."

"Excuse me?"

"I don't eat eggs."

"So you want toast."

"Okay. But no butter."

Dorothy is incredulous. She's never met a vegan, or even heard of one. "No butter either?"

"Right."

"You still want the fries?"

"Yes, please. And the coffee. Do you have almond or oat milk?"

"Honey, they don't even make that."

"Okay, I'll have it black then. Thank you. I have money, by the way." Chumpy lays the hundred-dollar bill on the table. "Can you break this?"

Since she works for tips, Dorothy no longer cares that Chumpy has an odd diet. "Sure thing, big spender! I'll be right back."

After he eats his dry toast sandwich, Chumpy leaves and heads to the UCLA Faculty Center, where he wanders around asking the other waiters about Will as "Sweet Dreams" by the Eurythmics plays on the sound system. They're busy cleaning up and getting ready to go home. Apparently, Will is not working right now ("he's never actually *working*," a waiter named Louis says), and he isn't back on the schedule for a couple of days, unless, of course, he gets fired remotely, as a preemptive precaution.

Uncertain what to do or where to go next, Chumpy walks back into the Village and impulsively decides to see *Blade Runner* at the Westwood Bruin. The door is open, so he walks right in. Oddly, there's no ticket taker, no one at the concessions counter, and no one else in the theater, so he has it all to himself. He does find a bag of free popcorn, conveniently without butter, and a soda on the counter of the concessions stand, and since no one is watching, he takes them into the auditorium. The lights go down, and the movie plays as if by magic. When it's over and he exits the Bruin, Chumpy notices they've already changed the marquee after an apparently private screening. The streets of Westwood are bustling with early nightlife even though it has begun to rain. There's already a line for the next show of the replacement movie, and someone is selling tickets in the booth. It's as if Chumpy watched this dreamlike movie inside a dream.

Chumpy walks down Gayley Avenue and orders black coffee at a pleasantly spacious place called Cafe Casino. He sits quietly sipping black coffee on the enclosed patio and looking out at the rain as "Chariots of Fire" by Vangelis plays on the sound system, feeling melancholy but content. The music and the rain remind him of *Blade Runner.*

While lost in this reverie, Chumpy notices a movie called *The Road Warrior* is playing across the street at the Mann National Theater. Intrigued, he walks over to buy a ticket, but once again, no one is in the booth. There is, however, a ticket just sitting on the counter. Realizing this is the new normal, at least for now, Chumpy takes it and walks into the theater. As expected, no one else is around, but there is yet another box of popcorn waiting for him. Once he takes his seat, the lights immediately dim, and *The Road Warrior* begins, much to his enjoyment.

After this equally entertaining sci-fi movie, Chumpy returns to the crowded wet streets and notices that a different film is advertised on the marquee of the National Theater, the same supernatural switch as the Bruin. Adding to the surreal nature of the situation, it's as if no time has passed at all in the outside world, since the light of the night remains the same as when he entered the theater. He doesn't think much of it, since he is accustomed to inexplicable events.

Chumpy continues to follow his randomly reliable instincts. He heads down Gayley to Wilshire Boulevard, walks past the Who's Who, continues down Veteran Avenue to Ohio Avenue, turns right, and walks a few blocks before he hits Cotner Avenue, which runs parallel to the San Diego freeway, also known as the 405. There's a modest-sized, nondescript apartment building on the corner. Chumpy feels like his creator is close. However, it's a security building, so he has no access. He sits and waits in the rain for over an hour, hoping something will happen.

Finally, feeling hungry again, Chumpy gives up and walks down Cotner to Santa Monica Boulevard, turns right, walks beneath the 405, and sees a diner called Dolores' across from a movie theater called the Nuart, which also triggers vague feelings of familiarity.

At Dolores', which is sumptuously cozy, Chumpy instinctively orders the eggplant parmesan without even looking at the menu, though he asks them to hold the cheese, so it's just fried eggplant with tomato sauce. He still likes it, though the fluffy bread is the best part of the meal, even without butter. He likes the song "Fade to Grey" by Visage playing on the sound system. It suits his current mood of romanticized oblivion.

After his strangely satisfying meal, Chumpy crosses the street to the Nuart Theater and decides to buy a ticket for a midnight screening of a movie called *Eraserhead*. This time, other people are present, but he still has some cash, so it's not a problem.

Chumpy enters the timeless time capsule and takes a seat on the aisle about halfway down the auditorium. A PSA asking patrons not to smoke during the movie plays as the lights go down. The man in the PSA is thin and balding with a mustache, exuding elegant panache and irreverent sarcasm. He introduces himself as John Waters. The irony that he is himself smoking in the PSA is not lost on Chumpy or the audience, who all laugh. This is followed by a movie trailer for a movie called *Pink Flamingos*, which is the Nuart's midnight movie on Saturdays. It's directed by the smoking guy.

Just as the lights dim, two shapely silhouettes take seats right in front of Chumpy, and he moves over so he can see the screen. That's when he recognizes them as Linda and Tessa.

"Hello," Chumpy says, tapping Linda gently on the shoulder. "Remember me? I'm Chumpy."

"Oh my god, it's *you*!" Linda says. "How's your penis?"

"It's fine!" Chumpy says.

"*What*?" Tessa says.

"This is the guy who got shot in the crotch at Dukes!" Linda tells her.

"Really, *wow*!"

"You only know me as a walnut you retrieved from your toilet," Chumpy tells Tessa, who freezes.

The audience shushes them into silence, and they agree to discuss this matter after the movie.

"I'm so glad you're okay!" Linda whispers to Chumpy. "And glad we ran into each other."

"Me, too."

"*Sssssshhhhhh*!"

Chumpy is enthralled and traumatized by the movie *Eraserhead*, which is like a surrealistic nightmare caught on film. It's directed by David Lynch, a name that strikes a chord deep within Chumpy's soul.

Outside the Nuart, Chumpy is telling Linda what happened after the shooting.

"So that guy is in jail now?" Linda says.

"Yes. Do you know how Tanisha is?"

"I visited her in the hospital. She's recovering. It was all so awful!"

"Please give her my love. And tell her I miss her."

"I will!"

"So how do you know about that walnut in my toilet?" Tessa asks, since she was thinking about this all throughout the movie.

"Because I *was* the walnut in your toilet."

Tessa stares warily at Linda, who just shrugs, saying, "I've stopped asking questions and just learned to roll with it."

"That's a good way to be," Chumpy says.

"Would you like to come over?" Linda asks Chumpy. "I live right next to Dukes, so it might make you uncomfortable to return to the scene of the crime. But you'll be safe with me. Promise."

"But will *you* be safe with *him*?" Tessa whispers to Linda.

"Yes," says Linda. "Don't ask me how I know, but I know. We're meant to meet. Like when I sat in front of Will right here at the Nuart when I came to see *How to Marry a Millionaire* with Daryl.*"

"I thought it was *Gentlemen Prefer Blondes*."

"No, that was already over. Daryl and I only went to see the second feature."

"You remind me of Marilyn Van Mansfield," Chumpy says to Linda.

Tessa laughs. "You mean Marilyn Monroe. You're throwing Mamie Van Doren and Jayne Mansfield into the blonde bombshell blender!"

"You're a blonde bombshell, too," Chumpy tells Tessa.

"Well, thank you! But please don't make a smoothie out of me!"

Chumpy laughs. "Well, in my dimension, there's an actress named Marilyn Van Mansfield. They call her Marlyn the Maneater. Because she literally eats men."

Tessa stares at Linda again, then they both laugh.

"I'm a vegetarian, sweetheart," Linda tells Chumpy.

"Really? I'm a vegan!" Chumpy says proudly.

"Like Jane Goodall!" Linda says. "That's even better! We seem to have a lot in common!"

"Yes, we do!" Chumpy says. "I can see why Will is in love with you."

"*What*? You know Will, too?"

"I know he's in love with you."

"What makes you say that? I just met him a few months ago! And he's so much younger than me!"

Chumpy tries to backtrack since the ladies don't realize

his creator's life experiences are slowly seeping into his psyche, and their minds are melding into one pulpy blob of confusion. "Oh, well, um, well, I mean…who wouldn't be in love with someone who looks just like Marilyn? *Any* Marilyn!"

"Well, thanks, I guess. However, I don't want to be perceived as a Marilyn Monroe clone for the rest of my life. I have my own unique identity."

"I understand," Chumpy says. "I'm trying to find myself, too."

"So am I!" Tessa says.

"I didn't know you were missing, Tessa!" Linda says teasingly.

"I feel lost in place sometimes," Tessa says. "Sometimes everything seems weird to me. Just normal things I take for granted. You know what I mean? Life is just so *weird*!"

"I definitely know what you mean," Chumpy says.

"Me too," Linda says. "But you just have to follow your heart. It's like when Will followed me out to this parking lot and asked for my number, and Daryl kept telling me to ignore him because he could've been a total psycho. But instead, he led me toward my spiritual path, even if that wasn't his intention."

"Everything bounces off something to make something else happen," Tessa says. "It's like a big pinball machine."

"So you know how to get in touch with my creator, Will?" Chumpy asks Linda.

"Will Viharo is your creator?"

"Yes. I'm pretty sure. I have no reason to suspect anyone else, and he fits the profile."

"Profile of what?" Linda asks.

"Serial killer!" Tessa offers, tentatively joking.

"My demented creator," Chumpy says.

"That's what I call spiritual!" Tessa says. "I didn't know Will was demented!"

"Trust me," Chumpy says. "He's a bigger nut than I am.

Literally."

"Well, yes, I do have Will's number, all right," Linda says. "I can connect you with him, if you'd like."

"Yes, I'd like that very much!" Chumpy says. "I'm on sort of a spiritual quest myself. And only he can help me."

"Although the fact you say he's demented is suddenly concerning," Linda says.

"Demented but harmless," Chumpy reminds them.

"That's a relief since he knows where I live!" Tessa says, once again half-kiddingly.

Linda says to Chumpy, "Okay then, I'll get in touch with him and tell him to contact you, but where?"

"Hm. I don't currently have a residence. That's part of the problem."

"Aren't you staying in a motel or anything?" Tessa asks.

"I don't have enough money, I'm afraid. Not the right kind of money, anyway. I'm sort of a vagabond here, like my friends Goosey and Jinx."

"Can't they help you?" Linda asks.

"I have no way of contacting me, and they wouldn't know what to do here, anyway. They'd be lost, too."

"Oh, your poor thing!" Tessa says. "You can stay with me! I have extra room! I mean, for a little while. And I don't mean my toilet!"

"Why, thank you," Chumpy says. "But I have to keep moving. I can't rest until I've completed my mission."

"I understand," Linda says. "I mean, I don't *really* understand, but I can tell you need this. I'm so glad I didn't listen to Daryl and trusted my gut instinct so Will and I could become friends. And now I can pay it forward to you!"

"Who is Daryl, anyway?" Chumpy asks.

"Daryl Hannah, the actress. She's in *Blade Runner*."

"Interesting. I just saw that movie earlier tonight. It was really good. I liked the mood."

"Really, where?" Tessa says. "It came out this summer."

"At the Bruin."

"But it's not still playing there, is it? Not since like June?"

"I was wondering about that," Chumpy says. "But it played for me, anyway."

"*Wow,* that's *amazing*! You must have friends in high places!"

"Just a high friend in a place I can't find," Chumpy says.

"Well, anyway, Daryl plays one of the replicants," Linda tells Chumpy.

Chumpy nods. "I know who you mean now. Everything is connected, even if it doesn't make sense right away, like a puzzle with missing pieces. It's frustrating but also inspiring."

"That's what I always say," Linda says. "Well, something like that. I'm not as eloquent as you."

"I know. I annoy myself sometimes, but I can't help talking this way."

Abruptly, they are accosted by a man wearing a tight button-down shirt accentuating his pecs and equally tight jeans accentuating his insecurity, which partly explains the gun he's brandishing. Without a word, he grabs Chumpy as Linda and Tessa scream, then drags Chumpy into his car, a silver 1955 Porsche 550 Spyder, and peels away. Chumpy recognizes him as Vain Vinnie, the bartender from Trader Vic's.

"*Not again*!" Linda cries as the car vanishes into the impenetrable night.

"You must be bad luck for him!" Tessa says.

"I hope not," Linda says. "I'm bad enough luck for myself. At least he wasn't shot this time."

"Not yet!"

"We'd better call the police, Tess. I hope they believe me when I tell them the guy I witnessed getting shot at Dukes by a pimp just got kidnapped at gunpoint at the Nuart by a totally different jerk, right in front of me, *again!* They'll think I'm in on some sort of white short guy slavery conspiracy!"

"*Totally*!"

Linda and Tessa walk back toward the theater to use their phone, but it's already closed, just a bit early due to the commotion.

"Someone needs to invent a phone you can just carry around in your pocket," Linda says with frustration.

"They probably will one day," Tessa says. "Just not tonight."

"Poor Chumpy," Linda says.

"His name is really Chumpy? Like in Will's book?"

"That's what he says, Tess. I'm thinking Will stole the name from this guy or something, and now he wants to confront Will about it."

"Or maybe he's a crazy fan and stalking Will! And then *he* has a crazy fan who is stalking *him*! L.A. is full of crazy stalkers stalking each other!"

"No way, Tess, it's not even published! This guy could only know about the manuscript, and I have one of the only copies, which Will gave me after we met. Plus, in the book, Chumpy is only a foot tall. This guy isn't very tall, but he's taller than that. He had a big bulge in his pants back at Dukes, but it's gone now. I guess the bullet deflated his penis."

"Oh, no, that's *terrible*!" Tessa says. "In any case, it does seem like trouble follows this Chumpy everywhere he goes. And he's always going towards *you*!"

"Now *that's* a creepy thought, Tess!"

"Plus, Linda, remember that Chumpy also told me he really *was* the walnut in my toilet!"

"Yeah, I know. That's really weird. Maybe he *is* crazy. But he seems so sweet and innocent. It is an odd coincidence that he got shot at Dukes right when I was going to show the walnut to Tanisha before *she* got shot. Then that walnut just disappeared, and this guy shows up out of nowhere in its place, bleeding all over the sidewalk next to Tanisha. It's too bizarre to make any sense, so maybe the most outrageous explanation is the truth."

"Sometimes I think we're imagining all of this."

"So do I. But just in case he's real, we need to help him."

"Even if he isn't!" Tessa says. "I mean, I don't even know the difference anymore!"

Flustered, Linda and Tessa walk down to a payphone on the corner. After Linda picks it up, she looks at Tessa and says, "Wait, what are we doing? Am I calling someone? A taxi?"

"But I drove us!" Tessa says, equally disoriented. "Last thing I remember is going into the Nuart, but I can't remember anything after that."

"Me either!" Linda says. "Good thing we've already seen *Eraserhead* before!"

"Oh my god, Linda! Do you think we were abducted by aliens?"

"If so, I wish they'd dropped us off closer to my place. Let's call it a night."

"Yes, let's!"

In the car with Vain Vinnie, Chumpy is trying to turn either invisibly short or into a sentient walnut, but for some reason, his self-transformative powers are not operational. "One Thing Leads to Another" by The Fixx is blasting from the car radio.

"Have you been following me?" Chumpy asks Vain Vinnie, who turns the volume of the music down.

"Huh?"

"*Have you been following me?*"

"No! I mean, yeah. Just a little. I was driving home and just happened to see you coming out of Dolores', walking right in front of me in the crosswalk, so I got a good look at that doll face of yours since nobody else looks like you outside of *Alice in Wonderland*. Then I watched you buy a ticket for the movie, so I bought one and sat in the back. I was going to hustle you out the side door, but then you started gabbing with those two hot broads. I could tell from the sewing circle tone of the conversation you weren't gonna get laid, so I was waiting it out, but you were taking too long yakking it up about the meaning of life and all that highfalutin' hippie bullshit, so I had to make an executive decision."

"People get fired for making executive decisions."

"Not when they're the chief executive."

"What's your rush?"

"I'm in a hurry. Life is short."

"I usually am, too."

"I just gotta do what I gotta do, and do it *now*. Seeing you was a sign."

"Of what?"

"An alternate future for both of us."

"I don't have a good history with alternate futures."

"Tough shit."

"Are you going to shoot me?" Chumpy asks.

"Hell no, this is a prop gun. I mean, not with this, anyway. I just needed it so I could kidnap you. I'm no criminal. I mean, not deep down. I'd love to play one sometime, though. I definitely have the background for it."

"So you're an actor?"

"Of course, who isn't around here? Well, I'm trying to be, like every other pathetic loser in this town."

"Where are you from?"

"What the fuck is this, an interview?"

"Yes. I always like to know my kidnappers, so it feels more personal and not so random."

"How many times have you been kidnapped?"

"A few."

"Not by someone like me, though. Someone with a heart and vision."

"They were *all* people like you. Heartless and blind. Some were gangsters, too, *real* gangsters. Real in my world, anyway."

"What, you don't live in the real world with the rest of us, fuckface?"

"No. I'm just visiting. I must say it's a pretty lousy vacation so far."

"Hey, look, I could be a real gangster, I mean the *best*, but I chose a higher path, so you better show me some respect."

"Higher path? You mean Santa Monica Boulevard?"

"Aw, fuck you, you little dipshit fuck goon. Anyway, we're on Pico now. I actually live in Venice. I just say Santa Monica to strangers. I got too many enemies."

"Okay, *that* sounds intriguing. Please. Just tell me about yourself. I'd really like to know. Explain to me how you're different from all my other kidnappers."

"Well, okay, since you asked, and I love talking about myself. I mean, since we're gonna be partners and all, I might as well, right? I was saving myself for the *Hollywood Reporter* and Carson, but I guess I can practice on a captive audience. My name is Vincent Vincerelli. I'm from New York, in case you can't guess from the accent. Bensonhurst, to be exact. My father is in the Mob. I mean, like, the fuckin' *Mafia,* man, like in the movies and shit, only for real. Not as much violent action, unfortunately. Anyway, my father was an asshole to my mother and brothers, fuckin' all these broads on the side, so I didn't want any part of him or that business, though I did pick up some good tricks for when you're in a jam. Like this one, for instance. I'm a big movie fan, see, and I'd rather play mobsters than *be* one, so I wouldn't land in the can, where my asshole father is and deserves to be. He'll die there, but not before the prison shows at least one of *my* movies, so I can rub it in his stupid, smug, fuckin' greaseball goombah face."

"But you also have a stupid, greaseball, goombah face. I guess it's genetics."

Vain Vinnie smacks Chumpy in the back of the head.

"Shut the fuck up and let me tell my fuckin' tale, willya, Jimmy Olsen? So anyway, like I was sayin', proving to my Pop I don't need his fuckin' business to succeed, except for all the money I stole from him over the years, is my goal in life. Well, that and to fuck a movie star. If I can accomplish those two things, I'll die happy, even if I'm young. As long as I die pretty. There's probably a hit out on me, but I don't care. I mean, there's a hit on everybody eventually, if you get my drift. So *that's* why I seem like I'm in a hurry. I have a mission to complete."

"See? We have something in common. I'm also on a mission."

"Oh yeah? What's your mission statement?"

"To find my creator so he can explain my life choices to me, whether they were mine to make, or if I messed it up myself."

"*What*? Fuck that New Age shit, man. What the fuck is *wrong* with you pansies out here? What the fuck difference does it make? Suck it up and deal with the way it is without pretending any of it means shit beyond what you can see. We're here, and we gotta make the most of it while we can. First, you gotta figure out your goals. Then do what you gotta do and don't let anybody stand in your way. If they do, you need a prop gun that you stole from a street set."

"What exactly are your goals, if I may ask?"

"You can't tell?"

"You talk too fast."

"Sex and revenge, man. And money. And fame. The basics. That's all I live for. I mean, what else is there? You want the meaning of life, pipsqueak? Here it is. Just two things." Vain Vinnie makes a fist, then counts down the components one finger at a time. "*Sex. Revenge. Money. Fame.* There. That's it, man, that's what it's all about. Mystery solved. So stop whining and man up. We got work to do."

"That's four things."

"So?"

"You said two."

"Money and fame are part of the revenge. So it's like, you know, whatcha call it. Consolidated."

"Some people would say you're just petty and shallow."

"Well, some people can kiss my ass. *Most* people."

Chumpy shakes his head. "I asked how you're different, but you're just like most people."

"Yeah, well, so what? I won't be part of the riff-raff once I have a hit movie. I'll still be petty and shallow, like most people, but also rich with a harem of choice poon tang at my beck and call, which *ain't* like most people. But I realize I need to write, produce, and direct my own movie, because nobody will hire me otherwise. When I overheard the treatment for your movie, and all those famous broads creamed all over it, I knew I had just found someone else's winning lotto ticket."

"I told you, it's not a screenplay, and it's not for sale. To anyone. Even those nice ladies."

"Man, you don't know what you're saying. All the shit you talked about is like golden pussy on a silver platter. I've seen a lot of movies, man, so I know a hit when I smell one. And I smell golden pussy."

"I've seen a lot of movies, too. My whole life is a movie. A horror movie, with lots of sex. Though that wasn't the original plan."

"See? *Now* you're talkin'! Horror and sex! That's what it's all about, man!"

"I thought it was all about sex and revenge?"

"Horror is part of the revenge, don't you *see*? Or maybe it's part of the sex, I don't know, who the fuck cares? It's all baked into the recipe for success, man! That is the simple truth of *everything*! And people wanna see the *truth*, man, even if it's made up! It's not a mistake we met, even if it's currently under unfriendly circumstances. Our partnership will pay off big. Trust me. Just let me help you make my dreams come true, that's all I ask."

"How many movies have you actually been in?"

"None yet. Not technically. I walked by when they were filming around town and might be in some of the background shots. The problem is I can't act worth a shit. But I have presence. Or so an agent once told me."

"So you have an agent?"

"Fuck no. She was coked up and I fucking her at the time, so she wasn't thinking clearly. But I took the compliment anyway, even if it was given under duress."

"But you're really just a bartender."

"Nobody's really anything in L.A., man. It's all fuckin' make-believe in this fucked-up town."

"I saw you tending bar. By definition, that makes you a bartender."

"Yeah, well, whatever, that's all over with now, thanks to you. I guess I owe you. And you'll get your taste of that sweet, juicy golden pussy, so don't worry."

"But your plan won't work."

"It will as long as you play ball, pal."

"I don't like sports."

"What're you, gay?"

"Not particularly, why?"

"Not that I care. I'm sure my father takes it up the ass all the time in prison. Shit happens. As it were. I just need to know for your sleeping arrangements tonight, even though you'll be tied up anyway. I don't want any awkwardness between us since we're gonna be partners now."

"Do all people here hold guns on their partners?"

"Eventually, yeah. Even if it's metaphorical. I'm just speeding up the process."

"Where are you taking me?"

"My pad in Santa Monica."

"I thought you said you live in Venice."

"I don't fuckin' know, man, it's by the beach, what the fuck's the difference? Well, kinda near the beach. Bottom line is I won't hurt you as long as you cooperate."

"What exactly do you want with me?"

"Nothing sexual, so relax."

"So why will I be tied up?"

"So you can't escape before I make our movie.

"That sounds like it'll take a long time."

"Don't worry, I'll feed you, and you can crap in a cup. I just need your screenplay, or at least the concept. I'll pay you with your freedom. Much later."

"What about golden pussy?"

"I said a *taste*. Like you can lick the spoon."

"But it's my life, not a screenplay!"

"Whatever! I'll adapt it! That crazy shit writes itself!"

"I told you it's not for sale! All rights belong to my creator!"

"Your *what*?"

"My creator! It's all *his* idea, not mine!"

"I think you had too much fuckin' rum, man. My fault. I *knew* you couldn't handle it. No wonder they fired me. But you can make it right."

"Why did you get fired?"

"Because I served an underage kid a drink, what the hell do you think!"

"I'm not underage, and you didn't serve me! I sipped from the bowl already on the table!"

"Same thing! Not like you were a stray kitten sipping someone else's milk! That was enough. Also I bugged Ann-Margret about my headshot and resume, which is a huge no-no in the local restaurant business. I do it all the time anyway, but this time the manager witnessed it. Or she told him. Bitch."

"So why are you blaming me?"

"I don't give a shit about *any* of that now! All that matters now is making that movie!"

"But why?"

"What do you mean, why? So I can sell it and make a

fortune, and never have to work any shitty jobs again. Plus, I'll have a shot at nailing Stella Stevens. You can introduce us formally as your partner, even if it happens to be at fake gunpoint. I'll take it from there."

"Not very far you won't. I don't think she likes you."

"Oh no? You don't get broads, man. It's all about building sexual tension and knowing when to pull the trigger. She'll *love* me when I introduce her to my big Cable Hogue and pop a cap in that golden pussy of hers."

"Oh, yeah?"

"*Fuck*, yeah!"

"You mean it's bigger than *this*?"

Chumpy unbuttons his shorts, and his twelve-inch piston springs out, fully loaded. Vain Vinnie is so shocked that he loses control of the car and crashes into a telephone pole on Pico Boulevard, near Rae's coffee shop. Vain Vinnie's final words to himself are, "*I could be the next James Dean...except I haven't starred in any movies yet...except that one where I'm an accidental extra...maybe someone will notice it, and...aw, fuck you, Pop.*" Vain Vinnie looks in the cracked mirror at his demolished face, coughs up blood, and croaks.

The next morning, Greg, who recently moved into a cozy house around the corner, is walking into Rae's for breakfast with Nina when he finds a cracked walnut on the ground. For reasons he can't understand, he picks it up and puts it in his pocket as he walks into Rae's, where "One Way or Another" by Blondie is playing on the sound system.

Tanisha Alopecia is in the hospital, still recuperating from her flesh wound. She is in no pain due to legal drugs for a change. She is passively watching daytime TV, wondering what she'll do next, since she doesn't feel safe now at the beauty salon.

Flowers arrive, and surprise, surprise, they're from Fate the Pimp, who is in police custody, and with the various charges against him, he is not going back on the street anytime soon. She figures out right away that this is what he did with his one phone call from the station. There is an envelope with a note, which is a simple apology, without further explanation, as well as a storage locker number with the lock combo and address, written in their private code. Tanisha Alopecia is familiar with it. It's at the Greyhound Bus Station where Fate the Pimp keeps his private stash of emergency getaway reserve cash. Last she heard, he had a hundred thousand dollars in there, stuffed inside a big carnival teddy bear, which she won back when he was nice to her one halcyon day in Venice Beach.

Tanisha Alopecia smiles as a tear streaks down her face. She is happy to be relatively rich as compensation for her trauma, even if it's with illicit funds, though she helped to earn them. Still, she misses Chumpy and prays that he's in good hands. Fate the Pimp is in his cell, also crying. He misses something that Tanisha Alopecia has, which he doesn't: freedom. Plus his getaway cash. His remorse is real, just belated, and self-centered, so worthless.

Tanisha Alopecia plans to pick up the loaded teddy bear right after she's released from the hospital. Then, the long-range plan is to return to Hawaii to start a new life, or rather to restart the old one, and take care of her mother with her ill-gotten gains, with which she can afford the operation to cure her alopecia, and maybe have enough left over to open her own salon in Honolulu.

"Nice flowers," says the nurse who delivered them from the front desk. "Who are they from?"

"My ex-husband," Tanisha No More Alopecia says sadly. She isn't sad because her ex left her his entire guilt fund, which can only mean he's going to be locked up indefinitely on multiple charges (including two previously unsolved murders and a slew of unpaid parking tickets) and has no further use for it. She's sad because she misses someone dear to her, but suddenly can't remember who it is, and all she wants to do is thank this person for making such a profound difference in her life.

Chapter Six
DIORAMA OF A DIRTY MIND

One afternoon, a few months later, Tom Waits is at the Formosa Cafe enjoying a Chinese dinner with his friend Charles Bukowski when Greg walks in with Nina. "Teenage Enema Nurse" by Killer Pussy is playing on the sound system.

"Look who's here," Greg says to Nina as they sit in one of the famous red booths near Tom Waits and Bukowski.

"That makes sense," Nina says.

"I'm glad something does," Greg says.

"Why, what's wrong?"

"Nothing. It's just this walnut I've been carrying around. I can't seem to let it go. I don't know what significance it has, but it feels magical or something."

"That walnut in your pocket right now."

"I'm not just happy to see you, baby."

"Let me look at it again."

"Here?"

"The walnut, stupid."

Greg reaches into his dark jeans and pulls out the walnut. Nina inspects it closely.

"You want to know what I think?" Nina says.

"In this case, yes."

"It's a fucking walnut."

"Aw, forget it. Give it back. Order our drinks. I gotta go spray paint some enamel."

"Mystery is a dead art."

"Better than a live fart."

"How rude. You owe me an apology."

"I'll give it to you later, in private."

Greg goes to the restroom and sits in one of the stalls. As he's vacating remnants of the greasy enchiladas he had for lunch, he thinks about his friend Will. He wants to show Will this walnut for some reason that makes no sense to him, but lately, whenever they make a plan to get together, something always comes up, and yes, that often means spontaneous sex.

His pensive thoughts are interrupted when the bathroom door swings open (the worst feeling when you think you have the place to yourself), and Greg sees a pair of dirty shoes strut by and occupy the stall beside him. A cacophony of competing flatulence follows. Finally, feeling exhausted and embarrassed, Greg hurriedly wipes himself and pulls up his pants, unaware that the walnut has fallen out of his pocket and rolled over to the next stall. Bukowski exits his stall moments later, holding the walnut that rolled his way, as if by divine providence.

Back at their booth, Bukowski shows the walnut to Tom Waits. "Hey, I *know* that walnut!" Tom Waits exclaims, grabbing the walnut from Bukowski.

"All due respect to your musical genius and all that crap, but fuck you, Tom, that's *my* walnut!"

"But it's the one I've been looking for!" Tom Waits says. "I mean, not looking in a literal sense, just hoping I'd find it anyway. I guess it was looking for me, too!"

"How do you know that's *your* walnut?" Bukowski asks.

"It's cracked," Tom Waits says. "Like me. I want to write a song about it."

"Well, it rolled under the fucking stall when I was taking a shit, and now it belongs to me. I feel a strong connection to it, and I want to write a poem about it."

"Well, too late and too bad, Hank. I saw it first. Well, I heard about it first, and I've been hoping it would turn up ever since. I had a feeling it might, so I've been on the lookout for it. It's Fate."

"Who the fuck told you about a cracked walnut that

hangs out in public crappers?"

"A friend of mine named Tanisha."

"Tanisha Alopecia?"

"Yeah, you know her, too?"

"No, but I fucked her a couple of times."

"I never fucked her, I just know her. From Dukes."

"Coffee shop?"

"Yeah, over near Barney's Beanery, down Santa Monica Boulevard way."

"Yeah, of course I know it. Dukes is a cathouse now? Although in a way it was always like a cathouse lobby."

"No, Tanisha was moonlighting there."

"As a waitress?"

"What else, a mannequin?"

"A hooker."

"I don't think she was on the menu, Hank."

"So she served either coffee or blowjobs, depending on the menu of the venue."

"It's tough to make ends meet these days."

"That's how she made a living. Making ends meet."

"Not any more, Hank. She finally got her alopecia operation and opened up her own beauty salon back in her home state of Hawaii."

"Does she still fuck?"

"Not for money."

"What a waste of a fine piece of ass."

"She doesn't need to sell her ass anymore, not after Fate left her a pile of his dough."

"Fate again. The one thing that scares me."

"Not literally. Fate is the name of her Pimp. Nobody knows his real name. He says he forgot it, too."

"I know. I owe him money, so I avoid him. His namesake can go fuck itself."

"Well, avoiding him will be easy to do from now on. He got busted for shooting Tanisha, and then right after he left her his fortune, he hung himself in his cell with his sequin leather belt."

"He was pretty hung from what I hear."

"Well, now he's all hung up for the foreseeable future."

"Tom, I didn't even hear a peep about any of this shit on the street."

"There are many interesting things that happen we never hear about, Hank."

"Then how do you know they happened?"

"You don't, really. It's an assumption made out of a desperate need to believe in something interesting."

"Fuck all this. Did the pimp leave a note?"

"Yeah, it said you still owe him money and he'll collect on the other side."

"So he's dead after shooting his wife, like Burroughs, only he got away with it. That's some dirty business."

"Yup. Even dirtier than Notes of a Dirty Old Man'."

"But not as life-affirming."

"True." Tom Waits pensively sips his coffee as Bukowski pensively sips his beer. The walnut tends to inspire pensiveness.

"Last time I saw that gorgeous caramel-skinned whore was at Musso," Bukowski says. "She wanted me to meet this strange John of hers who was on a quest to find his creator."

"Who's his creator?"

"I have no fucking idea, but he looked like a cartoon character, so I'm guessing Walt Disney. Definitely not mine or yours."

"Walt Disney is dead, Hank."

"So is God."

"He checks in with an earthquake now and then, at least. But Disneyland is a mortuary."

"It doesn't matter anyway because this guy was nuts."

"Yeah, well, nuts seem to be the theme lately," Tom Waits observes.

"In fact, this guy's name was in the nut family."

" Nut family'? Like Charles Manson?"

"No, I mean his name. Peter Peanut or Alfred Almond or some shit."

"Was it Chumpy Walnut' by any chance?"

"*Yes*! How the fuck did you know?"

"That was the name Tanisha gave her walnut."

"Tanisha's so-called walnut is this Looney Tunes turd I met."

"So he wasn't actually a walnut."

"No, I keep telling you, Tom. Just some creep who thought I could point him in the right direction."

"To the bathroom?"

"To his creator."

"Did you point up or down?"

"I pointed at my cock."

"But your cock never created anything, Hank. Nothing memorable, anyway."

"Maybe it did, but I never heard about it."

"From here to maternity, Hank."

"I plead innocent of all discharges."

"The only mystery that concerns me is the meaning of this walnut," Tom Waits says. "It's driving me crazy. I've been in an existential crisis ever since this complete stranger predicted my imminent death. Somehow it's all connected."

"What the fuck are you talking about, Tom? You've always been in an existential crisis. That's your muse."

"I'm talking about the guy who got shot along with Tanisha. Blonde kid. He looked like a…wait a minute."

"A cartoon character?"

"Now that you mention it, Hank, yeah, he did. I didn't get a good look at his face, though. Just his cock. It was like something out of a Ralph Bakshi flick."

"His *cock*? What the fuck? Was he wearing a raincoat?"

"No, he wasn't a flasher. I don't *think*. Fate the Pimp shot Tanisha in the gut, but the bullet passed right through and hit this guy's cock. It was spraying blood like a paint gun."

"At least he didn't shoot his cartoon cum all over you."

"I'm always thankful for the little things like that."

"Look, that walnut belongs to me now, Tom. Let it go and move on already. It's obviously bad luck for you."

"How do you know it won't be bad luck for you, too, Hank?"

"Hard luck is my stock in trade, Tom."

"Mine, too."

"Just give me the god damn walnut already. It belongs to me since I saw it first."

"You didn't see a walnut, you saw some hopped-up Disney freak."

"So did you. You just said they're connected. I'm the connection."

"How's that, Hank?" "Because I met the funhouse fucker first, and just now some asshole just crapped out a walnut and rolled it my way, that's why. Maybe it was this living cartoon character, though I haven't seen him around lately. Maybe he got erased from the panel like a Robert Crumb reject because his job here is done."

Tom Waits sniffs the walnut. "Well, sorry, but I don't see or smell any shit on it, which makes your assertion scatalogically incorrect, my good sir."

"It's probably plastic toy shit. Doesn't stink and washes off easy."

"Maybe it was passed to you, so to speak, just so you could give it back to me."

"Only one way to find out, Tom. Let me have it and I'll tell you what turns up."

"The only thing that's gonna turn up is your cock."

"That's regardless of the walnut. I can at least tell you if the walnut sprouts its *own* cock. Give it to me."

"No."

"*Please,* god damn it. Or else I'll take back all the inspiration I gave you."

"Sorry, Hank, but I already cashed that check."

"Aw, fuck you, Tom."

"I love you, Hank, but fuck you, too. This is my walnut, end of story."

"Why don't we let Tanisha decide?"

"Funny, last time I talked to her, just before she left, I asked her if she was taking her walnut with her over there, but she had no memory of it whatsoever. She doesn't remember telling me all about it, what its name was, nothin'. It's like none of it ever happened. Maybe she's in denial."

"Maybe you lost your fuckin' mind."

"I didn't lose it. I hocked it for a piano."

"Regardless of its history, I still think that walnut is meant for me, Tom. It's like a chain walnut. And it's my turn."

"Nope."

"I gave you inspiration for all your fuckin' music, and now you won't even give me a fuckin' *walnut*?"

"That wouldn't make us even, Hank."

"What would?"

"Nothing, Hank. So why bother?"

"Can I borrow it then?"

"Can I trust you to return it?"

"Fuck, no."

"Well, there you go then. You'd just chop it up and put it in your salad."

"I don't eat salad, for Chrissake. I drink it. Olive salad with extra gin dressing."

"The basic food groups. Good for you."

"*Hey!*" Greg exclaims, making everyone's head turn. "My walnut! It's *gone!*" he laments loudly, feeling all his pockets.

"Funny, I overheard the two bards talking about a walnut just now," Nina says. "I thought it was just a coincidence, but then I remembered there's no such thing."

"*What*?" Greg exclaims.

"Aw, shit," Tom Waits says. "Here we go."

"*He's* got it!" Bukowski says to Greg over his shoulder, pointing at Tom Waits.

Greg gets up out of his seat and grabs the walnut from Tom Waits.

"Hey, that's my walnut now!" Tom Waits says, grabbing it back.

"Fuck the both of you, it's mine!" says Bukowski as he grabs it from Greg.

Bukowski and Greg wind up in a tussle that quickly turns into an impromptu wrestling match as Nina laughs and "Rebel Yell" by Billy Idol plays on the sound system. Glasses are shattered and chairs overturned as the waiters try to break it up, to no avail. The two continue to trade wild punches as Bukowski, a more seasoned barroom brawler, pins Greg against the Formosa's iconic green backlit bar counter. As Bukowski downs stolen beer between punches, the walnut slips away from both of them and rolls under Tom Waits' table. Taking it as a sign of affirmation from the other Fate, Tom Waits picks it up and quickly hurries out of the restaurant.

In the meantime, Bukowski and Greg finally stop fighting, with no memory of what caused it. The only reason they're not 86'd is because a Bukowski bar fight is anecdotally good for business. They shake hands and sit back down with Nina and share some beers like nothing ever happened, because as far as they can tell, nothing did.

Later that night at Norms Coffee Shop on La Cienega Boulevard, Tom Waits sits and drinks his coffee, just staring at the walnut for a long time, as if daring it to speak. Finally, Tom Waits has an epiphany.

A few days later, Tom Waits and his wife, Kathleen, are having dinner with Will Viharo at Musso & Frank. They had just come from a screening of a short *noir* film called *Tarzana*, by a filmmaker named Steve De Jarnatt, later lauded for the apocalyptic romance classic *Miracle Mile*.

Steve appeared in person with his film. Will met Tom through Mickey. Tom and Mickey both star in the forthcoming film *Rumble Fish*, for which Will auditioned half-heartedly. He keeps insisting to everyone who will listen and even those who don't that becoming a successful writer is his only dream and goal in life.

Will is wearing a shirt that looks like an American flag, which Mickey bought for him since he thinks Will looks like the "All-American Boy." Tom finds it amusing. As they eat, Will is telling Tom Waits and Kathleen all about his unpublished book.

"My novel—which I finished last year in Houston when I was staying with my schizophrenic mother's family that raised me my first six years and gave me a solid foundation before my father showed up out of the blue and took me to Los Angeles, where he then hooked up with his fourth wife Anne Helm while still married to his third wife, who wound up raising me even though she was crazy and abusive—"

"Oh no!" Kathleen says, putting her hand to her mouth, as Will keeps right on talking.

"—so anyway, my novel is about a guy only a foot tall who is found tucked inside a bird's nest on the doorstep of a barren couple's home after a forest fire and raised in this conservative small town of religious hypocrites before he runs away and is discovered by two hoboes in the woods, who take him to the big city where he's exploited on the nightclub circuit by gangsters, and he meets all kinds of Runyonesque characters, like showgirls and juvenile delinquents, before he finally meets his one-and-only true love, whose name is Cupey Honeysuckle, who is a half inch shorter than he is, because she's the only other survivor of the forest fire, *phew*, and it's a creative reaction to my upbringing in my stepmother's right-wing guru cult back in New Jersey."

"Just breathe, dear," Kathleen says, gently patting Will on the shoulder.

"That's not a sentence I've ever heard before," Tom Waits says.

"Really? I say it all the time," Will says. "Though it's a run-on sentence."

"More like a life sentence," Tom Waits says.

"Sorry. Usually, I break it up. I'm just nervous."

"Why?" Kathleen asks

"I'm a busboy hanging out with celebrities."

"Don't be!" Kathleen says.

"I can't help it. I need a job."

"No, I mean don't be nervous!"

"Look, Will, I'm just a dreamer, just like you," Tom Waits says. "When I was around your age, I'd be sweeping up in some dive and staring at the jukebox, wondering how to get from here to there."

"But you made it. I haven't."

"You're still sweeping up. Give it time."

"Thanks, Tom. Your music is such an inspiration, and it would be great if my novel ever became a film someday and you wrote the score."

Tom nods in agreement without committing.

"Sounds like something the whole family could enjoy," Kathleen says. "Like *E.T.* "

"Thanks," Will says. "I'm hoping it will be my *Catcher in the Rye.*"

"As long as it's not your *Confederacy of Dunces*," Tom Waits says.

"That would be pretty dark, like Steve's movie," Kathleen says.

"It's one thing to watch film noir, and another thing to live it," Tom Waits says. "I know, because I've done both."

"Me too," Will says.

"I can tell," Tom Waits says. "That's why we like you."

"I can't believe you wrote a book about someone named Chumpy Walnut,'" Kathleen says. "Small world."

"So to speak," says Tom Waits.

"You like it?" Will says.

"Yes, but there's more to it."

"Like what?"

"Tell him already, Tom," Kathleen says to her husband.

"Like this," Tom Waits says, reaching into his pocket and handing Will the dormant walnut. "I think this probably belongs to you. In fact, I *know* it does. I can just feel it. I think people have been trying to give this walnut to you, consciously or intuitively, for a year now. I'm going to succeed where they failed. This is the real reason I asked you to join us tonight."

"Why do people keep giving me walnuts?" Will says with a puzzled but flattered smile. "It must be an omen."

"I think it's all the same walnut," Tom Waits says. "Not a bunch of different walnuts. That's the ominous thing about all this. There's something about *this* walnut. People get a sense of it but can't figure it out. Neither can I, frankly. But that's because it's not mine. It's your turn. Last stop."

Will takes the walnut and studies it. "It has a crack, like the other one Linda tried to give me."

"Exactly," Tom Waits says.

"What does that mean?"

"It's injured and needs your care, I guess," Tom Waits says.

"Hey, I bet Tanisha named this walnut after your book!" Kathleen says. "So that *must* be the connection!"

"Who's Tanisha?" Will asks. "Oh, wait. You mean the prostitute who almost blew me in a parking lot around here?"

"Well, she is a fan," Tom Waits says.

"Except I'm the one who blew it," Will says.

"You mean when Mickey and Lance took you out," Tom Waits says.

"Yes, how did you know?"

"Word gets around, especially when it's sordid. People generally like anything sordid, even if they don't admit it."

"Did you tell Tanisha about your book?" Kathleen asks Will.

"No, I didn't have a chance. When I ran into her on Halloween, I didn't even realize she was the one who almost took my cherry."

"In exchange for a walnut," Tom Waits says. "Fair trade."

"I already have two," Will says, then blushes. "Oh. Sorry, Kathleen."

"No need, Will. I'm married to a musician. They talk like that."

"I don't!" Tom Waits insists. "At least not in front of you. Not on purpose, anyway."

"This conversation is getting weird," Will says.

"It started weird," Tom Waits says. "And it just keeps getting weirder. That's why it's hard to stop."

"I'm used to weird, too," Kathleen says.

"Not *this* weird," Tom Waits says.

Will is staring at the walnut. "Anyway, this time I'll accept the walnut, just to see what happens."

"Maybe it'll talk to you," Tom Wait says. "I've heard things."

"From the walnut?" Will asks.

"No, other people have, and they told me," Tom Waits says.

"Tom, you told me you thought you heard it crying once," Kathleen says.

"I thought so, but it was just the wind," Tom Waits says.

"The wind doesn't cry," Kathleen says.

"The wind makes all kinds of sounds, apparently, depending on the situation," Tom Waits says. "That's why it always gets the blame."

Will puts the walnut in his pocket. "Well, mission accomplished. Thanks, Tom!"

"You're welcome, Will, and good luck," Tom Waits says. "You know, that's some shirt Mickey got you. I'm not exactly a patriot, but it looks good on you."

"Neither am I. Mickey got it for me because he thinks I look like the All-American boy."

"You do," Kathleen says.

"I guess he thinks I look like Marlon Brando, too, since he dressed me up like *The Wild One* on Halloween."

"You're like his personal Ken doll," Tom Waits says.

"Now I just need my own Barbie," Will says.

"You look a lot like this guy I know who got shot in the penis," Tom Waits tells Will. "Except he's even prettier. With a much bigger penis than anyone I know, based on the law of averages, but now it has a big hole in it, so maybe it's just another discarded jumbo condom by now."

"How did you know him?" Will asks.

"Well, I didn't know him exactly, but I did witness an intimate milestone in his life, so I feel some sort of kinship. Plus, I saw his dick."

"Why did someone just walk up and shoot him in the dick?" Will asks.

"Actually, they drove up. It was a hit-and-run blowjob, only a different kind of blowjob, since it almost blew him away."

"You boys just can't help yourselves when it comes to penis talk," Kathleen interjects.

"I think it was an accident, anyway," Tom Waits says. "He was aiming at Tanisha."

"I heard about this from Linda," Will says. "I didn't know you were talking about the same shooting."

"All shootings sound alike after a while," Tom Waits says. "*Bang*, *bang*, that's all she wrote."

"Do you know whatever happened to him?" Kathleen asks Tom. "The boy who got shot."

"Don't worry, he's fine, Kathleen. I'm not worried about him. I *am*, however, a tad worried about *me*."

"Is the same guy going to shoot you, too?" Will says. "That would make him a legend! And make you a legend, too."

"Tom's already a living legend," Kathleen says.

"I prefer the living' part," Tom Waits says. "You can have the rest. Anyway, the guy who shot Tanisha and the penis is now dead. But Tanisha's fine and living well in Hawaii."

"So why are *you* worried?" Will asks Tom Waits.

"Well, the funny thing is, right before he got shot, the penis warned me that I was in danger of being rubbed out by his creator."

"You mean God?" Will say.

"His penis wasn't *that* big."

"So you mean God, as in *our* creator."

"It was lower level than that, I think."

"Well, I'm pretty low level," Will says. "But I didn't create a Frankencock. Not on purpose, anyway."

"Maybe you dreamed him into existence," Kathleen says.

"I didn't say it was you," Tom Waits says to Will.

"Then what are you saying?"

"So here's the other thing which ties it all together, even if it keeps unraveling once you pull a string: that walnut I just gave you was also at the scene of the crime. That can't be a coincidence."

"Just rolling by?" Will asks.

"No, someone in Dukes must've dropped it, either Linda or Tanisha. I almost tripped over it. Then *bang!*, the shooting out front."

"At least we know the walnut and that penis guy aren't the same person," Kathleen says.

"The walnut could be a bad omen," Will says. "Now I'm worried. Maybe you're just passing along a curse."

"Like a voodoo walnut?" Kathleen says.

Tom Waits shakes his head. "Except both the penis and Tanisha came out fine, while the pimp who shot them died in jail, so maybe it's a good luck charm, after all. Except for the pimp, of course."

"Then if you feel your life is in danger, you should keep it," Will says, fishing the walnut out of his pocket and handing it back to Tom Waits.

"No, no, no, it belongs to you," Tom Waits says, rejecting it. "If it gives you any trouble, let me know. I'll kick its hard little ass and chuck it in a compost bin."

"But it always seems to find its way back somehow," Kathleen says.

"To who?" Will asks.

"To *you*," Tom Waits says.

Will nods, feeling an odd mixture of comfort and dread, which is his life's usual recipe.

After Tom pays the check, they head back to the Musso parking lot and pile into the front seat of the Thunderbird.

"I've always liked these big dashboards with the powerful radio sound," Tom Waits says, while Kathleen, who is sitting between Will and Tom Waits, admires the blue upholstery.

"Mickey gave me this soon after I learned how to drive," Will says, turning the key and revving the old school engine. As they pull out of the lot and turn up Las Palmas, Will continues, "Mickey, Debra, Lance, and Lenny were at the apartment on Maple when Mickey handed me the keys. Matter of fact, I'd just seen *The Wild One* down at the Rialto! Anyway, we barely made it around the corner before a Beverly Hills cop stopped us. And I don't mean Eddie Murphy."

"Why?" Kathleen asks as Will stops at the intersection of Franklin Avenue, straining to look past her head to see any perpendicular traffic from the right.

"The registration had expired or something," Will says before he abruptly makes a fast left turn.

"*Whoa!*" Tom Waits exclaims as Kathleen gasps and Will swerves wide to avoid a collision. They had almost been broadsided by a police car coming down Franklin, whose lights are now flashing red, redder than Will's face. Shaking, Will pulls over to the side of the road as Tom and Kathleen console him.

"I almost killed you both!" Will says, fighting back tears.

"You mean all three of us," Tom corrects him. "But yeah, me first, most likely, since I'd have taken the direct hit."

"Yeah, but I'm nobody," Will says. "So that wouldn't even matter."

"You're nobody till somebody loves you," Tom Waits says. "And we love you. Even if you did almost fulfill that prophecy of doom."

"Wait, this must mean Will *is* the Creator!" Kathleen exclaims. "I mean, of the walnut, not us."

"I think you're right," Tom Waits says as Will rolls down the window and the cop asks for his license and registration, which Tom Waits takes out of the glove compartment. Will is almost crying, and profusely apologizes to the stone-faced officer.

"This is my first ticket," Will tells the cop. "I just learned how to drive, and this is my first car. Mickey Rourke gave it to me. That's Tom Waits, by the way."

"So it's your first offense," says the cop, unimpressed and unmoved by Will's desperate name-dropping. "I mean, as a driver, not as a person."

"Yes."

"And your first defense is to drop a bunch of famous names like that will matter to me."

"Yes."

"Well, son, if I hadn't hit the brakes as hard as I did, it would've been the last. For you and your passengers."

"Give him a break!" Kathleen pleads.

"Yeah, officer, look at him!" Tom Waits adds. "He's the All-American boy, for Chrissake!"

The officer carefully considers the garishly jingoistic shirt and nods in approval, finally impressed. Miraculously, the officer, who, unlike Will and Tom Waits, actually *is* a nationalistic neofascist and cares more about his country than celebrities, lets Will off with a warning.

"See?" Tom Waits says.

"See what?" Will says, still trembling.

"That walnut is your good luck charm after all."

"And it means you really are the creator of the guy who got shot," Kathleen points out. "At least he thinks you are. You need to find him and figure out what it's all about. At least for *our* sakes, because it's driving me crazy!"

"What makes you so sure it's me?" Will says.

"Because he warned me about you, and about this incident," Tom Waits says. "Then that walnut rolls its way to me months later, and it was in my possession or at least my presence right when I needed it, to prevent me getting bumped off by the penis maker."

"But it was an accident!" Will says.

"*Almost* an accident," Tom Waits says. "That's how a good luck charm works. If nothing bad almost happened, but *didn't* happen, you'd never know how lucky you are."

"That's why the walnut was there, to protect both of you," Kathleen says.

"So it's *all* our good luck," Will says.

"No, we just benefitted by proxy," Tom Waits says. "It's definitely your walnut, and it's definitely a good luck charm, and this definitely proves it. Case closed. Congratulations."

"Congratulations to you, too, Tom and Kathleen, for surviving a night on the town with me," Will says sheepishly.

"Any time!" Kathleen says sincerely.

Will quietly ponders the seemingly coincidental yet possibly providential ramifications of this rusty chain link of events as he continues to drive Tom and Kathleen home. They change the subject back to *Tarzana*, agreeing it's the promising start of a stellar career for Steve De Jarnatt.

(Unbeknownst to Will at the time, Steve De Jarnatt had

worked with Mickey Rourke a couple of years earlier on Mickey's passion project about a boxer Mickey knew back in Miami. Like the private eye protagonist of *Tarzana*, Steve played a real-life *noir* gumshoe and tracked down a photo of the boxer for Mickey's reference. Later, Will would work a little on the script of Mickey's movie, called *Homeboy*, which came out in 1988, co-starring Debra and Christopher Walken. Decades later, Will became Facebook friends with Steve, and they put all those pieces together when Will remembered Mickey showing him the photo of the boxer, and Steve took the credit.)

"Thanks for the walnut!" Will yells, waving at them as they walk toward their front door.

"What walnut?" Tom Waits says, turning around with a curious frown, then looking at Kathleen, who is equally baffled.

Hoping it's a joke, Will reaches into his pocket to make sure he didn't hallucinate the entire evening, but he can't find it. Will figures it was just a walnut, anyway, and it's the thought that counts, even if the thought itself is immediately forgotten. The walnut had fallen out of Will's pocket when he climbed into the driver's seat back at the Musso and Frank parking lot, where it became lodged in the crevice of the seat between Will and Kathleen. Then, when the car lurched, the walnut was shot forward and landed beneath the gas pedal before it rolled backward and beneath the front seat, where it remains unconscious and undetected.

Will parks in the lot on Ohio Avenue in Westwood, across the street from his tiny apartment in the building on the corner of Cotner Avenue. He is looking forward to visiting that pretty waitress named Nancy at the Good Earth Restaurant the next day, so he can finally give her the book of poems that he wrote for her, which he has titled "Diary of a Dreamer." If she likes it, maybe she'll go out on a date with him. He already has his eye on an upcoming revival of *Annie Hall* and *Manhattan* at the Nuart. It's one of his favorite double bills because they're so quintessentially New York, where he was born and spiritually, never left. Nancy is from Long Island. He's really hoping that she turns out to be his Cupey Honeysuckle. She is shorter than him, at least.

Just as he's about to enter the apartment building, Will stops short because he thinks he hears the wind crying, and it gives him a chill.

A couple of months later, a swarthy, masculinely handsome, ambiguously ethnic-looking actor named Robert Viharo drives to the parking lot on Ohio Avenue near Will's Cotner Avenue apartment and swaps his nondescript car for the stylish Thunderbird so he can arrive at the Playboy Mansion in vintage style. But first, he drives to the Tropicana Motel to pick up Linda Kerridge, whom he's been seeing, something he hasn't yet confided to Will. Meantime, Will is now living with Nancy, the waitress from the Good Earth who looks like Nastassja Kinski.

"I feel guilty," Linda tells Robert in Will's car. Robert's most recent ex-wife, Jeane Manson, was an ex-Playmate and is presently a major singing star in France. Will knows her as one of the stars of the Roger Corman exploitation film *Student Nurses*. Due to his relationship with Jeane, Robert met Hugh Hefner, and they became friends. The Mansion is open to outsiders by Hef's personal invitation only, and despite his son's pleas, Robert never agreed to bring Will.

"I don't feel guilty at all," Robert says as "Harden My Heart" by Quarterflash plays on the car radio. "It's all Karma and Destiny. I'm going to tell him soon, before he hears it from anyone else, out of respect for his feelings. He's a sensitive kid."

"Well, Will might see it as a betrayal," Linda says with empathy. "I know he really liked me before he started dating Nancy. I think he sees our meeting as some kind of karmic event that changed his life or something."

"Well, it wound up bringing *us* together. So there you go.

Karma and Destiny."

"I don't think Will meant to bring together Karma and Destiny. I didn't either, frankly. Will led me to my spiritual path. That's the only reason I can think of that matters or makes any sense for me. I don't see what Will gets out of it, though. Certainly not me. He's very handsome, but he's so young."

"You weren't meant to be romantically involved with Will. We were."

"I don't know. I just think it's really odd that the title of your movie, *Hide in Plain Sight,* is on the marquee of one of the movie theaters Dennis passes while walking around Westwood in *Fade to Black.* It creeps me out!"

"Why? We're not hiding in plain sight or fading to black anytime soon."

"Still. It has to mean something. Everything does."

"Hey, babe, forget about it," Robert tells Linda as the gates open and he pulls into the winding driveway of the Playboy Mansion. "He's living with Nancy now, anyway. You met her at the play."

"Oh, you mean the one-act play that Will wrote about a writer celebrating his recently published book with a drive to Las Vegas but on the way he picks up a hitchhiker who turns out to be his Guardian Angel because he's about to die in a car crash, which you directed and that I starred in as the Angel after Victoria Jackson had to drop out at the last minute to be on Johnny Carson."

"Well, uh, that's unduly expository, but yeah. That's the one."

"I don't even know why I said all that. Not like anyone else is listening."

"I am," says a voice in the back seat. "Sounds pretty good."

Startled, Robert slams on the creaky brakes of the Thunderbird, nearly hitting the valet approaching the car, who gives it a wide berth. Robert turns around to see

Chumpy Walnut, in full-sized human form, wearing his customary aloha shirt (though in a striking new tiki pattern) and cabana shorts, accompanied by loafers. Chumpy has no idea who they are, or, as he looks into the rearview mirror, who he is, either.

"Who the hell are you, and how did you get in the fuckin' backseat without me noticing?" Robert demands of Chumpy.

"I feel like I know him," Linda says, though all memory of her past interactions with Chumpy has been involuntarily erased from her mind. "He looks like Will! Only handsomer! I think this is a sign!"

"A sign of what, me punching this shrimpy stowaway fuck in the fuckin' face?" Robert fumes in the tough guy style of his leading role as Zachary Kane, Modern Day Bounty Hunter in the film *Bare Knuckles*. "Get the hell out of my car!"

"You mean Will's car," Linda says.

Nonplussed, Chumpy nods and obliges. Shoving Chumpy up against the Thunderbird, Robert is about to rough him up the way he rousted Nick Nolte in *Return to Macon County,* as Don Johnson sat inside a 1950s car. Then, just like Don Johnson, Linda gets out of the 1964 Thunderbird to intervene in the confrontation. But Robert's fuse has already fizzled. He takes a deep, long look into Chump's eyes and hugs him warmly.

"I'm so sorry, man. I didn't know who you were!"

"Who am I?" Chumpy asks.

"You're Chumpy Walnut!" Robert exclaims.

"You mean the little guy in Will's book?" Linda says.

"Yeah, can't you tell?" Robert says. "He's just a life-sized version! Well, relatively life-sized!"

"Who is Will?" Chumpy has been trapped in a car-wreck-induced, cracked-walnut-encased coma, lost in an endlessly spiraling whirlpool of right-wing guru cult nightmares, so he has no recollection of his creator, his quest, his past, his present location, or his identity.

"Will is Robert's son!" Linda tells Chumpy.

"I've always wanted to meet you, man!" Robert enthuses.

"Me or your son?" Chumpy asks.

"Both!" Robert says. "But I met Will already!"

"So you *must* know Will!" Linda says to Chumpy. "Why else would you be in his car?"

"I have no idea. I just woke up there and heard you both talking about your secret affair."

"Oh my god!" Linda says. "He's a spy in the house of love! He's going to tell Will all about us!"

"I keep saying, I don't know Will, I don't know you, or you, I don't know me, and I don't know where I am."

"This is the place to be, kid!" Robert says as he hands the wary valet the keys. "C'mon, I'll introduce you around!"

"But he isn't on the guest list," Linda says to Robert.

"Forget about it, babe, I'll vouch for Chumpy Walnut anytime! Hef will *love* this kid!"

"You aren't the only one who knows Hef," Linda says. "Remember, I was in a promotional Playboy spread for *Fade to Black*."

"Yeah, I know! Will showed me that issue! That's one reason I cast you in his play!"

"He's not the only one with an issue," Linda says with a sigh.

They enter the luridly opulent, lushly ornate Mansion, and Chumpy is immediately aroused by all the scantily clad "bunnies" walking around the lobby. He springs a foot-long boner that breaks right through his zipper, causing quite a stir, which turns out to be his surprise guest pass. Soon, he is swarmed by Playboy bunnies as if he's a rock-cock star, which makes Robert rather jealous, and Linda very protective.

Hugh Hefner himself is alerted to the commotion and comes downstairs wearing his customary robe and smoking his customary pipe to see what all the fuss is about. The bunnies open a pathway to Chumpy, whose clothes have been torn off, so he stands naked and gloriously endowed before Playboy's megalomaniacal mastermind between Robert and Linda, whom Hef barely acknowledges. Moments later, Hef is showing his new friend Chumpy around his magnificent monument to Masturbation, telling an enrapt Chumpy all about his magazine and other enterprises, since Hef wants Chumpy to work for him in some capacity, the first being a photo shoot with the centerfold of the next issue.

Meanwhile, Linda tells her date for the evening, "Sorry, Robert, but I can't go on with this charade. I choose Chumpy. He's so much bigger than you! Or anybody I've ever met! Even Jack Nicholson!"

"But I love him too!" Robert says sincerely.

"Not in the same way that I will. Good night and goodbye, Robert. Our Karma and Destiny have run their course, and are now going their separate ways."

"*What*? You gotta be fuckin' *kidding* me!"

"At least Chumpy kinda looks like Will. Only handsomer and much bigger where it counts. That's the best I can do."

"You mean you fucking his fictional character is the best *Will* can do!"

"Well, it's better than his father, at least! Thanks for everything, Robert! It was sort of fun while it lasted! I'm going to catch up with Chumpy now."

"That's not *really* Chumpy Walnut, Linda! I was just *kidding*, for Chrissake! Well, sort of!"

"But I'm not kidding, Robert. Now, if you'll excuse me…"

Dejected, Robert returns to the Thunderbird and heads back to Ohio Avenue, where he drops off the Thunderbird, then he drives home to his Brentwood apartment. By the time he gets there, he can't recall anything of the evening besides picking the Thunderbird up, a memory lapse he can't explain and which scares him a little, so he chalks it up to Karma and Destiny, as always. Those two never let him down. At least as far as he can remember.

Back at the Mansion, Chumpy Walnut is the unchallenged center of attention as Linda tries to stay as close to his side as possible, but she is constantly being shoved aside by all the other fawning females.

"What's your name anyway, stud?" Hef asks Chumpy. "If I don't like it, I'll make one up for you!"

"Walnut. Chumpy Walnut."

"Perfect! Like Bond. James Bond."

"Who's that?"

"Funny you should ask, Walnut, Chumpy Walnut, since we're showing *Octopussy* in the theater tonight. The question is, who are *you*?"

"I have no idea, but at the moment, who cares?" The bountiful bunnies adoringly surrounding him keep touching and kissing his epic erection, which extends before him like a battering ram before it suddenly spurts semen like a liquid flame-thrower. As "Come On Eileen" by Dexys Midnight Runners plays on the sound system, Chumpy continues to euphorically ejaculate all over the artfully adorned walls, plush carpeting, and fancy furniture of the Mansion for roughly thirty seconds. Chumpy's synthesized semen seeps into the very fabric of this eroticized empire, spraying its founder, Hef, and all the bunnies with cartoon cum.

"I think we *all* need a bath!" Hef says with a wry chuckle, wiping cream off his face like he's been in a pie fight as the bunnies rub the buckets of sugary, sloppy substance into their flesh like it's organic mammary moisturizer. "Let's retire to the hot tubs, shall we?" Hef says. "Bring your cocktails! Chumpy, you just bring your *cock*! We'll tell the tales later!"

Later that night, as Hef and the bunnies are sprawled around the Mansion in intoxicated states of post-orgy bliss, an insatiable Chumpy and a smitten Linda are making love in one of the guest hot tubs.

"I feel so guilty," Chumpy says.

"I don't," Linda says.

Not much later, she wakes up alone in her apartment, vaguely recalling a strange, sexy dream with the main character of the manuscript sitting on her bedside table. Meanwhile, Hugh Hefner slowly stirs to consciousness on the sticky floor of his Mansion and wonders if that gooey stuff on his face is his own jizz or someone else's as the naked, equally amnesiac bunnies stretch, yawn, and laugh it all off as just another wild night at the Mansion.

A month or so later, Greg is cleaning out the Thunderbird he recently bought off his friend Will. It's now painted blue. While vacuuming the backseat carpet, Greg finds an empty walnut shell. He studies it closely, wondering what its story is and how it came to be there, then shrugs and tosses it away, since its contents are long gone, anyway.

Chapter Seven
LAY OF THE LAND

Chumpy wakes up disoriented and dismayed in a dank, musty, cramped room of the Hotel Europa at the intersection of Broadway and Columbus in the North Beach district of San Francisco. He is naked with a penis that looks like a punctured hot air balloon. Three naturally attractive but heavily made-up nude women are sleeping beside him on the creaky, mysteriously stained bed, their limbs intertwined, with two more sprawled out on the filthy carpet, snoring serenely. All but one are fellow residents of the hotel, employed as strippers in the infamous nightclub below, the Condor Club, next to Big Al's, which is the first all-nude bar in The City. The lady snuggling closest to Chumpy is luscious local legend Carol Doda, who is not a resident. Empty bottles of booze and beer are strewn around the floor amid burnt cigarette butts and broken condoms. The harsh red lights of the iconic neon sign flash harshly outside the dirty, open window as a barker on the street entices passersby to enter the decadent domain. "*It's showtime!*" he announces repeatedly, annoying the residents of the hotel.

"This is all very Charles Bukowski," Chumpy groggily mutters aloud to himself after taking in his sordid surroundings, unsure not only of his location, but the identity of the name he just dropped to nobody conscious. Chumpy then recalls the dreams he had of pain and punishment in a strange land called New Jersey, populated by strange people doing strange things. Everything besides that is a murky mix of cartoon sex and corporeal chaos in a different land of sunshine, palm trees, and desperation. In his heavy head, all these half-disturbing, half-stimulating images have meshed into a surrealistic stew that sloshes around his skull until it spills out of his eyes in tears.

Carol Doda slowly wakes up and nibbles on Chumpy's, then whispers, "Thank God, I thought it was just the nastiest dream I've ever had. You've got the biggest cock I've ever seen, and I've seen more than my share."

Chumpy shakes his head and says, "Thanks. It comes in handy. Not just for sex. Once it saved my life from a bullet, and another time, it rescued me from a kidnapper."

"Really?"

"I don't know. I don't know why I even said that. It just popped out."

"That ain't *all* that popped out!"

"It could be I only dreamed what I just said. All I can remember now are dreams I don't understand."

"Well, it makes no difference since you're putting it to much better use now anyway," Carol Doda says, mounting him for one more therapeutic orgasm before she passes out again on top of him, leaking his cartoon cum all over the sheets. Feeling spent, Chumpy keeps staring at the neon sign flashing outside his window, wondering where he is, who he is, and what he is. Clues buried deep in his subconscious break through, but only in bits and pieces, as if damaged by the effort.

"*Don't worry about it*!" booms a stranger who suddenly enters the room as if it's his, because in fact it is.

"Don't worry about what?" Chumpy asks the stranger, whom he does not recognize, even though the stranger greets him like an old friend or at least a friendly acquaintance.

"Don't worry about *nothin'*!" the stranger repeats, leaning on a thin, black cane.

"If you say so."

Unbeknownst to Chumpy, the stranger's name is Alfonso Calabrese, or Nice Try Alfie for short, since he

171

always botches his own schemes. Nice Try Alfie is a thin, pale, pockmarked, thirty-something, lifelong hood born and raised in Brooklyn. He is on the lam from some "people" in New York and living in San Francisco under the assumed name "Rocky Sullivan," since he's a big James Cagney fan. Everyone calls him Nice Try Alfie anyway, since he keeps letting it slip.

Nice Try Alfie is wearing his usual outfit: cheap dark sunglasses, a shiny fake leather jacket, tight black jeans, two-toned fake leather boots, and a white T-shirt, or rather it was white at one time. He is often confused with the singer Lou Reed, whom Nice Try Alfie knows from their days hanging out together at legendary punk/New Wave music venue CBGBs, before Lou became famous. They lost touch after Nice Try Alfie mugged a man in the Bensonhurst section of Brooklyn at knifepoint while strung out on heroin. There was a struggle, and Nice Try Alfie stabbed him in the face. Fortunately for the man, he survived. Unfortunately for Nice Try Alfie, the man was a Mafioso. Even more unfortunate, the man was Alfie's uncle, Nick "the Nice Prick" Vincerelli, who is Vain Vinnie's father. This is why Nice Try Alfie is now hiding in plain sight for almost three years, and with his uncle serving a life sentence, he finally feels free. Mostly. The cane is due to the hip injury inflicted upon him by a couple of his uncle's business associates, warning him to leave town for good. But Nice Try Alfie knows they'll never let him off this easy, and eventually, his uncle will send him his hospital bill, attached to a bullet.

Sitting on the edge of the bed, oblivious to the raunchy remnants of casual carnality, Nice Try Alfie takes out a wad of cash and counts it, tossing a few bills on the bed for Chumpy, who appraises it with apprehension. Nice Try Alfie feels safe to speak his mind, given the sensually inebriated state of his present company,

"What's that for?" Chumpy asks.

"What's it *for*? All of *this*! Three months and you're more popular than ever, American Gigolo! These bitches were literally lined up outside the door! The hallway was crowded like it was a fuckin' Sex Pistols concert, except there's only one Sex Pistol here, and that's *you*, a one-man fuckin' band, so I let them all in while I went out for pizza. This is your cut."

"It's not very much," Chumpy says, noticing they're all singles.

"As I keep telling you, I'm doing all the hard work while you're having all the fun, plus I'm covering your living expenses, so stop bitching. By the way, I didn't charge Carol. Celebrity discount. I got more comin' tonight, so to speak, including three hot tourist chicks from Northern Italy I met in some ice cream shop down at the Wharf. It's a drug front, so I know the owner. I also know enough Italian to get by, though the chicks spoke German too, so it got a little confusing since I don't speak Kraut. Doesn't matter. We set up the deal in the universal languages of Lust and Greed. At least I *think* we did. Anyway, you'll love em! They're clean and tan with long, sexy hair and bodies like Greek statues. I'd fuck them myself if they let me, but no chance of that. At least I can benefit from your blessings. So rest up, Pony Boy. It's gonna be another long, hard night."

"My name is Pony Boy?"

"You forgot your fuckin' name *again*? You can't hold onto any memory for more than five minutes. It's so sad. Like the ad says, this is your brain on drugs.

Chumpy carefully considers his situation. "Last thing I remember is…it's like…it's like I'm drowning in a sky of brightly colored bodily fluids mixed with alcohol or something, like a celestial cocktail, and I'm the garnish that fell in and is getting stirred around until I'm dizzy. No. It was…it's more like I fell into psychedelic quicksand at the end of a rainbow tornado. I can't explain it except with phrases that make no sense, even to me."

Nice Try Alfie shakes his head and chuckles. "Yeah, sure, whatever you say, Pony Boy. All any of *that* means is you're a fuckin' junkie like these other junkie whores. You shot up enough smack to drown in a liquid sky, *that's* for damn sure."

"*What*?"

Nice Try Alfie grabs Chumpy's arm as Carol Doda stirs, still delirious, not from narcotics, but biologically induced bliss.

"*Seriously*?" Nice Try Alfie says. "I've shot you up a *hundred* times and you don't remember *any* of it! *Look*!"

Chumpy glances down at the crook of his left arm and sees the faint puncture wounds. "*I* did that?"

"Well, I did it for you since when I asked if you wanted to take a quick trip to the Milky Way, you said, *Sure.*"

But while Chumpy and Nic Try Alfie are looking at them, the puncture marks suddenly fade away without a trace.

"Wait, where did they go?" Chumpy asks.

"You can't scar, you don't seem to feel pain, and you have the stamina of a fuckin' merry-go-round stallion. Like I always say, Pony Boy: *Don't worry about it!*"

"I don't understand."

"Neither do I, Pony Boy, neither do I. But I never look a Gift Horse Dick in the ass. I guess you don't remember how you got here, either."

"No."

"You don't remember being in L.A."

"What's that stand for?"

"To me? Lots of Assholes."

"I don't know what you're talking about."

"Really? *Nothing*? Not even the peepshow downstairs? We were both whacking off to the chicks behind the glass—one of which is laying cum-otose on the floor here—when you coated it with so much jisim I almost wanted to lick it like frosting off a spatula. Man, it was the most epic splooge in grindhouse history! I told some of my homies back on Forty-Second street, and they thought I was lyin'! I wish it could've been recorded for posterity. But no matter. It was the best single-shot promo gimmick I could've ever imagined. You're a lucky stiff, literally. But if there's any killing to be done, I'll take care of that, too. I'm your manager. You agreed to that, way back in Burbank, but I guess you have no recollection of that either."

"Manager of what?"

"Manager of that built-in leaf blower, that else?"

"No," Chumpy says defiantly.

"No? No, *what*?"

"No, I don't know who you are or whatever you say I agreed to, because none of this is the real *me*. That much I do know. I can't help it if my brain isn't functioning properly, probably because you poisoned it. But my soul is still all mine."

"How the fuck could you *know* anything if you can't r*emember* anything past five fucking minutes? Little late for an insanity plea, slick. That train has left the station and gone over a cliff."

"I know who and what I'm *not*, though."

"Are you fuckin' kidding me? Look around, Pony Boy! This is *all* because of you! Who cares who you used to be or where you came from? We both have pasts we'd rather forget, or at least pasts we hope will forget *us*. It's all about the future, Pony Boy! *Our* future! I was even gonna bring in my cousin Vinnie, but he bought it in a car accident a few months back. I told you that already, but I'm assuming you forgot that, too. So now it's just you and me."

Chumpy sits up. The off-duty strippers are aroused, too, in both senses of the word. They are caked with his saccharine semen, and want a second coat.

"I gotta pee," Chumpy says.

"*Whoa!*" Nice Try Alfie says, standing straight up, then almost tipping over, as he snags his cane leaning against the bed. "Please don't overflow my fuckin' sink anymore. You gotta drain your personal Godzilla down the hall in the communal restroom. Aim carefully and keep flushing so you don't make a mess. Take a shower while you're at it. I need you fresh and smellin' nice for the Italian babes from Germany, or wherever the fuck they're from. And come right back, or else I'll cut off your fix."

"My fix?"

"Once more time, Manchurian Candidate: *you're a drug addict, you have no free will of your own, your brain is mush, and you're under my control*. I take all the credit for it, at least. Now, go do your bathroom business, then hurry back. Make sure you drain that Swamp Thing, too. No water sports allowed, Chuck Berry."

"I thought I was Pony Boy?"

"Jesus, does it even matter?"

"My real name is Jesus? It seems to change sentence to sentence."

"That's because you're fuckin' impossible to describe! Just *go* already! Hurry!"

"*Don't leave!*" implores one of the strippers, grabbing Chumpy by the ankles.

"Jesus fuckin' Christ, it's like you shoot *smack* out of that fuckin' thing!" Nice Try Alfie says in envious awe. "It's like a whipped cream dispenser injected straight into their pussies! It's a freakin' *miracle,* just like the Late Fate told me when he tried but failed to turn you out. You must be from another planet. Like those Saucer Men with booze in their claws. Except you got a cock filled with *coke*! The junk I give these skanks is cake frosting, but you're the fuckin' cake!"

"You mean like the one the prisoner uses to get out of jail?" Chumpy says.

"I have no idea what you're talking about."

"Neither do I.'

"Well, that's why I'm the manager, and you're the

talent."

"Not any more." Chumpy sees an aloha shirt, shorts, and shoes on the floor, which he assumes are his since they seem to be his size. After his penis retracts into the recesses of his groin, Chumpy puts them on while Nice Try Alfie keeps ranting about lost profits and wasted opportunities.

Carol Doda, the only woman present who is not high on Nice Try Alfie's supply, looks suspiciously at Alfie's wad of cash and says, "Where the fuck did you get all that dough?"

Nice Try Alfie instantly pivots into desperate defense mode. "If you must know, and since I respect you, I scored it from their rooms, while you were all otherwise engaged. The locks here are easy to pick, and most of these dumb bitches never lock their doors anyway, so I went in and helped myself to their purses, but *only* took what they owed me. No more, no less. Scout's honor."

"*Owe* you?"

"Yeah? What, you think this first-class joy ride was *free* for these skanks?"

Carol Doda is immediately incensed by this information. "How long have you been doing that?"

"I don't know, a few months, why?"

"Oh my god, that's where all their money has been disappearing! *You're* the Mystery Thief!"

"How else would I bankroll this operation? I can't trust these bitches to pay their bills, can I?"

"What operation?" Carole Doda says, increasingly irate. "I thought you were just a dealer?"

"Not since I hooked up with Pony Boy here. Now I'm a one-man multi-media conglomerate. Okay, two men."

"Did I overhear you say you're shooting him up with smack?"

"Yeah, so? It's like giving steroids to a stud horse. No big deal. Sometimes Nature needs a stimulant."

A dismayed Carol Doda is wide awake now. "So that

dick isn't even *real*? Like it's some bionic banana?"

"It's real all right. I'm just trying to keep him in the right headspace so he can keep up with demand."

"This is our relaxation workout routine, not your fuckin' sci-fi sex racket!"

"How the fuck can a workout routine be relaxing? This isn't a fucking *yoga* class!"

"Who needs yoga with him around? I can get six orgasms flexing one muscle! And it's not even my muscle!"

"Carol, sorry, I could've sworn we had this conversation—"

"Well, we didn't! Did we, girls?" The somewhat stoned, sexually satiated strippers all agree, emphatically if drowsily.

"And what about me?" Carol Doda says. "When are you planning to snatch *my* mattress money? I don't even live in this dump!"

"I know, that's why *your* full access amusement park pass is *free*! Call it a professional courtesy. *Don't worry about it*! The rest gotta pay their fuckin' fair fares, including the party favors. Remember it or not, they agreed."

"*No, we didn't!*" chimes the discombobulated dissenters.

"Well, too bad and too late! I hooked you all up with primo sex and drugs, so this mint is *mine*!"

"You have no *right*!" Carol Doda says. "I *never* have to pay for sex, and neither should these women, since most are hookers anyway and people pay *them*, so fuck off, you scrawny fuckin' loser! I oughta drop dime on you to your friends back East!"

"You don't even *know* them!"

"I know *everybody* worth knowing in this world, buster! Now, give all that money back to these poor, love-starved sluts, *now*!"

Nice Try Alfie balks at her demand, so Carol Doda kicks him squarely in the balls and forcibly takes back all the cash, which she distributes as evenly as possible to the rest of the other ladies, who are grateful even though they are barely aware of what is happening.

"Goodbye, everyone," Chumpy wearily says in an exhausted monotone as he pulls his ankles loose and staggers toward the door, anxious for a change of scenery as well as company. "I won't be back. I'm blowing this scene, as they say, whoever they are."

"*Fuck you!*" yells Nice Try Alfie, still bent over in pain. Then the cane gives way under the pressure, and he crashes to the floor, cradling his crotch as Chumpy steps over him.

"*I love you, don't forget me!*" Carol Doda tells Chumpy with a blown kiss and a loving wave, and the rest of the smitten strippers echo her sincere sentiment.

Feeling shaky, Chumpy steps out into the hellhole's hallway, where he locates the communal restroom and urinates into a toilet, which quickly overflows. Chumpy gingerly steps out of the stall and back into the hallway. Nice Try Alfie is standing there with a switchblade, which he scored off Fate the Pimp.

Terrified, Chumpy runs down the hall and sees that a door to one of the rooms is slightly ajar. Without another escape route handy, Chumpy dashes through the door and locks it behind him. Inside the room, he finds a gray cat lounging on the bed. The cat just stares at him. But the cat isn't looking up. The cat is looking down.

That's when Chumpy realizes he's shrunken in size. The transition has resulted in full recollection of his recent history. If nothing else, he's relieved to have involuntarily reverted to his natural form, even if his true origins remain on the murky outskirts of his mental map. He turns to open the door, but he can't reach the knob. The cat hops off the bed and sniffs Chumpy from head to toe, then licks his face affectionately, cleaning off the tears from his cheeks. Lonely and fearful, Chumpy hugs the cat back. Then they both hop up on the bed and cuddle, gradually falling asleep together.

Outside the Europa, Nice Try Alfie is frantically hobbling about on his cane, looking for "Pony Boy" in vain, checking first inside the Lusty Lady, then bar-hopping, from Vesuvio to The Saloon, swilling one drink apiece to drown the dismay of his defeat and toast his possible demise. After an hour or so of fruitless searching, Nice Try Alfie tipsily returns to the Europa and is just about to walk back inside the hotel when a tall, foreboding man wearing a trench coat and a handkerchief covering his lower face walks up behind him and pops a bullet through his brain. As Nice Try Alfie falls, his cane clattering across the pavement, the hit man jumps into a car that speeds around the corner and out of sight. Witnesses scream and sirens wail. Carol Doda, wearing cat-eye sunglasses despite the twilight, a leopard print coat over her famous nude body, and snakeskin pumps, leaves the hotel and casually steps over Nice Try Alfie's lifeless body.

"Don't worry about it," Carol whispers with a smile as she walks over to the Condor for one of her final shifts before quitting the burlesque biz, immediately forgetting what she'd been doing in the Europa and why she feels so damn good, as if she's just had the full body massage of her life. She attributes it to relief about her pending retirement.

Meanwhile, Chumpy sleeps soundly in the stranger's room, without dreaming anything at all. The blackness is blissful.

When Chumpy wakes up beside the purring cat, which is much more comforting than his previous bedmates, he feels an unusual sense of personal empowerment now that his full memory has returned in tandem with his physical reduction, because knowing where he's been will help him to get wherever he's going. At the same time, he discovers he's not alone with the cat anymore, for sitting on the bed beside them is his elusive creator, Will Viharo.

Recovering from a state of existential shock, Chumpy stands up and shouts at Will, who apparently can neither see nor hear him, even though the cat, whom Will calls "Puss," is fully aware of Chumpy's presence but feels no sense of urgency. Puss casually lies back and watches Chumpy trying to communicate with his owner. Frustrated by the lack of response, Chumpy walks over to Will and pounds on his arm to no avail. Will can't feel Chumpy, either. Chumpy doesn't understand this, but he figures it might because Will is too enthralled by the kinetic images on the tiny color television propped precariously atop a portable trunk at the foot of the bed. It's a popular television series called *Miami Vice*. Will is just sitting there in a hypnotic daze, crying softly, so Chumpy sits beside him and cries too, as Puss quietly watches them both with feline puzzlement and sentient compassion.

While Chumpy continues softly sobbing within earshot of his selectively deaf creator, recollections of recent events leading up to this monumental moment rush back into his consciousness in one raging torrent:

Back in Los Angeles, Nice Try Alfie discovered Chumpy wandering the streets of Santa Monica, completely disoriented, while the feckless, felonious fugitive was down there looking for his cousin, Vain Vinnie, whom he hadn't been able to locate. Nice Try Alfie was emotionally, if not geographically, close to his cousin, and they kept in touch. Vain Vinnie told Nice Try Alfie he'd send for him when his latest scheme was hatched, so they could team up to humiliate Nick the Nice Prick. In fact, while growing up, Vain Vinnie and Nice Try Alfie were known as "the Prickly Pair," due to their relation to Nick the Nice Prick. This always annoyed them, which is my Nick the Nice Prick thought of it.

After making several inquiries into Vain Vinnie's whereabouts, a neighbor finally informed Nice Try Alfie of his cousin's tragic passing, so Alfie killed time just hanging out at the beach, gawking at girls in bikinis. That's when he saw Chumpy getting off a blue bus, which he had boarded in Beverly Hills, after leaving Playboy Mansion, clueless as to why he woke up in a hot tub surrounded by a harem of hedonists.

While in L.A., Nice Try Alfie also tried to look up his long-distance drug partner, Fate the Pimp, only to discover he was recently deceased, too. Fate the Pimp was one of Nice Try Alfie's West Coast cocaine connections, and the contraband was smuggled down from San Francisco to Los Angeles via one of Fate's "mobile mole ho's." Nice Try Alfie planned to dig up more dirt with Fate the Pimp's golden shovel concerning the fabled Cartoon Cocksmith, who sounded too good to be true.

When Nice Try Alfie saw Chumpy strolling aimlessly around the Third Street Promenade in Santa Monica, he immediately recognized him by Fate's description of Chumpy's incomparable countenance, and couldn't believe his stroke of good fortune. The fact that Chumpy had no memory of his prior existence only worked to Nice Try Alfie's nefarious advantage, since he planned to succeed where Fate the Pimp had failed. And where his cousin Vain Vinnie had failed, too, though this coincidence was lost on him since Vain Vince never spilled the walnuts on his own scheme, only sharing with Nice Try Alfie that he was working on something "big." The fact was, even though they shared a familial bond, they didn't trust each other when it came to money. Nice Try Alfie is unwittingly picking up where his cousin left off, while implementing Fate the Pimp's plans.

After picking Chumpy up in Santa Monica, Nice Try Alfie makes one last stop over in Burbank to drop off a delivery on the way out of town, and then takes Chumpy to Bob's Big Boy for a late lunch, where he lays out his own life story, since Chumpy can't remember his. "Planet Claire" by the B-52s is playing on the sound system.

"You'll dig San Francisco," Nice Try Alfie is telling Chumpy. "I'll show you the lay of the land. And then you'll *be* the lay of the land. *Don't worry about it*! But first, I gotta call you *something*. How about Pony Boy'?"

" Pony Boy'? That's my name?"

"Hey, I don't know *what* the hell you're fuckin' name is because you don't know it yourself. So it might as well be Pony Boy from that movie, *The Outsiders*, since you're so boyish and innocent. And if you're hung like a horse, like Fate the Pimp says you are, it's the perfect name for what I got in mind for you, and for us."

"I don't know any pimps, much less one named Fate," Chumpy insists, eating only dry toast and black coffee, since the idea of cream, butter, or eggs instinctively repulses him.

"How do you know if you can't remember anything past this morning?"

"That's a good point," Chumpy concedes. "What did this pimp you know tell you about me?"

"That you look like a cartoon character with a giant cartoon cock."

"I really have a big penis?" Chumpy opens the button of his shorts and feels around.

"*Don't* you?"

"I don't know. It doesn't feel like it."

Nice Try Alfie gets agitated. "Maybe you ain't my bitch after all."

"That would sure be a shame."

"But *nobody* else anywhere fits Fate's description of you. You're a fuckin' flesh-and-blood cartoon character, that's for sure. The big dick part might need some coaxing to bring it out of its shell."

"You mean, like a walnut?"

"I'm thinking more like a bomb."

"I guess I could check a little harder, which might *make* it harder."

"Well, I ain't gonna check for you. Go to the bathroom and confirm it yourself."

"Why?"

"Because I'm buyin' your fuckin' lunch, that's why."

"It's a piece of toast."

"Not my fault, you fuckin' rabbit! What're you, Bugs Bunny undercover?"

"Maybe. All options are open at this point."

"I need to confirm your dick size, preferably before our trip. Even if it's not that big, you're unique enough to put on the market. Do you fuck guys?"

"I don't know."

"That's not an offer, just wondering what our audience potential might be. No need to limit our target demographics. Me, I'll fuck anything that can stand me for two messy minutes."

"I do have to pee."

"Knock yourself out. Then report back your findings. Shouldn't be hard. Scratch that. *Make it hard.*"

Chumpy sighs, nods, then gets up and locates the restroom, where in the privacy of a stall, he studies his penis and deduces it is commensurate to his height, which is not very tall by locally conventional standards, but adequate enough so he doesn't stand out from the crowd.

On Chumpy's way back to give Nice Try Alfie the disappointing news, a man with big hair, big eyes, a big smile, and a big heart stops him politely. The man is sitting alone in a booth, drinking coffee and a chocolate shake, and eating cherry pie, with a pile of napkins in front of him, on which are scribbled copious notes. There is a good deal of sugar spilled on the table, like it's Tony Montana's office desk.

"Hey, young fella, do I know you?" the man asks Chumpy.

"I don't know. I don't even know myself."

"Few people do. Do you know me?"

"No, should I?"

"Only if you like weird movies. Ever seen *Eraserhead*

or *The Elephant Man*?"

"I don't know. *Eraserhead* seems to ring a distant bell in a forgotten tower, though."

" A distant bell in a forgotten tower.' I like that."

"Thank you, I guess."

"I think that you may like *The Elephant Man*. It's the true story of a beautiful soul with a tender heart, born into a tragically deformed body, and how he survives, and then transcends, a harsh but poetic world of both cruelty and charity."

"Hm. That does sound interesting. I will try to remember to look for it, though my memory is not what it used to be. At least as I recall."

"Understood. For the moment, I'd only like you to remember my name. It's David."

"Hi, David."

"Hello," says David Lynch. "You're not from around here, are you?"

"I don't know. But it doesn't feel like it."

"Then you're probably not. Neither am I, not really. Please, have a seat. Sorry about the mess, but I get excited when I'm on a creative roll, and I knocked over the sugar, which is what sent my system into overdrive in the first place."

"You eat sugar?"

"I don't mainline it like Mickey Rourke in *Diner*. But yes, filtered. This is my fifth chocolate shake of the day. It's my rocket fuel."

"What are all those napkins for? To clean up the mess?"

"Those are my notes. Sit down and I'll tell you all about them."

"But I'm with someone."

"Yes, I know. I've been watching you both. That character can wait. He looks pretty shifty from where I'm sitting and is probably up to no good."

"I get that idea, too. Should I make a break for it/"

"And go where?"

"I have no idea."

"Then just stay on the path you're on, but pay attention to the signposts. Right now, that guy is your traveling companion. But not for too long. He's just a catalyst or a conduit to advance you on your journey.

"What journey?" Chumpy asks with extreme curiosity.

"We're *all* on a journey. And all life journeys are circuitous, so just accept that fact, and you won't be overly anxious to get where you're going. Just trust that you'll arrive right on time."

"Even if I don't know where I'm going?"

"None of us knows where we're going or where we're from. That's why it's so much fun, trying to figure it out. The mystery doesn't need a solution, because the mystery is the whole point. Once you resolve it, it's over with, and so are you."

"What if you never solve the mystery?"

"*Now* you're getting it!" David Lynch says, giving Chumpy a thumbs-up.

"I am?"

"Yes, but it'll take a while to sink in. There's no hurry. Just have fun with it as much as you can. And if you're not having fun, remember it's all a dream, anyway."

"That answers almost all my questions."

"Glad I could help!" David Lynch says with a gregarious grin.

Chumpy is still feeling lost without a compass, and he feels he can trust this stranger much more than his captor. "I've been having very strange dreams lately. I think they're someone else's nightmares, and we got our wires crossed."

"Could be. We're all connected to the same higher consciousness. Dreams are subconscious reminders that Life is a dream. When we wake up from this dream called Life, we'll find that this world wasn't our real home anyway, like we do when we wake up from our nightly dreams and find ourselves back in *this* waking world, which is all we know for now. Think about it."

"I'm thinking as you speak," Chumpy says, contemplating the concepts. "Please. Go on."

"See, when you're dreaming, you think that dream inside your head as you sleep is your only reality. You have no consciousness of anything else. Then, when you wake up, you're relieved to find that *this* world is your reality, and the dream doesn't even make sense anymore. This world doesn't always make sense either, but it just *feels* more real, at least, because dream logic doesn't apply in this realm. We're just dreamers passing through multiple dreams that all seem real to us in the moment, until we get back to the true reality."

"Then no more dreams."

"No more need for them."

"I think I understand."

"Of course you do!"

"Is that why you're so interested in me?"

"Not really, because we're *all* dreamers. You remind me of a friend of mine, and I have a few things to tell you, if you don't mind. Please. Just for a moment. This might be important to both of us."

"Who do I remind you of?" Chumpy asks as he sits opposite David Lynch.

"Ronnie Rocket."

"Who's that?"

"He's a creation of mine."

"So he's not real."

"He's real to me, in my mind. If I can ever get his movie made, he'll be real to everyone else, too, because then they'll be able to see what I can see."

"What is your movie about?"

"It's about this guy, named Ronnie Rocket."

"What is your movie going to be called? Ronnie Rocket'?"

"Well, my working title is The Absurd Mystery of the Strange Forces of Existence.' Some have suggested that's not a very commercial title. But I say fuck em."

"Somehow I can relate."

"Of course you can, or we wouldn't be talking. This is why I like you, even though we just met. I feel like I already know you. You and Ronnie would get along great, too, if you ever get a chance to meet. But right now he's trapped inside my head. Once I find a way to get him out, you never know what can happen. Raising money is a lot harder than putting a saw inside a cake."

"I'm not sure I get the reference."

"Picture a jail cell, with a very sad prisoner in it, imprisoned for something he didn't do or didn't know he did. Also, picture a cake with a saw inside it that someone brought him, maybe his mother or his girlfriend. He's very lonely inside that cell, desperate to be free. So he eats the cake, finds what's inside after maybe cutting his lips a little, then saws through the bars, and escapes. He is reunited with his loved ones. This is how Ronnie Rocket will feel when he's been busted out of the prison of my mind and let loose in the world for all to meet and enjoy. You know what you call that?"

"No."

"*It's a piece of cake!*"

"I see. A piece of cake. Yes. I mean, I can see it in my mind."

"You could also call it a slice of Life, but that might conjure the wrong imagery."

"So you're saying trying to finance your movie is harder than trying to saw your way out of a jail cell."

"Yes. It's more like trying to bite through the bars with your teeth."

"That sounds pretty hard. They'd just break."

"Exactly."

"*Ouch*, I can see and feel that, too."

"That means I painted a good picture in your mind. I'm a painter, that's why. But if I want to paint that picture for a lot of minds, unlimited minds, I need to use a movie screen as my canvas. Or else Ronnie Rocket will remain a picture in my head, but no one else's."

Chumpy feels like he has found his spiritual advisor. "How is it I can see images inside my head, and in my dreams, like they're movies, when my eyes are on the outside of my head?"

"Because the mind's eye sees beyond the temporal, that's why. If you ever learn how to meditate, your mind's eye will show you a lot more. It will show you things you can't see with the naked eye."

"Including myself?"

"Including your *real* self, yes. It'll be like looking through this mirror that's really a portal to Eternity, where all dreams merge into one. This is why, in dreams, if you notice, there's no sense of time passing, even though the events are sequential. You have no memories. Just awareness of how things are, and your acceptance of this constant reality, regardless of how nonsensical it is by our standards, comes without any doubts or questions. It all exists in the moment. Because in eternal space, there is no time as we experience it in this realm."

"Wow. What else can you see that no one else can see?"

"I can see *you*, Chumpy Walnut."

"Chumpy Walnut?"

"Yes. That's your name."

"I don't remember that. But it's better than Pony Boy'."

"You don't remember your real name because you're not your true self right now, I can tell."

"Why can't anyone else but you see the real me?"

"Because they're not looking in the right place. Your soul."

"Why can't I see it?"

"You must have lost touch with your spirit. But it's there,

all right. It happens to everyone now and then, sometimes permanently. But not you. You'll reunite soon with your creator, and it will all become clear."

"What will become clear?"

"Your true self. In reality, or at least what you know to be reality, you're only a foot tall. Ronnie is only three feet tall, another reason you'd get along. And you live in a town called Thrillville, though you grew up in another town called Lonesome Grove. You were raised by a lumberjack and his wife when they found you inside a bird's nest, after a forest fire destroyed your race of little people. When you grew older, you ran away to escape persecution by the small-minded townspeople, and two hoboes found you. They wanted to take care of you, but also help themselves, so they put you on the nightclub circuit in the big city of Excelsior. One way they promote you is at a baseball game, where you hit a walnut and run the bases. But then a gangster named Johnny Romance and his gang take a piece of your action. Other people, like a juvenile delinquent named Tiger Willie, his girlfriend Peachy Creamola, a burlesque dancer named Hotsie Totsie, and others, help you out along the way. Everything turns out temporarily fine after you survive a gun battle and another fire, this time a cabin where you're being held, and when you recover, your hobo friends take you to a nightclub to see a new act, and it turns out that she's the other surviving member of your race. Her name is Cupey Honeysuckle, and she's a half inch shorter than you."

"Wow. So then we live happily ever after?"

"No. Nobody does. Not down here, anyway. And your dimension is a reflection of this one, but reflected in a funhouse mirror."

"Hm. So then what happens to me in this story?"

"I don't know, and you don't want to know. Not yet. But I sense that eventually, after a lot of really weird, sexy stuff—too weird and sexy even for me, almost—you'll meet your creator and he'll explain everything, and ultimately you'll be fine. You just have to have faith in that eventual outcome as you struggle down the pathway to your final destination. I keep telling Ronnie Rocket the same thing. The difference is I'm his creator. But I'm not your creator. If I were, you'd probably end up being a lot better known."

"I only want to know who I am."

"I just told you."

"But why should I believe you?"

"Because it's true. But it doesn't matter. There's no reason to trust me, or certainly not that guy over there, or anybody except your own heart, and if you follow it, you'll find not what you want, maybe, but what you need or deserve, which can be either better than or worse than what you were hoping for. The truth has no credibility until you discover it for yourself."

"I understand. I just hope I can remember it. My memory is not working so well lately. In fact, it's totally broken."

"You'll forget what I'm telling you right now, Chumpy Walnut, then remember it when you're ready. I'm planting the seed in your subconscious so it can bear fruit later, when you need it most. That's how it works. Meantime, you'll keep assuming different shapes and roles to suit your evolving circumstances. We all do, whether we realize it or not. Since you're an extraordinary being, it's more extreme for you."

"That doesn't make sense. Like a dream doesn't make sense. Except now I know I'm dreaming, so maybe it will make sense when I wake up."

"Nothing will make sense until it needs to, and by the time it does make sense, you still won't understand it. So don't waste time trying to figure out the meaning of everything all at once. The reason for everything is revealed piecemeal, to keep it interesting."

"What the hell is *this*?" demands Nice Try Alfie, standing by the table after he went to see what was keeping

Chumpy for so long. "Who the fuck is *this* perv?"

David Lynch grins at him. "I was telling your newfound friend Chumpy Walnut here that he can't trust you, but he can trust his heart, wherever that leads him."

Nice Try Alfie is unable to process this information, so he says, "I'm more interested in where his cock will lead me."

"You can never trust a cock," says David Lynch. "It will get you into nothing but trouble."

Chumpy laughs, then stands up out of the booth. "C'mon, let's go to San Francisco, and I'll be your bitch, as you so thoughtfully offered," Chumpy tells Nice Try Alfie.

Nice Try Alfie is pleasantly stunned. "What? I thought you were too nervous to go with me?"

"I guess because your car is so old and crappy. And you're so young and creepy."

"Both will make the trip intact, trust me. I've done it a dozen times for these business trips."

"Okay. It looks cool, anyway. By the way, I checked, and I have a small dick. Sorry."

"You're just scared," Nice Try Alfie says. "It shrivels when you're scared." Then he looks at David Lynch and says, "Right, pervert?"

David Lynch keeps smiling as he gives Nice Try Alfie the thumbs up, but then lets his thumb slowly sag, until it's thumbs-down.

"You're a fuckin' weirdo, man," Nice Try Alfie tells a stubbornly smiling David Lynch.

"I'm ready to go now," Chumpy says impatiently to Nice Try Alfie. Then he reluctantly says goodbye to his *real* new friend, David Lynch.

"Don't worry, you'll be okay," David Lynch tells Chumpy as they shake hands. "I can't say the same for your temporary traveling companion. I know his type. I've written about guys like him. They never land on top."

"Fuck you, creep," Nice Try Alfie says to David Lynch

with a menacing glare.

"One last thing before you go, Chumpy," says David Lynch, looking right past Alfie as if he doesn't even exist. "I have a message for your creator that I'd like you to pass on for me when you finally meet him."

"But I won't remember it," Chumpy says.

"Yes, you will."

"Okay, if you say so. What is it?"

"Tell him I said, If you love what you do, do what you love.'"

"You mean do who you love, and make them love it,'" Nice Try Alfie says, though he is ignored.

"Okay," Chumpy says with a shrug. "I'll try. Let's go, Alfie."

Nice Try Alfie turns around and flips David Lynch the bird as they head toward the exit. Unfazed, David Lynch keeps smiling and gives Chumpy Walnut the thumbs-up once more. Chumpy returns the gesture.

By the time they get into Nice Try Alfie's beat-up old Dodge Dart, Chumpy can't even remember his own name or the identity of the guy driving him. But he does remember that nice, wise man he met in the coffee shop, whose advice is all he has to guide him. Somehow, he's confident it will be enough, even though as soon as they hit the 101 north, Chumpy can't remember what it is. He can still feel it, though.

Eight hours later, the neon lights of North Beach beckon them to hedonistic hell, which only feels like heaven in spurts. Chumpy has slept most of the way, dreaming about the New Jersey right-wing guru cult. As soon as Nice Try Alfie illegally parks his Dart, he wakes Chumpy and leads him directly into the Lusty Lady Peep Show beneath the Hotel Europa to conduct a sexperiment. The blasé ladies behind the grimy glass are slowly gyrating, making lewd gestures at the drooling customers, or staring blankly into space as if in a mystical trance while "Relax" by Frankie

Goes to Hollywood plays on the sound system.

After beholding the bouncing bosoms for a minute or so, Chumpy's boner gradually expands to its full twelve inches as "99 Luftballons" by Nena plays on the sound system. Moments later, he is hosing down the booths with his seedless sperm to the gleeful delight of the performers, affirming the late Fate the Pimp's account. Word quickly spreads about Chumpy's mythical member, and Chumpy Walnut, AKA Pony Boy, quickly becomes the hotel's resident gigolo for the next several months, which pass by in a hallucinatory blur once Nice Try Alfie introduces Chumpy to David Bowie's metaphorical "China Girl." Hotel management is fully aware of this arrangement and collects a portion of the proceeds for its compliance.

Feeling paranoid and protective of his investment, Nice Try Alfie hides Chumpy in his room, telling him someone is trying to kill him, and so he needs to stay inside for a while. Chumpy doesn't ask many questions because he is enjoying his new status as a stationary stud, which requires very little effort on his part. The women do all the work as Chumpy remains motionless, like a stiff board with a hard nail sticking straight up out, impaling wet vaginas like a jackhammer through gelatin. Nice Try Alfie attributes his boy's doped-up demeanor to his innate shyness, which appeals to many maternal instincts. Eventually, the board grows bored, and the nail gets rusty. During this perversely profitable period, Chumpy never wears protection, nor is he concerned with contracting a disease, because his body composition is alien to this dimension's denizens. In this relatively real world, he can't get sick, he can't be killed, and any wounds heal quickly without a trace. He can't impregnate anyone because his seed is synthetic, not organic, so it's biologically incompatible with the human womb. He is a living, breathing fictional character, making any physical interaction on this plane transient at best. Nice Try Alfie thinks he's some kind of vampire, which is one reason he never lets Chumpy leave the room. Chumpy's deepening depression makes him apathetic and resigned to his circumstances, a willing prisoner of Fate, even though Fate has left the building.

Though he sometimes hears the cries of female ecstasy down the hall, only listening to them long enough to pop his own wad in the privacy of his room, hotel resident Will Viharo never sees his creation Chumpy in this state, never imagining the little character in his manuscript is pleasuring dozens of women of every size, shape, and color, nearly around the clock, as Chumpy often dozes off during the constant copulation. Even if Chumpy dared to venture outside of Alfie's room, Will still wouldn't see him, since he is too deeply entrenched in his own despair.

This remains true even once Chumpy reverts to his normal size and takes expedient and unexpectedly fortuitous sanctuary in Will's room, remaining invisible to everyone but Puss, who communicates with Chumpy telepathically. Their regular conversations reveal a lot of valuable intel about Chumpy's creator's life. For instance, Puss was adopted when he was living with Will and his girlfriend, Nancy, the UCLA student and Good Earth waitress. They lived together in that tiny Cotner apartment for over a year before they broke up and Will decided to start over alone in San Francisco to pursue his dreams of becoming a successful writer. He chose the Hotel Europa from a listing in a Los Angeles paper, unaware of the depravity that was in store for him. Per the amicable breakup agreement, Will took Puss with him, smuggling him into the hotel in a blanket per the unspoken "unseen and unheard" policy, which blatantly breaks the No Pets rule. Will was too lonely to let him go. To pay his rent, Will works the graveyard shift as a desk clerk, counseling off-duty strippers and traumatized Vietnam vets simply by listening to their woes, with no advice to offer beyond passive commiseration.

The only time Chumpy witnesses Will's happiness is when his creator brings three sexy, female Italian tourists back to his room since they need a place to crash for the night. Will met them at his job serving ice cream at a shop down in the Cannery on Fisherman's Wharf. They shower Puss with affection, but there is no human sex. Chumpy is privately relieved since it would bring back unsettling memories, but he is sad that his creator isn't getting any relief from his incessant masturbation, especially when Chumpy happens to be sitting too close and gets creamed.

Soon after this, Will goes to work as usual at the ice cream parlor, but the owner just hands him the keys and asks him to lock up behind him, as the authorities take him away, and the place is blocked off with yellow tape. Will is without a steady job again, besides his graveyard gig as a desk clerk for the hotel, which only covers his weekly rent.

Presently, in Will's hotel room, Chumpy is serenely asleep inside a soothing void, without any disturbing dreams. Despite the cherished company of his beloved cat, Will is perpetually lonesome and depressed. He forces himself to get out of bed and get dressed, then he walks out the door, leaving Chumpy alone with Puss. When Chumpy wakes up a bit later, he is not afraid despite the discordant sounds of traffic and tourists on the streets below, because this depressing little hovel feels more like his true home than anywhere else he's been in this demented dimension. Of his different incarnations here, his present state of diminutive invisibility is his favorite, because it restores his original height, and because he cannot be seen, which gives him a stealthy operational advantage.

Will returns to his hovel in the late afternoon and sets up his portable typewriter atop his portable refrigerator, typing furiously while sitting on the floor and leaning against the bed. Chumpy is instantly captivated, wondering if Will is working on the original draft of *The Romance of Chumpy Walnut*. In fact, Will has already finished it, and the manuscript is packed in his beat-up travel trunk, which doubles as a TV stand. Instead, Will is working on something that will never be published called "The Sea and the Stars," which has nothing to do with Chumpy, so it is of little interest to him, other than another peek inside his creator's head, which increasingly appears to be a scary place, even scarier than his physical surroundings.

After an hour or so, Will puts away the current manuscript and the typewriter and heads back out to grab a burrito and then watch *Day of the Dead* for the third time at the Embassy Theater, a grindhouse on Market Street with cheap admission, which allows drunks and derelicts to spend hours indoors to safely sleep on the uncomfortable chairs, privately masturbate in the dark, and urinate on the floor. *Day of the Dead* is playing on a triple bill with *The Howling* and *Humanoids from the Deep*. This will keep Will out till rather late, giving Chumpy time to open that trunk and read the contents.

As Puss looks on, Chumpy stands on the edge of the bed and manages to gently push the TV from atop the upright locker, where it lands safely on the bed beside him. Then, with great effort, Chumpy pushes the locker over, and after several strenuous attempts, he is finally able to snap open the lock, releasing all the contents, which fall all over the filthy floor.

Chumpy is overwhelmed.

He sits down and reads pieces of several manuscripts, assiduously propping the individual pieces of typewritten paper up against the bed like they're menu boards. The pile of manuscripts includes "Diary of a Dreamer," the original "Chumpy Walnut," "The Sea and the Stars," and, of course, "The Romance of Chumpy Walnut." Chumpy is astonished to find out the sequel is just as innocent and charming as the first book, with only a few gently ribald passages, but nothing objectionable to the average reader. Chumpy is more determined than ever to find out why the definitive version published decades later was so different on every level, though the decadence of the current environment offers a few clues.

When Chumpy hears the door open about midnight, he scampers to the corner while Will chastises Puss for knocking over his locker and spilling all his hard work on the floor. Will is mystified by the fact that his precious TV—his only regular companion besides Puss—is still intact, carefully sitting on the bed as if Puss moved it himself, which is impossible. Too tired to care, Will turns on the TV and watches a late-night rerun of the British crime series *Dempsey and Makepeace* before crying himself to sleep. Chumpy apologizes to Puss, who doesn't seem to care, either. Puss is merely an observer, not a participant in human activity.

The following morning, Chumpy makes sure to wake up when Will does so he can tag along behind his creator and witness his daily routine, which he finds fascinating despite its impoverished mundanity, soaked in suffocating solitude. Will is wearing an oversized green Army jacket and is wearing headphones attached to something called a Walkman. It is foggy and cold outside, and Chumpy is shivering in his customary cabana wear, but it doesn't bother him. He is warmed by the clandestine proximity to his creator.

In the cafe downstairs next to the Lusty Lady, which, unlike Chumpy, Will has never entered out of sheer dread, Will sits quietly by himself (or so he believes) eating a tomato and cottage cheese omelette while reading Joe Bob Briggs' movie column in the Pink section of the *San Francisco Chronicle.* "Take On Me" by A-Ha plays on the sound system. Chumpy is enthralled.

After his poor man's Sunday brunch, Will walks to the Alhambra Theater on Polk Street to see a bargain matinee of a new movie called *To Live and Die in L.A.,* which strikes Chumpy as ironic. On the way, Will is listening to a cassette tape of the soundtrack for a movie called *The Breakfast Club*. His favorite song on the album is "Don't You Forget About Me," by Simple Minds, since he feels so forgotten. Naturally, Chumpy gets to sneak in for free, sitting in the seat beside Will in the mostly empty theater. Chumpy enjoys the movie, and, enhancing the irony, he recognizes one of its stars, Will's friend Debra Feuer, who is married to Will's friend Mickey Rourke. Chumpy feels this makes them his friends, too, at least by proxy.

After the movie, Will walks back toward the hotel but detours through Chinatown, with Chumpy close behind, both carefully navigating the narrow, crowded streets. Will walks down Grant, crosses Broadway, and enters a falafel shop where he orders his usual meal to go. Chumpy can sense his creator's deep melancholia and doesn't understand the source of it. Will's life seems very different now than it was in Los Angeles, and Chumpy is quite curious to find out what happened, because that might help explain the radical course change in his own journey.

This goes on for several days, as Chumpy follows Will everywhere, eating Will's scraps when he isn't looking, or, due to his invisibility, stealing food from whomever he can, wherever and whenever he can, climbing up and pissing in the sink at the hotel, and doing his other dirty business in alleyways. Chumpy sits with Will as he drinks coffee and writes in a notebook in Caffee Trieste. He wanders with his creator around City Lights Bookstore, reading the enticing spines of the myriad tomes, and wondering when his life story will join them on the shelves. When Will goes into Specs Bar, a beatnik landmark, he only orders coffee, never beer or booze, which puzzles Chumpy, who has to resort to stealing alcoholic sips from other patrons. Wherever he goes, Chumpy's creator is lost in a book, lost in his notepad, lost in thought, lost in dreams. Chumpy feels his creator's sadness intensely and wonders if the nightmares he's been experiencing, about being trapped in a cult, have anything to do with it, even though they were in the distant past.

One day, Will decides that this pent-up lifestyle is not conducive to Puss's well-being, and he's also missing L.A. and might give it another go. Nancy travels from L.A. to visit Will in the hotel, the arrangements remaining strictly platonic, and brings Puss back with her to Venice, where she is living with her new boyfriend. Chumpy misses Puss and their conversations, since now Chumpy has no one else to talk to that will listen, because no one else can hear him.

With his feline companion gone, Will is lonelier than ever in his self-imposed isolation from mainstream society, still oblivious to the fact that he is never alone. Chumpy decides to find a way to enlighten and perhaps console his creator.

In the wee small hours of the morning, after his desk clerk shift, Will notices a walnut sitting on the pillow next to Puss, who seems to be safeguarding it. It looks familiar because of the cracks, but it couldn't be the same one multiple people keep trying to give him, because how could it possibly get all the way up there? Will decides to draw a little face on his new inanimate companion to sustain the comforting illusion that he has constant company in his travels.

"I'm going to call you Chumpy," Will tells the walnut. "And I will take care of you and never lose you, no matter what."

"*Finally*," Chumpy the Walnut says to himself, hopefully for the final time, but he's not holding his cartoon breath.

Chapter Eight
LURID LOUNGE

Will is at the Berkeley Flea Market on Ashby Avenue, where he often goes to buy rare VHS movies from his friend, Professor Curtis, who would soon open his own store, Professor Curtis' Famous Cult Videos on San Pablo Avenue. While browsing the tables of vintage collectibles, Will finds a tiny, plastic, towheaded figurine painted in yellow, black, and red lying on the ground. Since Curtis doesn't claim ownership of the figurine, Will puts it in his pocket next to the walnut, which is Will's constant companion. While Chumpy still can't communicate with his creator, he hears and senses everything, and thanks to the eyes Will drew on his face, he can see everything, too. The walnut instantly imbues the figurine with Chumpy's spirit, so together, the walnut and the figurine share Chumpy's silent perspective.

Will moved to Berkeley after leaving Los Angeles for the second time in the summer of 1986. He worked for Mickey Rourke as his assistant while living in Mickey's Mandeville Canyon home with Mickey's wife, Debra Feuer, Mickey's brother, Joey, and Linda Kerridge. Will and Linda almost moved into their own place elsewhere, on a strictly platonic basis, at least according to Linda. But Will still secretly carried that water-resistant torch for his dream girl, and he had returned to L.A. to either snuff it out for good or fan the eternal flames of his burning love, which were finally doused by the firehose of reality, and are now nothing more than an ash heap of smoking embers. With sagging spirits and a soggy heart, Will moved back to the Bay Area, landing in a residential hotel in the Tenderloin before his friends in Berkeley helped him get his own place. He's been here a couple of years now. Puss is back in the mix too, living with Will and Chumpy in a rented room on Dana Street, just off Telegraph Avenue, a few blocks from the UC Berkeley Campus. Puss, who can telepathically converse with Chumpy in any form, has caught Chumpy up on everything about his creator's life since he was adopted by Will and Nancy in 1983, back down in Westwood. Will is much more pathetic than Chumpy realized. He almost feels sorry for his creator. By comparison, Chumpy's life is a blast.

So far, Will's malaise has proven impenetrable to any communication from Chumpy. Chumpy attributes this stubborn wall of depression to his upbringing in that New Jersey cult. Puss has overheard many conversations between Will and Nancy about that traumatic experience, and Chumpy can see the parallels with his own story, to a point.

Currently, Chumpy is content as a portable voyeur, enjoying or enduring his creator's many misadventures from a relatively secure vantage point. Even though he's hitching a ride inside Will's pocket, which prevents him from seeing much of the action, he can still vicariously appreciate it from what he can hear, and when he's just idling on a shelf, he's afforded a front row seat to his creator's personal and artistic angst, as well as his obsession with movies, providing Chumpy with a lot of resonant revelations about his own journey.

"I never heard of this movie," Will is saying to his friend Curtis, who is a genuinely gentle, soft-spoken, middle-aged African American man with glasses, kind eyes, and an infectious grin, not to mention a shared affinity for offbeat cinema.

"It will change your life," Curtis says. "This is a very rare copy."

"A bootleg,"

"Almost any movie worth seeing is bootlegged right now. The video makers are having trouble keeping up with demand, especially for connoisseurs like you and me."

"I can't wait to watch it." Will hands Curtis a twenty-dollar bill, part of his tip money from waiting on academics at the UC Berkeley Faculty Club. Then he reads the title aloud. "*The Swimmer*. I really like Burt Lancaster, especially in *Sweet Smell of Success*."

"This is just as good, trust me. You will be able to relate to it on a certain level."

"Burt must be pretty bummed in this one, then."

"He is. It's very existential."

"Okay, I'll also take *Werewolf vs. the Vampire Women* and *Dracula vs. Frankenstein*. I hope you can track down *I Was a Teenage Werewolf*. That was my favorite when I was growing up in New Jersey. Also the other one, *I Was a Teenage Frankenstein*. I used to watch them playing together on Doc Shock's Mad Theater and Horror Theater out of Philly. I was raised by this crazy, angry woman who beat me and punished me all the time for no reason other than she was miserable herself. Horror movies helped me cope with these real-life nightmares, and luckily for me, her cult meetings were on Saturday afternoons, so I could watch The Bowery Boys and Doc Shock almost every week. It seriously saved my life at the time."

"Sorry to hear that, man. Movies have always helped me deal with my life, too, so I understand. What about that Jean Rollin vampire movie I was telling you about? *Requiem for a Vampire*? Very rare. It's not a great copy, but it's the best anyone can find."

"Another one from Video Search of Miami?"

"I'm afraid so. But it's very sexy. You'll be able to see enough of the sexy stuff, trust me."

"Okay," Will says. "I'll take whatever I can get. That's my motto."

"That's a good motto these days. And the other movie?"

"What other movie?"

"The Japanese gangster movie. *Tokyo Drifter*."

"Oh, yeah. Shit."

"It's pretty great, but I don't want to pressure you."

"I know, I know. I saw it as part of a Suzuki retrospective at PFA. I loved those movies so much that I went out and bought a used sharkskin jacket at Sharks on Telegraph."

"Makes sense."

"Yeah. It's very Rat Pack style. Well, more Mickey Mouse Club than Rat Pack, but I'm on a budget. I saw them perform at the Oakland Coliseum. It was like a religious experience. Those guys know how to enjoy life. I want to be like them, eventually."

"You're developing your own style, my man. It takes time. You'll get there. The ladies like a man with personal style. The ones worth their while do, anyway. There's no one else like you, so you need to stay in the game until someone appreciates you just for who you are. In the meantime, you just need a little encouragement and inspiration. "

"Okay. I'll take it. The video *and* the inspiration. I'll need a bigger bag."

"Of course, so you can put those in there too," Curtis says, nodding at the batch of vintage cheesecake magazines tucked under Will's arm. Will nods in fiscal defeat, somewhat undermining the short-lived elation from his purchases. He's already in debt from the VCR he bought recently, after finally obtaining a credit card. Although he's impulsive, he does his best to put as little on the card as possible. His best sucks, though.

Given his low wages and wide range of interests in pulpy pop culture, this financial plan falls apart rather quickly. Within fifteen minutes at the flea market, Will has spent almost all of his tip money, but he still has enough for a burrito, which is his go-to, since they're both cheap and filling, and as a vegetarian, he's okay with rice and beans.

After another solitary lunch, spent sadly staring into space, trying to picture a better future, Will heads over to Comic Relief, the comic book store on Shattuck, where he buys a Batman graphic novel and a monster/girlie pinup magazine, putting them on his credit card. Fortunately, he hasn't cashed his check from the Faculty Club yet, though rent is almost due. Regardless, after he deposits it in the bank, he takes out another twenty bucks to watch *Cafe Flesh* on a double bill with *Liquid Sky* at the UC Theater on University Avenue. Afterward, he heads down the block to one of his frequent hangouts, the Au Coquelet Cafe, where he consumes a sandwich and a cappuccino while leafing through his lurid literature, trying not to visually stalk any of the cute coeds. Then he returns to the theater and buys a solo ticket to see the regular weekly midnight screening of *The Rocky Horror Picture Show*, presented by a performance troupe called Barely Legal Productions, whose members are dressed up as the cast while performing along with the songs. The fact that Will is sitting alone in the back of the theater as the rest of the audience cheers and sings along doesn't detract from his appreciation, because he's become accustomed to his self-isolation, imposed by his innate non-conformity.

When he gets home, it is almost 3 a.m. Unable to fall asleep right away, partly because of the nightmares he must endure on a semi-regular basis, Will cuddles with Puss a bit and then re-reads the letter from his literary agent in New York, the one Paul Zindel hooked up for him when Will was briefly in the Writer's Unit of the Actor's Studio in West Hollywood. She can't sell anything he sends her, but he likes her name, Marilyn Marlow, a combo of his favorite actress and favorite detective, and he considers it a sign to continue. The letter explains that she can't interest anyone in his latest submission, called "Lavender Blonde," though she personally believes it's his best manuscript so far, and his friend Greg down in L.A. agrees. Her faith in his idiosyncratic work, as well as the sincere support of people like Greg, keep Will going, even as the futility of his ambition eats away at his heart. He needs any affirmation he can get. But he's sad that Marilyn has pretty much given up on both "Chumpy Walnut" and its sequel, "The Romance of Chumpy Walnut." It was the first novel that piqued Paul Zindel's interest and spurred the recommendation to his agent.

Will takes his Good Luck Walnut out of his pocket and kisses it before setting it on his writing desk, next to the little plastic figurine he found at the flea market. Chumpy's consciousness instantly splits between the two, so his spirit inhabits two different physical forms, exponentially increasing his surveillance capabilities. Will had picked up the figurine, which represents the corporeal manifestation of Chumpy as a foot-tall human, to keep the walnut, Chumpy's initial conception, company. Will has always attributed human feelings to inanimate objects, as well as animals. Little does he know this is a correct attribution, at least in this case.

The following Monday, Will walks up Telegraph Avenue to meet with his friend Kyle, a funny, smart, handsome black dude with whom Will works as a "waitron" at the UC Berkeley Faculty Club. The previous year, they had dressed up as Crockett and Tubbs for Halloween. Their current rendezvous is Caffe Mediterraneum, a legendary coffeehouse seen in *The Graduate*. Kyle is telling Will about their friend Catherine's dream of one day opening a movie theater that serves food, beer, and wine, which customers can consume while they recline on comfortable couches. Catherine discovered this business model when she was living in Washington, D.C., and discussed her dream with Kyle, who is about to graduate with a law degree, before moving to Los Angeles with his wife, an aspiring jazz singer.

"That sounds like a great idea," Will says. "Maybe I can

be a part of it."

"We might need your movie expertise, so maybe."

"I don't know what to do with my life."

"You're a writer."

"No, I'm a dreamer who records his dreams in fictional form."

"Not many people can do that."

"It's a useless talent."

"It's saved your life. You have an art that expresses who you are and what you feel. Many people would kill for that. I know I would."

Will and Kyle sit and watch the pretty girls walking past the cafe as "Road to Nowhere" by the Talking Heads plays on the sound system.

"Time is going by so fast," Will says.

Kyle nods. "This is why you can't waste time just dreaming. Keep writing your dreams down on paper, and someday they'll manifest as reality."

Will shrugs. "I don't have anything better to do." After Kyle leaves, Will visits his usual haunts: Blondie's Pizza, Amoeba Music, Rasputin Music, Moe's Books, and Cody's Books. He puts his purchased books (by John Irving, Kurt Vonnegut, James Ellroy, and Paul Auster), VHS tapes (John Woo, Woody Allen, and some classic film noir), and CDs on his credit card and tries to tell himself that when he's a famous author, he can easily pay it all off. Then he goes home, masturbates, and cries before heading down to Shattuck Avenue to watch another movie. Puss and both Chumpys' wish they could help, even though they already are, simply by supplying spiritual sustenance.

Chumpy, both the figurine and the walnut, experience a lap dissolve like in a movie.

When the lap dissolve stops, Will is back in his room, sitting on his frameless mattress while his friend Debra Feuer, visiting from Los Angeles, sits on the chair at his writing desk. They've just come from the Ashram on San

Pablo Avenue, where Debra's guru is appearing in person. Will is excited because he just had lunch with both Debra and the actress Lisa Bonet, from *Angel Heart*.

"I remember when I was working for Mickey after he'd just come from New Orleans," Will is saying to Debra. "He was telling me how much I'd like *Angel Heart* because it was about a nineteen-fifties private eye who sells his soul to Satan. I said, So it's a fantasy.' And he said seriously, No. It's not."

"He's like that," Debra says. "Oh! That review of *Barfly* you sent him?"

"From *The Daily Californian*, yeah! It was my first movie review. They published my first short story, too. It's called The In-Betweeners.'"

"You sent me that. I really liked it. Reminded me of Beckett."

"Thanks. Mickey told me when we were walking around Westwood once that he thought the script for *Nine and a Half Weeks* reminded him of Pinter."

"Whatever."

"You're just jealous of Kim Basinger."

Debra laughs. "If I wasn't jealous of Lisa, I'm certainly not jealous of her."

"But you were jealous of Daryl Hannah when they made *Pope of Greenwich Village*, I remember."

Debra shakes her head and lets that slide. "Not really. Anyway, Kim *hated* Mickey. He told me she said kissing him was like kissing an ashtray."

"Yeah, well, despite the rumors, I wouldn't know."

Debra laughs. "I barely know either, anymore."

"You told me he was jealous of Willem Dafoe when you made *To Live and Die in L.A.*, so now you're even."

"Hardly."

"I *love* that movie."

"Thank you. It was fun to make. Anyway, anyway, that *Barfly* review? You trashed it, but he liked it so much that he has it framed and mounted."

"Get out!"

"I swear."

"That's so cool. I saw it again and liked it much more. I was just in a bad mood back then. Plus, as someone who has actually lived the Bukowski lifestyle out of sheer desperation, I resent when it's glamorized by suburbanites."

"Mickey likes that about you because he comes from the same squalor and never forgets it. Sometimes I think he misses it."

"Did I tell you, I was on a bus in San Francisco soon after I came back to the Bay Area, and saw a movie marquee playing Linda's movie *Downtwisted* on a double bill with *Angel Heart*, and it just said Twisted Heart.'"

"Your life," Debra says. "I hope you're writing all this down."

"Yeah, in so many ways. Linda was in this other movie called *Mixed Blood* that was really good. I saw it like fourteen times at Ghirardelli Square when I was living at the Hotel Europa in North Beach."

"It's that good?"

"Yeah, it's good. More like I was that lonely."

"I didn't see it, but I remember when she was filming it in New York shortly after you left the Mandeville house."

"How's Linda doing? Is she still living at the house?"

"She's moved out and moved on. She's doing fine. As far as I know. We don't really keep in touch anymore."

"It's so weird how we wound up living in the same house. She was the reason I went back to L.A. that summer."

"She really likes you, Willie, but as a friend. Or a brother, like I do."

"I know that now. I even knew it then. That's why I could never say anything to her. I just can't get over the way we met. It must mean something."

"Why? Maybe it's just karma."

"Karma has no meaning in of itself, Deb. It's all just a

system of checks and balances that never ends by design."

"No meaning we can remember, Willie. That doesn't mean it has no meaning."

Will is weary of trying to figure it all out, so he keeps gossiping, dropping familiar names. "I think I told you, while we were still in the middle of apartment hunting together, how Linda and I ran into Sean Penn and Madonna at Musso and Frank while I was living at the Bowl Motel around the corner. Linda said it was like meeting the Statue of Liberty."

"Have you talked to Sean since?"

"No. He gave me his number at Musso. I called it from a payphone near the nearby hooker motel where I was staying the next morning, but the number had been disconnected. Story of my life."

Debra laughs as Will hears the Madonna song "Live to Tell" from the Sean Penn movie *At Close Range* in his head, playing over a mental montage of the summer of '86. Chumpy can actually see and hear it, even if Will can't see or hear him. Everything in his creator's life is a movie to him, and vice versa.

"How are you and Mick getting along?" Will asks Debra after he snaps out of it.

Debra shrugs. "We got along while making *Homeboy*, because we had to."

"That's so sad. It's a great movie, though. Mickey's dream came true. All of his dreams come true."

"He still seems pretty miserable most of the time. He loves the work but hates the business."

"He seemed okay to me when I was working for him. I had fun showing that guy from Ireland around San Francisco. It made me kind of miss it, one reason I came back."

"The Irish guy?"

"Yeah, Brendan, who was helping Mickey with his brogue for *A Prayer for the Dying*."

"Right. I thought you'd just stay up there after that."

"It was only a weekend. Mickey sent us up there because Brendan wanted to visit San Francisco. I also met this actual dude from the I.R.A. in Mick's office. And the head of Hell's Angels here in Oakland."

"Those guys idolize Mickey. He loves it."

"Well, that was in between guys like Dice Clay and Treat Williams popping by, or Frankie Valli calling to leave a message, so it's not all dangerous dudes."

"Just guys who play dangerous dudes."

"Like Mickey."

"I think Mickey prefers the real-life tough guys because he actually respects them. After *Homeboy* wrapped, he talked a lot about getting back into boxing."

"I know, he always did, though, even when we were working on the script a little together. I only contributed a couple of lines, but they didn't make the movie."

"I remember that."

"You character was named Ruby Brown back then, and I wrote this exchange where Mickey called you Ruby Blue' by mistake, and you correct him, and he says, Well, in any case, I can tell you have a very colorful personality.'"

Debra nods with a smile. "I was named Ruby after Red Ruby, Mickey's production company."

"Or was it the other way around?"

"Yeah, maybe it was."

"Anyway, after Brendan and I got back to L.A., I realized my mission to find out once and for all what my connection to Linda is all about was just another delusion of a desperate mind."

"*Finally.*"

"So I came back up here, lived in another cheap hotel in the Tenderloin, then some friends helped me get a room in this house, where another friend lives."

"I'm glad you have friends here, at least."

"Me, too. But I'm still lonely."

"Of course you are, you're a romantic."

"Yeah, I'm pretty fucked. Just not literally."

"Oh, Willie, you're such a drama queen. Anyway, so what are you doing tonight?"

"Watching the season finale of *Miami Vice*."

"Oh, c'mon! Really? No wonder you can't get laid!"

"Sorry, I never miss an episode, and this is a big one. If the show's not renewed, it could be the last episode *ever.*"

"Then what will you do with your Friday nights?"

"Beats me."

"You mean jerk off."

"Yeah, but I already do that *every* night."

"I can't believe you'd rather watch some stupid show than hang out with me."

"Just tonight. I can see you tomorrow before you leave town."

"Whatever, Willie." She gives him more crap to no avail, then she gives up and leaves.

That night, Will watches the *Miami Vice* fourth season finale, called "Mirror Image," with Chumpy also watching, from two angles. In the episode, Sonny Crockett, mourning the death of his wife (Sheena Easton) at the hands of a criminal he busted but then was tricked into helping off Death Row with falsified evidence, is undercover as his alias Sonny Burnett on a boat. There's an explosion, and when Crockett wakes up, he thinks he's a drug dealer named Burnett and goes on a murderous crime spree, even shooting his partner, Tubbs, but not fatally. After killing a crooked cop, Burnett drives off into the horizon on a speedboat, as Tubbs frantically calls to him from the dock, *Sonny*!'"

As a fellow amnesia victim who got sucked into a cesspool of smut and scum, Chumpy can relate to Sonny's situation. Chumpy really, really hopes the show is renewed so he can find out what happens next, almost as much as Will does.

Lap dissolve.

Will, Chumpy, and Puss are watching the fifth season premiere of *Miami Vice*, called "Hostile Takeover." Still in his violently amnesiac state, Crockett, as Burnett, is taking over the crime family he was once investigating, and his love interest is the drug lord's sexy mistress, Celeste, played by Will's friend, Debra. Chumpy finds the irony amusing. His creator considers it cosmic torture.

"What does it all mean?" Will says aloud in the darkness of his empty room, or the room he believes is empty. "It can't all be a coincidence. It must be a clue. But to what? Why am I so lonely? Why can't I get laid? Why can't any of my books get a break? Why did I have to be raised in a fucked-up cult and have all these fucking nightmares? When will my life change?"

Chumpy wishes he knew the answers, because he has the same questions about his own existence. But even if he did think of any solutions, he'd be unable to convey them to his maudlin maker. It's as if Chumpy's mission and his creator's mission have converged. Or else, they've always been the same mission.

Lap dissolve.

Will is in the Bensonhurst section of Brooklyn, New York, visiting his schizophrenic mother, Charlotte, whom he has not seen since he was a child. Chumpy the walnut is sitting on the coffee table in her dark apartment. Will is lying next to the coffee table on the couch, pretending to be asleep, as his mother stands silhouetted in the doorway, smoking a cigarette, the light glowing in the dark like a one-eyed demon. But Will's mother is not herself a demon. She is only possessed by one. This does not prevent both Will and Chumpy from feeling terrified.

Lap dissolve.

Will is saying goodbye to Charlotte at her workplace, the Cuckoo Clock Company in Manhattan, where she's employed as a secretary. Will has a stack of neatly typed letters from his mother on stationery with the company's letterhead. Though Chumpy has never read any of them, he could tell from his creator's response to them that they were quite disturbing. This situation caused Chumpy to think about his own birth parents, who perished in the forest fire that destroyed his race, except for Cupey. He can't remember them, but he misses them just the same.

"Goodbye, William," Charlotte says to Will in a stoic monotone, as if in a trance, unable to look him in the eye, since she's trying not to cry, like Will and Chumpy do all the way back to the airport. Will wishes he could help her, but he can barely help himself.

Lap dissolve.

Chumpy the walnut is sitting on the counter of the front desk at The French Hotel in Berkeley, where Will has been employed as a desk clerk for about a year. Will is telling his friend PM about how a current guest, actress Sonia Braga, asked him out to dinner across the street at Chez Panisse. PM looks like a cynical hippie but is really a punk Elvis fan with a wry wit, long beaded hair, and sharply observant eyes, always assessing the human condition from a critical distance. He's one of Will's best friends. Besides Greg. And the walnut.

PM doesn't hold back from telling Will the truth, which is why he's a good, if occasionally annoying, friend.

"Dude, I can't believe you're always complaining about these other college girls breaking your heart, but then a movie star asks you out and you tell her to go fuck herself," PM says in his gently patronizing tone.

"I didn't tell her to go fuck herself."

"You might as well have."

"I can't just leave my job."

"Why? I leave my job all the time."

"But you work here, too."

"Well, I leave, then I come back. The door swings both ways. Like our boss."

"Do you?"

"What, swing both ways?"

"Yeah."

"Why not?" PM says with a smirk, which makes it hard to take anything he says seriously. "Is that an offer?"

"No, just wondering."

"About what, your options?"

"Nothing, forget it."

"Let me ask you something, and be honest."

"No, I'm not gay."

"Not that. I know you're not gay because gay guys always get laid. All the ones I know, anyway."

"What then?"

"Why do you carry that walnut around wherever you go?"

"It's my good luck charm."

"It's obviously not working."

"Hey, I met Sonia Braga, didn't I?"

"But then you blew it."

"So it's my fault I'm a bum."

"Well, you're not a punk, that's for sure. A punk would be on a Caribbean cruise with Sonia Braga right now, not sitting in this dump talking to a bum like me."

"We can't all be punks like Frank Sinatra."

"Frank's not a punk. He's not a bum. He's just frank about calling out punks and bums."

"What was Dino?"

"Bum. But he was Head Bum, so sort of a hybrid."

"Sammy?"

"Full-on Punk. Head Punk."

"Anyway, I found this walnut and drew a face on it to remind me."

"Remind you of what?"

"Chumpy Walnut. I never want to forget him."

"Why not?"

"I created him when I was in New Jersey. First, he was

a talking walnut in a comic strip. It helped me cope."

"I thought he was a little guy, like a foot tall or something?"

"Yeah, he was when I wrote the novel. That's why the figurine reminds me of him, too."

"What figurine?"

"It's at home, keeping Puss company."

"Can I meet him?" PM asks.

"Who, Chumpy?"

"Who else? I already met Puss. He's a cool cat."

"The walnut or the figurine?"

"The *real* one."

"He's not real."

"He's real to you, obviously."

"No, he's just a figment of my warped imagination."

"Maybe *you're* just a figment of your warped imagination."

"Maybe *you* are."

"Maybe you're a figment of *mine*!" PM says.

"That would explain a lot, actually. Okay, I told you about the walnut. Now you tell me something that's really been bugging me."

"Anything."

"What does PM stand for? The truth this time."

"Pretty Much."

"Pretty Much what?"

"Pretty Much whatever you need it to mean."

"So like life itself."

"Pretty much."

"You're never gonna tell me, are you?"

"First, do me a favor, or rather, make me a promise." Ironically, "The Promise" by When in Rome is playing on the sound system.

"What now?" Will says.

"Next time a movie star asks you out, ask yourself, What would Elvis do? '"

"I'm not Elvis."

"And you never will be until you start following his commandments."

"What're you, high priest of the Church of Elvis?"

"Yeah, I am actually."

"Really?"

"Would I ever lie to you?"

"Never mind," Will says, flustered. "So which Elvis commandment did I break?"

"'Don't.'"

"'Don't'? Don't *what*? Be Cruel?"

"That's a different commandment. You know the Elvis song 'Don't', right?"

"Dude, please. I'm a much bigger Elvis fan than you are."

"You're a much shorter one, I'll say that much for you."

"Well, I don't see how the commandment 'Don't' applies here, when I *didn't*."

"Two ways of looking at that. You either didn't take Sonia Braga up on her offer, or you didn't stop being a pussy long enough to have dinner with a movie star instead of going home and jerking off to *Kiss of the Spider Woman*."

"How did you know?"

"Because I know *you*."

"Okay, what about Return to Sender'? Isn't that a commandment?"

"Of course it is! But so is Now or Never.'"

"So if the commandments are all open to interpretation, how can you say I broke one?"

"You didn't break anything from a bum's interpretation. Only from a punk's interpretation. Which one do you think is the right interpretation from The King's perspective?"

Will thinks for a bit, then says, Now and then there's a fool such as I.'"

Chumpy must concur.

"Now one last time: what does PM stand for?"

"Pre-Meditated. Or Pre-Med for short."
"Aw, fuck."
"Partially Mutilated."
"Forget it."
"Primo Sexo."
"You're a pain the ass. So maybe it's Pain in the…um…"
"Peach Marmalade."
"Shut the fuck up."
"Pristine Mammogram."
"Okay, okay, I'll tell you."
"What?"
"Punk Motherfucker."
Sigh.

Lap dissolve.

Chumpy the walnut is in Will's pocket, while Chumpy the figurine is back in Will's recently acquired studio apartment on McKinley Avenue, across from the Berkeley Police Station and more conveniently around the corner from the UC Theater and Au Coquelet Cafe. Both the walnut and the figurine keep their telepathic feline friend, Puss, company when Will is not around. After a few minutes listening to Will's conversation, Chumpy correctly deduces that Will is talking to his friend Professor Curtis inside Famous Cult Videos. Some time has obviously passed since the Berkeley Flea Market days. "Nothing Compares 2 U" by Sinéad O'Connor plays on the sound system.

"I hope I won't get caught using the company car on weekends to come see you," Will says to Curtis. "But I need the therapy. Both your friendship and the videos. I don't know if I ever told you, but you were right about *The Swimmer*. It didn't change my life because I couldn't relate to that guy much, who was swimming in money and pussy. But I love the beautiful sadness of it, and the midcentury malaise, which at least *looks* pretty. I've watched it several times, and it's one of my favorite movies now."

"I told you it would broaden your perspective of

humanity."

"You did?"

"Well, I meant to. Or that's what I meant when I said whatever it is I actually did say."

"I hope it gets a proper release someday."

"Everything happens eventually, just not always when we want it to. Hardly ever, in fact."

"Yeah, I've had some sex recently, so that's a rare example."

"See? This is why I believe I miracles. You just gotta keep plugging away. So to speak."

"Yeah, I know. Meantime, you're my connection for illegal cinematic contraband."

"Happy to be your pusher, my man. That car outside is the one you use for your delivery job?"

"Yeah. I'm supposed to drop it off at work, but sometimes I take it home after they're closed, then bring it back before they notice and take the bus back home."

"What is it called again?"

"Pathology Institute. Or P.I. for short. It's a medical lab. I deliver various bodily fluids to various hospitals around the East Bay."

"All that I know. I just didn't know you moonlighted as a car thief."

"Don't tell anyone."

"My lips are sealed, my friend. Say, speaking of P.I., you should write a private eye novel."

"I've been thinking about it. The name of the detective would be Vic Valentine. And you'd be Doc, the owner of a video store that is also a bar."

"Hey, I like that!"

"Thanks, Doc!"

"Just write it down, man!"

"I will. I write everything down."

"Good. Keep at it. Something good will happen. I can feel it."

Lap dissolve.

Still at Famous Cult Videos, but a couple of years later. "The Fly" by U2 plays on the sound system.

Will says to Professor Curtis, "Have you seen Tom Savini's remake of *Night of the Living Dead*? It's on a par with the original, I think."

"I agree," Curtis says. "Romero wrote it, too."

"That's one reason. Really tight script. It couldn't have been any better if he directed it. Savini did a bang-up job, including the makeup. Great score, too. It's up there with the first three *Dead* movies in my book."

"Mine, too. When you say my book,' I take it you're not referring to your detective novel."

"Not yet."

"Damn!"

Will holds up a video case in his hand. "Hey, how is this movie here, *The Sinful Dwarf*?"

"Oh, I love it! Not a bad copy, either."

"So it's a good movie?"

"I wouldn't go that far. Lots of gore and gratuitous nudity, though."

"I'll take it."

"All right! Just toss it here on top of the trash heap."

"So anyway, remember that girl at the blood bank I like who is very shy, and I'm insecure, so I can't even get up the nerve to talk to her?"

"Yeah, so what else is new?"

"Well, I went around with a Polaroid and took pictures of where I *would* take her on a date: a movie theater, a restaurant, a cafe, a park, a movie theater, and whatnot, and pasted them into an album with hand-written captions, and gave it to her. It's called The Date That Never Was.' And now it's The Date That Will Never Be.'"

Curtis laughs. "So I guess the Polaroids made her paranoid?"

"Something like that."

"Did she call the cops?"

"No, she just gave it back. I'm putting it in my detective novel. Starting it soon."

"Finally! Am I still in it?"

"Of course! I'm hoping Judith Regan will like it as much as Chumpy Walnut.'"

"Oh, so she likes that one?"

"Well, it's the reason Wally Lamb recommended me to her after I interviewed him. Her assistant told me that whenever Judith is having a hard day, she says she feels like just Chumpy Walnut."

"Wow."

"But she seems to like my letters more than my manuscripts. She says I should write a memoir in my own voice."

"What? You seem a little young for a memoir. But what the hell? She wants it, get on it!"

"I'd rather write my life as fiction."

"Well, your life is stranger than fiction," Curtis says as "Unbelievable" by EMF starts playing on the sound system.

"Anyway, so my detective novel already has a title. It came up in a recent phone conversation with my father. Pop was asking me about my latest failed romance, and I said to him, I don't want to talk about that now. Love stories are too violent for me.' He laughed and said that should be the title of my next novel. I agreed, and so it is."

"Love it! Judith Regan probably will, too. What company is she from again?"

"Senior editor at Simon and Schuster."

"Man, that's the big leagues!"

"I know. I'm almost thirty, and my ship has finally come in. I just hope it doesn't back out of port without me."

"It won't."

"I hope she likes my latest. She didn't say much about my crime novel, Down a Dark Alley.'"

"The one inspired by those letters from your hot cousin

in jail back in Florida?"

"Yeah. My agent Marilyn likes it a lot, but says I'm not really a crime writer. She says I'm more the literary type. I don't know what I am; I just write what I feel. In any case, I still want to get Chumpy Walnut out there someday. I haven't forgotten about him."

(If Chumpy the walnut could cry inside Will's pocket, it would be like Will just peed his pants.)

"You will," Professor Curtis says with his usual optimism. "Just hang in there and keep the faith."

"I'm trying, Doc."

"Doc? Oh, right. That's me! Doc Schlock! What's my place in the book called again?"

"The Drive-Inn."

"Yes! Love it!"

"Oh, I was gonna tell you. That thing, The Date That Never Was'? Vic Valentine does the same thing for a girl he likes at the blood bank. Only he's just there to donate his own blood, not deliver everyone else's to hospital labs. She turns him down, too. But he doesn't care. He's more concerned about the case he's working on. This down-and-out baseball player hires Vic to find his missing wife, only when the baseball guy shows Vic a picture of her, Will realizes it's *his* long-lost love, the whole reason he became a detective in the first place."

"You mean Vic realizes it."

"Yeah! What did I say?"

"You said Will realizes it.'"

"Oh, sorry. Yeah, Vic. Not me. Definitely not me."

Curtis chuckles as he shakes his head. "In any case, that all sounds great! Maybe it'll be a movie someday!"

"Let's not get ahead of ourselves. I still have to get it published first."

"You will. One way or another. Trust me. I just know."

"Anyway, got any more of those seventies lesbian vampire movies from Europe? I need a date for the weekend."

"Of course! Comin' right up! I got some more Bettie Page loops for you, too!"

"Awesome! I'll spend Christmas Day watching them!"

"Please don't tell me that."

Lap dissolve.

Will is placing Puss inside a pet carrier. He is obviously devastated beyond description. Puss is no longer communicating with Chumpy because he's too sick and weak. Will walks out of the little apartment with the carrier containing Puss, and an hour or so later, returns with the empty carrier. Will is sobbing uncontrollably, and Chumpy desperately wishes to console him, even if he's lost his only friend in the world, too, at least the only one aware of his existence.

Lap dissolve.

Kyle and Catherine are talking to Will in the Bowker Room of the UC Berkeley Faculty Club. It's after lunch, and "Come As You Are" by Nirvana is on the sound system.

"Catherine and I are starting our own publishing company, Wild Card Press," Kyle says. "We'd like to publish your book."

"Which one?"

"You pick," Kyle says.

"Are you sure? I found all my manuscripts in the bushes outside my apartment building once Judith Regan left Simon and Schuster to start her own imprint. She didn't even explain what changed her mind."

"Well, we're not Simon and Schuster, but we'll do what we can," Catherine tells Will.

"I appreciate that. Really. What are you going to call your company?"

"Wild Card Press," Catherine says.

"Yeah, that's me, all right."

"So now choose just one, and give it to us to read," Kyle

says.

"Okay. Chumpy Walnut.'"

"Not commercial in today's market," Kyle says. "At least from what I know of it. Plus, you wrote that as a kid. Anything more recent and relevant?"

"Okay. I think *Love Stories Are Too Violent For Me* is more commercial."

Kyle nods and shakes Will's hand. "We'll read it and let you know."

Lap dissolve.

Will is wearing a cheap tux as he stands with a cheaply made-up woman wearing a cheap wedding dress in the rather cheap comedy section of a relatively cheap video store called Movie Image in downtown Berkeley, where Will is cheaply employed as a clerk. It's after hours, his shift has ended, and the store is closed. Will somehow convinced himself it would be appropriate to secretly borrow the store for his private wedding ceremony so he can marry the colorful and very pretty customer he's been dating for about a month, even though she's bipolar and has recently decided she will only have sex with her husband. Will is slowly dying of loneliness and horniness, so he concludes expedited nuptials are the only possible solution to his pain. PM is standing before them as minister from the Church of Elvis, Greg from L.A. is at Will's side as his best man, and Chumpy is in Will's pocket, wondering what the hell is going on as Will and his new bride dance to the wedding scene of *Goodfellas* playing on the store's TV. Chumpy remembers Greg and wants him to stop it, but it happens anyway. The newlywed's first couple of weeks are blissful; the following month is brutal. Chumpy finds it torturous to witness.

Lap dissolve.

Will and Kyle are in a bar called Spats on Shattuck Avenue in downtown Berkeley. "I'm Only Happy When It

Rains" by Garbage is playing on the sound system. Kyle is saying, "Catherine and I are finally opening a movie theater, and we'd like you to program and host your own show to help promote the book."

"I have no experience with that."

"I have faith in you. You host those annual Elvis parties with PM and Cory all the time, so I know you can do it."

"Okay, thanks! I'll try. It beats hauling boxes in a travel guide warehouse or working in a bookstore." Will is referring to his most recent employment failures at the Lonely Planet distribution center in Oakland and Half-Price Books on Solano Avenue in North Berkeley.

"Any ideas?" Kyle asks. "I'm wide open."

"I think I'll assume the identity of a swingin' lounge lizard and call myself 'Will the Thrill.' That's what one of the other drivers at the blood bank called me."

"You mean after Will Clark."

"Who?"

"Jesus, dude, seriously? Will fuckin' Clark! First baseman for the Giants!"

"I know, but I'm not a sports fan, you know that."

Kyle shakes his head and sighs. "At least you know about movies, that's all that matters to me right now."

"I'd like to show a lot of old cult movies, plus some newer ones."

"Like what?"

"*Blue Velvet* would definitely be my first."

"That'll work."

"I can give out prizes and shit and have my new wife be my lovely assistant."

"Please don't."

"Give out prizes?"

"Only if your so-called wife is one of them."

"Why?"

"She's crazy, Will."

"No, she just has an unusually, um…well, an unusual

personality."

"To put it nicely. And she's an alcoholic."

"Not a practicing alcoholic. She's in AA, as you know. For years now. She really works the program, and it's the most helpful organization I've ever seen. She hasn't had a drink in years."

"Won't she be tempted since we'll be offering beer and wine?"

"No. She's not gullible and easily susceptible to temptation."

"Unlike you, apparently."

Chumpy sighs to himself in complete accordance with Kyle. "She Drives Me Crazy" by Fine Young Cannibals plays on the sound system.

Lap dissolve.

Will is wearing cheap sunglasses even though he's indoors, a vintage smoking jacket he bought at Stop the Clock in downtown Berkeley from his friend Karen, a wrinkled aloha shirt, and ill-fitting black slacks. He is standing on the stage of the refurbished Parkway Theater in Oakland, addressing a small crowd of patrons anxious to get to the movie. There is a big carnival wheel behind him. Chumpy is in the pocket of the smoking jacket, wondering what the hell any of this has to do with *him*.

Will speaks with natural assurance as he introduces the feature. He's not nervous because he just doesn't care anymore. "Tonight's movie, as you know, is the Elvis classic *Jailhouse Rock*. Since my first lovely assistant and ex-wife split up, I've been auditioning new lovely assistants and possibly new wives by selecting candidates from the audience. I met the perfect candidate in the lobby just now. She looks like Scarface's sister. Monica, would you like to come here and spin my wheel? I'll give you this Elvis blanket as a reward."

"It's not a blanket, it's a towel," Monica yells back as she heads toward the stage.

Lap dissolve.

Will is standing alone in the doorway of the Ivy Room in Albany, California, depressed as usual, considering walking away from his own public Elvis Birthday Party, when a stunning Latina about to enter the bar walks up and says to him, "Hey, I know you! Aren't you that guy who gave me an Elvis towel at the Parkway, but you called it a blanket?"

Lap dissolve.

Will, now employed full-time as the Parkway's Programmer/Publicist, is standing before an altar outside of the Cal-Neva Lodge & Casino, inside a gazebo facing glistening North Lake Tahoe on a bright, sunny day in May. By his side is the same gorgeous woman he chose to be his lovely assistant exactly three years earlier. Though it wasn't her initial ambition, she eventually got the wife gig, too. Will the Thrill is wearing a real tux patterned after Sean Connery's white jacket in the opening segment of *Goldfinger*. Monica—better known around the Bay Area as Monica Tiki Goddess, co-host of Will the Thrill's popular Thrillville Theater show at the Parkway—is wearing a glamorous wedding gown as she passionately recites her vows before an audience of family and friends. They have all traveled great distances for this very special occasion, even though it's a Thursday. But this date, May 31, 2001, happens to be the precise fourth anniversary of Monica spinning the wheel before *Jailhouse Rock* on stage at the Parkway, so it just had to be. Will's best man is Greg, and one of his groomsmen is PM. Chumpy recognizes their voices. Their pastor is a Dean Martin impersonator friend named Robert, who presides in Dino style as mariachis from Oakland perform Elvis and Sinatra songs in Spanish, both before and after the ceremony. Afterwards, there is an epic reception in the Frank Sinatra Celebrity Showroom, with an open martini bar. The cocktail menu is filled with customized cocktails named after the showroom's storied performers, like "The Dean Martini" and "The Ann-Margretini," as well as lounge lizard libations like "The 007" and "The Tiki-Tini." Scenes from the original Rat Pack classic *Ocean's 11* play silently on a big screen behind the mariachis. Later, during the cake cutting, it switches to scenes from *Blue Hawaii*, where the couple is about to spend their honeymoon.

"You really are my good luck charm," Will whispers to his walnut while he is dancing with his bride to Elvis singing "Can't Help Falling in Love." Will programmed the entire reception and wedding soundtracks, so it's chock full of lounge, jazz, soul, and exotic classics.

"You're mine, too," Monica smiles, thinking her husband was talking to her.

"You're the result of my good luck charm in my pocket."

"Well, don't flatter yourself *too* much."

Then they embrace as if they will never let go now that they've finally found each other and made it official. The next song is "The Best is Yet to Come," by Frank Sinatra, then "More" by Bobby Darin.

Chumpy is happy for his creator because, after years suffering one heartbreak after another, Will has finally found true love and happiness, just as Chumpy did at the end of the first book, before the second book was written over two decades later, and Chumpy's life as he knew it was destroyed, seemingly forever. Now Chumpy is more confused than ever about why his romance was ruined. It's just not fair, and Chumpy won't rest until he evens the score.

Chapter Nine
ATTACK OF THE CUBAN TIGER SHARK

Chumpy the figurine falls out of the breast pocket of Will's guayabera shirt as he slips on the slippery surface of the fishing boat off the coast of Miami. Will sees the figurine flying through the marine air in slow motion, landing into the gaping mouth of the shark, thrashing around on the stern, as Christian Slater tries to stop his beautiful fiancée, Brittany, from getting too close to its gnashing teeth. While this maritime melee is unfolding, the fishing boat's skipper, who looks just like a fishing boat skipper—in fact, he looks a bit like Will's sailor statue, Ivar—explains that it's a rare Cuban Tiger Shark, and per local laws, it must be thrown back into the ocean. Of course, no one present will actually climb down, pick up the shark, and toss it back in the broth. Eventually, the shark rolls off the boat into the water, and Chumpy the figurine is left stranded inside the shark's stomach, like Pinocchio inside the whale. Will is distraught as he explains to Christian the significance of the fallen figurine.

"Don't worry, you can get another one," Christian Slater tells him. "It wouldn't be as easy to get new fingers."

"But that was a very special figurine," Will says.

"Aren't your fingers special?"

"Yeah, I guess. Especially when I'm alone."

"Exactly! I need you to have your fingers intact so you can type up our screenplay. I have a whole display case of *Star Wars* figures at my place. Maybe I can find one for you."

Will nods sadly in phony appreciation. His new friend, Christian, doesn't understand why that particular figurine can't be replaced with a miniature Stormtrooper. Will isn't even a *Star Wars* fan, but he doesn't admit this to Christian. They do share common interests in the original *Star Trek* series, Frank Sinatra, and, best of all, Vic Valentine, and that's all that matters.

It is the momentous year of 2012, and not just due to the alien invasion foretold by *The X-Files*. Chumpy's creator is having the time of his life, as all of his dreams seem to be coming true at once, while Chumpy is languishing in a state of listless limbo, his creator's life flashing before his virtual eyes without revealing any further, tangible clues to Chumpy's own existential dilemma, including the fact he currently has no way of returning to his own life, and his own wife.

As the tragic shark situation unfolds clear across the country, Will's wife, Monica, and their cats, Tiki and Googie, are resting obliviously in the Capri condo complex, a midcentury modern building on Shoreline Drive in Alameda, CA. Before Googie, there was Bubba, who sadly passed away the day the first book about Chumpy's life was officially self-published by Will, an irony that haunts both Will and Chumpy. Meanwhile, Chumpy the walnut is safely back inside Will's hotel room at the Shelbourne on Miami Beach, where Christian put Will up in a luxury suite. The walnut knows exactly what happened to his twin and feels the figurine's fear, since they share the same soul, but he can do nothing to stop it. Chumpy worries about what will happen to him if the figurine is not rescued and simply discarded as just another piece of plastic debris polluting the sea. Seeing no positive outcome, Chumpy braces himself for the worst. As the figurine is flailing about inside the shark's nasty stomach, Chumpy sees memories of his epic journey playing like a memorial reel in his mind's eye, even though, as a walnut, he technically has neither.

The most upsetting memory is his creator's first trip to Miami in 1992, to visit Charlotte, who was then living with her mother, also named Charlotte. Though still suffering severe schizophrenia, she was medicated enough for a pleasant visit, unlike the one in Brooklyn, where she was sedated, but slightly scary. Will is deeply unsettled by her ongoing, incurable condition, and this hopeless sadness trickles down to Chumpy.

Otherwise, Chumpy has enjoyed the last decade or so, which, from his temporal vantage point, passed relatively quickly. It has been especially edifying since he now has two feline companions. At first, Tiki tried to maul the figurine, then Googie tried to swallow the walnut, but in both cases, Chumpy's squeaky pleas for mercy prevailed. But he doesn't think the shark would be as open to negotiation, since sharks are not normally keen on compromise. Chumpy hopes that if the shark consumes and digests the figurine, his walnut iteration will absorb the twin soul, and he'll be whole again, or he will simply disappear, and his soul will return to his dimension. This will be unfortunate, for several reasons, mostly because Chumpy has not yet discovered the mysterious misfortune that befell his creator, beyond the childhood traumas and various non-lethal setbacks that might have influenced Chumpy's tragic trajectory.

Besides this perpetually gnawing discontent with how his own life turned out in his dimension—one reason he is hesitant to return, as much as he misses Cupey—there is also the increasingly intense jealousy of his creator's other protagonist and doppelgänger, Vic Valentine, the subject of the book, *Love Stories Are Too Violent For*, which is now in the process of being adapted to a film by Christian Slater, who plans to both star as Vic and direct. Chumpy keeps rhetorically asking their shared Universe, "What about me? Where's *my* movie?" He feels he's been completely sidelined by Vic Valentine, whom he has personally met in an alternative incarnation back in Thrillville. Chumpy liked that version of Vic, but would like him more if he were a character in *Chumpy's* movie.

Speaking of movies, one of the benefits of physically residing in his creator's home and being carried around in his creator's pocket is that they both love movies. Chumpy has many happy memories of listening to, if not actually watching, hundreds of films over the years. His three favorite filmmakers of this realm are David Lynch, Jim Jarmusch, and Russ Meyer, which also happen to be his creator's three favorite filmmakers, which Chumpy acknowledges is by psychic design, not random coincidence. The burning question is how much of his sentient existence is comprised of these two elements, and to what extent does each deserve the credit, or the blame, for his soul-searching sojourn.

It is obvious to Chumpy that Jim Jarmusch movies like *Stranger Than Paradise*, *Down by Law*, *Mystery Train*, *Dead Man*, and *Ghost Dog* had some influence on the second book of his life (yet to be written at this juncture), in their idiosyncratic tone and feel if not content, but not as much as the films of David Lynch like *Eraserhead* (which Chumpy first watched when it was new), *The Elephant Man*, *Blue Velvet*, *Wild at Heart*, *Twin Peaks: Fire Walk with Me*, *Lost Highway*, *The Straight Story*, *Mulholland Drive*, and *Inland Empire*. While he loves all of these movies, he is saddened by the fact that his old friend David still hasn't been able to find financing for "Ronnie Rocket," with which Chumpy would no doubt relate the most.

Chumpy can vicariously sense the visceral resonance of certain films with his creator, like *Repo Man*, *Ghost World*, *American Splendor*, *Sideways*, and *Swingers*. Stylistically, Chumpy sees parallels to his world in the films *Sin City* and *Sin City: A Dame to Kill*. Robert Rodriguez is one of Will's top 10 favorite filmmakers. Chumpy is particularly a fan of *Machete*, *Machete Kills Again*, and *Once Upon a Time in Mexico,* as is Will, of course.

It's quite clear to Chumpy that the frenetically frolicking

films of Russ Meyer—such as *Faster Pussycat, Kill! Kill!*; *Common Law Cabin*; *Good Morning...and Goodbye*!; *Finders Keepers Losers Weepers*; *Cherry, Harry, and Raquel*; *Vixen*; *Supervixens*; and *Beneath the Valley of the Ultra-Vixens*—provided direct inspiration for the women of his dimension. This influence is particularly evident when it comes to the Bombshell Ballbreakers, a socially conscious squadron of voluptuous vixens that includes his old friend Hotsie Totsie, Lola Lovejoy (formerly Moxy Galore), Paige Pinup, Queen Exotica, and Cupey Honeysuckle. Collectively, they are the proprietors of the Monster Sex Motel back in Thrillville, an enterprise they founded more out of fiscal prudence than pity, once their progressive political coalition, the Bombshell Party, failed miserably at the ballot box, and their attempt to enslave the oppressive patriarchy and propagate the species with stockpiles of semen, obtained via duplicitous fellatio and stored in the basement of Ivar's Tiki Bar, bombed spectacularly.

One of Chumpy's favorite experiences during this period of surreptitious co-existence with his creator was the time Will hosted a birthday party for the star of *Faster Pussycat, Kill!, Kill*!, Tura Satana, whose company Chumpy had previously enjoyed earlier, when Will was introduced to Tura by her friend and manager, Siouxzan. Chumpy was the third happy nut in Will's pocket when he was posing for a picture of his creator romping with Tura on her hotel bed. The birthday party took place at Will's favorite haunt, Forbidden Island Tiki Lounge, in Alameda. Will's friends, Michael and Mano, were the proprietors. Will often hung out there with other mutual friends like Otto and Dorinda, AKA Baby Doe, producers of the annual Tiki Oasis event, first held in Palm Springs and later in San Diego. Chumpy, who misses his aloha shirt and his mai tais, vicariously soaked up the Ohana there when Will and Monica attended, often to host "tiki movie" screenings.

At Tura's birthday party, Will went to the bathroom to scratch an itch on his inner thigh. He sometimes sweated too much in the California heat and was already contemplating a move north. Monica called his itchy thighs and buttocks "diaper rash." But Will didn't want his wife patting his thighs down with baby powder in a public bathroom, even if she had some handy. While soothing his red, bumpy thighs with a damp toilet paper, the walnut fell out of Will's pocket and rolled behind the toilet, unseen by Will.

Right after that, a drunken patron barged in and pushed Will aside, trying to make it to the toilet before it was too late, but he vomited all over the floor instead. Repulsed but unsullied, Will tells Michael, AKA Conga Mike, because he also co-owned the Conga Lounge in Oakland with his brother Mano. As he was mopping up the mess, Conga Mike found the walnut on the floor, covered in bile, and, for reasons that weren't clear to him, he cleaned it off with a towel, then, unable to simply dispose of it, he set it down on the bar of the busy tiki lounge, while he tended to customers who had been waiting to order, like Otto, noticed the walnut right away. Being a vegetarian, Otto dropped the walnut in his cocktail as an impromptu garnish, incidentally soaking Chumpy in premium rum while spiking his drink with residual puke. After a sip, Otto gagged, plucked out the inebriated legume, and tossed it to the floor, where it rolled beneath Tura's table.

Tura felt the walnut under one of her feet, picked it up, and, smiling at the little face painted on it, put it inside her tight black top as a souvenir of this special celebration in her honor. A tipsy Chumpy was happily ensconced within Tura's famous cleavage for the duration of the event, feeling he could die happily there, as the aromatic ambrosia of her bountiful bosoms negated all lingering puke fumes. Chumpy even managed to wish her a happy birthday, and Tura thought she heard him, but wasn't sure.

When Tura rose to leave the lounge as the party ended, the walnut slipped down to her belly. Feeling the irritation, Tura slightly lifted her tight black top, and the walnut dropped out, landing on the floor beneath Will's feet, who immediately picked it up.

"I didn't know that was yours!" Tura said to Will.

"Neither did I!" both Otto and Michael, standing behind Will, said in unison.

"For some reason, I wanted to take care of it," Tura explained, "so I put it between my breasts for protection."

"I'm glad you did!" Will said, kissing the walnut. "It's like it's been blessed!"

"*Go, baby, go!*" said Siouxzan, standing beside Tura.

Chumpy later saw Siouxzan and her partner Helen at the Tonga Hut in Palm Springs, along with author David J. Schow and his lady Kerry, and Will's old friends Mel and Jessica, for Will's 59th birthday dinner. This shindig was of particular interest to Chumpy because he finally got to meet, from a pocket perspective, Mel and Jessica, who gifted the sailor statue later dubbed "Ivar" to Will as a gag. Ivar, as a sometimes sentient but always suspiciously supernatural statue, became a regular in the Vic Valentine series and is now the owner of Ivar's Tiki Lounge, which resembles a more spacious version of Forbidden Island Tiki Lounge, in *The Romance of Chumpy Walnut*. Ivar the statue kept psychic tabs on Cupey in Chumpy's dimension, where Ivar's core consciousness is currently manifested.

Chumpy also indirectly met Raven de La Croix, star of Russ Meyer's *Up!*, not to be confused with the Pixar film of the same title, during a Thrillville event at the Parkway, which featured a debut screening of the film *The Double D Avenger*, directed by William Winckler, on a double bill with *Mark of the Astro Zombies,* a sequel to Tura's film *Astro Zombies*, shown separately in a different Thrillville show. Both *Astro Zombies* movies were directed by another of Will's cult movie acquaintances, Ted V. Mikels, whom

Chumpy had encountered when Will and Monica visited the eccentric filmmaker in his film studio/warehouse in Las Vegas, where Monica marveled at Ted's economical ingenuity, such as a common fan painted to look like a rocket ship console. Chumpy could literally feel Will's excitement as he shared the stage with Raven, whom, as Chumpy knew, was one of Will's secret crushes.

So far, Chumpy has not yet been exposed via voyeuristic osmosis to the erotically surrealistic *oeuvre* of Jean Rollin, Will's fourth favorite filmmaker. This alone is worth sticking around in his creator's dimension, as Chumpy is quite curious why these films were in his consciousness upon arrival to this dimension, three decades earlier.

Quentin Tarantino is fifth on the list of his creator's favorite filmmakers, and while Chumpy finds QT's films highly entertaining, he fails to see any direct correlation with his own conception. Chumpy figures Vic Valentine would probably feel artistic resonance with the films *Reservoir Dogs, Pulp Fiction*, *Jackie Brown*, *Kill Bill* Volumes 1 and 2, and *Death Proof* (half of the Rodriguez/Tarantino double-bill-in-one-film *Grindhouse*, another of Chumpy's personal favorites). Tarantino's most recent films at this point, *Inglorious Basterds* and *Django Unchained*, were also quite enjoyable, but Chumpy doesn't feel that either WW2 or Western aesthetics suit his world, or Vic's, or his creator's, for that matter. However, Fate the Pimp, Vain Vinnie, Nice Try Alfie, Nick the Nice Prick, and Tanisha Alopecia definitely seem like dual residents of Tarantino's cinematic universe, so perhaps there was some indirect influence on his life story, on this third book if not the second. From what he has secretly read, Will's gratuitously pulpy crime/sex novel *Down a Dark Alley* is the most Tarantino-esque of his books, even though it was written in 1992, before Will saw *Reservoir Dogs*, released later the same year, so the incidental resonance is retroactive. Tarantino wrote the screenplay for Chumpy's favorite of his films besides *Pulp Fiction*, called *True Romance*, starring Christian Slater. Will saw it when it premiered in 1993, a few months after he wrote the ironically, similarly titled novel, *Love Stories Are Too Violent For Me*.

Chumpy is intrigued by the fact that his creator has so much in common, at least superficially, with Quentin Tarantino, except for the fact that Tarantino is successful and Will, so far, is not, though perhaps the Vic Valentine movie will change that. For one thing, Will once worked in that video store called Movie Image in Berkeley. Though he appreciated all the movies played on the store's TV during business hours, Chumpy was also forced to listen to the insipid banter of Will and his friends and co-workers, Robert and Jeremy, which grew quite tiresome. Later, Chumpy bore witness to Will's makeshift wedding in the store's comedy section, as already chronicled. Additionally and perhaps more disturbingly, Will has a female foot fetish, as evidenced by the uncomfortable fact that Will and Monica were featured in a foot fetishistic segment, called "Tootsie Roles," of the 24th episode of the HBO series *Real Sex*. Chumpy isn't sure whether he is proud of his creator or embarrassed by him.

Speaking of sleazy sex, one genre beloved by his creator that seems to have decided the descent of Chumpy's dimension into carnal chaos is grindhouse cinema, the inspiration for the movie *Grindhouse,* as well as his creator's novels, *A Mermaid Drowns in the Midnight Lounge, Freaks That Carry Your Luggage Up to the Room,* and *Lavender Blonde*; the novella *Things I Do When I'm Awake*; and the short story collection *VIHORROR! Cocktales of Sex and Death*. This factor particularly applies to the lurid European exploitation films of the 1970s and '80s by the likes of Jess Franco, Dario Argento, Lucio Fulci, and Paul Naschy. Chumpy assumes Jean Rollin, a French filmmaker who apparently reveled in ribald raunchiness, will be seen as a key ingredient in this same sumptuously sleazy stew. Chumpy's incidental and unavoidable psychic absorption of these films has greatly increased not only his awareness, but also, to his hesitant chagrin, his appreciation of the wanton world-building of the second book. A final verdict verifying and justifying this abrupt shift in narrative dynamics remains to be revealed.

Furthermore, Will's personal experiences with real grindhouse filmmakers like Ray Dennis Steckler seem to have contributed to the deterioration of his creator's increasingly deranged imagination, leading Chumpy to suspect no particular event warped his creator's psyche so much as his strong affinity for the strange, the sensual, and the psychotic in underground and alternative world cinema. Will's preoccupation with the graphic sex and violence from this particular era in film history remains unexplained, unless he's simply a sick fuck, as Chumpy is wont to suspect.

Chumpy had a blast being a pocket-bound party to the time Will, wearing a latex mummy mask and wielding a plastic axe, both from original road shows, chased Ray Steckler around the Parkway Theater during a screening of *The Incredibly Strange Creatures That Stopped Living and Became Mixed-up Zombies*, playing on a double bill with *The Thrill Killers*, promoted as "Valentine's Day with Ray Dennis Steckler," since the occasion indeed took place on February 14, 2002. Ray always brought his own worn-out 35mm prints from his home in Las Vegas to show in Thrillville Theater, and the print for *Incredibly Strange Creatures* (which was actually alternatively entitled *Teenage Psycho Meets Bloody Mary*) was not only faded pink but very fragile, breaking several times during the show. It was during these unscheduled interludes that Will, Ray, and some cast members of Barely Legal, presenters of the weekly *Rocky Horror Picture Show* screenings at the Parkway, whom Chumpy had first encountered at the UC

Theater in Berkeley, ran about the packed auditorium like rabid lunatics to the audience's delight. Chumpy actually fell out of Will's pocket during the chase, retrieved by Monica Tiki Goddess, who at the time was unaware of the walnut's secret sentience, knowing only how much her husband cherished its symbolic significance.

One of Barely Legals' founding members, Mick Turpel, became one of Chumpy's biggest champions after the first book was published, going so far as to contact his pals at Pixar in Emeryville about a possible film adaptation, which excited Chumpy. Tragically, Mick died suddenly in an accident at his home, so this plan never reached fruition. Once, when Mick was hanging out at Forbidden Island Tiki Lounge with Will, Chumpy managed to telepathically thank him for his support, and Chumpy knew the message got through, because Mick responded to Will, "You're welcome." Will wasn't sure what he meant, but Chumpy did. It was another instance where a person other than his creator was receptive to, if not cognitive of, Chumpy's shell-bound presence.

Another public event that directly connected Will's world to Chumpy's was the time Will read from his "grindhouse" novels *A Mermaid Drowns in the Midnight Lounge* (which Will has proclaimed as his personal favorite, within Chumpy's earshot, eliciting more envy) and *Lavender Blonde* (which is Will's friend Greg's favorite, another point of prideful pain for Chumpy) at a staged literary showcase hosted by Naked Girls Reading, the San Francisco chapter of the national organization of libertine ladies promoting literature while undressed before an appreciate audience of equally open-minded book lovers. Will and Monica wore robes, though, even though Will had been tempted to wear only his customized Thrillville fez hat. The reason this correlated with Chumpy's cross-dimensional consciousness was that the Bombshell Ballbreakers routinely read from books while nude at Ivar's

Tiki Lounge in Thrillville.

Throughout this period, Chumpy was elated to be reunited, even by pocket proxy, with actresses Stella Stevens, Deborah Walley, Julie Parrish, and Yvonne Craig, whom he remembered from his initial meeting with them back in Los Angeles. Additionally, Chumpy enjoyed the company of another "Elvis babe," Joan Blackman, who co-starred in *Blue Hawaii* and *Kid Galahad*. Will knew them all via his stepmother, Anne Helm, whom Chumpy finally met when she came up to Oakland from her Los Angeles home to appear with her friend Deborah Walley for a screening of Deborah's film with Elvis, *Spinout*. Unfortunately, all of Elvis's musical numbers were mysteriously missing from he 35mm print supplied by the distributor, so Will pitched it as "The Thespian Cut," since the print exclusively highlighted Elvis's acting skills.

But now, in the present, Chumpy is sitting alone on a bedside table in a dark Miami hotel room, feeling very film noir, as Will's friend Eddie Muller, the "Czar of the Noir," a big fan of the first Chumpy book, would put it. But then his inner retrospective suddenly jumps cut to visions of his creator at this very moment…

Will is inside Christian's luxurious penthouse pad a few miles away, and the three accidental shark hunters are eating the fish they actually did catch and keep, skillfully prepared by Brittany. (Will is not yet a vegan, but a pescatarian, though he's had no red meat since he was a boy in Houston. Both Will and Monica will not assume Chumpy's naturally vegan diet till a few years later, and Chumpy takes all the credit, feeling he subconsciously influenced their decision to steal his own ethical diet.) After dinner, throughout which Will quietly mourns the loss of his figurine, Christian walks his dog Dexter, with Will joining them, which is ironic, considering Will will eventually become a full-time dog walker, and Christian will star on the TV series *Dexter: Original Sin*. Then, back in the penthouse, Christian shows

Will an episode of his short-lived TV series *Breaking In,* which he also directed, titled "Episode XIII." Being Christian's directorial debut, the episode is a tribute to *Star Wars*, featuring a guest appearance by Peter Mayhew, who played Chewbacca. Christian is very excited about it, even if this is the final episode that will air, which is one reason he finally contacted Will to collaborate on the long-simmering adaptation of *Love Stories Are Too Violent For Me*, first optioned in 2001, a few months after Will's wedding.

"I was thinking we'd dedicate our script to Dennis Hopper," Christian says to Will. "You know, because he did that stage reading of an early draft of mine that he read with Bradley Cooper."

"Works for me. I love that he played Doc, even though Doc is black. Bradley Cooper would be perfect as Tommy, though."

"I've also talked to Ving Rhames for Doc, and I'm thinking Travolta for Luke Brandon if Mickey passes."

"I like Crispin Glover for Bobby Bundy."

"That would definitely be ideal. I just hope Tony plays Simon like he basically promised, in so many words."

"Tony?"

"Hopkins."

"Oh, right." Will is trying not to hyperventilate with euphoric anticipation. "This all seems too good to be true. I hope it works out."

"Me too, Will. I put a lot of work into this, as you know. It's worth it. It means a lot to me, too."

"Wow, thank you, man." Then Will tells Christian, "You know, when I first saw *True Romance*, I thought it was made just for me."

"That's how I felt when I read your book," Christian replies sincerely.

"Amazing. So you found it in that bookstore in Brentwood where my father's wife, Paige, was manager?"

"Yeah. Though I didn't know your father's wife even worked there."

"Yeah, she stocked the book."

"Small world," Christian says. "Anyway, I saw it on the shelf and was immediately intrigued by everything about it. The cover, the title, the few bits I read, you know. I put it on the pile of books my wife and I had chosen. When we left the store, I looked in the bag of books for it, but couldn't find it. I asked my wife where it was, and she said, Oh, you actually wanted that? I put it back!' Obviously, I went back inside to buy it. And here we are."

"Here we are." But Will really wanted to know where the figurine was. He figured it was a piece of plastic shark poop floating deep in the Atlantic Ocean by now. Will tried not to focus on it and remain in the unprecedented magic of the moment.

"You're still bummed about that thing you lost to the shark, huh?" Christian observes.

"Yeah. I'm sorry."

"No, I get it. I'm pretty sentimental myself about certain things. Here, let's go look for a replacement."

Christian proudly shows Will his collection of five and six-inch figures from the *Star Wars* universe, displayed neatly behind glass. Will pretends to be interested until he sees the Chumpy figurine standing between C3PO and R2D2.

"Hey, that's Chumpy!" Will exclaims, trying to open the glass case.

"No, don't!" Christian says. "I mean, please, be careful. Who's Chumpy'?"

"That's the name of the figurine, after the character of my first book. It's my good luck charm. I'm very sentimental about it."

"I get it, but that *can't* be it, because…wait a minute…"

Christian opens the case and carefully removes Chumpy, the figurine, and hands it to Will.

"How did this get in here?" Will asks the Universe.

"That's what I'd like to know!" Christian says.

"Oh, wait, that's the same one the shark ate?" says Brittany, walking up behind them after overhearing their conversation from the kitchen.

"Yes!" Will says. "How did you know?"

"I didn't! When I was cleaning the fish for dinner, I found it just lying on the floor, so I put it in the case because I thought it was Christian's."

"Honey, that's not from *Star Wars*!" Christian tells his bride-to-be.

"Yeah, I don't even like *Star Wars*!" Will says in a potentially fatal slip.

"What? The movie is *off*!" Christian says, temporarily torpedoing Will's elation. Then he slaps Will on his crestfallen shoulder. "Just kidding, buddy! C'mon, I want to show you the action figures I had custom-made of me as Vic!"

"Hey, don't you want to know how that thing got from the shark to here?" Brittany says. "I sure do!"

"To quote *This is Spinal Tap*, some mysteries are best left unsolved," Christian says.

"I wonder if the fish we caught was in the shark's belly, and the fish swallowed the figure," Will says. "The shark belched out the fish. We caught it. Then, when Brittany sliced it open, the figurine fell out."

"That's what Vic Valentine would probably deduce!" Christian says.

"No, he's not that good."

"You're probably right."

In fact, this scenario is exactly how it happened.

"This is a miracle," Will says. "Right up there with you randomly finding my obscure book in a bookstore and optioning it for a movie."

"Life is a miracle," Christian says. "It's all meant to be, buddy. You just gotta roll with it, wherever it goes. Like a walnut falling out of a tree. Or in this case, a shark."

"Onward Christian Slater!" Will says.

Back in the Shelbourne, Chumpy the walnut is sleeping peacefully, dreaming of a better future for his creator and himself. In these dreams, Chumpy bears witness via pocket proximity to many adventures in many exotic places with exotic names like Palm Springs, Houston, Boston, Minneapolis, Chicago, Atlanta, Vancouver, Mexico, Hawaii, and Memphis.

The most exhilarating travel experience for Chumpy was in February of 2017, when his creator was honored with an invitation to be an instructor at the Writer's Retreat of San Buenas in Costa Rica, organized by writer Ezekiel Tyrus. Will missed his home, wife, and cats back in Seattle so much that he didn't enjoy the trip as much as he thought he would, except for the new aspiring author friends he made, which included actor John Kapelos, famous for playing the janitor in *The Breakfast Club,* among many other roles, including a guest stint on *Miami Vice*, which seemingly connected more breads crumbs on Will's seemingly wayward trail.

Still, Will was grateful for the experience and appreciated the adventure, which inspired his novel *Vic Valentine, International Man of Misery.* Chumpy accompanied Will as the walnut this time, and likes to think Will absorbed some empathy via pocket osmosis. Chumpy didn't get to see much of the local scenery or soak up much of the atmosphere beyond the palm trees and exotic animals outside the window of Will's guest room in the luxurious compound. Will was too worried about losing the walnut after the shark incident in Miami, so he didn't venture out in the jungle or to the beach with his precious pal precariously placed in the pocket of his cargo shorts. Chumpy was rather relieved. He'd seen plenty of beach and jungle in Tikiti back in his dimension, and he didn't want his journey to end in this strange, alien world inside the belly of a snake.

Lap dissolve.

After a particularly long, blissfully dreamless rest, Chumpy awaken to see that Will is looking straight at him, holding the walnut in one hand and the figurine in the other, their spirits having separated at last. "Hello there, old friend," the creator says to his creation.

Chapter Ten
SHOOTOUT AT THE VAL MAR

"You've been with me all along," I tell little invisible Chumpy as he sits on the table of my booth at Twede's Cafe in North Bend, Washington, which is the "real" diner called the Double R on *Twin Peaks* and proudly promotes itself as such. It plays a prominent role in my Favorite Thing Ever, *Twin Peaks: The Return*. I have my iPhone out and am wearing an EarPod, so people (hopefully) think I'm remotely talking to someone real, just not at my present location. Everybody does it now. That doesn't stop Rachel, the owner, from giving me the side eye as she refills my coffee and notices my iPhone isn't even on.

By this point, I am 62 years old. I was 61 when I wrote *The Romance of Chumpy Walnut*, and I was 16 when I wrote the first draft of *Chumpy Walnut,* longhand on ruled paper in a binder. I've known him all of his life, and he's known me most of mine.

Chumpy hasn't aged a day, and never will. I envy him, although I feel as ageless as he is sometimes, at least on the inside. I'm enjoying a damn fine slice of vegan cherry pie with some damn fine coffee and damn fine almond milk, while Chumpy surreptitiously takes bites and sips when no one is looking. "Forever Young" by Alphaville is playing on the sound system.

"You just didn't know it," I add.

"Neither did you!" Chumpy fires back. "And you're the omnipotent one!"

"Only to you. Though my own life experiences all happened to me as described, I played a character in this book, just like you did. For narrative purposes, I blocked you out of my character's head until the revelation had ripened. But I really did keep that walnut and little toy figurine for decades, in your honor. I just didn't carry them everywhere I went, because I was afraid of losing them."

"Cut the crap!"

"*Chumpy*! Calm down."

"Why? No one here but you can see or hear me."

"But you're forcing me into a heated exchange with thin air. It's not a good look."

"Then why don't we go somewhere private?"

"Because this is the place where I'm supposed to reveal everything to you."

"A coffee shop?"

"It's not just a coffee shop. It's a place both wonderful and strange."

"Been there, done that," Chumpy says with a shrug. "Everyone who can see me in this world thinks I looked like a cartoon character, anyway. But in my world, we're as fleshy as you are."

"A matter of perception due to inter-dimensional transmigration. Personally, I think when you're our size and visible, you look more like a Gerry Anderson Supermarionette, like on *Thunderbirds* or *Captain Scarlet and the Mysterons*. Except, of course, with a big dick. So you're never for kids. I don't have kids and don't write for them."

"I don't get the reference. I don't get a lot of things you think about."

"All right. Ask me the questions I brought you here for me to answer."

Chumpy focuses. "Okay, let's start with this: I want to know why you waited so long to talk to me."

"I wanted to wait until after you experienced a carefully curated, selectively guided tour of our journey together in this dual dimension."

"Dual dimension?"

"By bringing you into my world, I created a dual dimension that subsists separately from both of our dimensions, that only exists in the imaginations of those who read it. And they'll all picture it differently, creating multiple imaginary variations."

"I thought I already lived inside your brain, like all of your creations."

"Yes, but I blended your consciousness with mine. Basically, I performed my version of the Vulcan mind meld, if you get the reference. I'm sure you overheard it once or twice when I watched *Star Trek*."

"I don't really get it, but that's okay. So now that our stories have been combined into a single universe, is my story now non-fictional, or is yours now fictional?"

"To the people in my world who might read this, all of *my* stories are true, but you're still fictional, including all your adventures in this dimension. Many of my old haunts—Ships, Dolores', the Cal-Neva, the Parkway—are gone, and, sadly, many of the people you met are gone, too. They only exist now in other people's minds, or in some cases, movies, or, for what it's worth, in the pages of this book. My memories are no more real than my imagination. In the end, it all might as well be fiction."

"But now that people in your world have seen me, in various forms, that means I exist here now, too. At least in their minds."

"You only exist in the minds of anyone reading this right now. None of the living people from my life you personally encountered have any memories of meeting you in any form. But you remember meeting them. It's subjectively selective by design."

"So you created an alternate timeline."

"No, a dual dimension."

"What's the difference?"

"I'm not sure. I just like alliteration."

"So it's all about subjective semantics."

"Absolutely accurate."

Chumpy ponders this premise, then says, "I guess the difference between a parallel or alternate universe and a dual dimension is that, in a dual dimension, we retain our unique identities, regardless of which one we're in, because there's only one of us wherever we go. Though some of the famous people in my world are a lot like the ones here, except in my world, they're zombies or perverts. Or both."

"That's not so different. The spiritual separation is selective."

"At least, *I* don't have a counterpart in this dimension. Right?"

"Right. And Vic Valentine is always the only Vic Valentine in existence anywhere, even with a virtual side trip to your world, which altered his persona a bit to suit the style and fit the frame. But he was just passing through someone else's dream."

"Or I was passing through his."

"He actually hallucinated you in *Vic Valentine, Lounge Lizard for Hire*, but he wasn't in his right mind and couldn't trust anything he saw."

"How can I trust anything *you're* telling me if you're a fiction writer and I'm just a figment of your imagination, and you're controlling all my reactions?"

"You shouldn't. I certainly don't. That's one reason I'm not religious. Those who think they have all or most of the answers are the ones I trust the least."

"Then why are you telling me all of this?"

"Because you came a long way to ask, Chumpy, and it's my fault. I owe you something. I can't verify its veracity. You'll just have to trust me."

"But you just told me not to trust anyone who thinks they have all the answers."

"I did. But you're going to trust me anyway."

"Why?"

"Because if you don't, you'll have no reason to continue in any dimension, because it will all feel like a meaningless dice roll."

"It already does."

"People need to have faith in something, Chumpy, even fictional people, even if what they believe in is fictional. I want you to live, and live as happily as possible, so I'm instilling your faith in me."

"I guess knowing you will take care of me no matter what happens does make me feel better. You have so far. But I have to believe you have my best interests in mind."

"I do and I always will."

"I know. I think I know, anyway."

"I'm being honest with you, but believing in a fabricated answer to a very real question often makes people feel better, at least good enough to keep going. Whatever works, I always say."

"I have been struck by how much the people of my world and yours are similar, but only in the worst possible ways."

"Of course. They're mirror images of each other."

"Both mirrors are cracked. Like my shell."

"Both are populated by lots of assholes, too."

Chumpy nods. "There are also a lot of weirdos in both our dimensions, it's true. I have to say, yours are weirder."

"I can't take credit for them because I'm not their creator, but thanks just the same."

"What would you change if you were their creator?"

"Nothing. They're all just working with what they got, like you. That's what makes Life so interesting. Diversity. To me, anyway. Nature is diverse, so diversity is natural. But, like empathy, a lot of people don't carry that accessory in their makeup bag. Especially when someone wants to buck the status quo and change what they started with, because it's not an accurate reflection of who they are or want to be."

"Change how they think, or how they look?"

"Either or both."

"Is that why you made Tiger Willie a werewolf? Or a werecat, that is?"

"Not really. I just dig werewolves. And cats."

"Me, too. Small world. Way too literally."

"You know, my original concept for this book was for you to wake up in your world normal-sized, but everyone else is small, like Jonathan Smith writing *The Amazing Colossal Man*."

"That sounds awesome! Why didn't you?"

"It wasn't enough for a whole book. I will probably put it in a short story, so to speak, and call it 'A Tall Tale.'"

Chumpy can't hide his disappointment. "Can't fuckin' wait."

"*Chumpy*! What's gotten into you?"

"Your mental illness, unfortunately."

"Look, as I was saying, I think this world, and yours, would be more harmonious if everyone just minded their own damn business. You see what I mean? That's what I try to do. I mean, if someone wants to cut themselves in half and have their upper body sewn onto the rear end of a cow and turn themselves into a minotaur, I'd only object because they killed a cow."

"So you're vegan, like me."

"No, you're vegan, like *me*."

"Why are there so few of us vegans? In either dimension?"

"Most people don't seem to enjoy their meals unless they know someone innocent suffered and died for it. It's human nature."

"It's human nature to be cruel?"

"Yes, it can be. People can't help being human. All we can do is try to rise above our own primitive impulses. Unlike animals, humans can make conscientious choices. Animals run purely on instinct, and one of those instincts is love. They don't deserve to be tortured and slaughtered for any reason. Not to me, anyway. So not to you, either. I've felt this way since I was a small boy and found out where meat comes from. I never got over it." I feel as if I am talking to my son because, in some ways, I am.

"Animals have feelings just like we do, even in my world," Chumpy says.

"I think many people feel it's a mistake to attribute sentient feelings to animals. I think it's often a bigger mistake to attribute sentient feelings to humans."

"Do you think you're a better person than they are because you don't eat animals?"

"No, but when they say that to me, I think *they* think I'm better than they are, and that must be what bothers them."

"What do you say to people when they criticize your diet?"

"I tell them to suck my cucumber."

Chumpy laughs. "What should I tell them? To suck my walnut?"

I laugh. "Sure. If they can find it."

"Why did you give me such a big dick?"

"*Whoa*, left field tonal shift. Though I've been waiting for that question."

"It's a big one. Question, I mean."

"Well, it's like this, Chumpy. When you transitioned to my crude dimension, your inescapable distinction as a character was translated into a normal guy but with a twelve-inch dick, at least when you were visible in human form, which was necessary for narrative navigation. I couldn't just have you inhabiting a walnut all the time, even though that's how I initially conceived you."

"As a walnut?"

"Yes. A sentient walnut in a comic strip."

"I remember. I experienced that firsthand in my nightmares of your nightmares."

"Right. But I decided I was a better writer than artist, so I made you human. But only a foot tall, so that you'd stand out. As it were. Then, when I brought you here, I had to find another way to make you stand out. So to speak. Because the theme of your existence is isolation from the status quo."

"But why make me so small in the first place?"

"I was picked on a lot for being short when I was a kid, so I passed that pain on to you."

"Gee, thanks."

"You're welcome. It's always a gift to be unique in a world of clones and chaos. That's what makes you so special: wherever you go, you don't fit in. Who wants to be just like everyone else? How boring and unoriginal. Conformity is for suckers."

Chumpy thinks, then nods in reluctant agreement. "I guess so. But it was nice to feel normal for a change, to mix in with other people without being belittled. Literally. But then I had the oversized dong, so I wasn't really normal. No matter how you create me, I'm still a freak. That's hard to deal with sometimes, even if I am, as you say, special.'"

"You're not just a freak, Chumpy, you're a freak of Nature, *my* Nature. Be proud of your individuality. Roll with it."

"But of all the ways I could stand out, why did you have to give me such a big dick that didn't even match the rest of my body?"

"Because you felt so sexually inadequate in your world. I guess I over-compensated."

"I think you just wanted an excuse to write more perverse sex scenes."

"I don't need an excuse."

"Do you feel sexually inadequate?"

"No. Just old. So generally inadequate."

"You don't look very old."

"Thanks. I still have all my hair, at least, and my skin doesn't look like rice paper, not yet, anyway. I feel ageless on the inside, which is where you were conceived, which is why you really are ageless."

"I'm not complaining. I'm just curious. Having an over-sized penis and being attractive to so many women for a change certainly had its upside. I think I appreciate it more now after this conversation. In fact, I appreciate my whole life more now, even the messed-up parts."

"Good! That's the whole idea of Life in *any* world."

"But something else is troubling my mind: why did you make me think of *Trouble in Mind* and Jean Rollin'? What did those things have to do with anything?"

"I didn't *make* you think of them. They both happened to be swimming around in my head at the time I started writing this story, so those elements seeped through the dimensional divide."

"Why these particular things, though?"

"After several viewings since I saw it first run, I've decided *Trouble in Mind i*s one of my favorite movies, which has a lot to do with living in Seattle for a decade plus. I also programmed a private Jean Rollin retrospective and confirmed he is one of my top five favorite filmmakers due to his dreamy mix of sex and surrealism."

"So what does any of that have to do with me?"

"Basically, my brain is like a stew of sex and surrealism, and you're just floating in it aimlessly."

"Like a turd in a toilet."

"Welcome to my world."

"So why were these thoughts of these films shared with me but not the other fifty million films in your head? There has to be a reason."

"Not everything has a reason where you're concerned. Sometimes I'm just going with the flow."

"Flow of what? Like when you flush the toilet?"

"Sort of. I mean my creative consciousness."

"So it *is* like flushing a toilet."

"That is metaphorically accurate, if rather insulting."

"But I think differently about some things than you do, and I don't know all the things that you know."

"Doesn't matter, Chumpy. You're not supposed to. Even though you're your own unique individual, you're still part of a collective consciousness. Our worlds are inextricably intertwined, and this dual dimension is a direct result of that barrier being broken. On purpose. By me. Just to see what would happen. Sometimes disparate elements randomly combine, like dropping your coffee in your soup. But in so doing, you create something new. Not necessarily good. Just new. And different. Movies offer clues to my personality, and you're a product of that personality, so naturally, you'd be curious. So I planted a few cryptic clues here and there, just enough to keep you guessing."

Chumpy's brow is furrowed with skeptical contemplation. "I look for clues everywhere. I can't help it. It's how you wired me. Sometimes I find them, sometimes I don't. It drives me crazy."

"Clues sometimes find you, Chumpy."

"Oh, that's cute."

Rachel refills my coffee as I pretend to pause my fake Zoom call. I almost ask Chumpy if he wants anything, but catch myself. After she walks away, I continue my philosophical conversation with my invisible fictional character.

"I know exactly how you feel, Chumpy. These seemingly magical coincidences and occurrences validate our existence. Sometimes the map of your journey reveals itself, just for an instant, to let you know you're on the right path. On my last birthday, I was celebrating right here in the real *Twin Peaks*. As usual, I went to the site where the Welcome to Twin Peaks' was located. Just as I got there, a rainbow appeared across the sky in front of the mountains, leading down into the river on the side of the road. Then, while I was marveling at this miracle, a second rainbow appeared above it, making it a double rainbow. It was like a direct message of hope and affirmation, possibly from David Lynch, your friend from Bob's Big Boy. This is why I've learned to appreciate the journey and trust in the navigator to reach my destination. Even if I'm my own navigator. I suggest you do the same."

"I'll try. I'm beginning to like the fact you turned my life into a horror movie, because I like horror movies."

"Of course."

"Can I meet some French lady vampires when I go back to my world, like the ones in Jean Rollin movies?"

"No. I'm saving that for Vic Valentine."

"*Fuck!*"

"*Chumpy!*"

"First, he gets his own movie, and now he gets his own sexy vampires!"

"But Vic *didn't* get his own movie because we got indefinitely sidelined at the goal line due to Christian's more pressing commitments."

"It's the thought that counts!"

"Not in Hollywood. Now it's just 'The Movie That Never Was.'"

"Like the 'Date That Never Was.' I remember you talking about that a long time ago."

"Exactly. In fact, as you overheard, Vic Valentine replicated this romantic, if slightly psychotic, strategy in *Love Stories Are Too Violent For Me*, so naturally it was also in the screenplay. Then, when Christian sent the script and storyboards to Winona Ryder, for the character of Rose, and she sent them right back without so much as a note of explanation, it became the Movie That Never Was."

"Weird."

"As usual."

"I'm sorry the movie didn't get made, even if it wasn't about me. That must make you sad."

I let out a long sigh. "It's hard to live with a dead dream. But I've learned to accept the fact that life doesn't always turn out as you want or expect it to, so it's important to appreciate the good things, large or small, as well as the irony of it all. All the bad stuff is merely anecdotal material for my books."

"Including mine."

"Don't worry, you have a lot more adventures in store,

back in your world, which I constructed, but it's now thriving independently of my oversight. I equipped you with everything you need to flourish. You don't need me to write your life anymore. You're free to make it your own."

"You still have a future, too. Maybe *you* should have faith."

"It's not that I don't have faith in the future," I reply. "It's just that I have less future to have faith in."

"You kept my dream alive by continuing my story. Thank you."

"You're welcome."

"I still want some lady vampires."

"Who doesn't?"

"Aw, c'mon, man, give me a break!"

"Okay, okay, maybe I'll turn some of your ladies into vampires. Like your wife."

"That'll work. As long as she's my height again, so she won't have to pick me up to bite my neck and wind up biting my head off."

"Done."

"I do like the fact my life is a fairy tale, so anything is possible because it's not restrained by your reality, which can be quite boring by comparison, I've discovered."

"Well, I have some interesting things in common with the famous fairy tale author, Hans Christian Andersen. First, we share a birthday, April second. We share the same middle name, Christian, as in Slater, although I no longer use it. And we both write stories about mermaids and little people."

"What do you think that means?"

"Nothing, so far as I can tell. Just another coincidence I can't explain."

"Or another clue."

"Maybe. Sometimes you're getting clues when you don't even know it's a mystery. Sometimes it's just a coincidence."

"How can we tell the difference?"

"By the actual outcome."

"What's a mystery that keeps you awake nights, pondering the possibilities?" Chumpy asks me.

"Besides Life?"

"Yeah, that's *everybody's* mystery. Specifically."

"Hmmmm…well, if I'm to be completely candid, I sometimes wonder whatever happened to Cristi Harris from *Night of the Demons Two*."

"That's *it*? Why?"

"You obviously haven't seen *Night of the Demons Two,* though you probably listened to it. She was pretty hot."

"You're pretty shallow for a Superior Being."

"Who said I was superior? If I were, I'd know what happened to Cristi Harris."

"The only big mystery I care about is why the first book you wrote about me was an innocent fairy tale, and the second one—the one that is published, anyway, therefore the definitive version—is a pulpy, perverted, sick, twisted, male-oriented horror fantasy."

"You forgot satire'."

"Oh, is that supposed to make it more respectable?"

"Look, don't take it so personally, Chumpy."

"How can I not take it personally when it's about me *personally*?"

"It's like this, Chumpy. I kind of did with the sequel to your first book what Tobe Hooper did with *The Texas Chainsaw Massacre, Part Two*. People were expecting it to be like the original *Texas Chain Saw Massacre*, one of the most raw and realistic horror movies ever made up to that point. It was like a documentary of the decadent decline of the nineteen-seventies. By the time Tobe Hooper made the sequel, it was nineteen eighty-six, which had a completely different cultural context, so he wanted to reflect that in the way the first one represented its own era. There was no way to replicate the organic grit of the first one, so instead, he created a kind of Neo-Pop-Art-Pulp fever dream with a totally different vibe."

"Neo-Pop-Art-Pulp Fever Dream does sound like the second book of my life, too."

"Yeah, that's my thing. It's not so bad, is it? I wish *my* life was a Neo-Pop-Art-Pulp Fever Dream, like a Mario Bava movie."

"Can we switch?"

"Too late now."

Chump shrugs. "So we're in the third book now, which I guess is your 'makeup' book for completely trashing my life in the second one. So what about the third movie in a film series? Was that ever the best one?"

"Hmmm…yes. But only subjectively speaking. *Return of the Living Dead, Part Three* is definitely my favorite of that series. But that's mostly because Brian Yuzna made it feel more like a *Re-Animator* movie. It's both the darkest and the sexiest of the franchise, at least in my book."

"My book too, unfortunately."

"Melinda Clarke is not in your book, though she is in my head sometimes, co-starring with Cristi Harris in *Night of the Return of the Living Dead Demons. Part Six.*"

"Who's Melinda Clarke?"

"Exactly. She's pretty hot, too."

"You're not inspiring confidence in your values. Maybe that's why I'm so disappointed with how my life turned out in the second book. Your artistic influences are not very noble."

"Well, as Ed Wood said, My next one will be better.'"

"By next one' you mean *this* book."

"Yes. It's now a trilogy. You have to admit, it's different. Isn't that better?"

"The first one was different, too. It just wasn't a pornographic cartoon."

"The second one is different from the first, like this one is different than the second. It's good to remix the formula.

Keeps the creative juices flowing. Along with all the essential bodily fluids, like blood and semen."

"You keep talking about horror movies. My life story wasn't supposed to be a horror movie. In my case, you completely changed my original genre." "It's still a fairy tale. Just an *adult* fairy tale. I've lost the innocence that created you, long ago, so no way I could credibly recreate that. I've been too corrupted by reality, like everyone else. To keep your fantasy going, I had to update it to my present reality. These are especially dark times for my world, so your world darkened in reflection."

"Your world has always been pretty dark. I've seen it up close now. Not very pretty. My world's actually prettier."

"My world is uglier and darker than ever, trust me. You've spent too much time in my pocket. As you know, I was raised in a cult. Now the whole country is controlled by a cult."

"Why is that *my* problem?"

"It isn't. One more reason you're lucky. Sometimes I wish I could transport myself to your dimension."

"Why don't you? Then we could hang out more often."

"I can't. My creator isn't as flexible as yours. All I can do is infuse it with my tastes and interests."

"So when you created me, your interests were innocent, even though you lived in a cult. Now you just like cult *movies,* which aren't as traumatizing as an actual cult. Generally speaking. Maybe just as influential, though."

"Agreed. Back then I was young, Chumpy, escaping into my childhood dreams, which were also very romantic."

"So then, as you grew older in this dark world of yours, your interests got darker."

"Because the light of your life is on a dimmer from the moment you're born."

"That's a cop out. Dreams are an escape from reality."

"You're talking about voluntary, conscious daydreams. Our involuntary subconscious dreams are merely a warped reflection of waking reality."

"So I'm the victim of your warped imagination, then. Nothing tragic or traumatic."

"Um…yes. That is correct."

"Well, that sucks for me."

"Sometimes."

"Why does everything have to be so lewd and lascivious?"

"It doesn't. It's just a personal preference."

"What does your wife think of this?"

"She tries hard not to."

"Well, sorry, but I think you have a serious mental problem and you're taking it out on me."

"Hey, look, it's not just me. This wasn't my motivation or inspiration, but when I finished, I realized I was incidentally part of the current trend in cinema to reimagine classic children's stories in the public domain as horror movies. In fact, the original Grimms' Fairy Tales are horror stories for children, so it wasn't really a stretch, just a purification. Relatively recent examples include *Winnie the Pooh: Blood and Honey*, *Peter Pan's Neverland Nightmare*, *Bambi: The Reckoning*, *Screamboat Willie*, and *The Death of Snow White*."

"So is this information meant to be an excuse for corrupting my tale of innocence?"

"No, just an explanation that I didn't invent the concept."

"Is this book meant to be an apology or an explanation?"

"Explanation to you, apology to no one."

"So why did you write it?"

"I don't know. Someone just put the idea in my head, and I was compelled to follow through."

"Are they any good?" Chumpy asks.

"What?"

"These fairy tales turned into horror movies."

"Some are okay. Not classic like the originals at any

rate."

"Then what's the point?"

"Making easy money."

"Oh. Well, that obviously isn't *your* motivation."

"Nope, it never has been, even when I was young."

"What do you miss most about being young?"

"Youth."

"You know what *I* miss about your youth? Your innocence."

"I don't."

"Well, I miss *my* innocence, anyway. Everything was so much simpler."

"We all have to grow up sometimes, Chumpy, and that means outgrowing our naive delusions about life and the world we live in."

"But I'm fictional. You could always rewrite my history."

"I already did. Mine, too. With this book. It's fantasy revisionist history, like *Inglorious Basterds* or *Once Upon a Time in Hollywood.*"

"Or *The Romance of Chumpy Walnut.*"

"*Touché.* In any case, it's all artistic fantasy that doesn't impact or change reality. It's just wishful therapeutic thinking."

"I know how much you love *Once Upon a Time in Hollywood* because it reminds you of your young days there. Can we go to your place and watch it together, side by side, instead of me on a shelf or in your pocket? I missed a lot of visuals along the way."

"Sure. I can think of several movies I'd like to watch with you while Monica is out of town visiting her nephew Ian and niece Ellie in Phoenix. You know, while writing your newer stories, I sort of thought of Ian."

"Is he short?"

"Yeah, he's seven years old."

"Is he smart?"

"Smarter than me."

"Low bar."

"The only bar either of us can reach."

Rachel brings the check. She smiles at Chumpy, or at least the spot where he is sitting on the table, then winks at me.

After lunch, we stop by scenic Snoqualmie Falls, next to the Salish Lodge, made famous as The Great Northern Hotel on *Twin Peak*s. There is no one else around at the moment, and we feel completely at peace in the spiritual serenity of the setting. Chumpy marvels at the mystical mist as I hold him close and we chat. It's like a sweet slice of eternity.

When we embark on the forty-minute drive back to my condo apartment in Seattle, Chumpy seems morose as he listens to the song "Death," by White Lies, playing on the Mini Cooper's sound system. The lyrics about the fear of mortality are speaking to him, even though he's essentially death-proof. His creator, however, is not. To change the mood, I switch to more suitably relaxing music: some of Angelo Badalamenti's score for *Twin Peaks*, Richard Ford's gently soothing "Obatala," and an achingly moody melody called "Hold On, We're Going Home" by Sly 5th Avenue.

"That is a very melancholy tune," Chumpy says of that last one.

"It reminds me of this little dog who recently died in my arms. Her name was Roo, and her housemate was a little dog named Harry, who is much younger. You've heard me walking them many times. Anyway, as you may recall, one day this past summer, right after our walk in the park, just as I was bringing her back and approaching the door to their home, Roo made a strange sound, then her head sagged, and she was gone. I could feel her soul leaving her body. As devastated as I was, I was honored she chose me to literally carry her over the bridge to the other side, even though I didn't know that till it was suddenly all over. She'd been sick for a long time, and it seemed like she was hanging on for one last walk in the park before she let go. It was one of the most profound experiences of my life."

Chumpy's eyes are misty, like the Falls. "I remember hearing but not really understanding this since I was in your pocket at the time. All your dogs love you. I know because they told me while I was in your pocket, stuffed between the treats and poop bags."

"I love them, too."

"They know. Do you like walking dogs?"

"Yes. It saved my life."

"I thought *I* did."

"That too. It wasn't just one thing that kept me going. It never is."

"What else saved your life?"

"My wife."

The song ends, and Chumpy asks to listen to something different, because this music is making him sad, too.

"I got just the thing." I navigate the CarPlay menu till I find "The Ballad of Chumpy Walnut" and "Blues for Chumpy Walnut," two original jazz numbers composed and recorded by famous jazz flugelhornist Dmitri Matheny.

"My friend Dmitri wrote these tunes just for you," I tell Chumpy. "They sometimes play them on Jazz Twenty-Four, the internet radio station that provides the soundtrack to The Thrillpad. Dmitri and his gal Sissy are big fans of yours."

"Cool. I dig jazz. I'm his fan now, too. You know, the Will the Thrill' in my dimension also calls his place The Thrillpad."

"No shit? I'll sue the bastard."

Back in my neighborhood of Capitol Hill, I drive past some of my favorite local date hangouts with Monica so I can show Chumpy their exterior, since he's only experienced them from a pocket perspective: Donna's, Dino's, Revolver, all-vegan Life On Mars, Hula-Hula Tiki Bar, Rumba, Canon, Lost Lake Cafe and Lounge, Linda's Tavern which has a picture of Laura Palmer behind the bar, and Bimbo's Cantina which has a vegan Mexican menu, and is right above a favorite bar called the Cha Cha Lounge and right next door to Big Mario's Pizza, which offers vegan slices. The final stop of the tour is Sol Liquor Lounge, where Monica and I go for their monthly tiki nights.

On the way home to The Thrillpad, we pass a midcentury apartment building called the Val Mar.

"I love the name of that apartment building," I tell Chumpy. "I plan to set a story there."

"What are you going to call it?"

" Shootout at the Val Mar.'"

"Why?"

"Because I like it. It sounds like a film noir or a Spaghetti Western. Two of my favorite genres."

"Will I be in it?"

"You already are."

"Is there going to be a shootout?"

"Not likely. But you never know around here."

"Should I be worried?

"No. You're fictional."

"That does seem to come in handy sometimes."

Back in The Thrillpad, I turn on the TV, and "Czar of Noir" Eddie Muller is hosting Noir Alley on TCM.

"That guy is a big fan of yours," I tell Chumpy. "You've met him, sort of. He used to co-host film noir festivals with me in Thrillville."

"I recognize his voice. Very distinctive. And he has good taste."

"In movies or books?"

"Both."

Chumpy is enrapt by the movie, *Sweet Smell of Success*, which, coincidentally or not, is my favorite film noir, but he can't help staring out the big living room windows at the spectacularly panoramic vista of downtown Seattle, Lake Union, and the Space Needle, as well as our meticulously decorated silver Christmas tree, making it feel like we're living inside a View Master.

"That looks like my dreams of Landoli, home of my ancestors," Chumpy tells me with a sweeping wave of his little hand. (He pronounces Landoli correctly as "Land-oh-lie.") Then he points at the Space Needle and says, "Especially *that* building. It looks like a rocket ship with a flying saucer on top of it, just like the ship that brought my ancestors to my world. Now it's a statue in the middle of Landoli's town square."

"I know. I put it there."

"Were my ancestors from another dimension, or outer space?"

"I want to leave you with at least a little mystery, to keep things interesting," I say, tapping my temple. "Use your imagination."

"Your imagination uses *me*."

"It's not imagination, it's creative visualization."

"What's the difference?"

"Well, I feel like I saw the Space Needle in a dream, and it came true. Sometimes I gaze at it and it feels like I'm looking at the Mother Ship, waiting to wake up and either save our race from self-extinction, or destroy it before our stubborn savagery becomes a cosmic contagion. In fact, in *The Space Needler's Intergalactic Bar Guide*, the Space Needle actually *is* a rocket ship."

"So I creatively visualized my own ancestors into existence?"

"You've only seen Landoli in your dreams, so it's a mystery you'll have to solve on your own. No spoilers, sorry."

"My whole life is a dream. Just not *my* dream."

"My point is, if you believe in a dream enough, it sometimes comes true. Not always. But sometimes. Your only duty is to dream. The rest is out of your hands."

"What other dreams of yours came true lately?" Chumpy asks me.

"Besides meeting you?"

"Besides that, of course."

"Well, I finally made it to Graceland on my sixty-first birthday. And Sun Studio. My old filmmaker pal John Michael McCarthy—you might remember he came out to co-host his movie *Superstarlet A.D.* in Thrillville with live burlesque by Dane's Dames a quarter of a century ago—anyway, he showed us around his hometown of Memphis, pointing out historic Elvis landmarks, also Martin Luther King sites, and *Mystery Train* film locations. It was perfect."

"Elvis is Rocky Rolemodel in my world."

"Sort of, just like the Pack Rats are parodies of the Rat Pack, not replicas."

"Got it."

"Want to watch a Rat Pack movie?"

"Okay!"

I whip out my Blu-ray of the original *Ocean's 11,* and we watch it while still in the living room. I tell Chumpy all about my infamous, unduly publicized "protest" of the remake. He doesn't really understand it, but then not many people did.

"I like them a lot better as people, not zombies," Chumpy says afterward.

"Most people do."

After lunch, we retire to my home office, which is filled floor to ceiling with lurid artwork, hundreds of movies on disc, books, old comics, old monster and cheesecake magazines, vintage collectibles, ViewMaster reels, a stuffed CD rack, LPs, tiki statues, and action figures, or as my wife calls them, "dolls." I also made an elaborate diorama with four and five-inch resin figures of grindhouse mutants and B-movie monsters carnally mingling with sexy, trashy scream queens, depicting an old-school orgy at a retro horror mansion. I call it "Monsterville." Chumpy calls it "Home." Monica describes the room as what the walls would look like if my brain exploded. After taking it all in, Chumpy stops at a poster for an old sci-fi monster movie called *It Conquered the World*, a favorite of mine.

"What is that movie about?" Chumpy asks.

"Basically, it's about an alien monster from outer space that looks like a cucumber and tries to take over mankind."

"At least it's vegan."

We sit on my sofa in my home office, facing the big TV, and Googie joins us. Googie not only hears Chumpy in this form, but he also sees him. He even lets Chumpy pet him. I put on the two movies that most inspired Chumpy's first book, the Jimmy Cagney gangster classic *Angels with Dirty Faces,* and my favorite movie musical, *Guys and Dolls*, starring Marlon Brando and Frank Sinatra. The parallels to his dimension are crystal clear.

Later that night, after we've done some more chatting in my cozy home office, I put on an early Abbott and Costello classic, *Hold That Ghost,* since Bud and Lou inspired Chumpy's hobo friends Goosey and Jinx, and then *Jinx Money*, a great old Bowery Boys movie. They started as the Dead End Kids in *Angels with Dirty Faces,* and both iterations were the inspiration for Tiger Willie and the Dynamite Kids, which is what I called my own little ragtag gang back in New Jersey. Chumpy clearly sees all the parallels with his pals back home.

"That's more like it," Chumpy says afterward. "I could relate to all those movies because they remind me of my world, like you said. I mean, before it got corrupted."

"I thought you'd like them for that very reason."

"Can we watch some horror movies now? With lots of sex and nudity, and gore? I mean, like the ones that inspired the second book? For a change of pace, and to round out my self-education." Neither one of us can sleep. I think it's because we're afraid that we'll wake up and realize we only dreamed each other.

"I was hoping you'd ask. But first, some refreshments."

I make some popcorn and mix a couple of mai tais, with Chumpy's served in a size-appropriate shot glass. Then I sit back down with Chumpy and Goosey, feeling cozy and trying to think of us ever parting.

First, we watch Tex Avery's *Red Hot Riding Hood* (1943) as a short subject before the next double feature, *Mad Doctor of Blood Island* (1968), and *Re-Animator* (1985).

"I get it now," Chumpy says later that night. "I mean how your mind works, and what turns it on."

"Did you enjoy them?"

"Yes, very much. But only as movies. Not as a lifestyle."

"Agreed."

"Discovering new movies and music feels like a gift."

"I agree with that, too."

Next, we watch *Once Upon a Time in Hollywood*, by request.

"I really liked that one," Chumpy says. "I can see why you do, too. What are some other recent movies that have nothing to do with my creation, but might tell me more about *you*. I mean, as you are now. Maybe something with strong, sexy women, which seems to be your type."

"Hm. Off the top of my head, I'd say *Mad Max: Fury Road*, *Ex Machina*, and *Under the Skin*. Those are the three that immediately come to mind anyway, just because I like them so much."

"Oh, right. I'm pretty sure I was on the shelf when you watched those before, so I couldn't see them too well, which was frustrating. I'll enjoy them much more in my normal form, with you sitting next to me."

I look at the clock, then back at Chumpy. "You're just delaying the inevitable with this marathon of movie marathons."

"You mean till I have to say goodbye?"

"Yeah. But that's okay. So am I. Let's do this till we can't do it anymore."

As we watch *Fury Road*, I tell Chumpy, "There's also a prequel called *Furiosa,* which is really good, too. It's also a Mad Max movie."

"I watched a Mad Max movie soon after I got to Los Angeles in nineteen eighty-two. It was called *The Road Warrior*."

"I know. We even saw it at the same theater. The National in Westwood."

"Just not at the same time."

"I was like your *Wizard of Oz*, making things happen from behind the scenes."

"Except as I remember that movie from when you watched it, that Wizard was trying to help the girl get home."

"That's what I'm doing."

"No rush. I have to complete my mission. And it doesn't feel quite done yet."

"You were on a mission to find me and find out about me. That's why I wanted you to see movies that impacted me around the time you were born, or came of age, I should say, so I arranged that private screening for you, since it had already left the National when you were there. I also arranged that private screening of *Blade Runner* at the Bruin, for the same reason. It was also the same theater where I first saw it."

"I liked that movie. Especially that line about in time all will be lost, like tears in rain.' That's how I'm feeling. Everything gets washed away."

"True. Though in your case, the cycle is set on repeat. One time I was at a party with Rutger Hauer, who played the replicant who said that line, and I danced to Jailhouse Rock' and he clapped along and gave me the thumbs up."

"Since he's not a celebrity where I come from, I'm not that impressed. So you can skip the name-dropping already."

"There's a sequel called *Blade Runner 2049*. It's just as

good."

"Can we watch it? And the other movies, too? We can finally watch them at the same time, and I've never seen them, and this is my only chance."

"That would take up the better part of an entire day."

"So? You have something better to do?"

"Well, it is the weekend. And I've always liked watching movies as often as possible. When I first got to Westwood and was on my own and finally free to go out to the movies whenever I wanted, to see anything I wanted, I watched *Dawn of the Dead* like five nights in a row. It was so horrifying to me that it was mesmerizing. Back in New Jersey, I had no privileges at all, so I took full advantage of my freedom to watch movies all the time, and still do."

"That must be a zombie movie. I know how much you like zombies because they're all over the place where I come from."

"Lucky you. Anyway, you and Googie chat while I put on a Martin Denny album and mix some more mai tais."

"I really like that kind of music."

"Of course you do. That's why your world has so many musical doppelgängers. Les Baxter, Esquivel, Henry Mancini, Xavier Cugat, Dave Brubeck, Sinatra, Sarah Vaughan, Nina Simone, Ella Fitzgerald, Julie London, all those swingin' cats 'n' kittens. That music helped me discover my true identity as Will the Thrill. That's why jazz and lounge are the soundtracks of our souls. And New Wave music, the music of my youth, because it still makes me feel so young."

As I'm preparing the drinks in the kitchen, Chumpy remains in my room, reading the framed City Council Proclamation of Mai Tai Day in Oakland, CA., August 29, 2009. When I return with our mai tais, Chumpy asks me why I was quoted in the proclamation.

"I lobbied for it in conjunction with Trader Vic's and Mike and Mano from Forbidden Island," I explain to him.

"Since then, every August thirtieth has been celebrated as Mai Tai Day around the globe, and the mai tai is finally recognized as the Official Cocktail of Oakland, which was our original goal, since it was invented there by Vic Bergeron in nineteen forty-four. My campaign slogan was Oakland, Home of the Mai Tai, Not Just the Drive-by. It wasn't officially adopted, though."

"So even the mai tais I drink in Thrillville were invented in Oakland?"

"Same basic recipe, yes."

"A cross-dimensional cocktail. That's what I call influential."

"Yes, it is. There's also a 'Vic Valentine' cocktail created by Susan Eggett for Forbidden Island."

"*What*?"

"*And* a 'Chumpy Walnut' cocktail created by Suzanne Long, also for Forbidden Island. I'd make one for us, but I'm missing the key ingredient of Nocello, which is a walnut-flavored liqueur from Italy."

"Can I get the equivalent back at Ivar's Tiki Lounge?" Chumpy asks, looking up at my Ivar statue, who seems to wink.

"I'll make sure all the imported ingredients are stocked by the time you return." I wink back at Ivar, but he ignores me as usual.

We clink glasses. I don't drink nearly as much as I once did. My aging constitution can't handle more than a couple or so cocktails a week these days unless we're on vacation, which isn't often since I hate leaving my house, much less the neighborhood, city, state, or country. It's crazy out there and getting crazier. But, for this special occasion, I revert to my somewhat more boozy lounge lizard ways, though even then I moderated my alcoholic intake. Well, mostly. I'm really more into the classic aesthetics of vintage cocktail culture than the actual booze. As a fictional character, Chumpy, like Vic Valentine, can imbibe without any health consequences whatsoever. It's the most I can do for them, given all the crap I put them through. My creator won't supply me with the same courtesy.

The next day, Monica returns from Arizona and cooks us a delicious vegan meal to enjoy as we sit at the dining table, looking out at the sunset behind the Space Needle. Chumpy tells Monica how much appreciates her midcentury modern decor, which reminds him so much of his home. Monica knows this is the first and last time she'll ever meet Chumpy, and she tries not to show her emotions. After dinner, she sits on the sectional living room sofa with Chumpy, and they talk for a long time while I catch up on text messages from my old friends Jon, Greg, PM, and Robert, as well as Facebook messages from Linda and Tessa. Chumpy asks Monica about her jobs as a college dean and adjunct professor, as I married way above my station. My brilliant, beautiful wife is also an accomplished theater actress, and Chumpy is intrigued by her anecdotes about performing in plays before live audiences, conveyed with a marathon of *Mad Men* playing in the background on the big living room TV, which Chumpy also finds both fascinating and recognizable.

Later, Monica FaceTimes her sister Erica in Australia so she can show Chumpy Erica's baby, Liliana. Erica can't see Chumpy, but apparently, Liliana can. When Monica calls her brother Quetzal and his wife Liz in Arizona, they can't see Chumpy either, but Ian can, and though Ellie cannot see anything very well due to her condition, she laughs and points at Chumpy through the portable portal of time and space. Monica shows Chumpy her photos of her beloved parents, Jaime and Elizabeth, both deceased, and their boxes of ashes, which are beside the ashes of Bubba and Tiki on top of a bedroom Elvis shrine.

The finality of it all sobers Chumpy. "This is what happens to everyone in your dimension?" he asks me after silently honoring the souls of the departed.

"Eventually."

"Even you?"

"Eventually."

"I don't want you to die."

"I don't want to die, either. But we all have to, to make way for the new cast members."

"Even me?"

"No. You're eternal."

"Why?"

"You're irreplaceable. You will live on in the world I created for you, which now has its own life, one that will continue through eternity in a continuous loop."

"Maybe yours does, too."

"Well, since I don't know what's true, I don't know what's *not* true. So maybe. I can wait to find out. No rush."

Chumpy nods sadly. Next, I talk with him about my own far-flung family, several of whom have known and loved Chumpy since I created him. I show him photos of my sister Serena and her sons, Phoenix and Zayden, who live in Los Angeles, along with her mother (and my stepmother) Annie, who signed her original poster of *Follow That Dream* hanging in The Thrillpad. "It's been a beacon to me ever since she gave it to me years ago," I explain to Chumpy.

I tell him more about my half-brothers, Rome (who has a son, also named Rome), and Zola, who lives in Nashville. They are the full-blood sons of the woman who raised me in the cult. Then there's Marc, the long-lost brother in Texas, recently found. Chumpy is more interested in hearing about my father, Robert, and his wife, Paige, who live in Santa Fe, New Mexico.

"I want to watch that movie sitting next to you," Chumpy says, pointing to a poster of *Bare Knuckle*s, starring my father as Zachary Kane, Modern Day Bounty Hunter. "Not on the shelf or in your pocket."

So we watch it, since it's the best possible introduction to my father for anyone, and Chumpy is impressed by his grandfather's rugged machismo. I tell Chumpy it was directed by Don Edmonds, the guy also also directed the notorious Nazisploitation masterpiece *Ilsa, She Wolf of the SS*. When he asks if we can watch that one next, I tell him no way, because I have to draw the responsible parental line somewhere, and that's a good place to do it.

After *Bare Knuckles*, I show Chumpy photos of my family in Houston, who raised me till I was six, because my mother was incapacitated due to her mental illness. This includes my late grandparents, Fred and his wife, Mamie, and my aunts, Mina and Carol, Charlotte's half sisters, all of whom were witnesses to Chumpy's birth when I wrote the novel while staying with them in 1981.

"Where is your mother now?" Chumpy asks.

"She's dead."

"I'm sorry to hear that. She's finally free, then."

"Hopefully. She died the same day as Herschell Gordon Lewis, both in Florida, except she was in a state ward."

"Who is Herschell Gordon Lewis?"

"I've shown his movies in Thrillville, like *Blood Feast*, which you could hear but not see."

"That was probably for the best."

The next day, I let Chumpy read the public letter I wrote to him in my epistolary memoir, *Graffiti in the Rubber Room: Writing for My Sanity*, wherein I promised to finally publish the sequel to the first book, *The Romance of Chumpy Walnut*, which I thought had been lost forever until I finally found the hidden manuscript. He finds the letter touching and illuminating, even though the published sequel has been vastly revised. I explain to him that this third book could not have been written if the second one didn't exist, and since Chumpy approves of this one in real time, he has come to see all three books as necessary chronicles of a complex journey. Chumpy also admires Shannon Wheeler's cover art for *The Romance of Chumpy Walnut*, feeling it captures the essence of his world and life.

It riffs off of Dyer Wilk's equally lurid cover for *The Thrillville Pulp Fiction Collection, Volume Two: Chumpy Walnut and Other Stories,* which I now consider to be the definitive edition of the first book in the series. It includes my original Thurberesque illustrations featured on the front cover of the Lulu edition. While he loves both covers because they depict him ensconced in cleavage, Chumpy appreciates my cruder drawings the most, since they were created when Chumpy's world was still as innocent as I was at that time.

Per his last request before departing our dimension, Chumpy and I sit quietly and sadly together watching *Trouble in Mind.* At first, he had expressed curiosity about Gaspar Noé's *Enter the Void*, another movie that popped mysteriously into his head upon entering the dual dimension. While it's a favorite of mine and reminds me of my own work, being a surrealistic depiction of sex and death as a fever dream, I didn't think it was appropriate for Chumpy. I couldn't think of any other Gasper Noe movies that would be appropriate so I just showed him a picture of Monica Bellucci, something that suits any occasion. Naturally, while Damien Leone's *Terrifier* series is also a nightmarishly nihilistic mix of sex and death, they are definitely the wrong choice to end anything, except perhaps an unwanted relationship. Ditto Michele Soavi's *Cemetery Man*, though that isn't nearly as extreme in its sadism. I figure where Chumpy is concerned, I've been sadistic enough.

If Chumpy hadn't already been inadvertently exposed to *Trouble in Mind*, which gave him a psychic itch that needed scratching before he left town, Yorgos Lanthimos's erotic saga of a creator losing control of his creation, *Poor Things*, might've been the one, though I think his recent film *Bugonia*, not yet on Blu Ray (I'm a strict physical media fiend), would've hit that sweet existentialist spot just as exquisitely. Briefly, I considered Darren Aronofksy's

Requiem for a Dream. Trippy but too heavy. In the end, I made the right decision. *Trouble in Mind* is perfect, and Chumpy agrees.

As the final credits roll, the song that had been playing in Chumpy's head, called "The Hawk (El Gavilan)," written by Kris Kristofferson and sung by Marianne Faithfull, makes us both cry, since the lyrics resonate with our pending separation.

"Time to get you back to your own dimension, Buckaroo Banzai," I say to Chumpy. He has seen the classic cult movie from a shelf in my room, so he gets the reference. Chumpy begins crying, but not because I called him Buckaroo Banzai.

"Why do I have to go back?"

"You don't belong here, Chumpy."

"Neither do you."

"But I have no choice. You have your life in your world, and I have mine."

"But I don't like my life in my world anymore. Not as much, anyway."

"You will, because from now on, you're going to make it anything you want it to be."

"I want it to be like it was before, and for Cupey to remain my size, and we live happily ever after in a fairy tale, even if the world around us is crumbling. You know. Like you and Monica."

"Done."

"Really? Just like that?"

"You'll see when you get back. You'll wake up next to Cupey back in Lonesome Grove on a beautiful day, and it will be as if no time has passed at all, and all memories of this dimension and all the events of the second book will vanish from your mind. And it won't be temporary, selective amnesia, like when Paige Pinup hypnotized you with her Magic Theremin. It will be a permanent reboot. You'll take vacations on Landoli, your ancient ancestral home, a peaceful paradise for your people. There will be no monster sex, no zombies, no mad scientists, no gangsters, no weird, horrific scenarios. And no loneliness."

Chumpy doesn't seem content with a complete overhaul, wondering if perhaps a healthy hybrid of romance and smut would be preferable. "I'm afraid I might get bored, though."

"Then you'll have to find a way to engage your own imagination. That's what I had to do. Still do."

"Will I still remember you when I'm back in my world? In this one, I kept getting amnesia, like the guy in one of your favorite movies."

"*Memento*. Right, very good."

"What's a movie that best represents your dimension, or at least how you see it?"

"*Night Train to Terror.*"

"*Night Train to Terror*? What's that about?"

"I have no idea, and nobody does, since it's comprised of scenes from several different cheap, lurid, B exploitation movies, some never even completed, economically edited down and then stitched together into a crazy-quilt of pulpy sex and violence, with random, MTV style music videos woven into the random fabric as God and the Devil sit in a train car discussing the rather arbitrary fates of the characters who are stuck on the same train which is going nowhere fast because it has nowhere to go but over a cliff into oblivion."

"How is that like this dimension?"

"Because it makes no sense, the depravity is gratuitous, and most of the characters are unlikable, but it's so terrible I can't take my eyes off it and never want to leave. It's totally incoherent, yet completely compelling despite its many flaws, or maybe because of them."

"That sounds familiar," Chumpy says.

"The movie?"

"The world."

"It should."

"Can we watch it?"

"No time. I'll beam it over to Will the Thrill's Thrillocitor sometime, and he can invite you over to watch it with him over cocktails. And you will definitely need cocktails."

"Wait. My Will the Thrill in his Thrillpad can watch movies from *this* Thrillpad?"

"When I feel like it, just for fun. He has no clue what they are or where they come from, but he likes them anyway since we have similar tastes. Of course, in Thrillville, these sleazy movies come off more like documentaries. I do it sometimes just to fuck with his fez."

"Isn't that like fucking with yourself?"

"More like mutual masturbation."

"Can I ask a favor?"

"Stop jerking off so much?"

"Besides that."

"Fire at Will."

"Can you change my destiny, or at least clean it up a bit, without me forgetting how I got there? So I remember everything, even the bad stuff? That way, I'll appreciate it more. And I want to live in Thrillville, not Lonesome Grove. As long as Cupey and I are together, as equals, I'll be happy."

"Understood. The second book will remain canonical, just a twisted detour on the road to blissful banality."

"Then what?"

"You'll live happily ever after."

"But what will happen to me when you die?"

"You'll go on living in the world I created for you. Or rather, the one you create for yourself."

"But will I still be able to hear your voice inside me?"

"No. But you'll be able to feel me. Forever."

Chumpy looks at me with his wet, luminescent eyes. "Why can't I stay *here* with you forever and feel your presence in person?"

"Because here I can't take care of you when I'm gone, Chumpy. I've learned the hard way never to overestimate the humanity of humans. You belong in your world, and I belong in mine."

Chumpy bows his head and sobs, and I hold him close, like a beloved childhood doll I lost as a child but found as an adult, only to lose again. Then Chumpy hugs Googie, and Googie licks away his tears. "I'll see you in our dreams," Chumpy tells his feline friend. He has a come a long way in more ways than one.

"What revelation from this journey means the most to you?" I ask my creation.

Chumpy has his answer ready. "The origin world of my creation and the truth of my existence is nothing I could've possibly imagined. It's so much more than anything I could've conceived with my limited perspective. I think when you finally meet your creator, whoever or whatever it may be, you'll have the same reaction."

"Yeah, that's why I try not to stress about it too much. Whatever any of us are thinking or hoping, it's probably way off the mark because of our stupid minds. *Stupid*! *Stupid*! As the alien in *Plan Nine from Outer Space* so eloquently put it. Anything else?"

Chumpy thinks carefully, then says, "The most important epiphany for me was discovering that you're on a mission in life, just like me. Except yours isn't over yet."

"As long as we live, Chumpy, the mission continues. And you'll live forever."

"You have a serious platitude problem."

For this emotionally fraught occasion, I put on "If You Go Away" by Frank Sinatra, who sings the most poignant version of it for my money.

"This sounds like a love song," Chumpy says.

"It is."

"So you love me?"

"Very much."

"But not romantically."

I smile. "No."

"Just checking," he says with a wan grin. His effort at levity in this moment is sweet but ineffective. "I just don't understand why I can't just stay here with you. You're healthy and not that old. We could have a long time together."

"What about Cupey? Don't you miss her? I know for a fact she misses you."

"My world is timeless. She'll barely notice I'm gone."

"But you've accomplished your mission. I answered all your questions. Now it's over. I'm sorry that I was such a tough nut to crack."

"But now my mission statement is to be your lifelong friend."

"You'll *always* be my friend, Chumpy, my best friend besides my wife, no matter where we are in the Universe of all Universes."

"I heard long-distance relationships don't work."

"The only distance between us is from my brain to my heart."

I pick my boy Chumpy up and hold him close to my chest as he hugs me tightly about the neck. "I want you to live forever, like me," he whispers in my ear.

"When I imagine myself as you, I feel immortal," I tell him.

"I just don't want to ever feel alone again, like when I was young."

"You won't. Cupey will always take care of you, even after I'm gone. And though you won't always live inside of me, I'll always live inside of you, so we'll always be together."

"Oh, wait!" Chumpy says, grabbing my arm. "I almost forgot! I have a message for you! From David Lynch!"

"I know. 'If you love what you do, do what you love.'"

"Aw man, you ruined it!"

As tears run down his face, Chumpy slowly fades away in my arms just as the song is ending, leaving only a walnut with a painted face in his wake, resting lifelessly on the couch beside me.

I pick up the walnut and put it to my ear. I think I hear Chumpy tell me he loves me before I kiss it and place it safely on a shelf.

Greetings from Los Angeles. 1980

"The Chumpy Walnut"

Created by Suzanne Long for
Forbidden Island Tiki Lounge
Alameda CA

CITY OF OAKLAND

City Council Proclamation

PROCLAMATION TO HONORING THE CREATION OF THE MAI TAI IN THE CITY OF OAKLAND

WHEREAS, the Mai Tai was created in 1944 by legendary restaurateur Victor J. "Trader Vic" Bergeron at the original Trader Vic's on San Pablo Avenue and 65th Street in the City of Oakland (formerly known as "Hinky Dink's"); and

WHEREAS, the Mai Tai "conjures universally positive images of retro-relaxation, portable Polynesia, a liberal lifestyle, multicultural mixology, exotic diversity, delicious creativity and the friendly spirit of Aloha — just like Oakland itself, the perfectly blended urban cocktail" said Will Viharo in an Oakland Tribune article recognizing the Mai Tai; and

WHEREAS, the Mai Tai, Tahitian for "the very best," is known worldwide as the quintessential tropical cocktail; and

WHEREAS, Oakland is a thriving, diverse and creative community which deserves its recognition as the Birthplace of the Mai Tai; and

WHEREAS, Oakland continues to be a destination for world class entertainment, food and drink, the home of an innovative and flourishing nightlife, and about which writer Herb Caen wrote that the "best restaurant in San Francisco is in Oakland,"

Now therefore I, Rebecca Kaplan, At-Large Council Member of the City of Oakland proclaim, on this thirtieth day of August two thousand and nine, Mai Tai Day in the City of Oakland.

Rebecca Kaplan — At-Large Councilmember

"I Finally Get Lucky at the Cal-Neva Resort in Lake Tahoe!" May 31, 2001

Aloha from Trader Vic's, Portland, Oregon, 2014

Greetings from Atlanta. GA
2017

Greetings from Chicago

December 2021

Kennichiwa from Hgoko
Boston. MA   June. 2022

Greetings from Veggie Galaxy, Cambridge, MA June 2022

Aloha from Trader Vic's, Emeryville, CA 2022

Aloha from Zombie Village

San Francisco, 2022

Greetings from the Orbit In Palm Springs CA 2024

Aloha from Trader Sam's
Disneyland. 2024

Aloha from Tiki Night at Sol Liquor Lounge
Seattle, WA
June, 2024

Aloha from the
Skull & Crown Trading Co.

Honolulu. HI. May 31 2025

Welcome to Twin Peaks
"The End of the Rainbow"

April 2, 2025

VIC VALENTINE SERIES

Classic Case Files:

Love Stories Are Too Violent For Me
Fate is My Pimp
Romance Takes a Raincheck
I Lost My Heart in Hollywood
Diary of a Dick
Hard-Boiled Heart

Mental Case Files:

Vic Valentine, International Man of Misery
Vic Valentine, Lounge Lizard For Hire
Vic Valentine, Space Cadet

Short stories/novella

Vic Valentine, Private Eye: 14 Vignettes
Vic Valentine Fever Dreams
All Souls Are Final plus *Panty-Stuffed Snakeskin Shoe*

Coming next:

Vic Valentine vs. the Vampires

CHUMPY WALNUT TRILOGY

Chumpy Walnut
The Romance of Chumpy Walnut
Chumpy Walnut Conquers the World

THE THRILLVILLE PULP FICTION COLLECTION

Volume One: *A Mermaid Drowns in the Midnight Lounge*
plus *Freaks That Carry Your Luggage Up to the Room*
Volume Two: *Lavender Blonde* plus *Down a Dark Alley*
Volume Three: *Chumpy Walnut and Other Stories*

SHORT STORY COLLECTIONS/NOVELLA

Things I Do When I'm Awake (novella)
VIHORROR! Cocktales of Sex and Death
One-Way Ticket to Thrillville

MEMOIR

Graffiti in the Rubber Room: Writing for my Sanity

SCI-FI WITH SCOTT FULKS (my pulp science fiction, his speculative scientific theories)

It Came from Hangar 18
The Space Needler's Intergalactic Bar Guide*
(*includes original and classic cocktail recipes)

www.willviharo.com
www.thrillville.net

Cheers to Chumpy!